WRITTEN BY AYUN HALLIDAY
ILLUSTRATED BY PAUL HOPPE

schwartz & wade books · new york

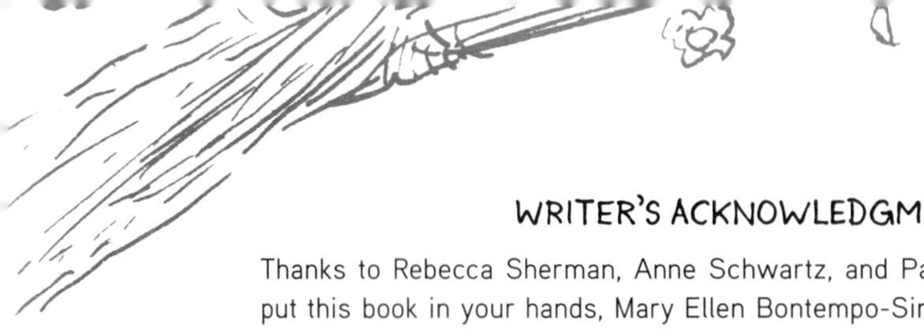

WRITER'S ACKNOWLEDGMENTS

Thanks to Rebecca Sherman, Anne Schwartz, and Paul Hoppe for conspiring to put this book in your hands, Mary Ellen Bontempo-Singer for providing character inspiration whilst serving as the World's Greatest School Nurse, Aeden Mlanao for reminding me to remain accountable to those with genuine peanut allergies, the staff of the late, great Gramstand for letting me spend upwards of six hours a day writing in their basement, Alex Cox for fueling my family's love of graphic novels, E. Lockhart for her ongoing good advice and encouragement, indie comic shops everywhere for bravely managing to exist at all, and all the lovely guerrilla marketeers who bring it on behalf of *The East Village Inky*.

A great big howdy-do to those who remember me from high school, both friends and former adversaries (some of whom I now claim as friends, thanks to the miracle of Facebook . . . which, like cell phones and for the most part peanut allergies, didn't exist back then).

As ever, my biggest thanks are reserved for Greg, India, Milo, and to a lesser degree, Mungo Kotis.

Dare to Be Heinie. —A.H.

ILLUSTRATOR'S ACKNOWLEDGMENTS

Thanks to Ayun for letting me lend my visuals to her wonderful story, and to Rebecca, Anne, Lee, and Rachael for making this all possible. It's been a long ride; I couldn't have done it without all your help, input, and patience.

Thanks also to my friends and colleagues for always being there with encouragement and enthusiasm, especially to Anuj for all those after-work sessions. A special thank-you to Lauren for opening my eyes to the publishing world.

Most importantly, I want to thank my parents for their love and support, without which I would not be where I am today. —P.H.

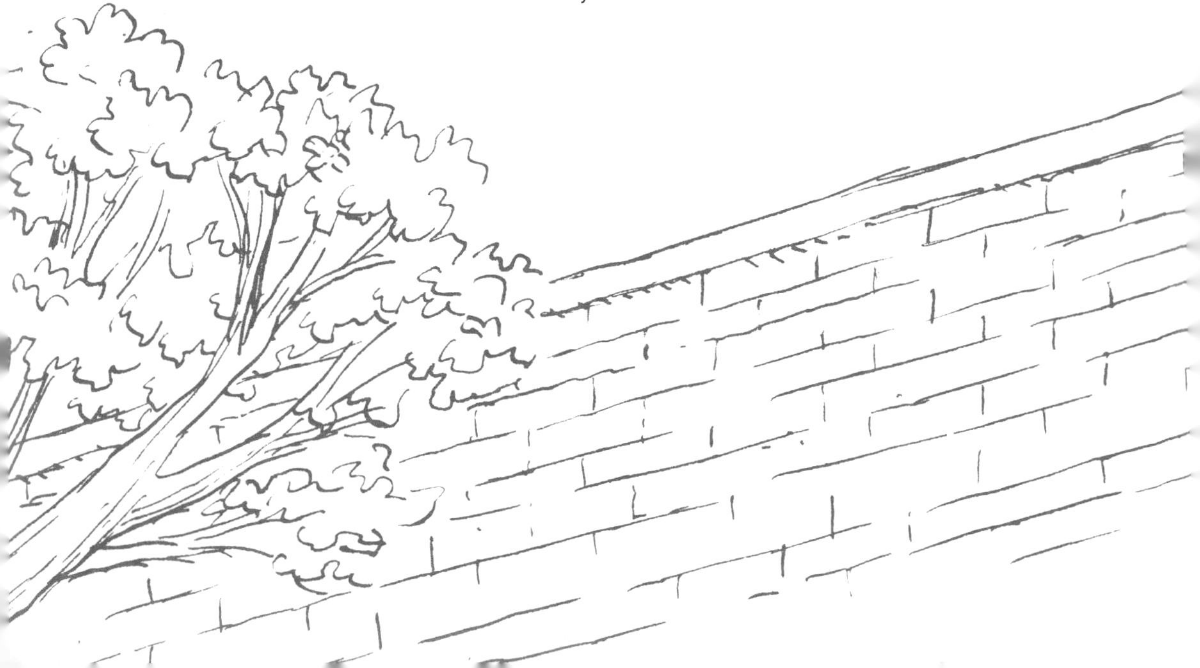

TO INDIA, MILO, AND ANYONE WHO'S EVER SOUGHT TO STAND OUT IN A CROWD —A.H.

FOR MY FELLOW CARTOONISTS OUT THERE, WHO INSPIRE ME TO DRAW —P.H.

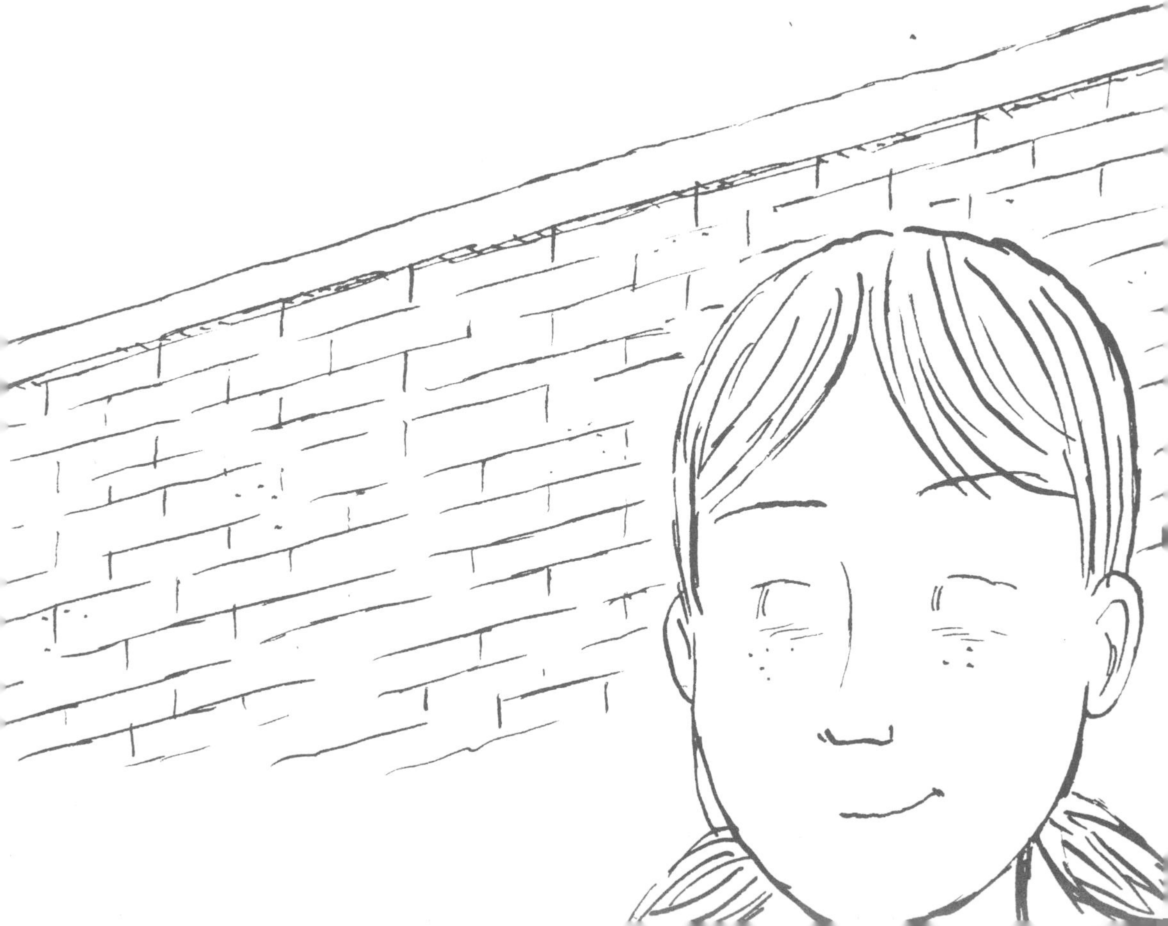

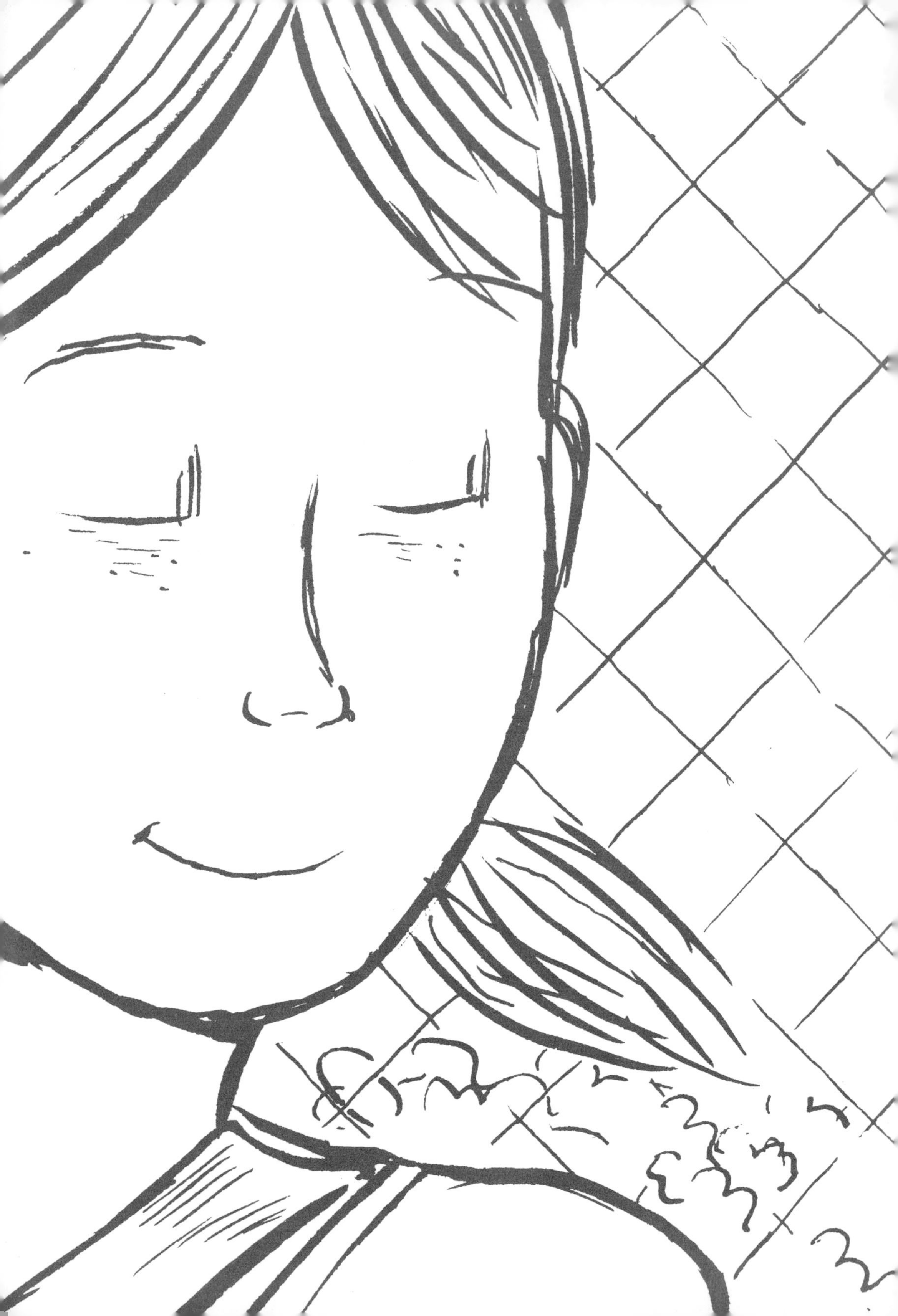

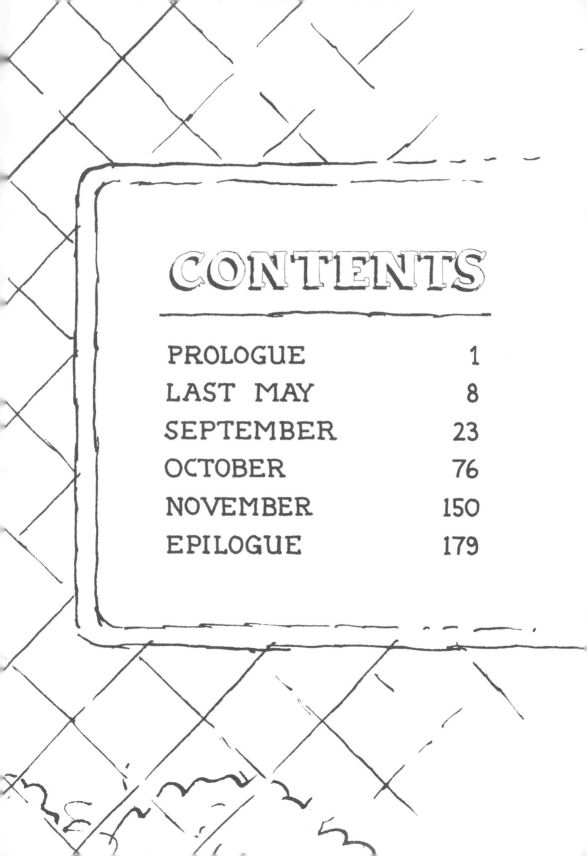

CONTENTS

PROLOGUE

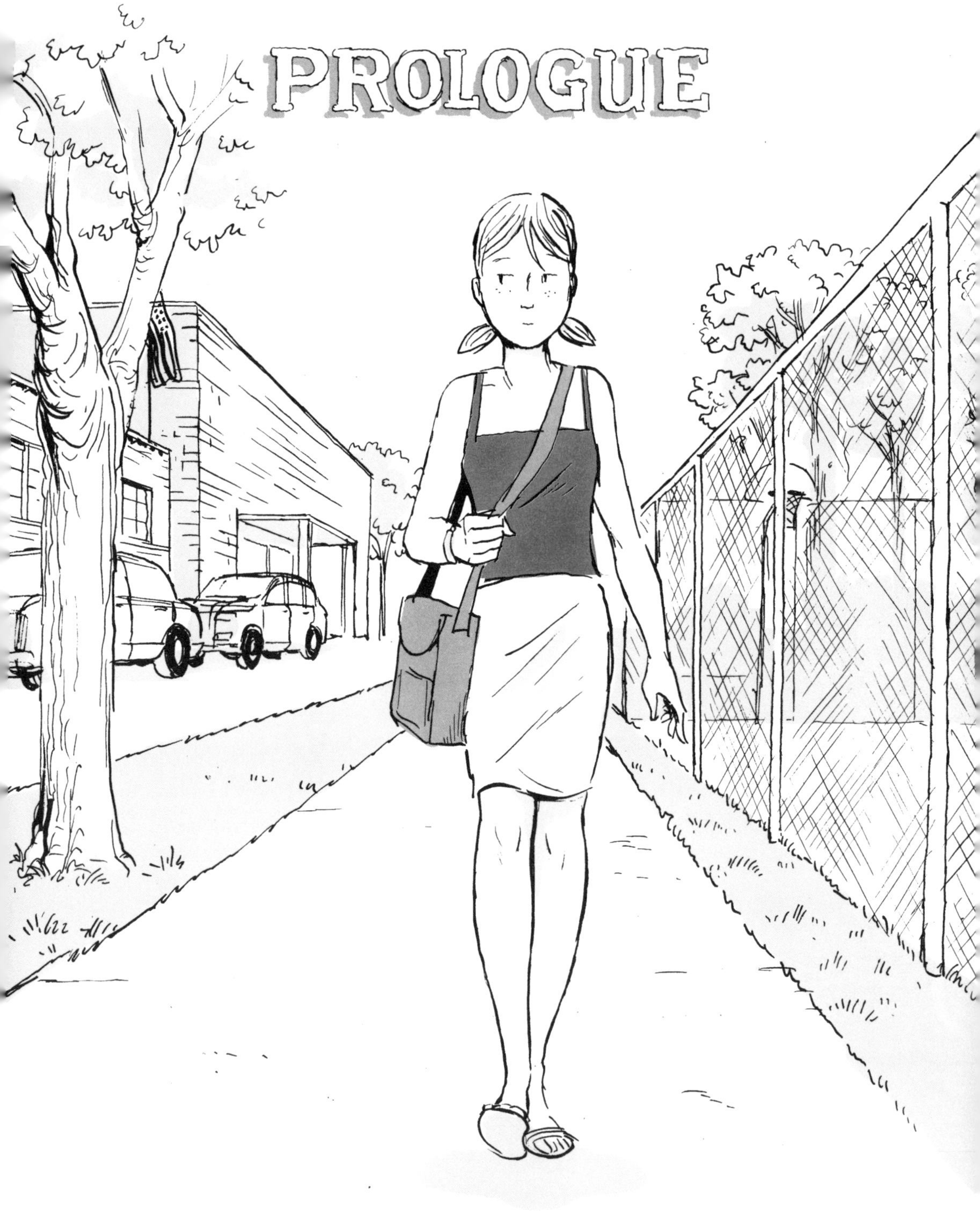

NO ONE AT MY OLD SCHOOL KNEW ABOUT
MY PEANUT ALLERGY. . . .

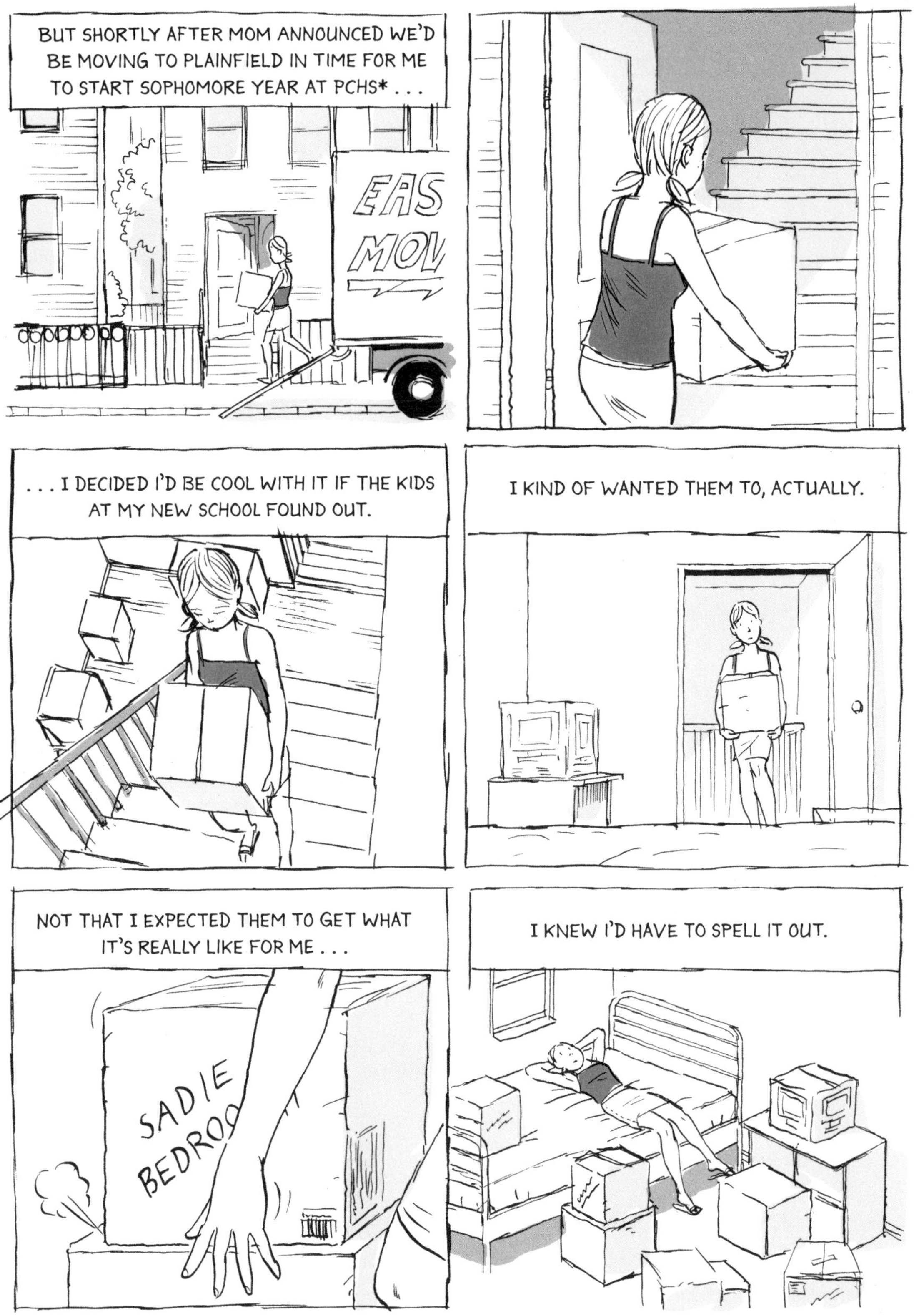
BUT SHORTLY AFTER MOM ANNOUNCED WE'D BE MOVING TO PLAINFIELD IN TIME FOR ME TO START SOPHOMORE YEAR AT PCHS* . . .
EAS
MOV
. . . I DECIDED I'D BE COOL WITH IT IF THE KIDS AT MY NEW SCHOOL FOUND OUT.
I KIND OF WANTED THEM TO, ACTUALLY.
NOT THAT I EXPECTED THEM TO GET WHAT IT'S REALLY LIKE FOR ME . . .
SADIE
BEDRO
I KNEW I'D HAVE TO SPELL IT OUT.

(*PCHS=PLAINFIELD COMMUNITY HIGH SCHOOL)

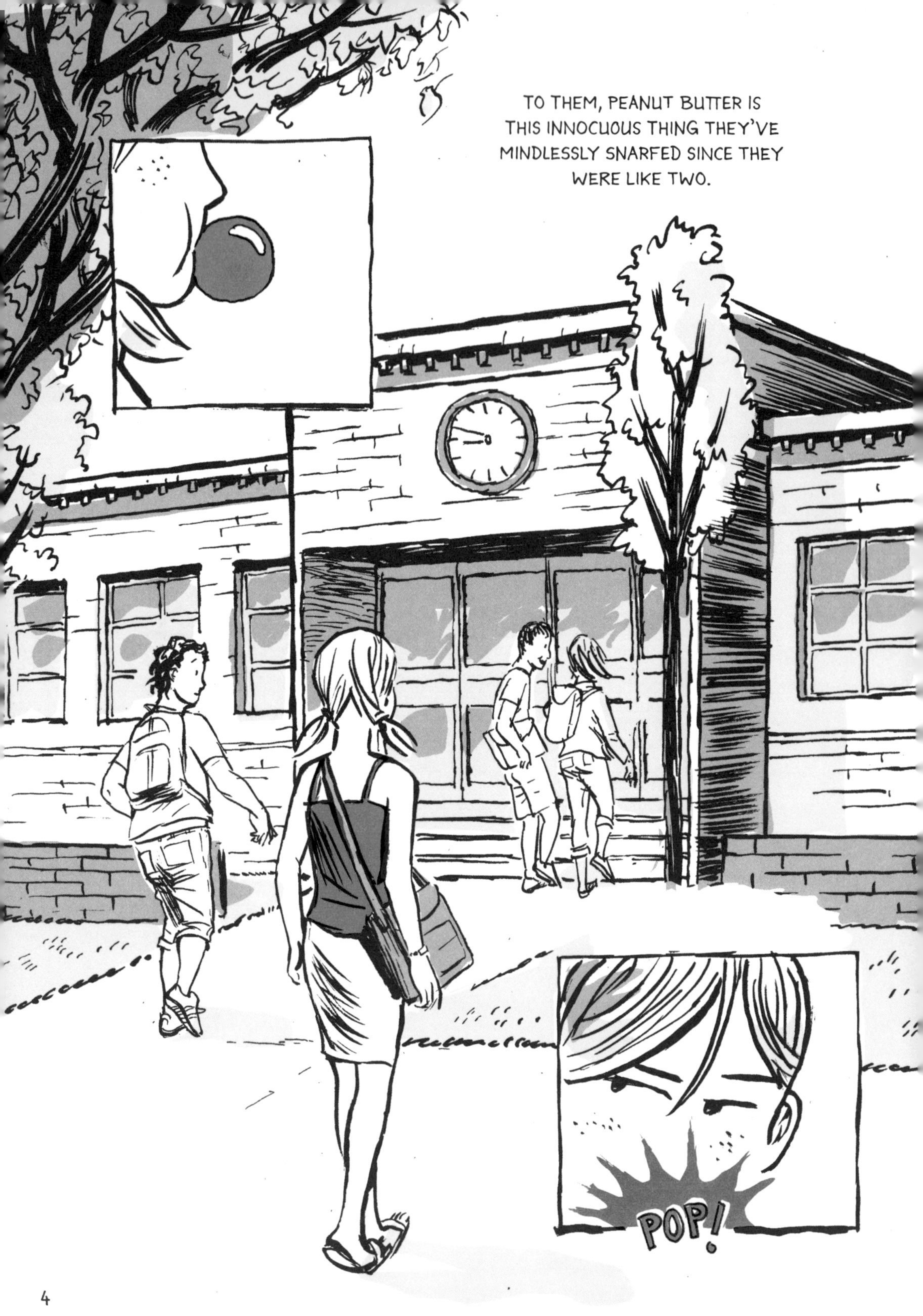
TO THEM, PEANUT BUTTER IS THIS INNOCUOUS THING THEY'VE MINDLESSLY SNARFED SINCE THEY WERE LIKE TWO.
POP!

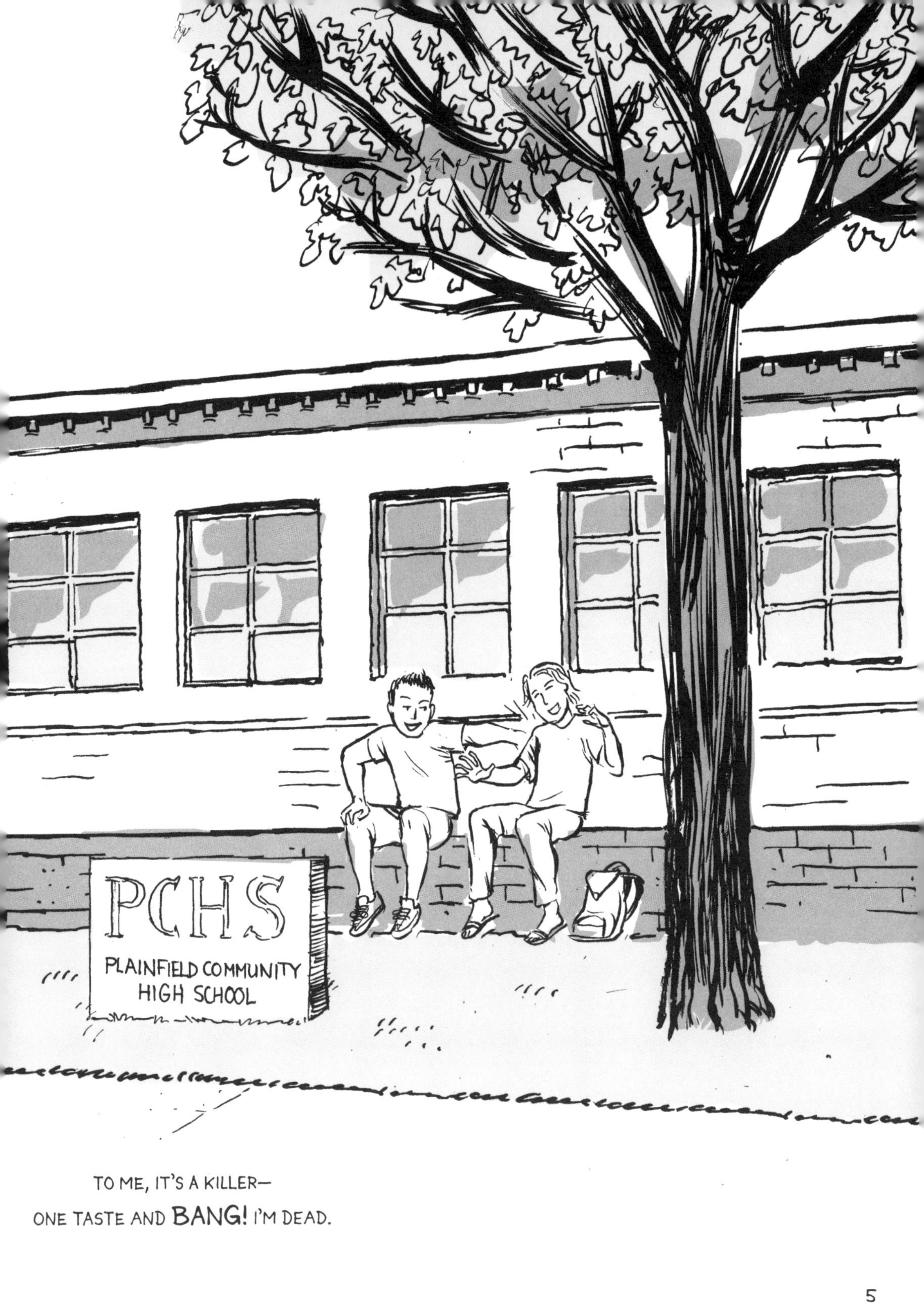
PCHS
PLAINFIELD COMMUNITY HIGH SCHOOL

TO ME, IT'S A KILLER—
ONE TASTE AND **BANG!** I'M DEAD.

ZOO GOT THAT RIGHT AWAY.

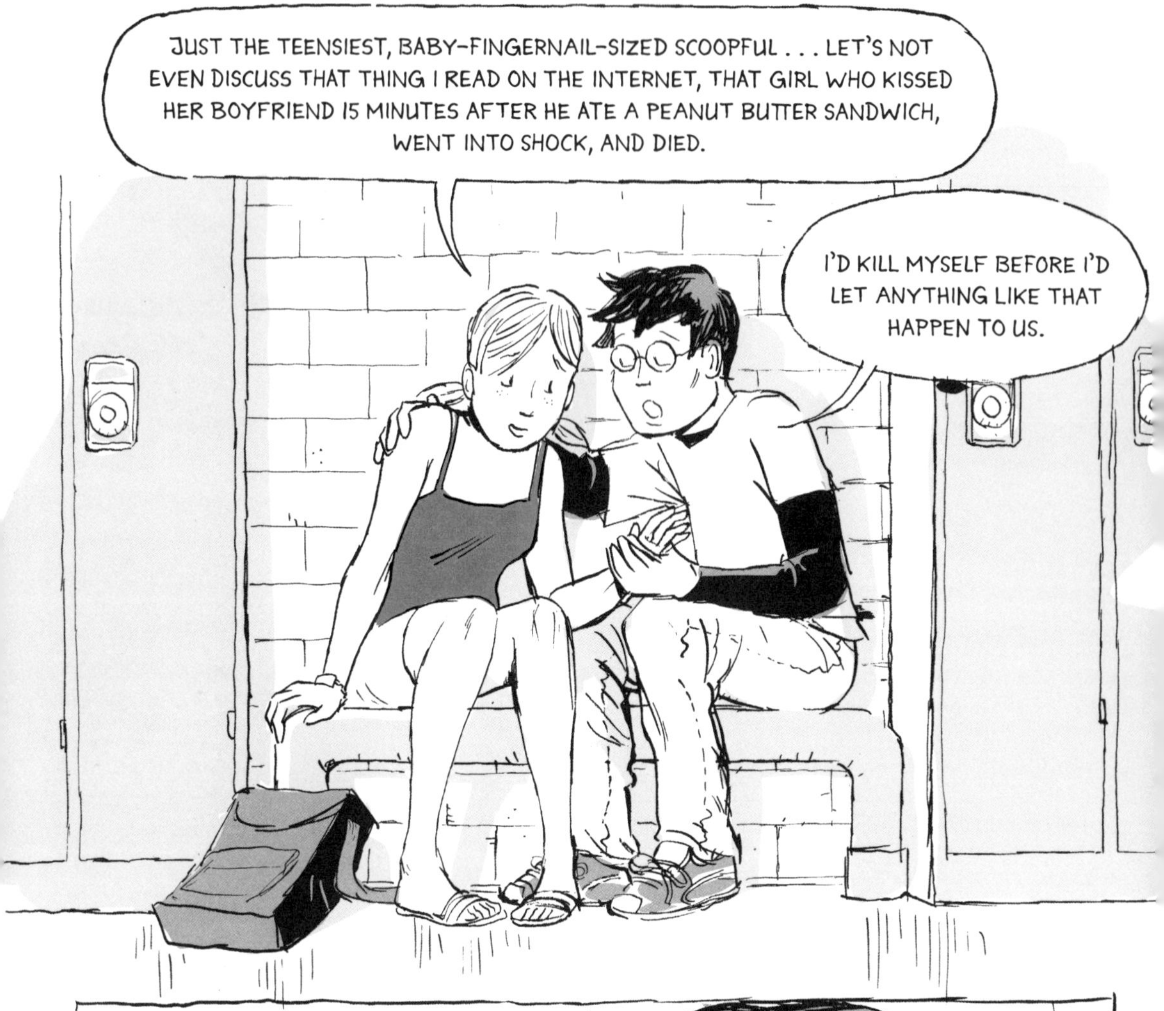
JUST THE TEENSIEST, BABY-FINGERNAIL-SIZED SCOOPFUL . . . LET'S NOT EVEN DISCUSS THAT THING I READ ON THE INTERNET, THAT GIRL WHO KISSED HER BOYFRIEND 15 MINUTES AFTER HE ATE A PEANUT BUTTER SANDWICH, WENT INTO SHOCK, AND DIED.
I'D KILL MYSELF BEFORE I'D LET ANYTHING LIKE THAT HAPPEN TO US.

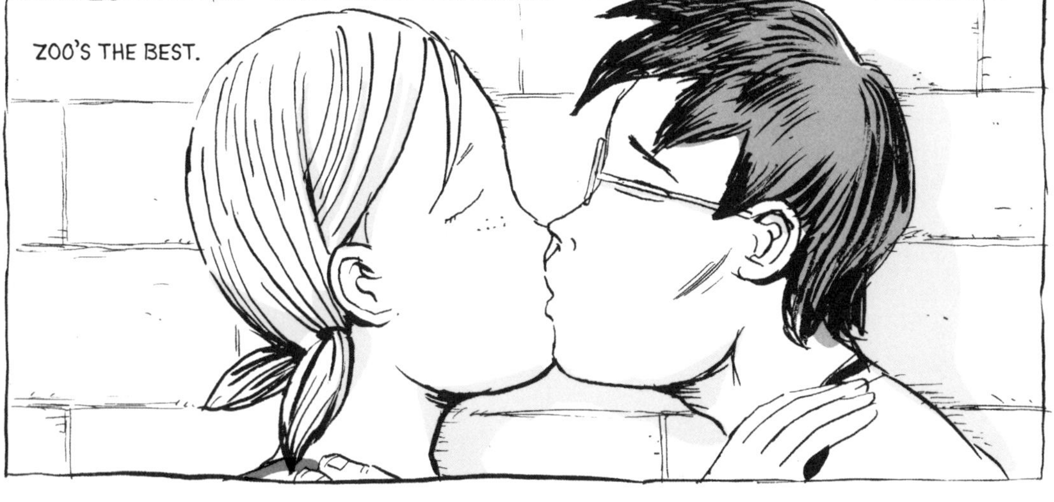
ZOO'S THE BEST.

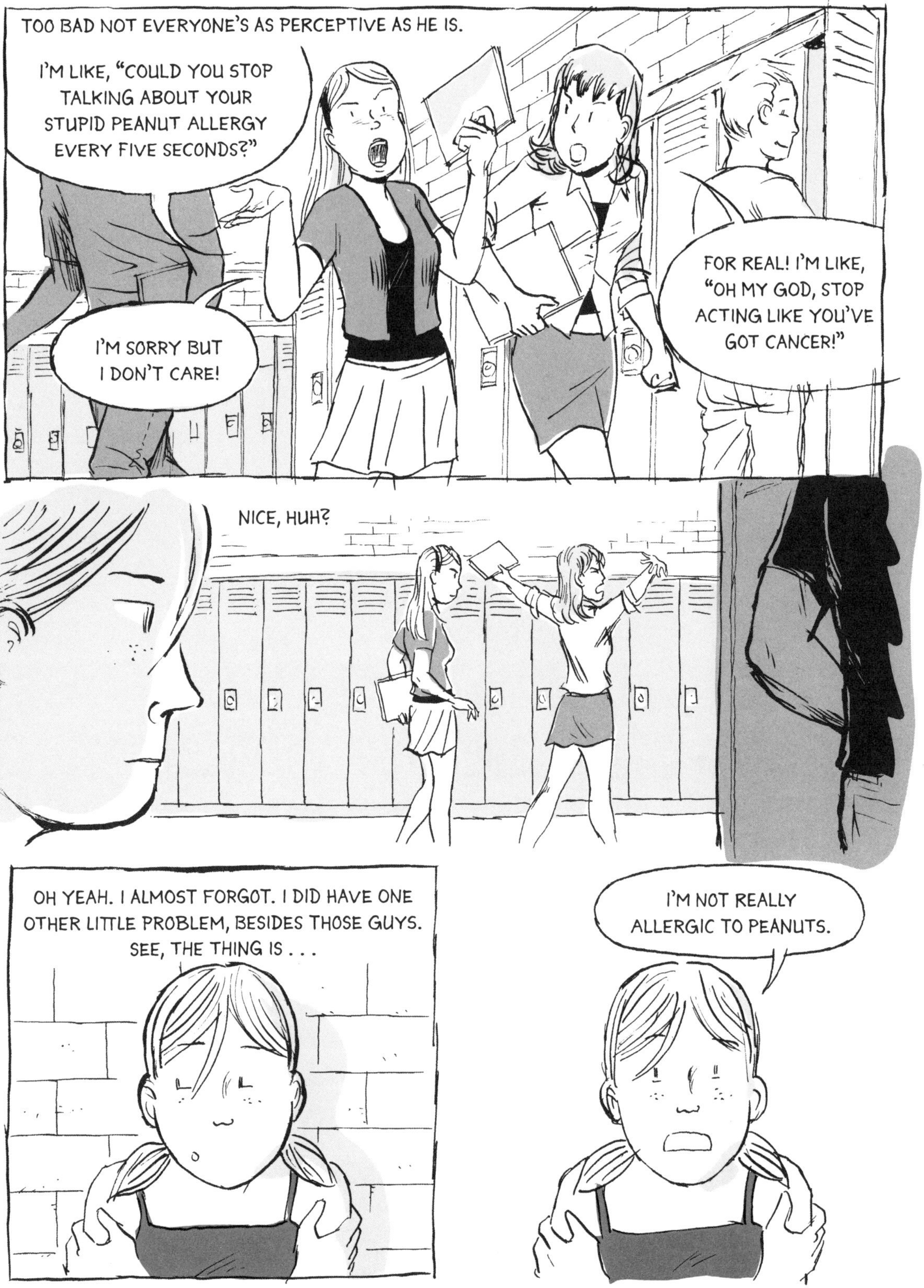

TOO BAD NOT EVERYONE'S AS PERCEPTIVE AS HE IS.
I'M LIKE, "COULD YOU STOP TALKING ABOUT YOUR STUPID PEANUT ALLERGY EVERY FIVE SECONDS?"
I'M SORRY BUT I DON'T CARE!
FOR REAL! I'M LIKE, "OH MY GOD, STOP ACTING LIKE YOU'VE GOT CANCER!"
NICE, HUH?
OH YEAH. I ALMOST FORGOT. I DID HAVE ONE OTHER LITTLE PROBLEM, BESIDES THOSE GUYS. SEE, THE THING IS . . .
I'M NOT REALLY ALLERGIC TO PEANUTS.

LAST MAY

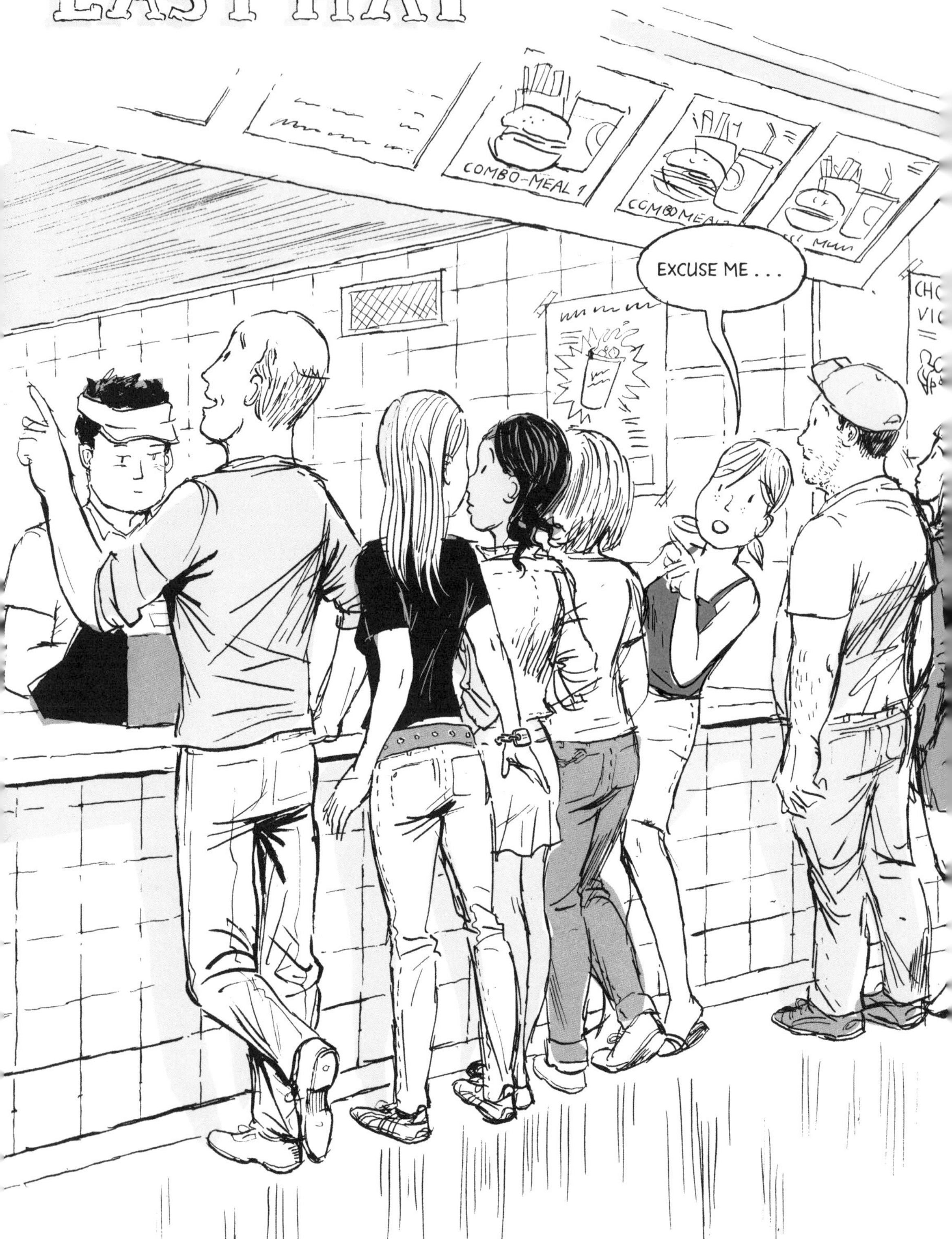
COMBO-MEAL 1
EXCUSE ME . . .

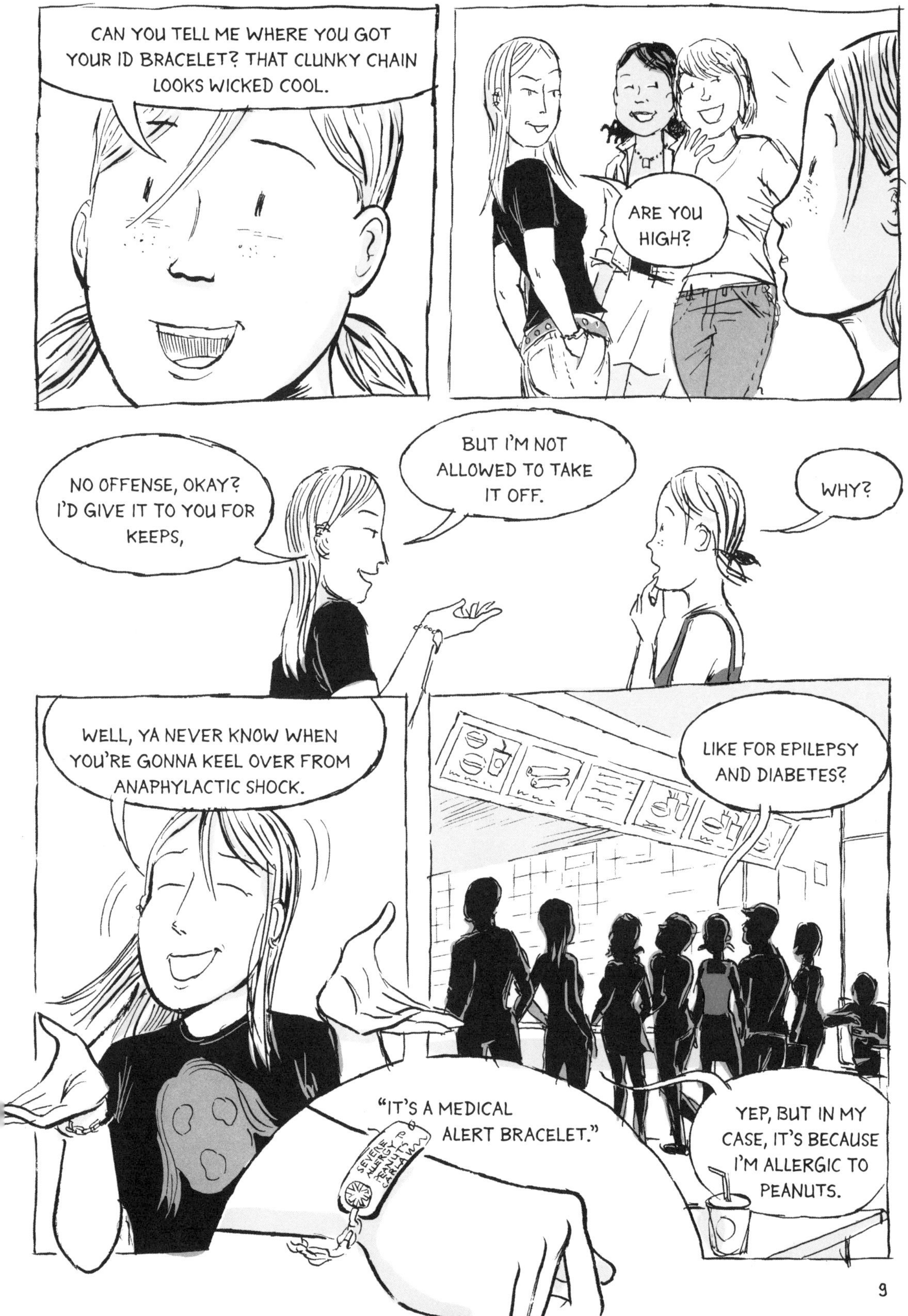
CAN YOU TELL ME WHERE YOU GOT YOUR ID BRACELET? THAT CLUNKY CHAIN LOOKS WICKED COOL.
ARE YOU HIGH?
NO OFFENSE, OKAY? I'D GIVE IT TO YOU FOR KEEPS,
BUT I'M NOT ALLOWED TO TAKE IT OFF.
WHY?
WELL, YA NEVER KNOW WHEN YOU'RE GONNA KEEL OVER FROM ANAPHYLACTIC SHOCK.
LIKE FOR EPILEPSY AND DIABETES?
"IT'S A MEDICAL ALERT BRACELET."
SEVERE ALLERGY TO PEANUTS
YEP, BUT IN MY CASE, IT'S BECAUSE I'M ALLERGIC TO PEANUTS.

OH . . . FORGIVE ME FOR BEING DENSE, BUT IF YOU KNOW YOU'RE ALLERGIC, CAN'T YOU JUST NOT EAT THEM?

PLEASE. YOU WOULDN'T BELIEVE ALL THE THINGS THAT CONTAIN PEANUT OIL . . .

. . . OR WERE PROCESSED IN A PLACE THAT ALSO PROCESSES PEANUTS . . .

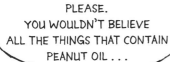

LIKE, MY FRIENDS ALL LOVE THAI FOOD, RIGHT? BUT WHENEVER WE GO TO A THAI RESTAURANT, THERE'S NOTHING FOR ME TO EAT!

EVERYTHING'S GOT PEANUTS!

BUT IF YOU TELL THE RESTAURANT YOU'RE ALLERGIC—

YOU MEAN ASK THEM TO HOLD THE PEANUTS?

HEY, GREEEEEAT IDEA!

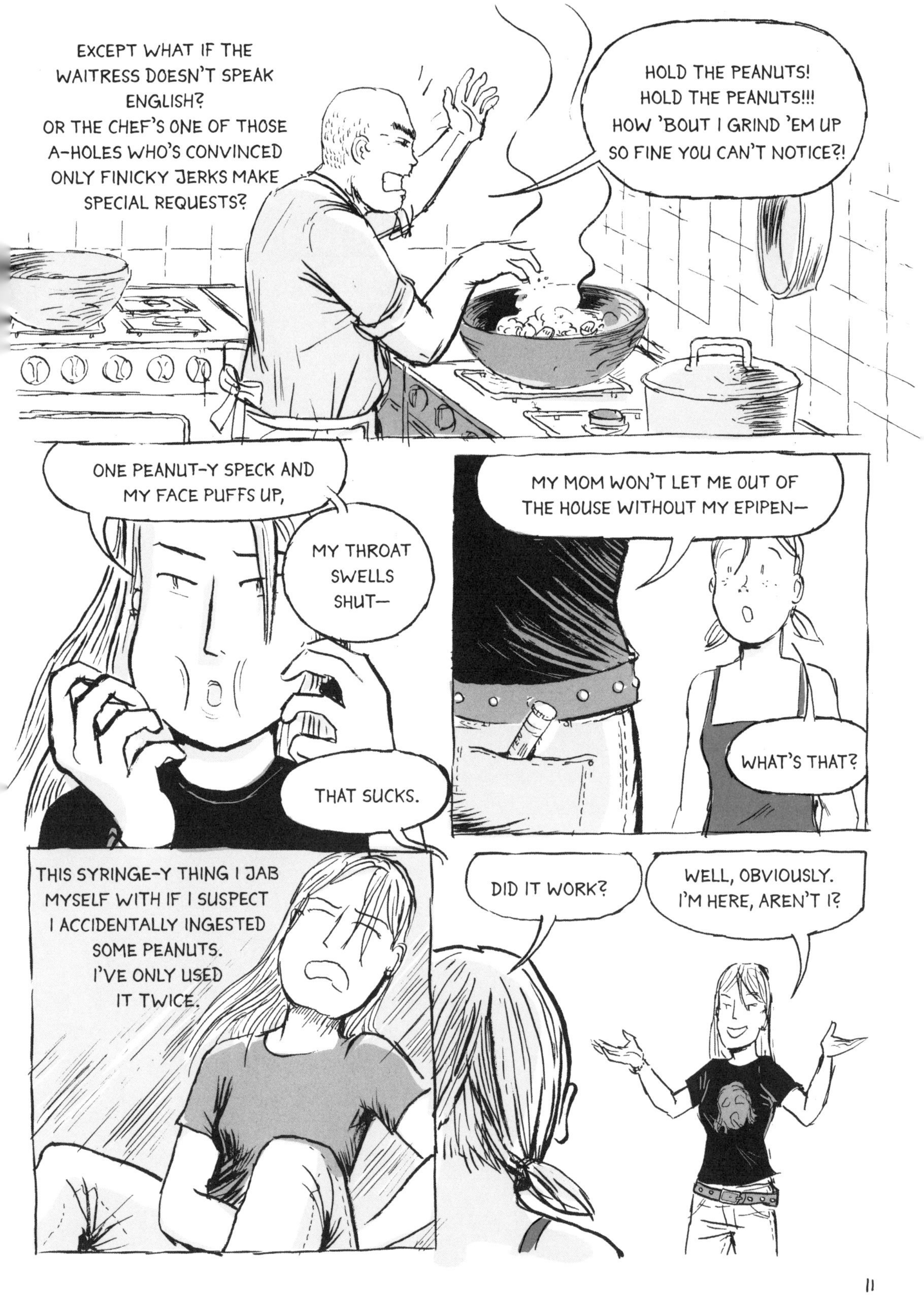
EXCEPT WHAT IF THE WAITRESS DOESN'T SPEAK ENGLISH? OR THE CHEF'S ONE OF THOSE A-HOLES WHO'S CONVINCED ONLY FINICKY JERKS MAKE SPECIAL REQUESTS?
HOLD THE PEANUTS! HOLD THE PEANUTS!!! HOW 'BOUT I GRIND 'EM UP SO FINE YOU CAN'T NOTICE?!
ONE PEANUT-Y SPECK AND MY FACE PUFFS UP,
MY THROAT SWELLS SHUT—
THAT SUCKS.
MY MOM WON'T LET ME OUT OF THE HOUSE WITHOUT MY EPIPEN—
WHAT'S THAT?
THIS SYRINGE-Y THING I JAB MYSELF WITH IF I SUSPECT I ACCIDENTALLY INGESTED SOME PEANUTS. I'VE ONLY USED IT TWICE.
DID IT WORK?
WELL, OBVIOUSLY. I'M HERE, AREN'T I?

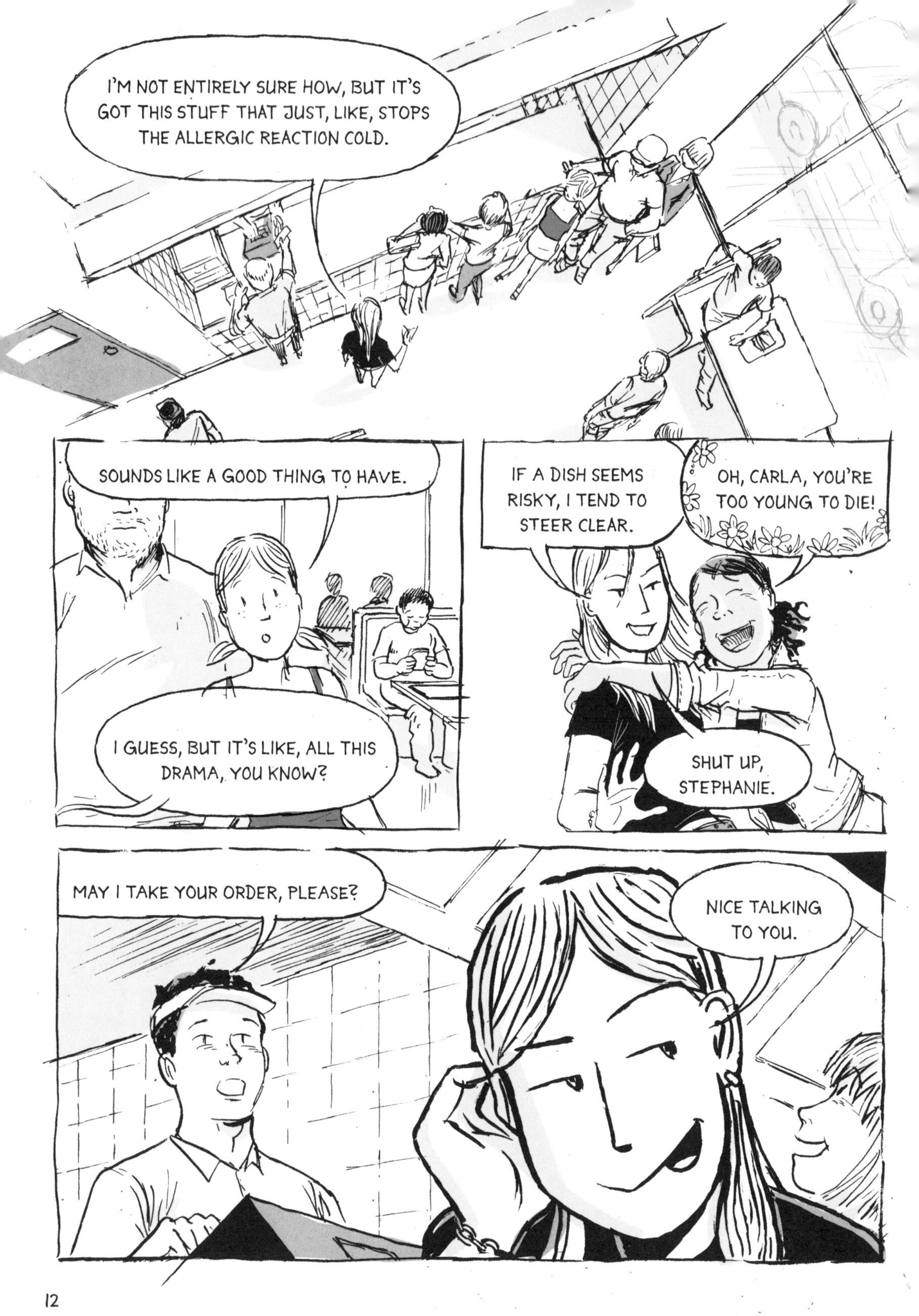
I'M NOT ENTIRELY SURE HOW, BUT IT'S GOT THIS STUFF THAT JUST, LIKE, STOPS THE ALLERGIC REACTION COLD.
SOUNDS LIKE A GOOD THING TO HAVE.
I GUESS, BUT IT'S LIKE, ALL THIS DRAMA, YOU KNOW?
IF A DISH SEEMS RISKY, I TEND TO STEER CLEAR.
OH, CARLA, YOU'RE TOO YOUNG TO DIE!
SHUT UP, STEPHANIE.
MAY I TAKE YOUR ORDER, PLEASE?
NICE TALKING TO YOU.

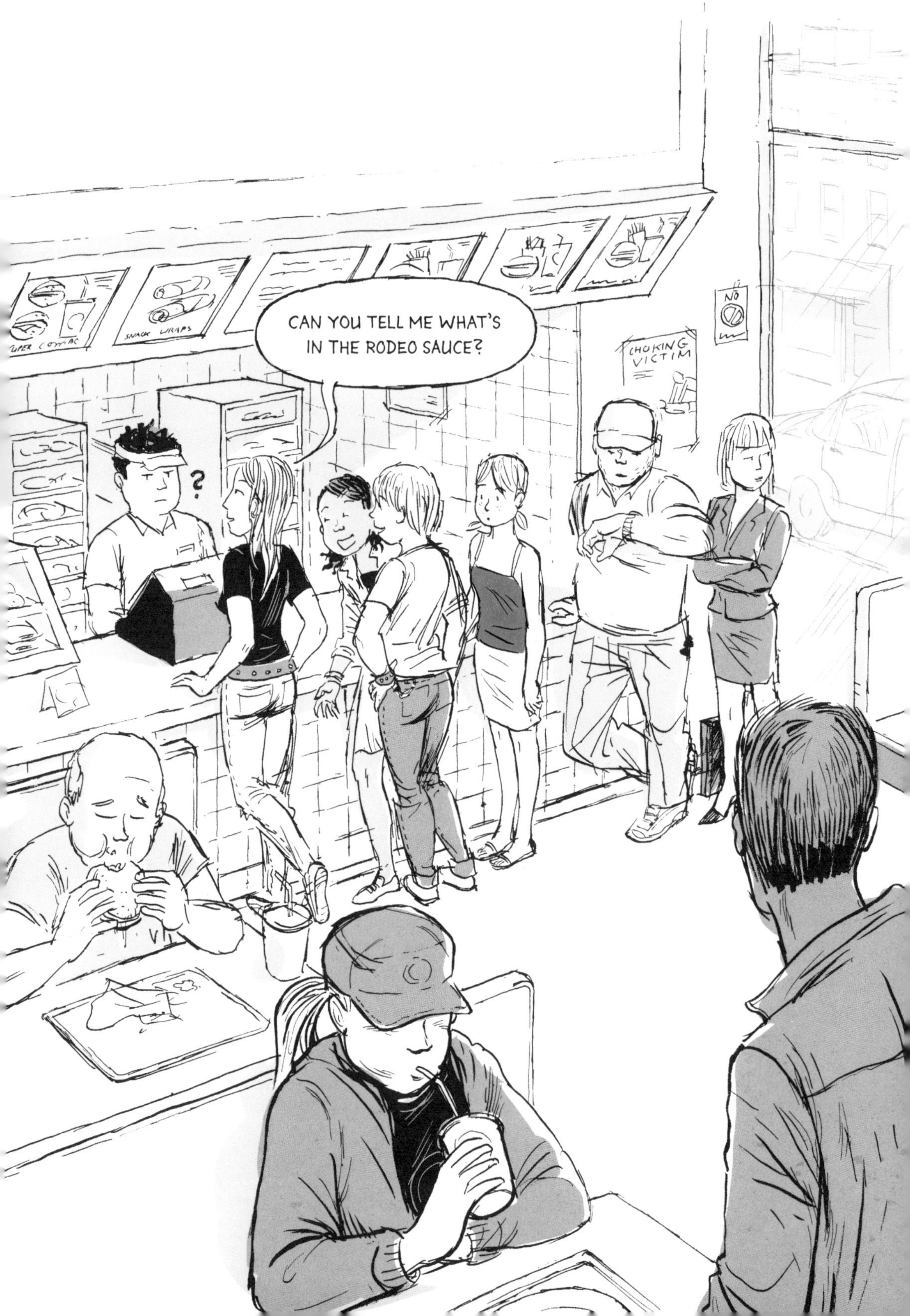
CAN YOU TELL ME WHAT'S IN THE RODEO SAUCE?
?
SNACK WRAPS
CHOKING VICTIM
NO

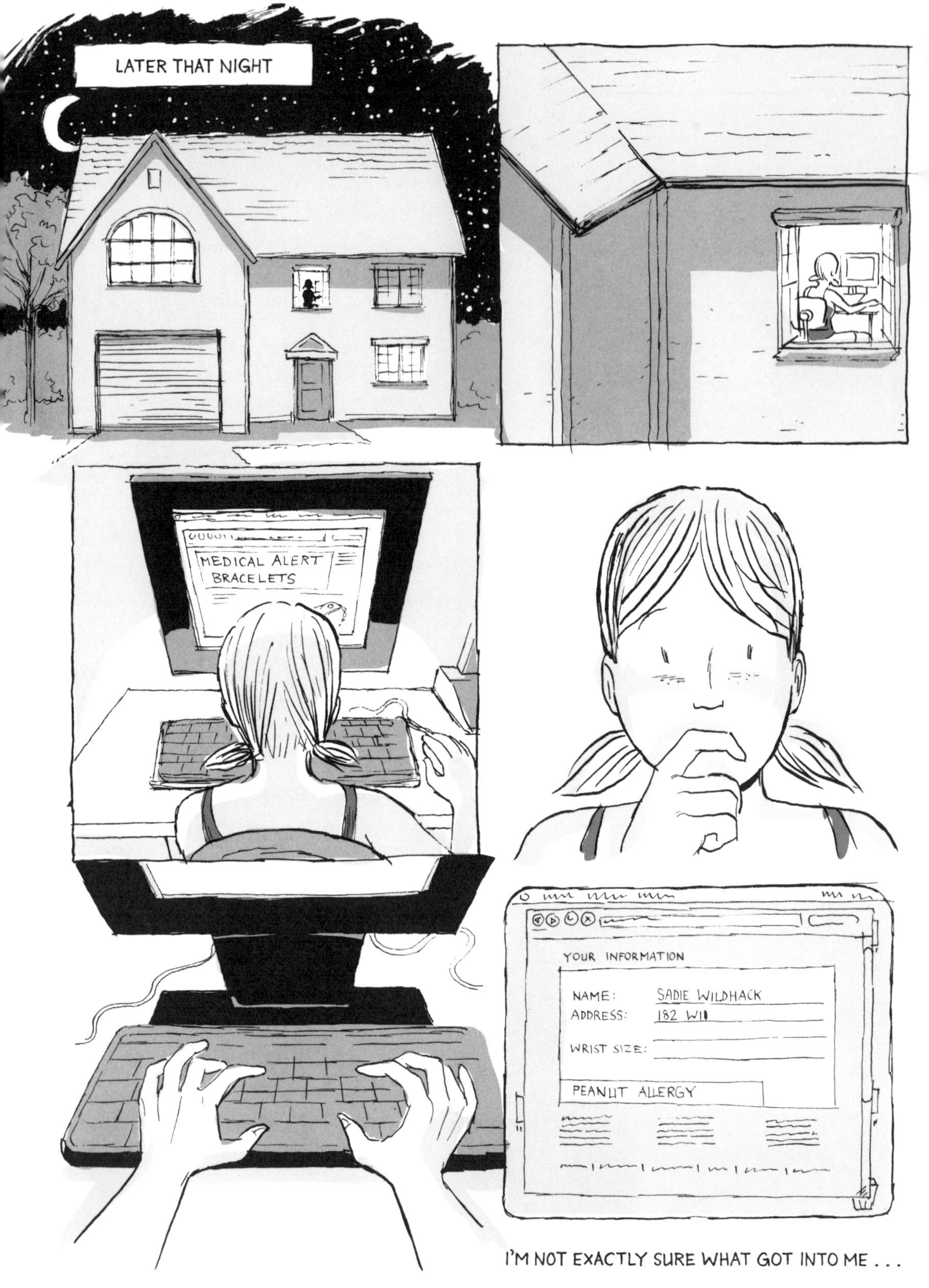
LATER THAT NIGHT
MEDICAL ALERT BRACELETS
YOUR INFORMATION
NAME: SADIE WILDHACK
ADDRESS: 182 WI
WRIST SIZE:
PEANUT ALLERGY
I'M NOT EXACTLY SURE WHAT GOT INTO ME . . .

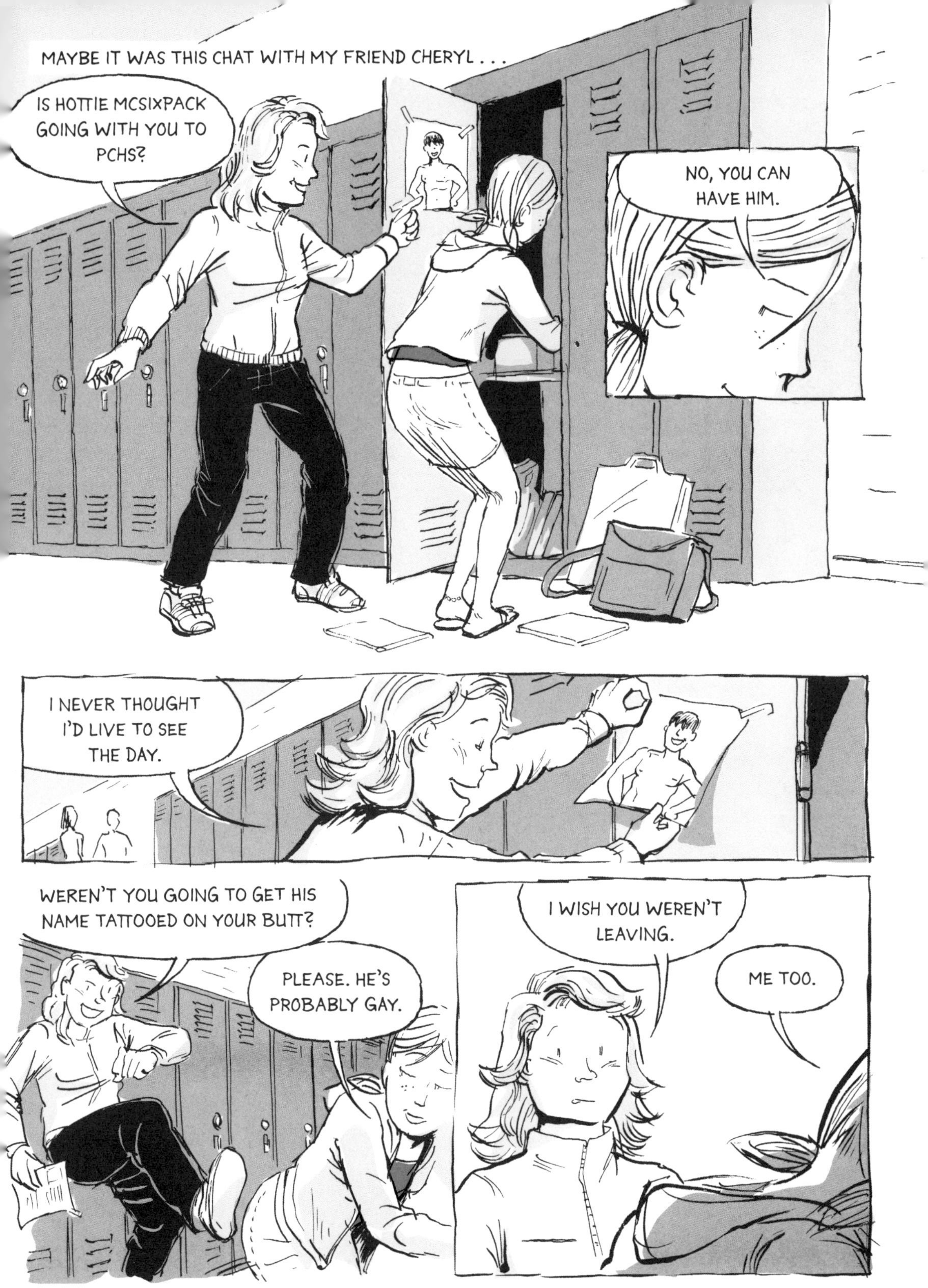
MAYBE IT WAS THIS CHAT WITH MY FRIEND CHERYL . . .
IS HOTTIE MCSIXPACK GOING WITH YOU TO PCHS?
NO, YOU CAN HAVE HIM.
I NEVER THOUGHT I'D LIVE TO SEE THE DAY.
WEREN'T YOU GOING TO GET HIS NAME TATTOOED ON YOUR BUTT?
PLEASE. HE'S PROBABLY GAY.
I WISH YOU WEREN'T LEAVING.
ME TOO.

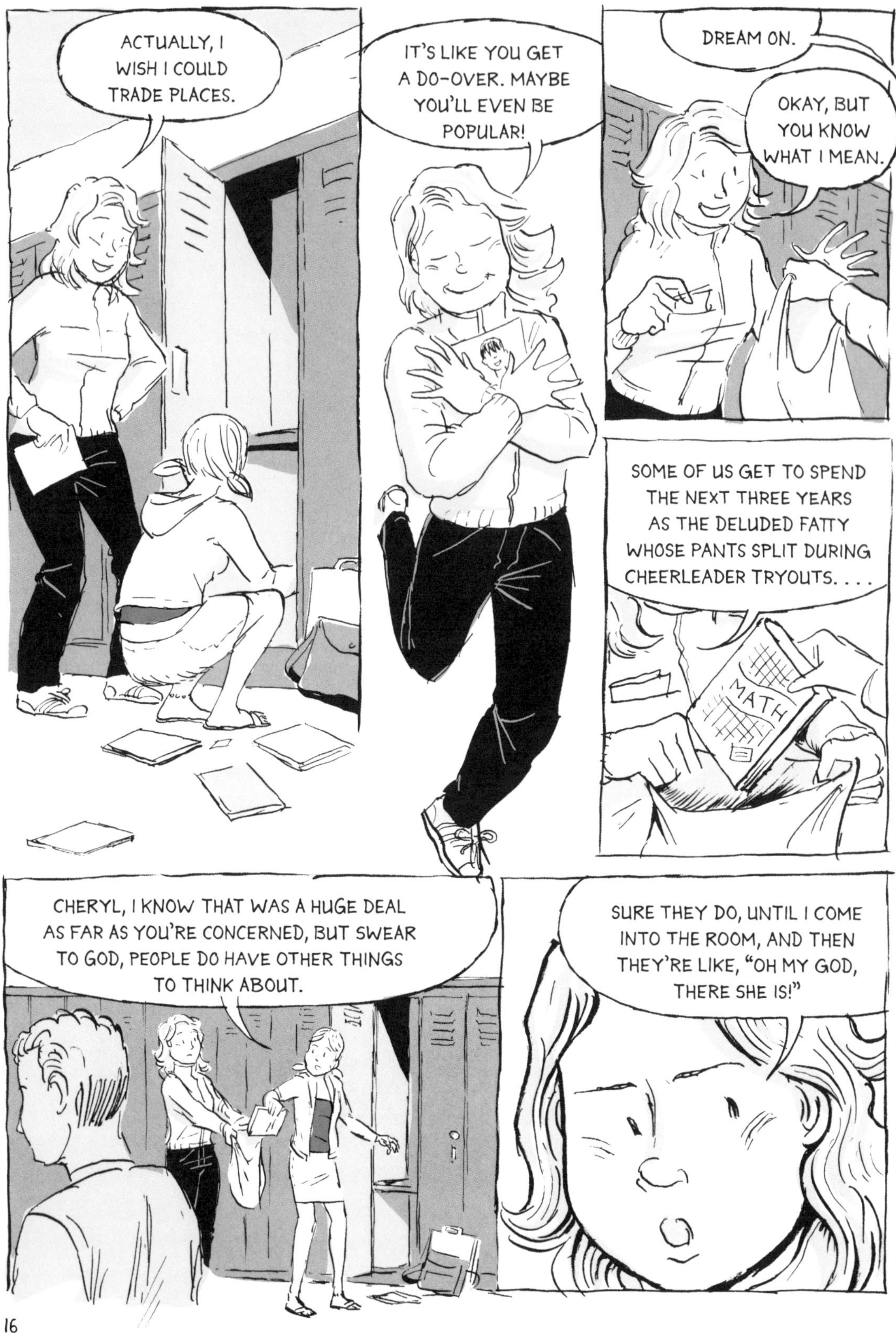
ACTUALLY, I WISH I COULD TRADE PLACES.
IT'S LIKE YOU GET A DO-OVER. MAYBE YOU'LL EVEN BE POPULAR!
DREAM ON.
OKAY, BUT YOU KNOW WHAT I MEAN.
SOME OF US GET TO SPEND THE NEXT THREE YEARS AS THE DELUDED FATTY WHOSE PANTS SPLIT DURING CHEERLEADER TRYOUTS. . . .
MATH
CHERYL, I KNOW THAT WAS A HUGE DEAL AS FAR AS YOU'RE CONCERNED, BUT SWEAR TO GOD, PEOPLE DO HAVE OTHER THINGS TO THINK ABOUT.
SURE THEY DO, UNTIL I COME INTO THE ROOM, AND THEN THEY'RE LIKE, "OH MY GOD, THERE SHE IS!"

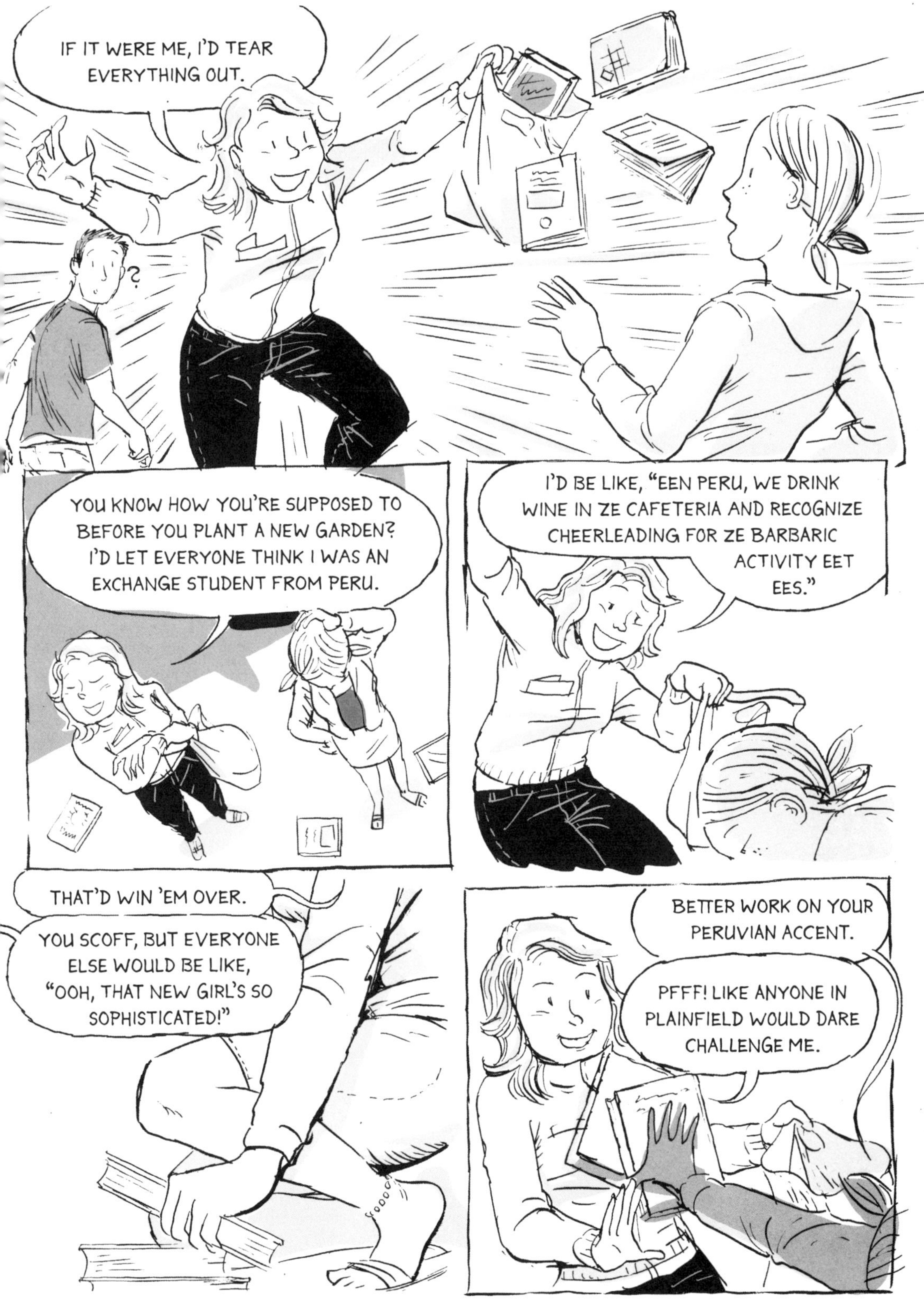
IF IT WERE ME, I'D TEAR EVERYTHING OUT.
YOU KNOW HOW YOU'RE SUPPOSED TO BEFORE YOU PLANT A NEW GARDEN? I'D LET EVERYONE THINK I WAS AN EXCHANGE STUDENT FROM PERU.
I'D BE LIKE, "EEN PERU, WE DRINK WINE IN ZE CAFETERIA AND RECOGNIZE CHEERLEADING FOR ZE BARBARIC ACTIVITY EET EES."
THAT'D WIN 'EM OVER.
YOU SCOFF, BUT EVERYONE ELSE WOULD BE LIKE, "OOH, THAT NEW GIRL'S SO SOPHISTICATED!"
BETTER WORK ON YOUR PERUVIAN ACCENT.
PFFF! LIKE ANYONE IN PLAINFIELD WOULD DARE CHALLENGE ME.

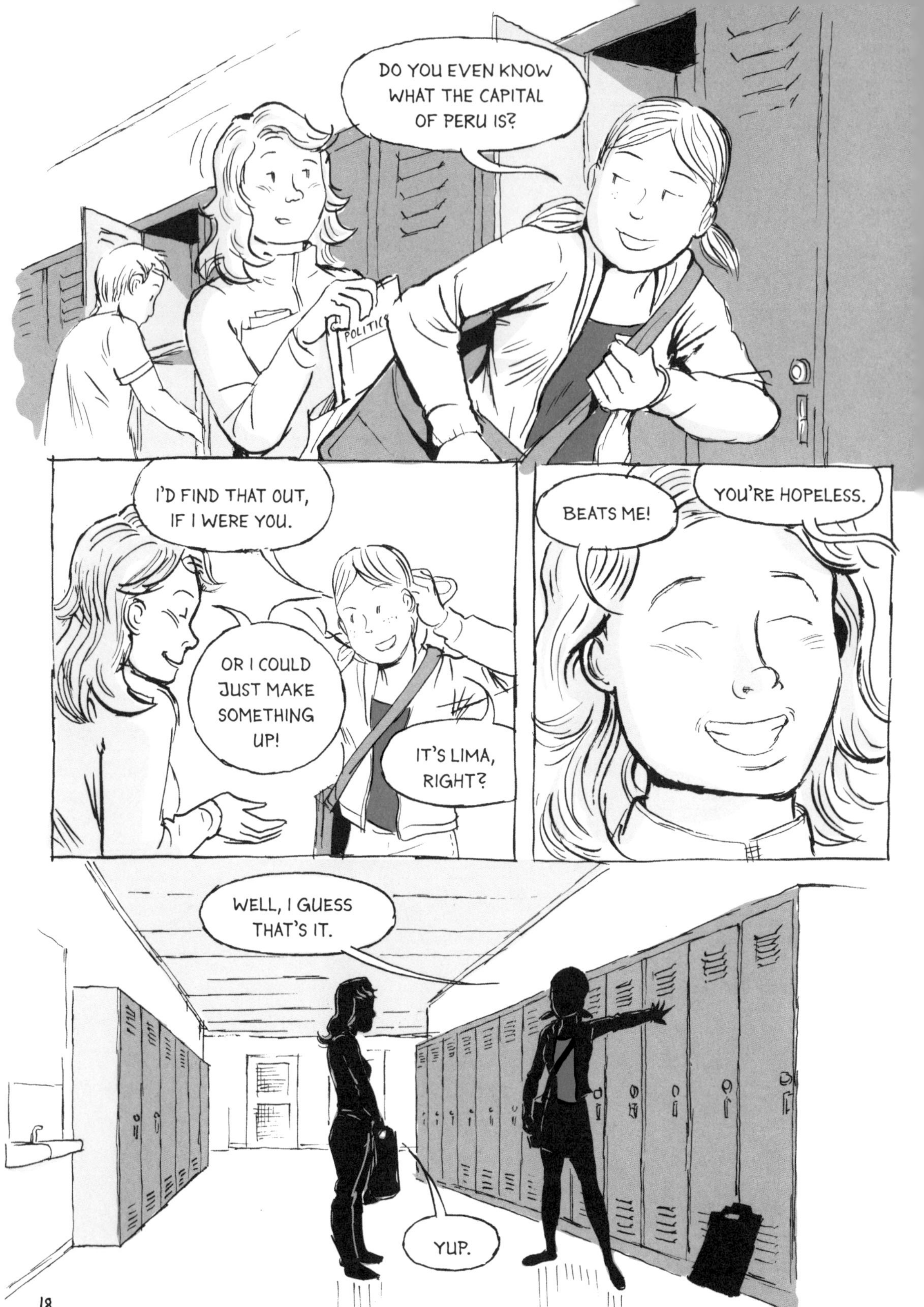

DO YOU EVEN KNOW WHAT THE CAPITAL OF PERU IS?
POLITICS
I'D FIND THAT OUT, IF I WERE YOU.
OR I COULD JUST MAKE SOMETHING UP!
IT'S LIMA, RIGHT?
BEATS ME!
YOU'RE HOPELESS.
WELL, I GUESS THAT'S IT.
YUP.

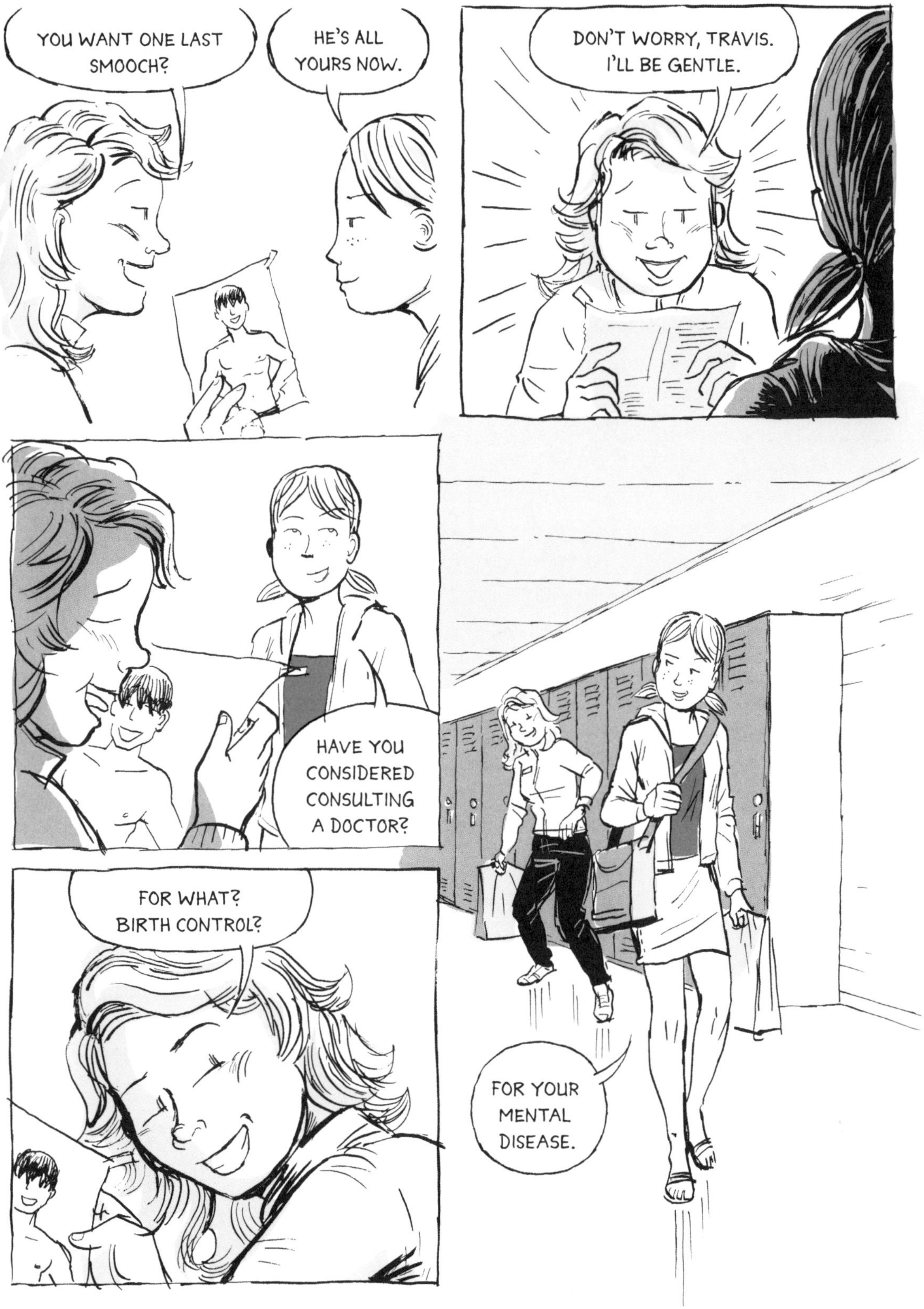
YOU WANT ONE LAST SMOOCH?
HE'S ALL YOURS NOW.
DON'T WORRY, TRAVIS. I'LL BE GENTLE.
HAVE YOU CONSIDERED CONSULTING A DOCTOR?
FOR WHAT? BIRTH CONTROL?
FOR YOUR MENTAL DISEASE.

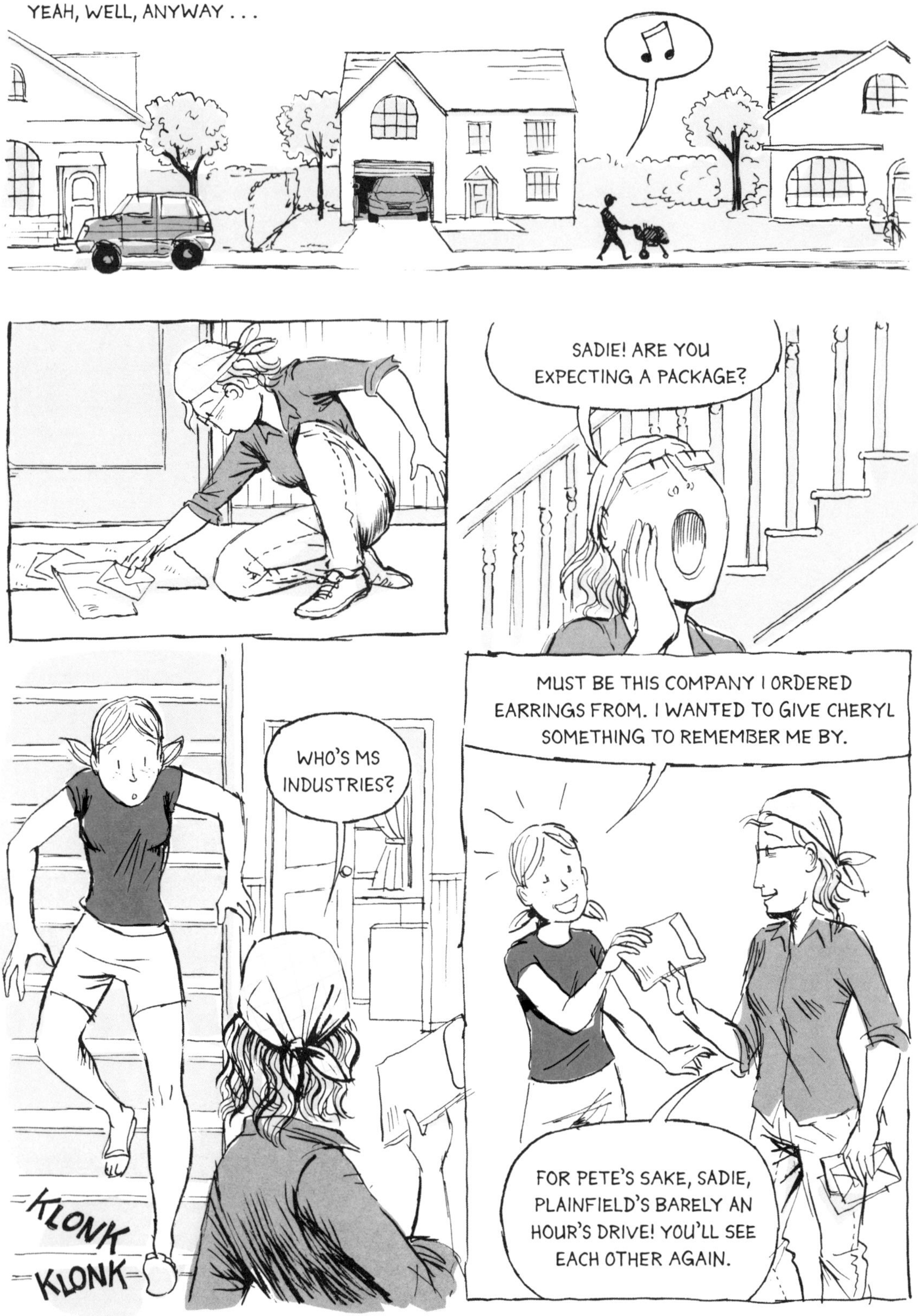
YEAH, WELL, ANYWAY . . .
SADIE! ARE YOU EXPECTING A PACKAGE?
WHO'S MS INDUSTRIES?
KLONK
KLONK
MUST BE THIS COMPANY I ORDERED EARRINGS FROM. I WANTED TO GIVE CHERYL SOMETHING TO REMEMBER ME BY.
FOR PETE'S SAKE, SADIE, PLAINFIELD'S BARELY AN HOUR'S DRIVE! YOU'LL SEE EACH OTHER AGAIN.

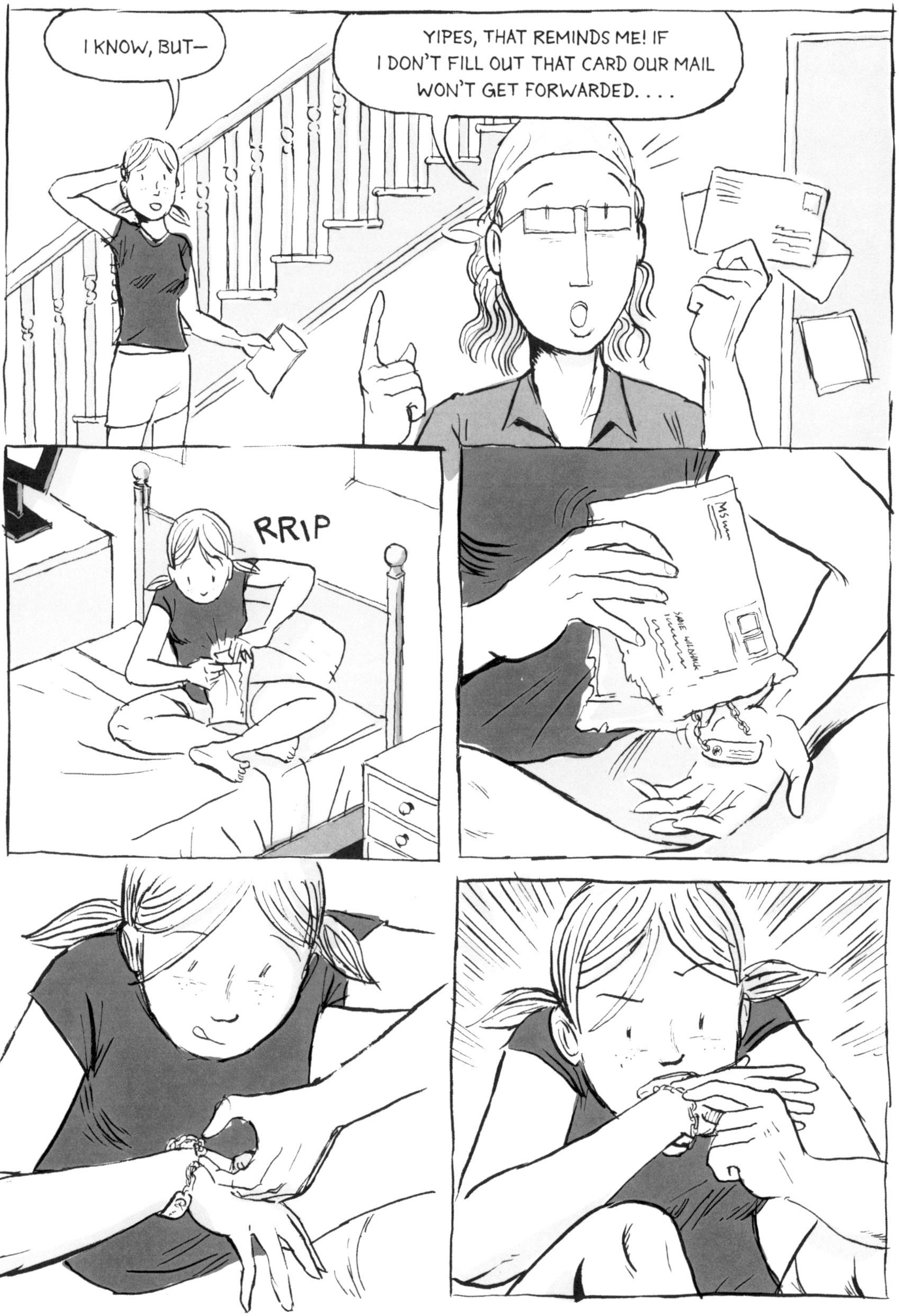
I KNOW, BUT—
YIPES, THAT REMINDS ME! IF I DON'T FILL OUT THAT CARD OUR MAIL WON'T GET FORWARDED. . . .
RRIP

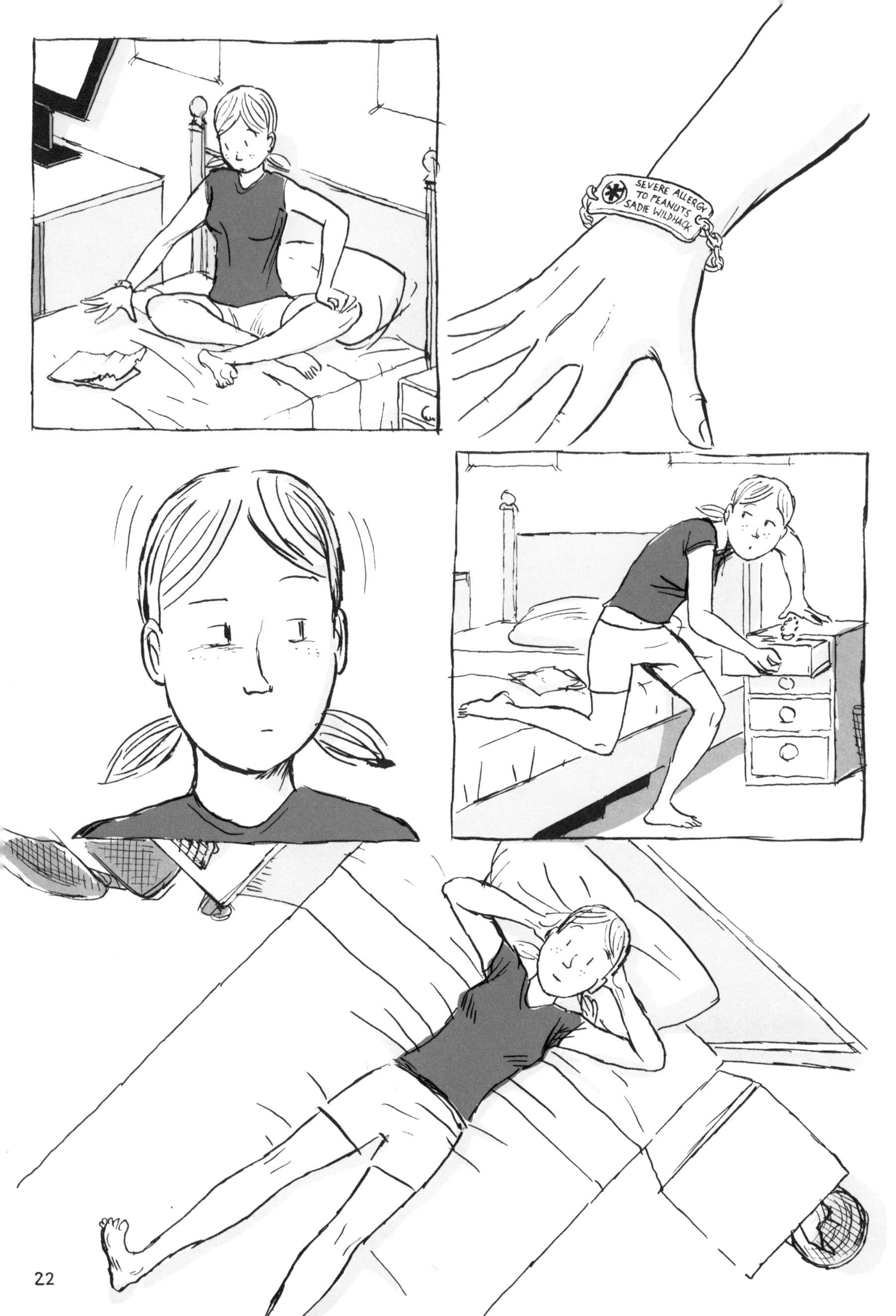
SEVERE ALLERGY
TO PEANUTS
SADIE WILDHACK

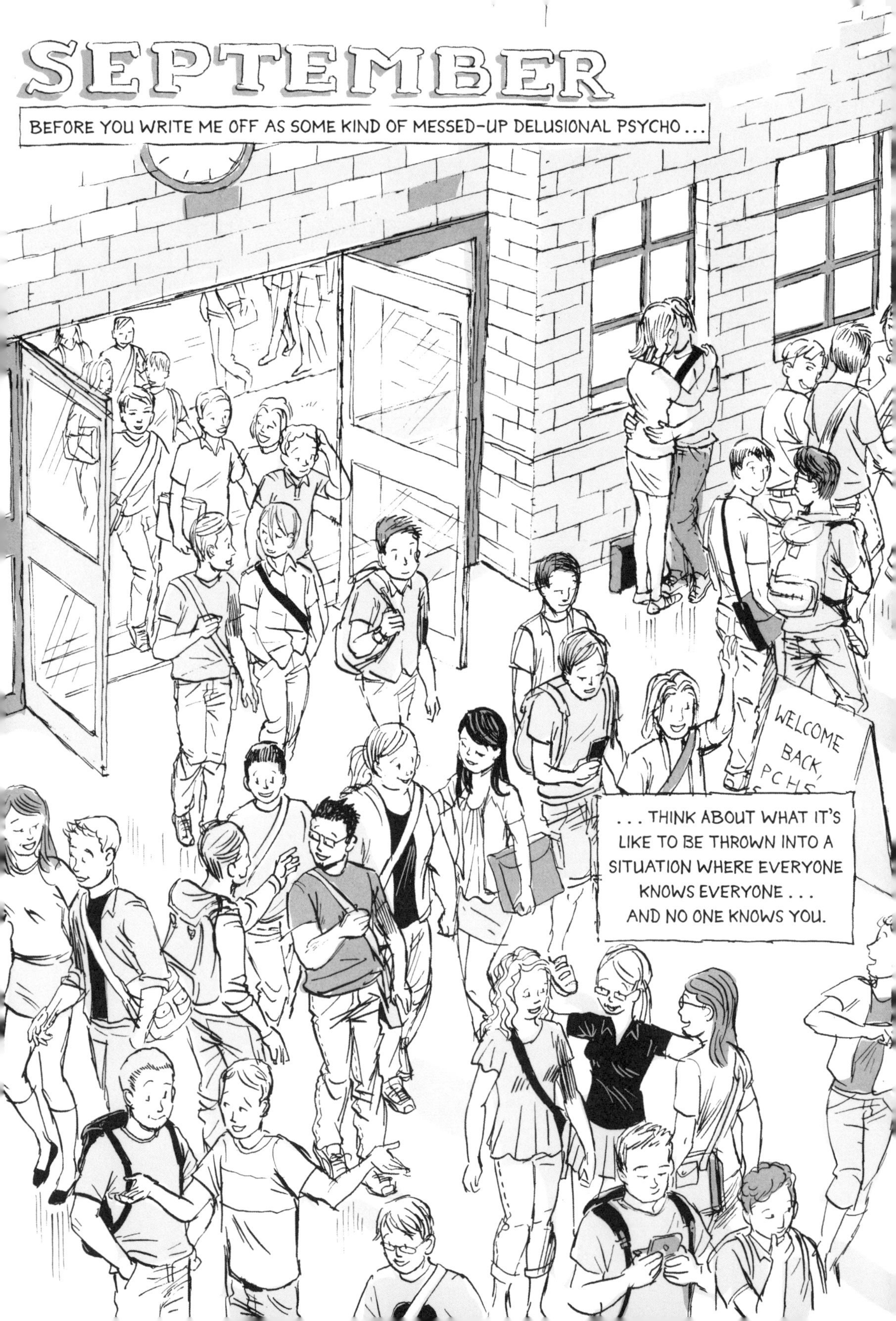
SEPTEMBER
BEFORE YOU WRITE ME OFF AS SOME KIND OF MESSED-UP DELUSIONAL PSYCHO . . .
WELCOME BACK, PCHS
. . . THINK ABOUT WHAT IT'S LIKE TO BE THROWN INTO A SITUATION WHERE EVERYONE KNOWS EVERYONE . . . AND NO ONE KNOWS YOU.

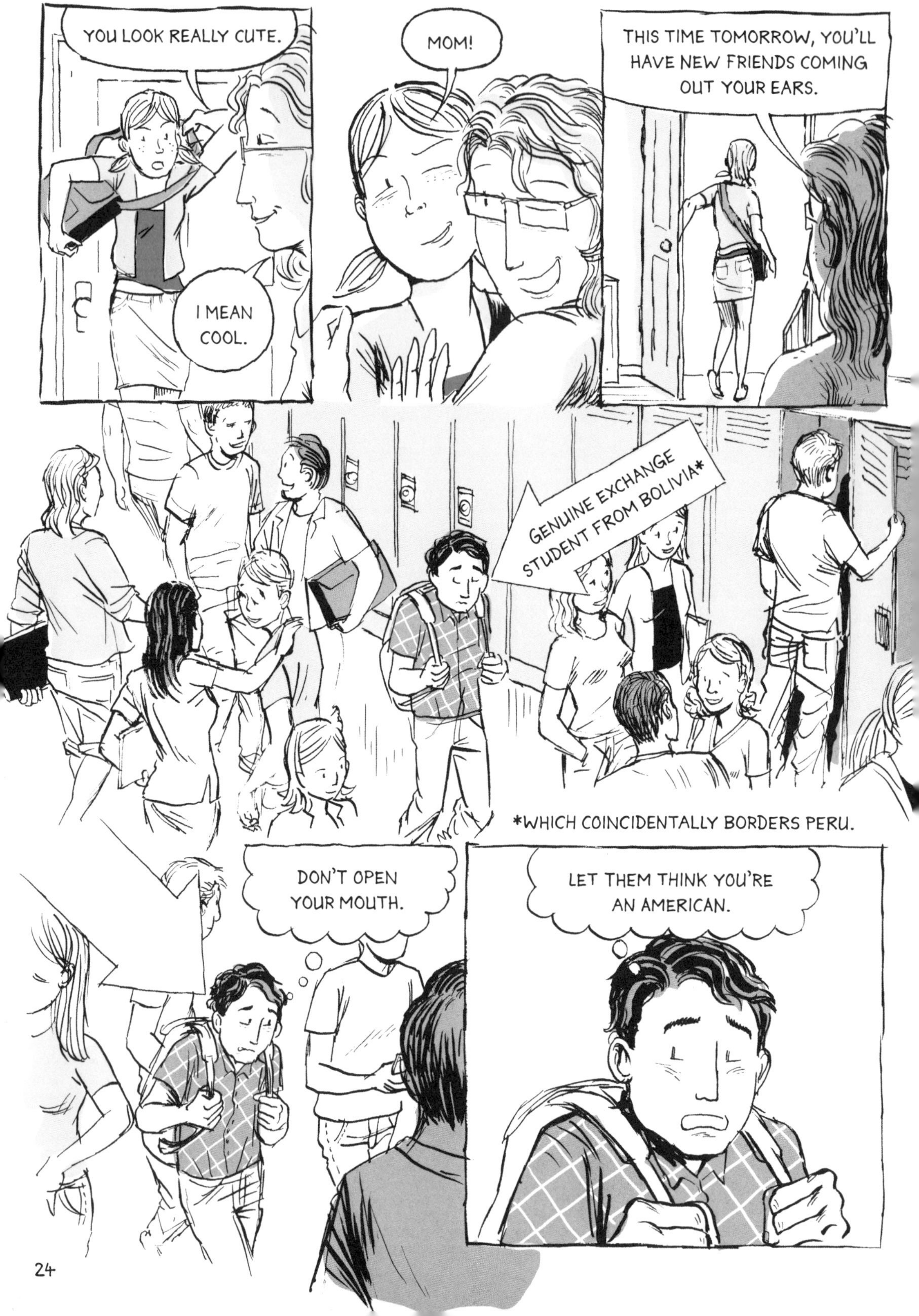
YOU LOOK REALLY CUTE.
I MEAN COOL.
MOM!
THIS TIME TOMORROW, YOU'LL HAVE NEW FRIENDS COMING OUT YOUR EARS.
GENUINE EXCHANGE STUDENT FROM BOLIVIA*
*WHICH COINCIDENTALLY BORDERS PERU.
DON'T OPEN YOUR MOUTH.
LET THEM THINK YOU'RE AN AMERICAN.

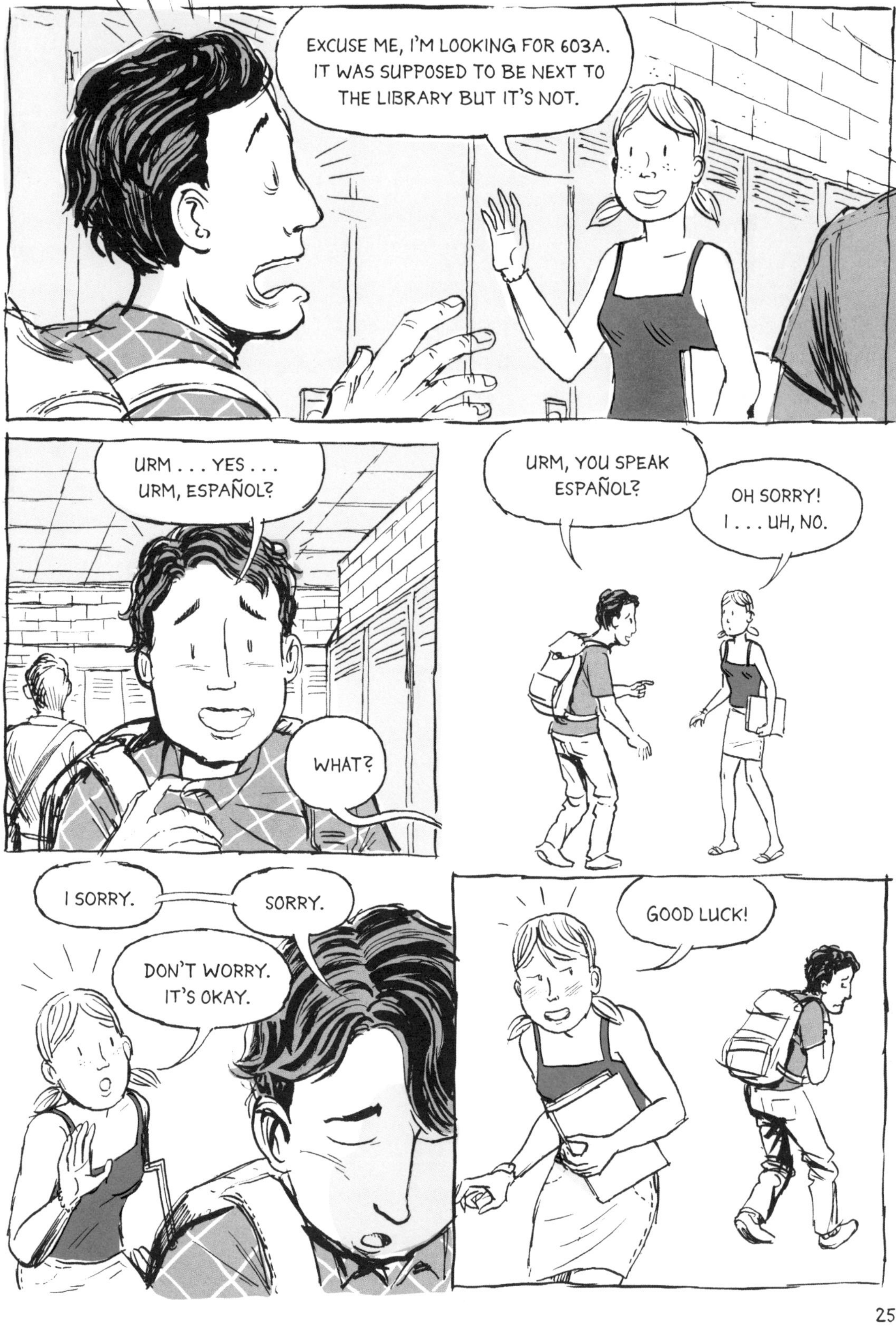
EXCUSE ME, I'M LOOKING FOR 603A. IT WAS SUPPOSED TO BE NEXT TO THE LIBRARY BUT IT'S NOT.
URM . . . YES . . . URM, ESPAÑOL?
WHAT?
URM, YOU SPEAK ESPAÑOL?
OH SORRY! I . . . UH, NO.
I SORRY.
SORRY.
DON'T WORRY. IT'S OKAY.
GOOD LUCK!

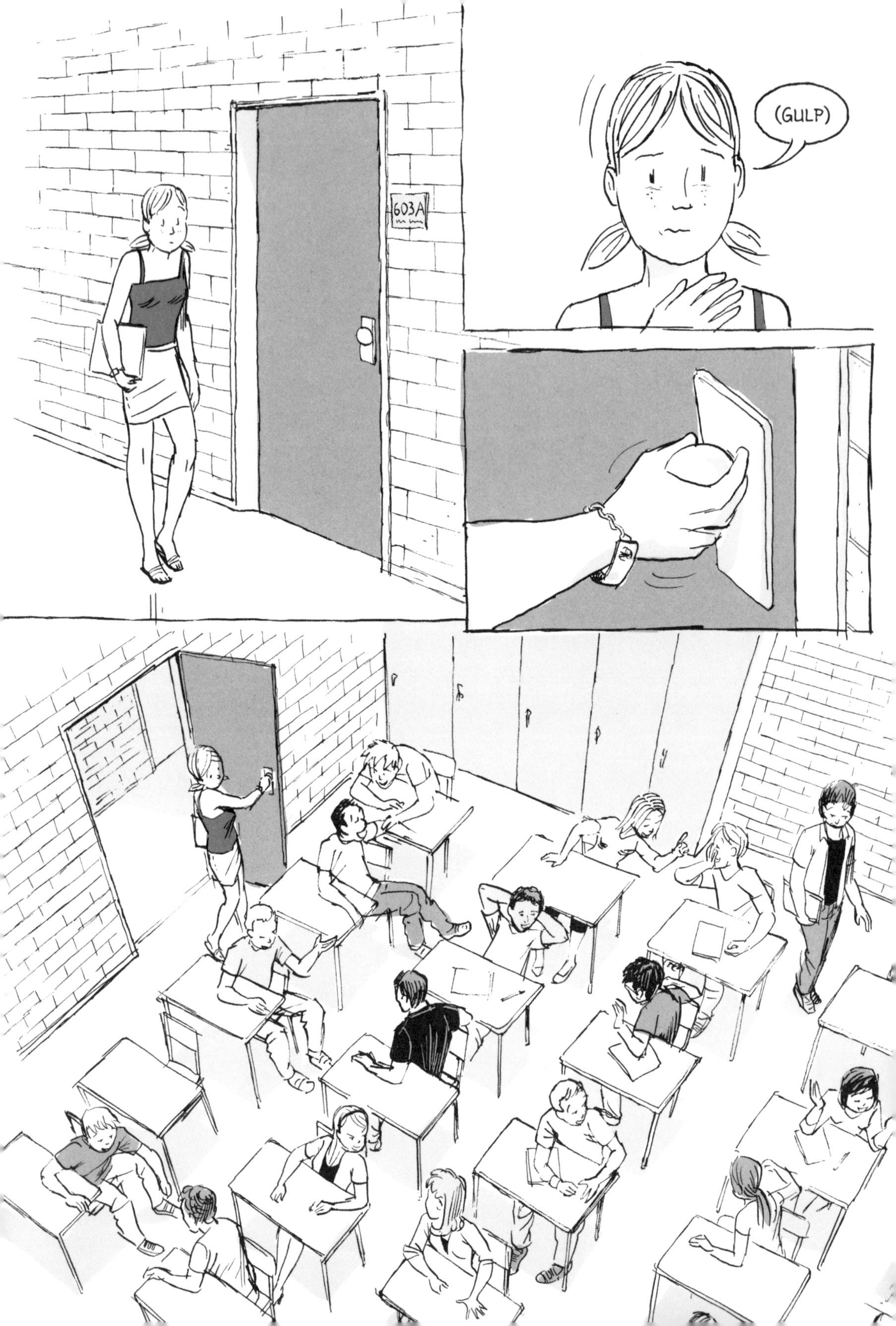
603A
(GULP)

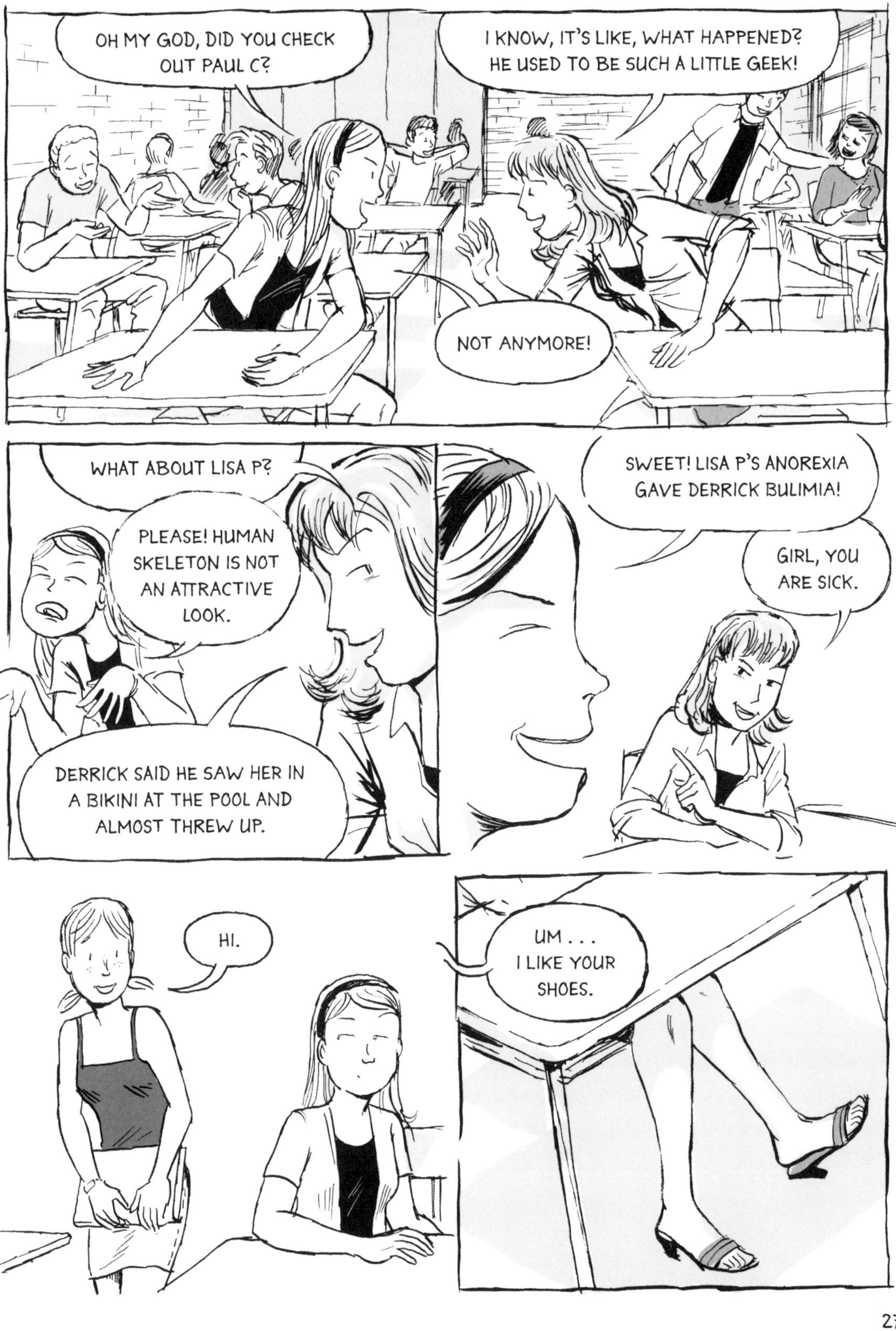
OH MY GOD, DID YOU CHECK OUT PAUL C?
I KNOW, IT'S LIKE, WHAT HAPPENED? HE USED TO BE SUCH A LITTLE GEEK!
NOT ANYMORE!
WHAT ABOUT LISA P?
PLEASE! HUMAN SKELETON IS NOT AN ATTRACTIVE LOOK.
DERRICK SAID HE SAW HER IN A BIKINI AT THE POOL AND ALMOST THREW UP.
SWEET! LISA P'S ANOREXIA GAVE DERRICK BULIMIA!
GIRL, YOU ARE SICK.
HI.
UM . . . I LIKE YOUR SHOES.

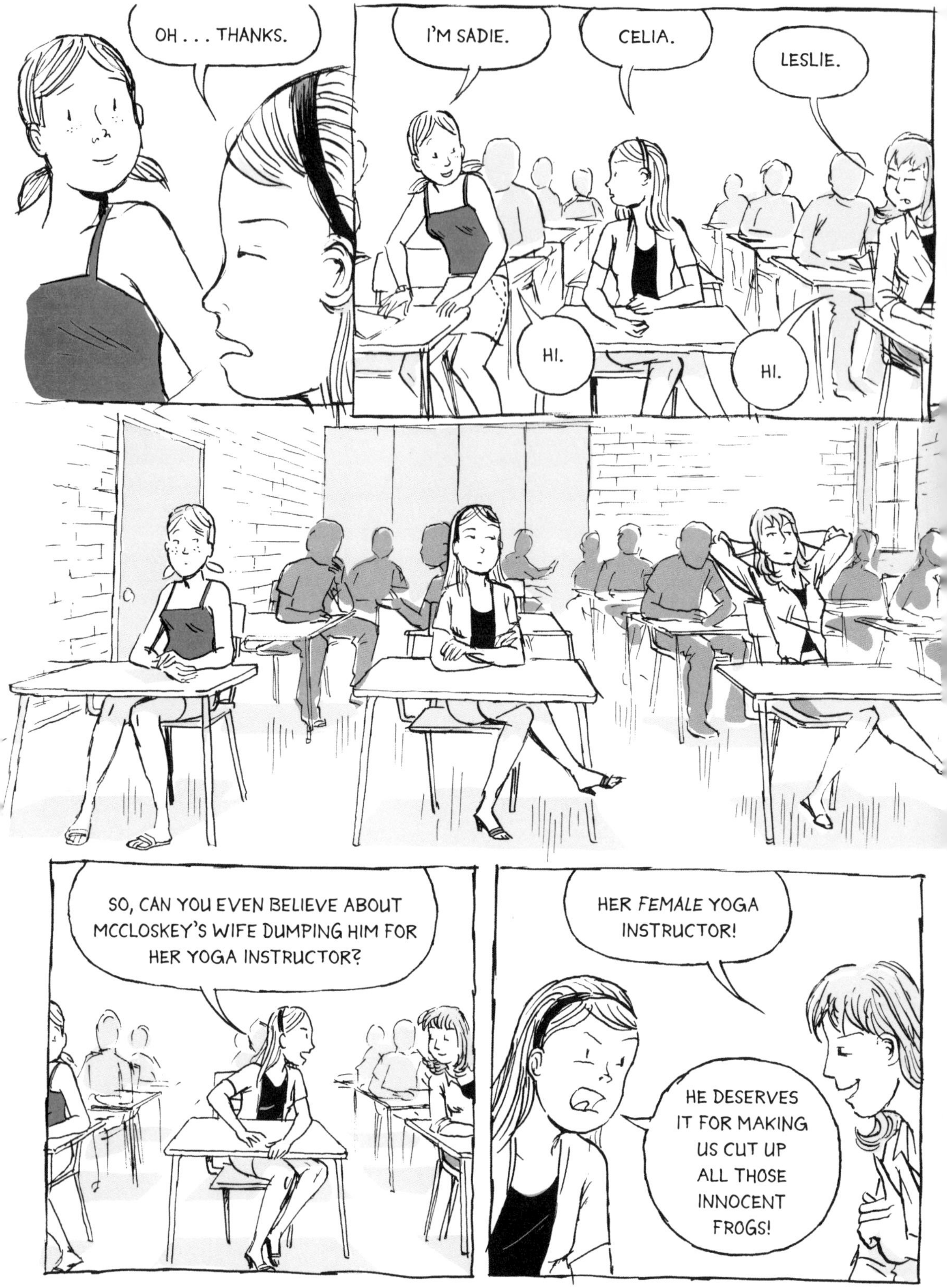
OH . . . THANKS.
I'M SADIE.
CELIA.
LESLIE.
HI.
HI.
SO, CAN YOU EVEN BELIEVE ABOUT MCCLOSKEY'S WIFE DUMPING HIM FOR HER YOGA INSTRUCTOR?
HER *FEMALE* YOGA INSTRUCTOR!
HE DESERVES IT FOR MAKING US CUT UP ALL THOSE INNOCENT FROGS!

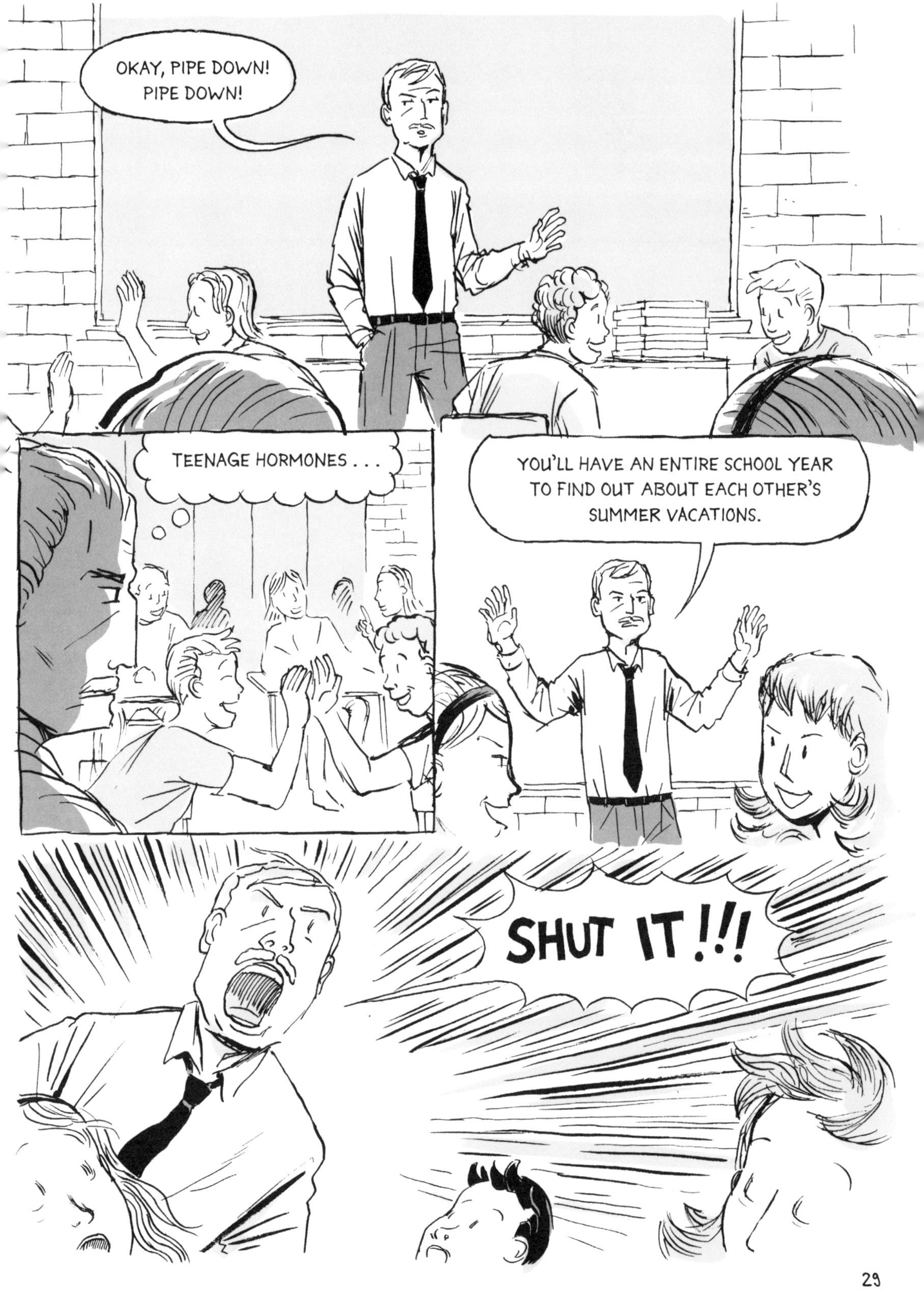
OKAY, PIPE DOWN! PIPE DOWN!
TEENAGE HORMONES . . .
YOU'LL HAVE AN ENTIRE SCHOOL YEAR TO FIND OUT ABOUT EACH OTHER'S SUMMER VACATIONS.
SHUT IT!!!

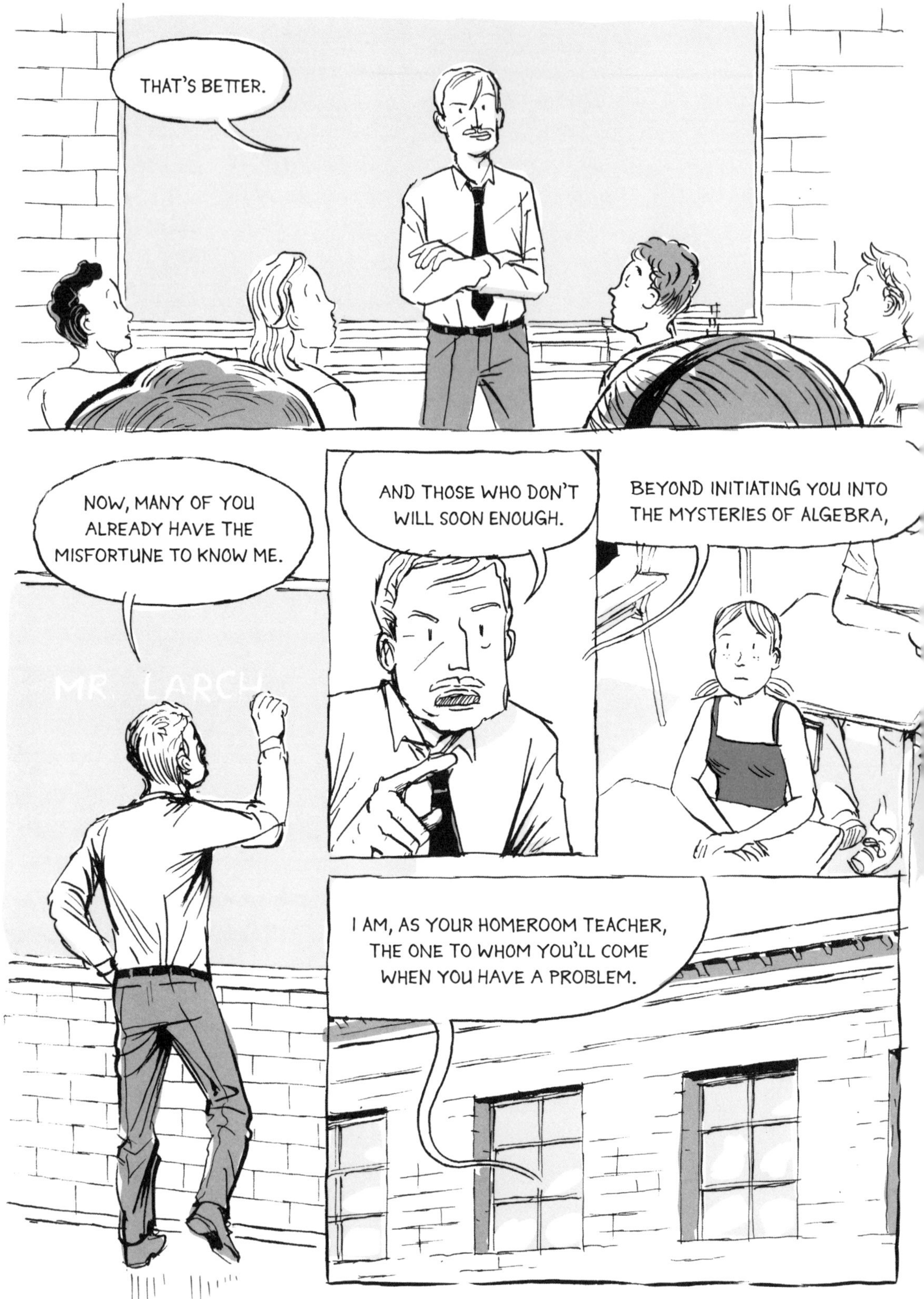

THAT'S BETTER.
NOW, MANY OF YOU ALREADY HAVE THE MISFORTUNE TO KNOW ME.
MR. LARCH
AND THOSE WHO DON'T WILL SOON ENOUGH.
BEYOND INITIATING YOU INTO THE MYSTERIES OF ALGEBRA,
I AM, AS YOUR HOMEROOM TEACHER, THE ONE TO WHOM YOU'LL COME WHEN YOU HAVE A PROBLEM.

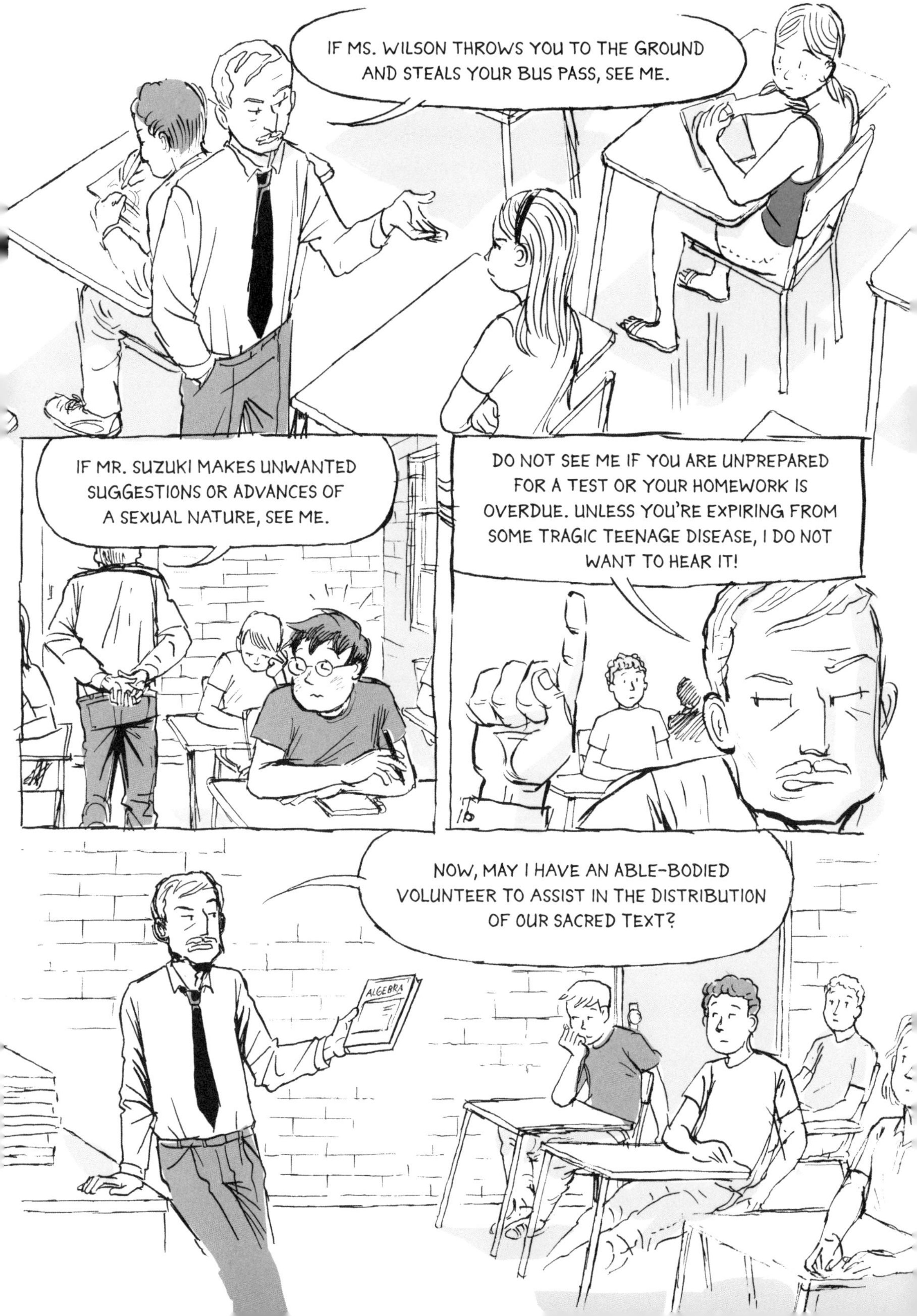
IF MS. WILSON THROWS YOU TO THE GROUND AND STEALS YOUR BUS PASS, SEE ME.
IF MR. SUZUKI MAKES UNWANTED SUGGESTIONS OR ADVANCES OF A SEXUAL NATURE, SEE ME.
DO NOT SEE ME IF YOU ARE UNPREPARED FOR A TEST OR YOUR HOMEWORK IS OVERDUE. UNLESS YOU'RE EXPIRING FROM SOME TRAGIC TEENAGE DISEASE, I DO NOT WANT TO HEAR IT!
NOW, MAY I HAVE AN ABLE-BODIED VOLUNTEER TO ASSIST IN THE DISTRIBUTION OF OUR SACRED TEXT?
ALGEBRA

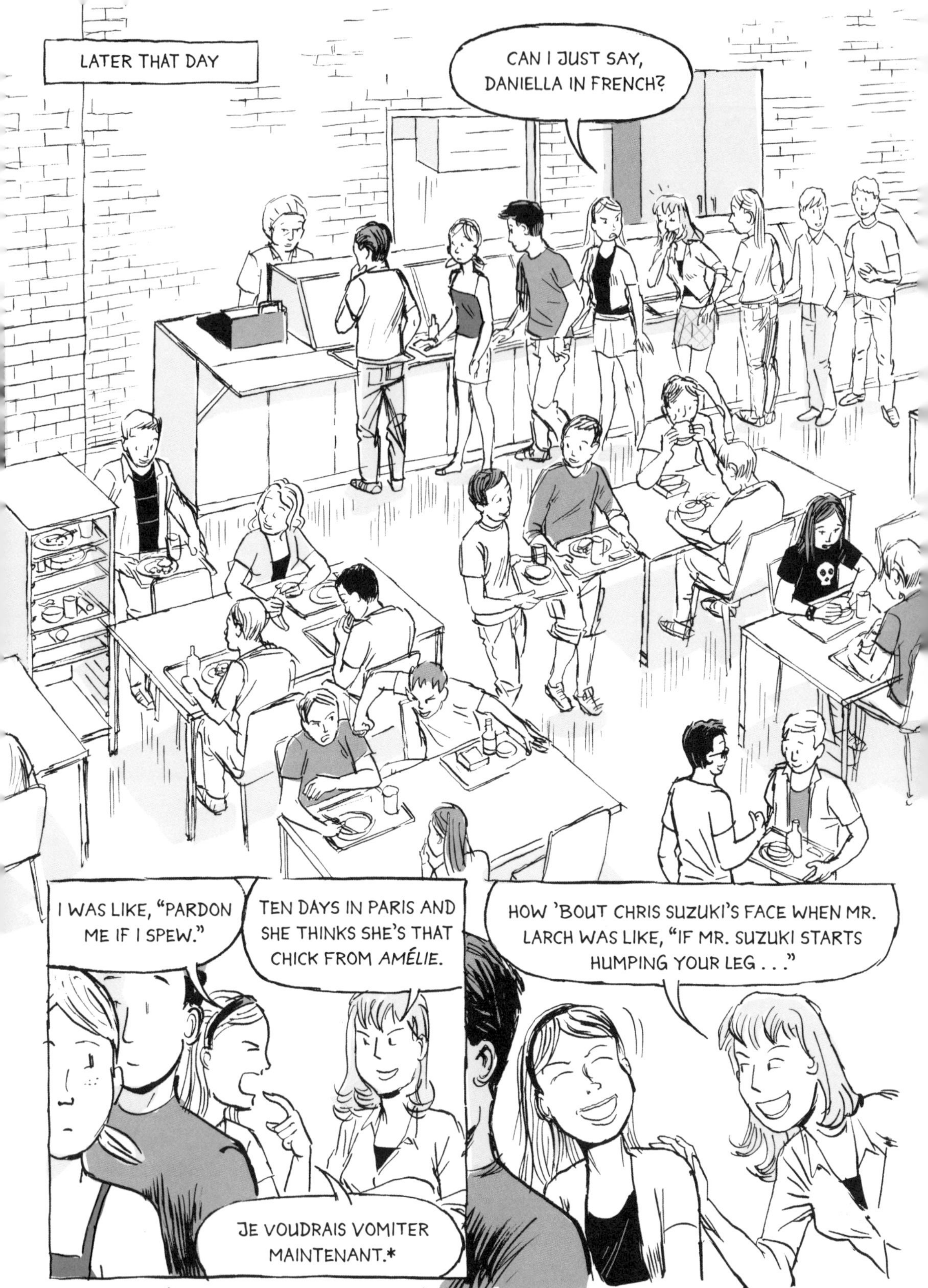
LATER THAT DAY
CAN I JUST SAY, DANIELLA IN FRENCH?
I WAS LIKE, "PARDON ME IF I SPEW."
TEN DAYS IN PARIS AND SHE THINKS SHE'S THAT CHICK FROM *AMÉLIE*.
JE VOUDRAIS VOMITER MAINTENANT.*
HOW 'BOUT CHRIS SUZUKI'S FACE WHEN MR. LARCH WAS LIKE, "IF MR. SUZUKI STARTS HUMPING YOUR LEG . . ."

(*I WOULD LIKE TO MAKE VOMIT NOW.)

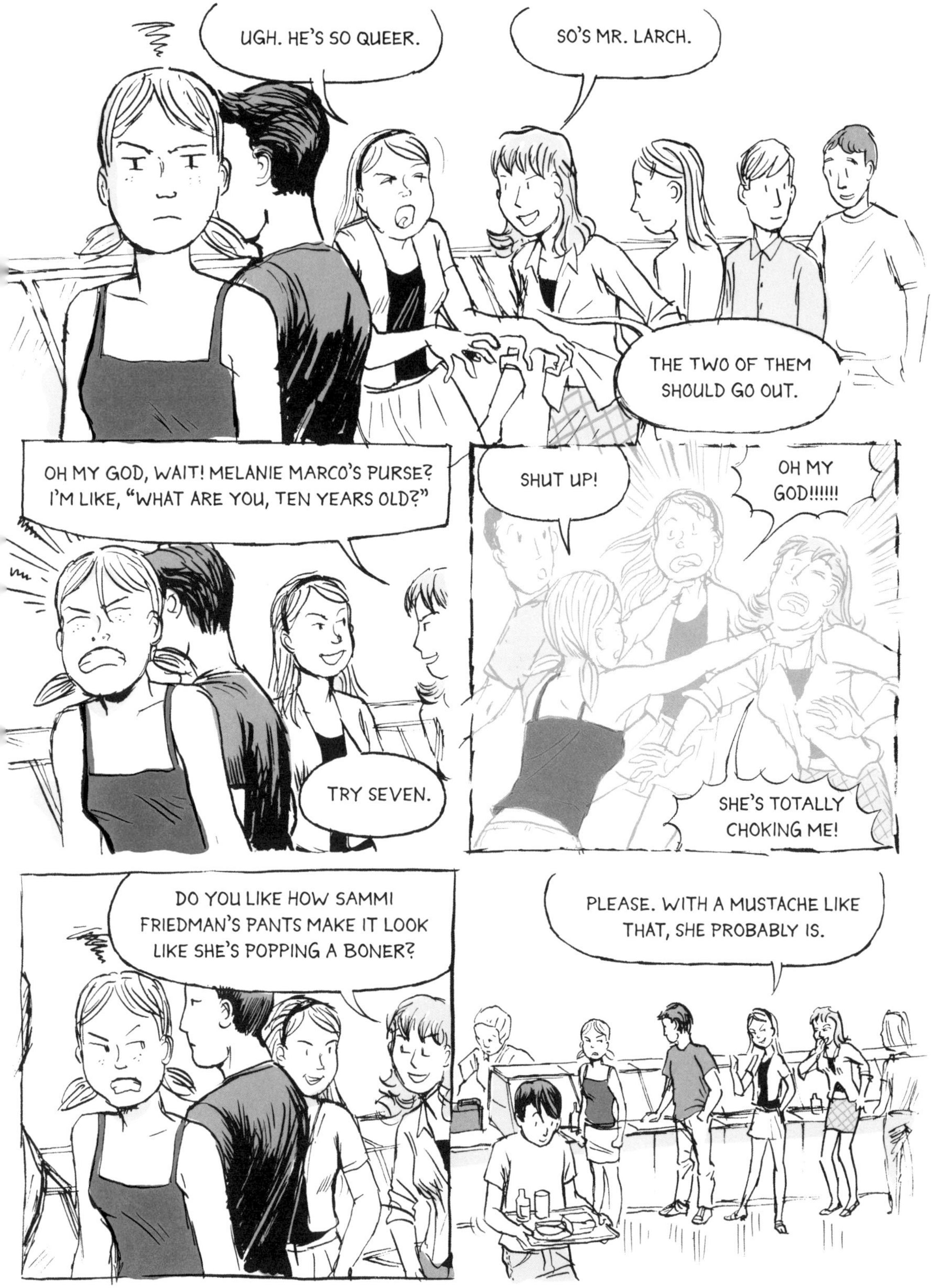
UGH. HE'S SO QUEER.
SO'S MR. LARCH.
THE TWO OF THEM SHOULD GO OUT.
OH MY GOD, WAIT! MELANIE MARCO'S PURSE? I'M LIKE, "WHAT ARE YOU, TEN YEARS OLD?"
TRY SEVEN.
SHUT UP!
OH MY GOD!!!!!!
SHE'S TOTALLY CHOKING ME!
DO YOU LIKE HOW SAMMI FRIEDMAN'S PANTS MAKE IT LOOK LIKE SHE'S POPPING A BONER?
PLEASE. WITH A MUSTACHE LIKE THAT, SHE PROBABLY IS.

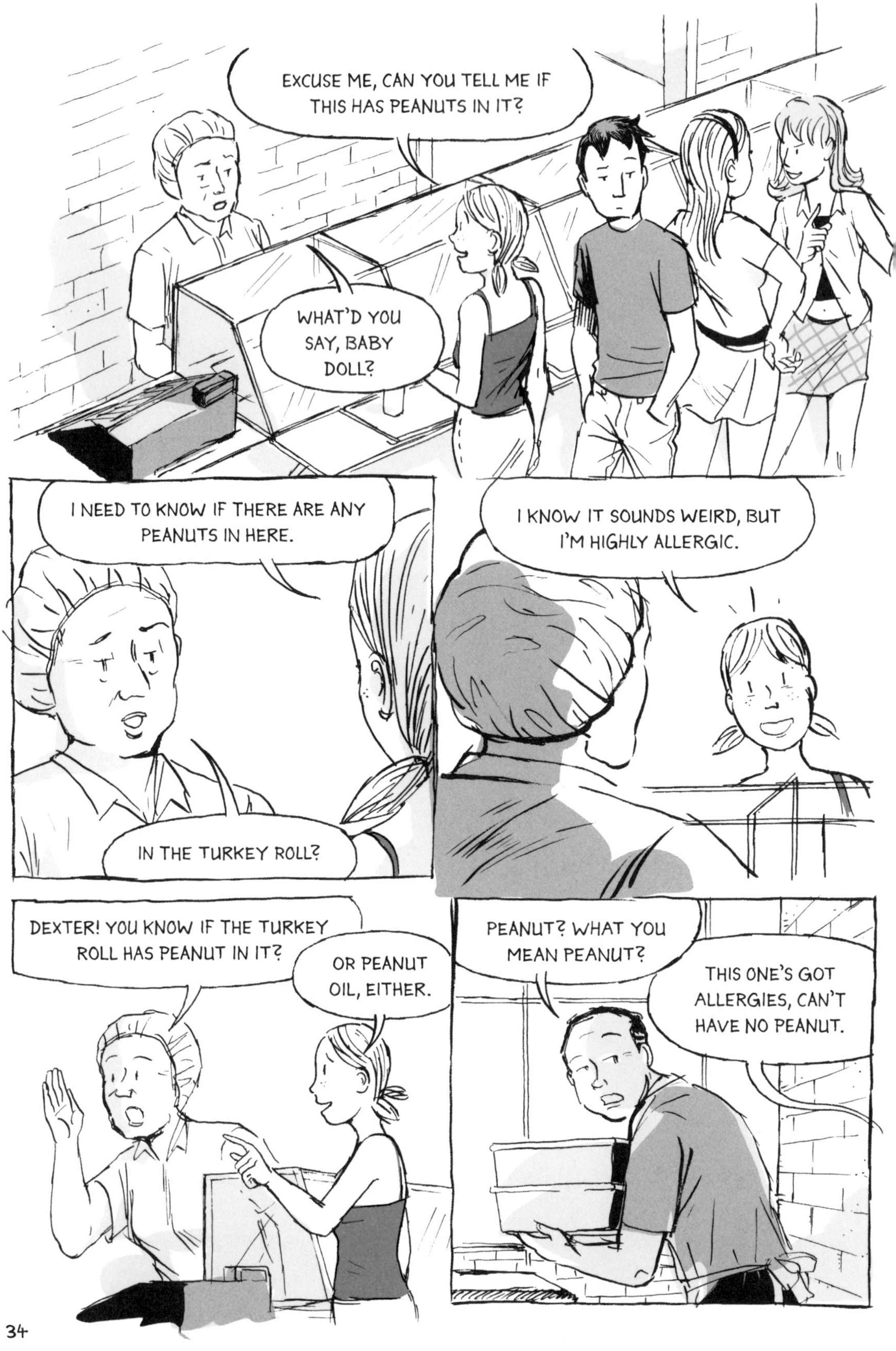
EXCUSE ME, CAN YOU TELL ME IF THIS HAS PEANUTS IN IT?
WHAT'D YOU SAY, BABY DOLL?
I NEED TO KNOW IF THERE ARE ANY PEANUTS IN HERE.
IN THE TURKEY ROLL?
I KNOW IT SOUNDS WEIRD, BUT I'M HIGHLY ALLERGIC.
DEXTER! YOU KNOW IF THE TURKEY ROLL HAS PEANUT IN IT?
OR PEANUT OIL, EITHER.
PEANUT? WHAT YOU MEAN PEANUT?
THIS ONE'S GOT ALLERGIES, CAN'T HAVE NO PEANUT.

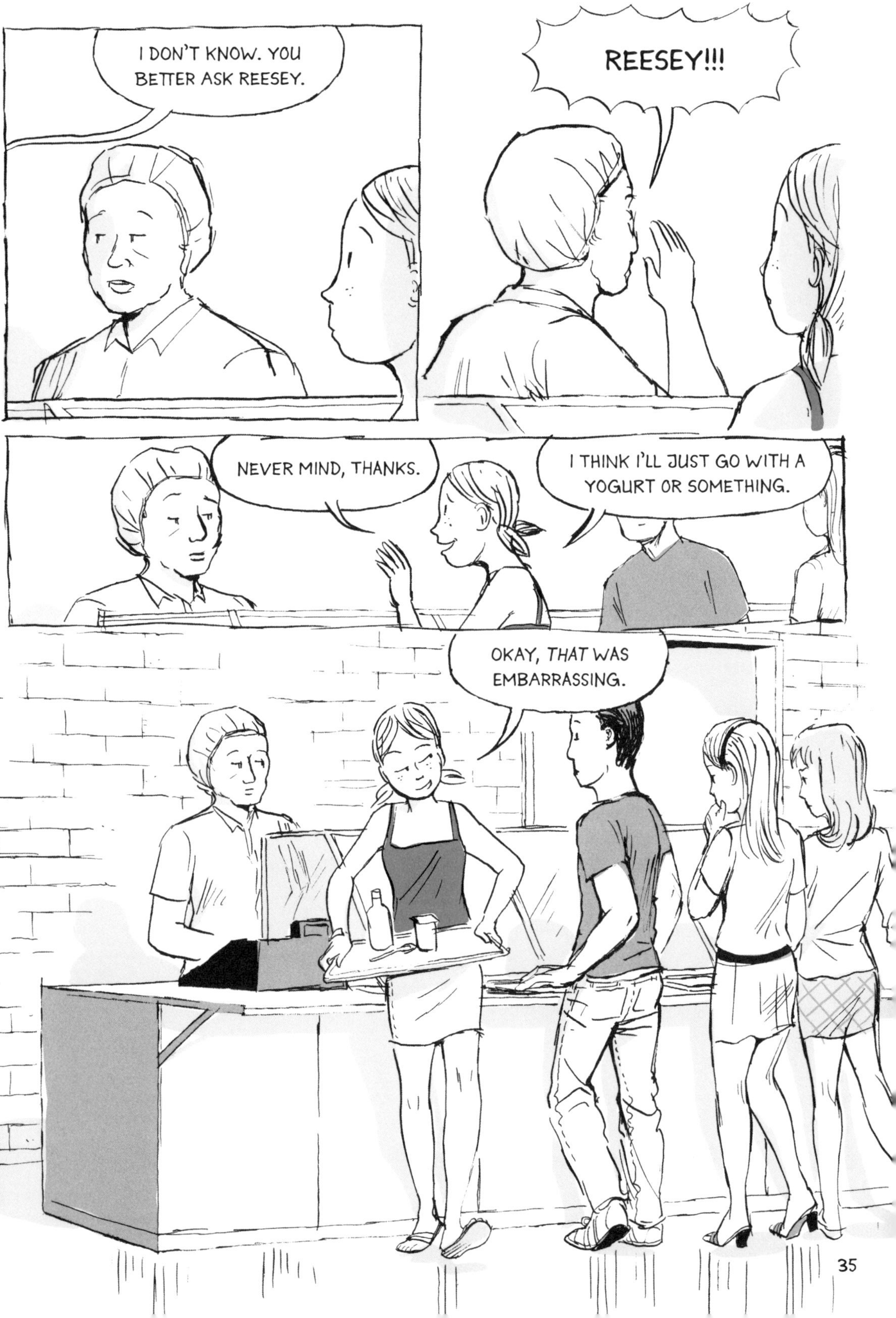

I DON'T KNOW. YOU BETTER ASK REESEY.
REESEY!!!
NEVER MIND, THANKS.
I THINK I'LL JUST GO WITH A YOGURT OR SOMETHING.
OKAY, *THAT* WAS EMBARRASSING.

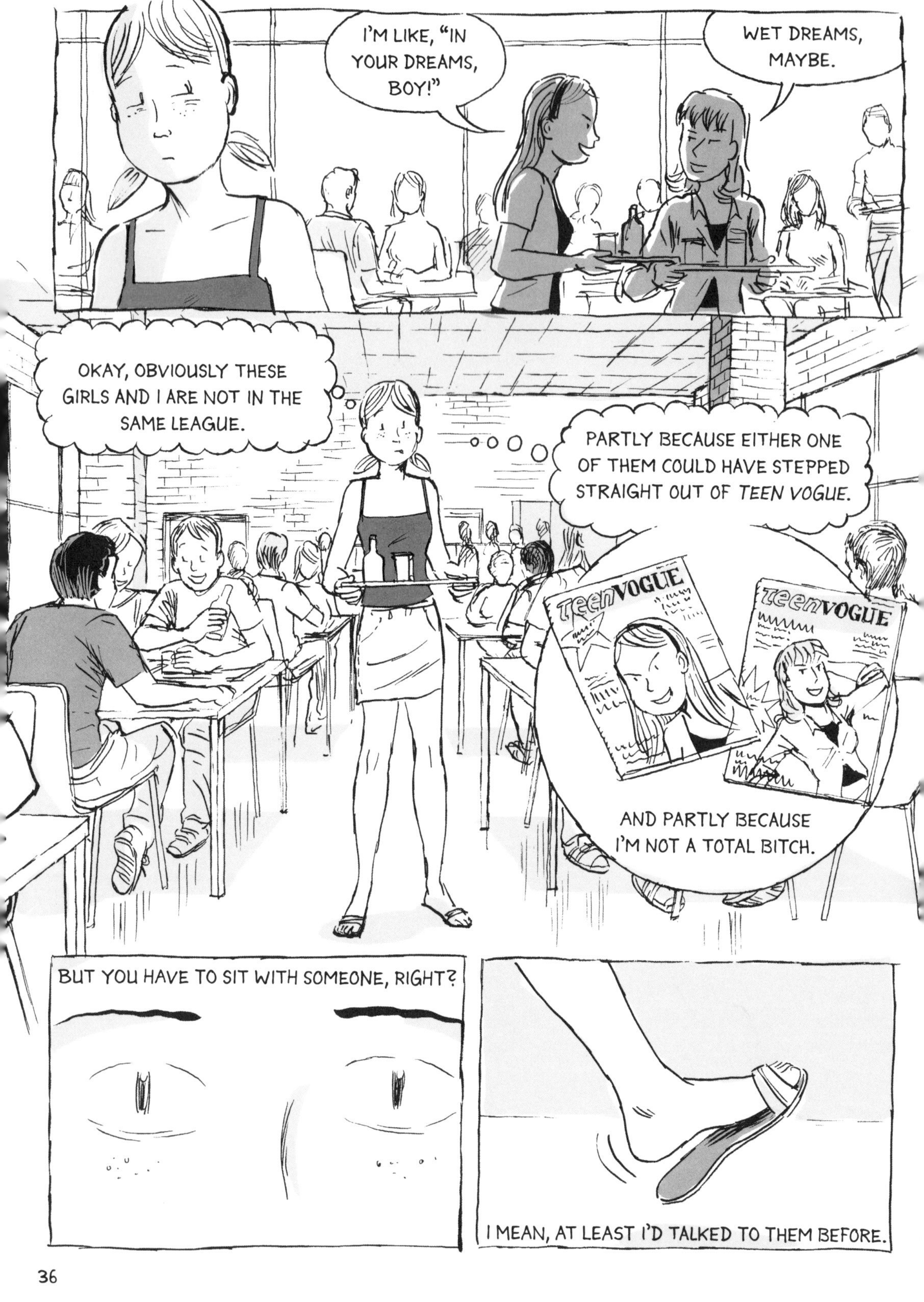
I'M LIKE, "IN YOUR DREAMS, BOY!"
WET DREAMS, MAYBE.
OKAY, OBVIOUSLY THESE GIRLS AND I ARE NOT IN THE SAME LEAGUE.
PARTLY BECAUSE EITHER ONE OF THEM COULD HAVE STEPPED STRAIGHT OUT OF *TEEN VOGUE*.
TEEN VOGUE
TEEN VOGUE
AND PARTLY BECAUSE I'M NOT A TOTAL BITCH.
BUT YOU HAVE TO SIT WITH SOMEONE, RIGHT?
I MEAN, AT LEAST I'D TALKED TO THEM BEFORE.

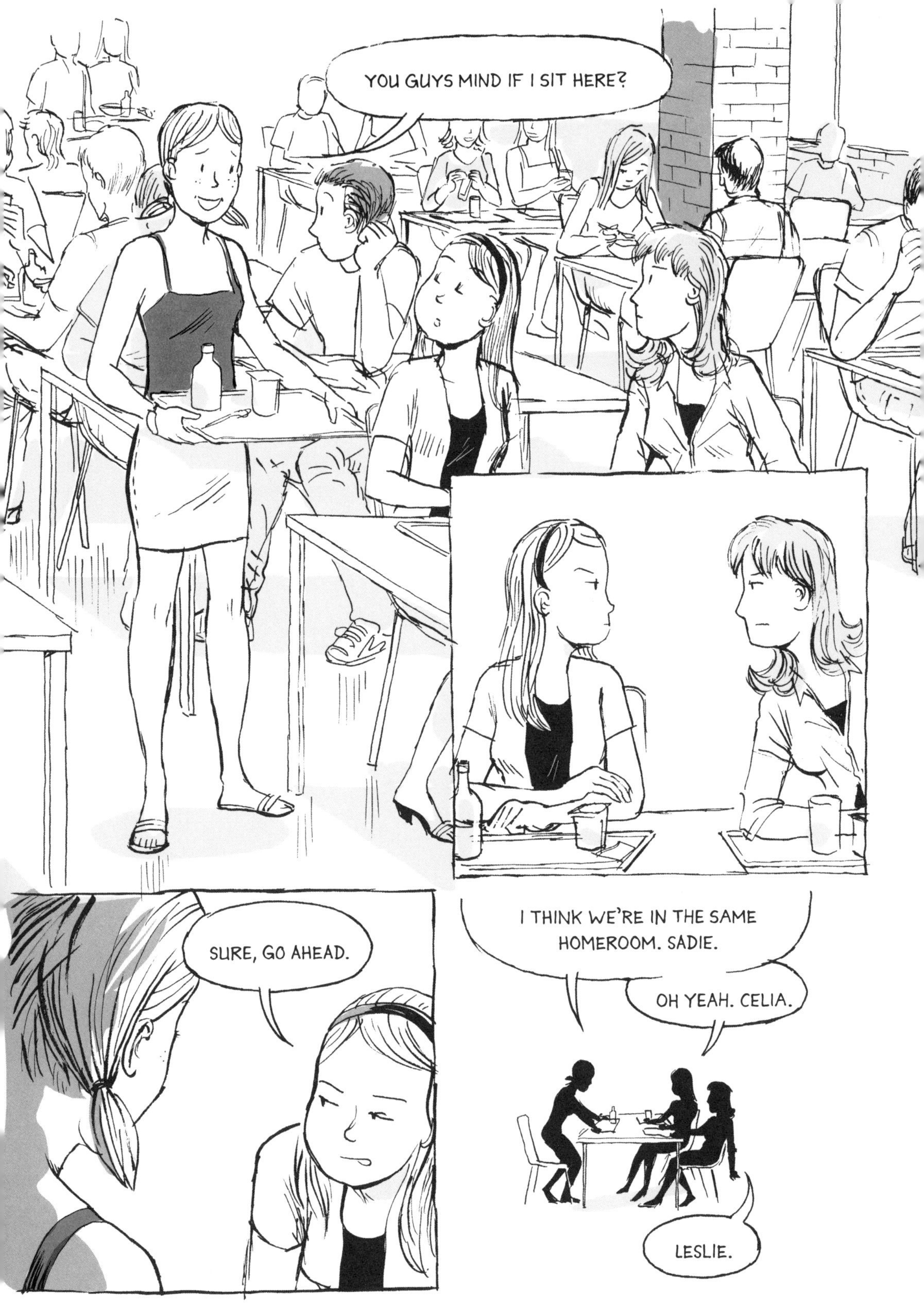
YOU GUYS MIND IF I SIT HERE?
SURE, GO AHEAD.
I THINK WE'RE IN THE SAME HOMEROOM. SADIE.
OH YEAH. CELIA.
LESLIE.

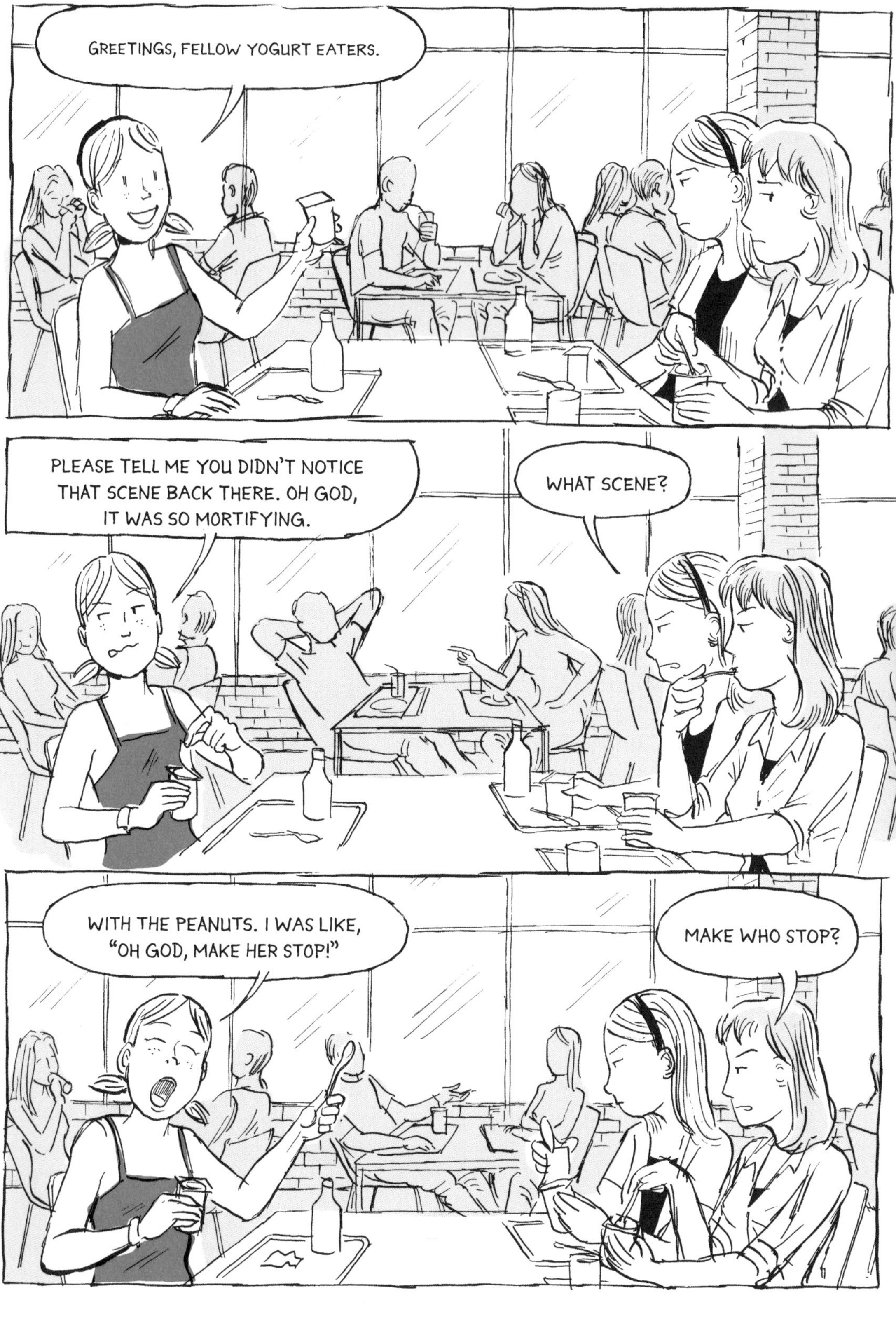
GREETINGS, FELLOW YOGURT EATERS.
PLEASE TELL ME YOU DIDN'T NOTICE THAT SCENE BACK THERE. OH GOD, IT WAS SO MORTIFYING.
WHAT SCENE?
WITH THE PEANUTS. I WAS LIKE, "OH GOD, MAKE HER STOP!"
MAKE WHO STOP?

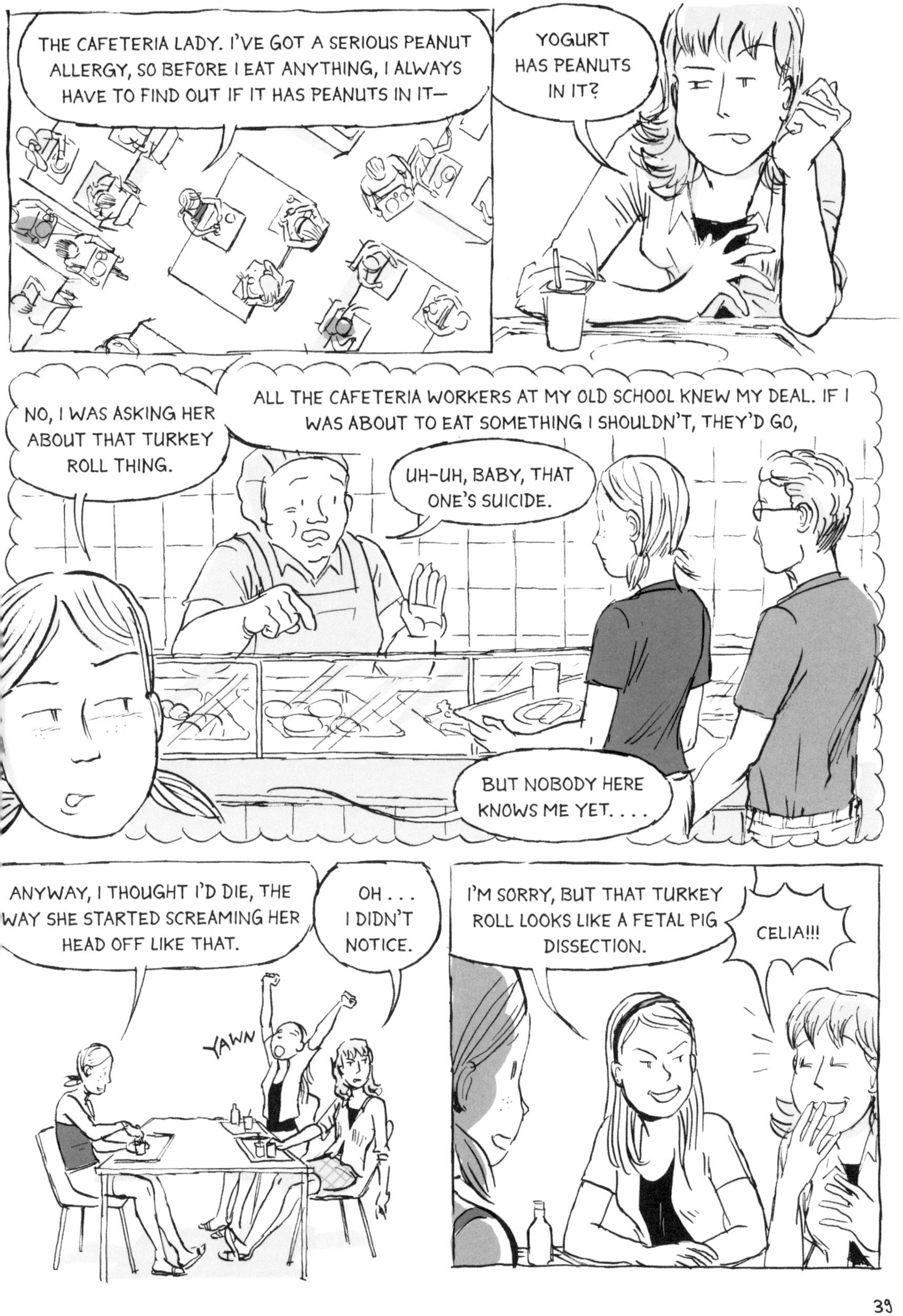
THE CAFETERIA LADY. I'VE GOT A SERIOUS PEANUT ALLERGY, SO BEFORE I EAT ANYTHING, I ALWAYS HAVE TO FIND OUT IF IT HAS PEANUTS IN IT—
YOGURT HAS PEANUTS IN IT?
NO, I WAS ASKING HER ABOUT THAT TURKEY ROLL THING.
ALL THE CAFETERIA WORKERS AT MY OLD SCHOOL KNEW MY DEAL. IF I WAS ABOUT TO EAT SOMETHING I SHOULDN'T, THEY'D GO,
UH-UH, BABY, THAT ONE'S SUICIDE.
BUT NOBODY HERE KNOWS ME YET. . . .
ANYWAY, I THOUGHT I'D DIE, THE WAY SHE STARTED SCREAMING HER HEAD OFF LIKE THAT.
OH . . . I DIDN'T NOTICE.
YAWN
I'M SORRY, BUT THAT TURKEY ROLL LOOKS LIKE A FETAL PIG DISSECTION.
CELIA!!!

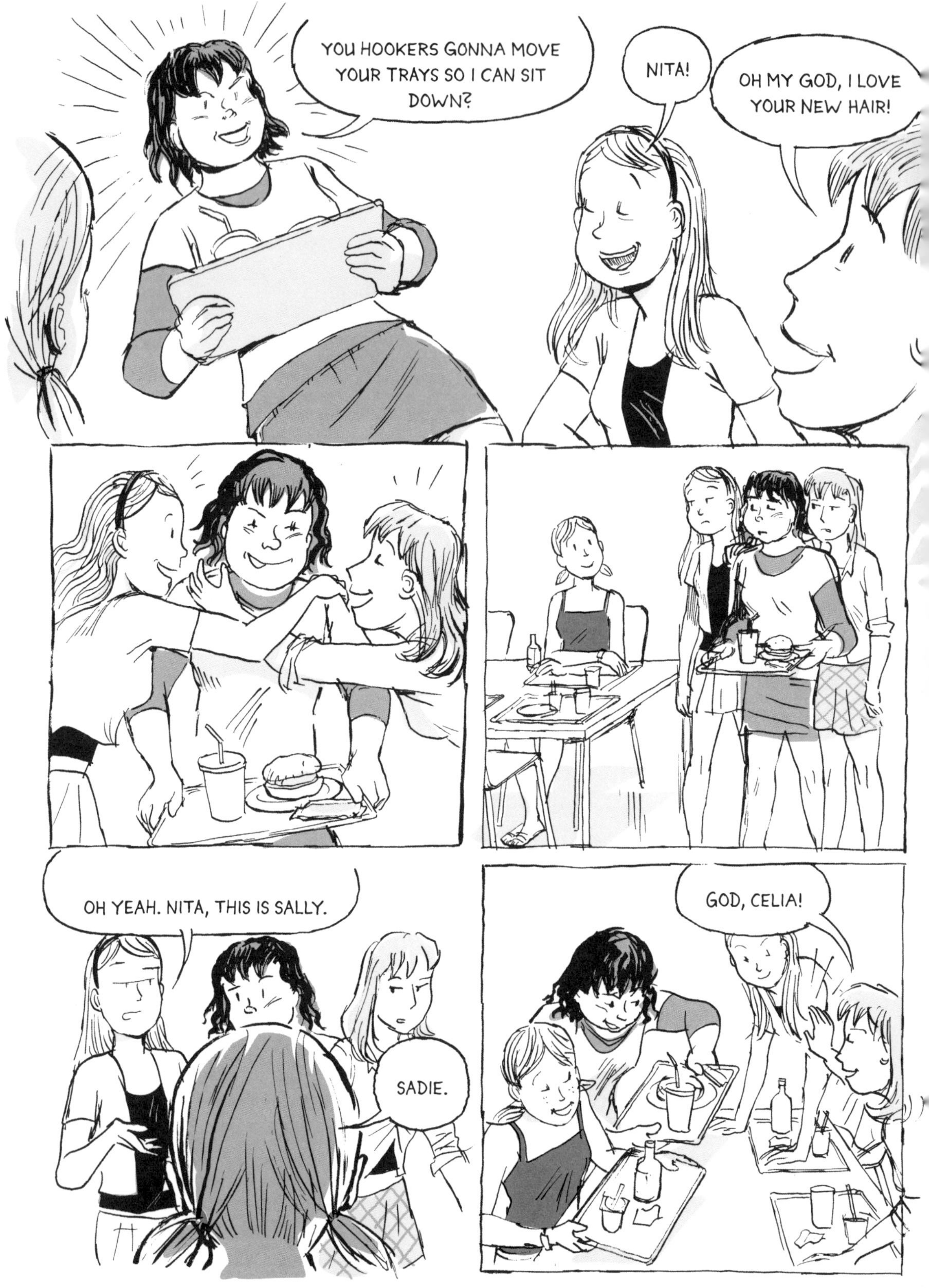
YOU HOOKERS GONNA MOVE YOUR TRAYS SO I CAN SIT DOWN?
NITA!
OH MY GOD, I LOVE YOUR NEW HAIR!
OH YEAH. NITA, THIS IS SALLY.
SADIE.
GOD, CELIA!

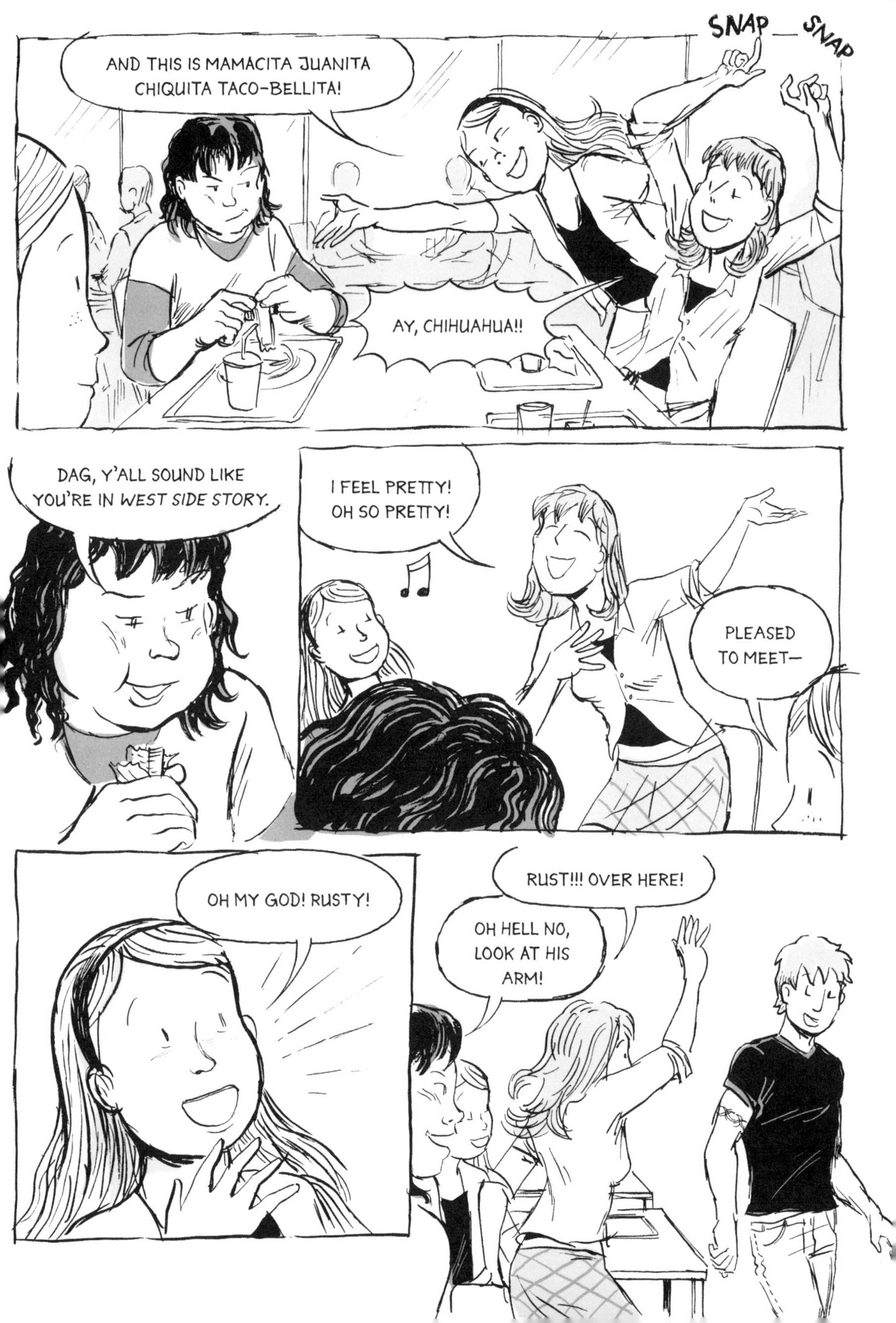

AND THIS IS MAMACITA JUANITA CHIQUITA TACO-BELLITA!
SNAP__SNAP
AY, CHIHUAHUA!!
DAG, Y'ALL SOUND LIKE YOU'RE IN *WEST SIDE STORY*.
I FEEL PRETTY! OH SO PRETTY!
PLEASED TO MEET—
OH MY GOD! RUSTY!
RUST!!! OVER HERE!
OH HELL NO, LOOK AT HIS ARM!

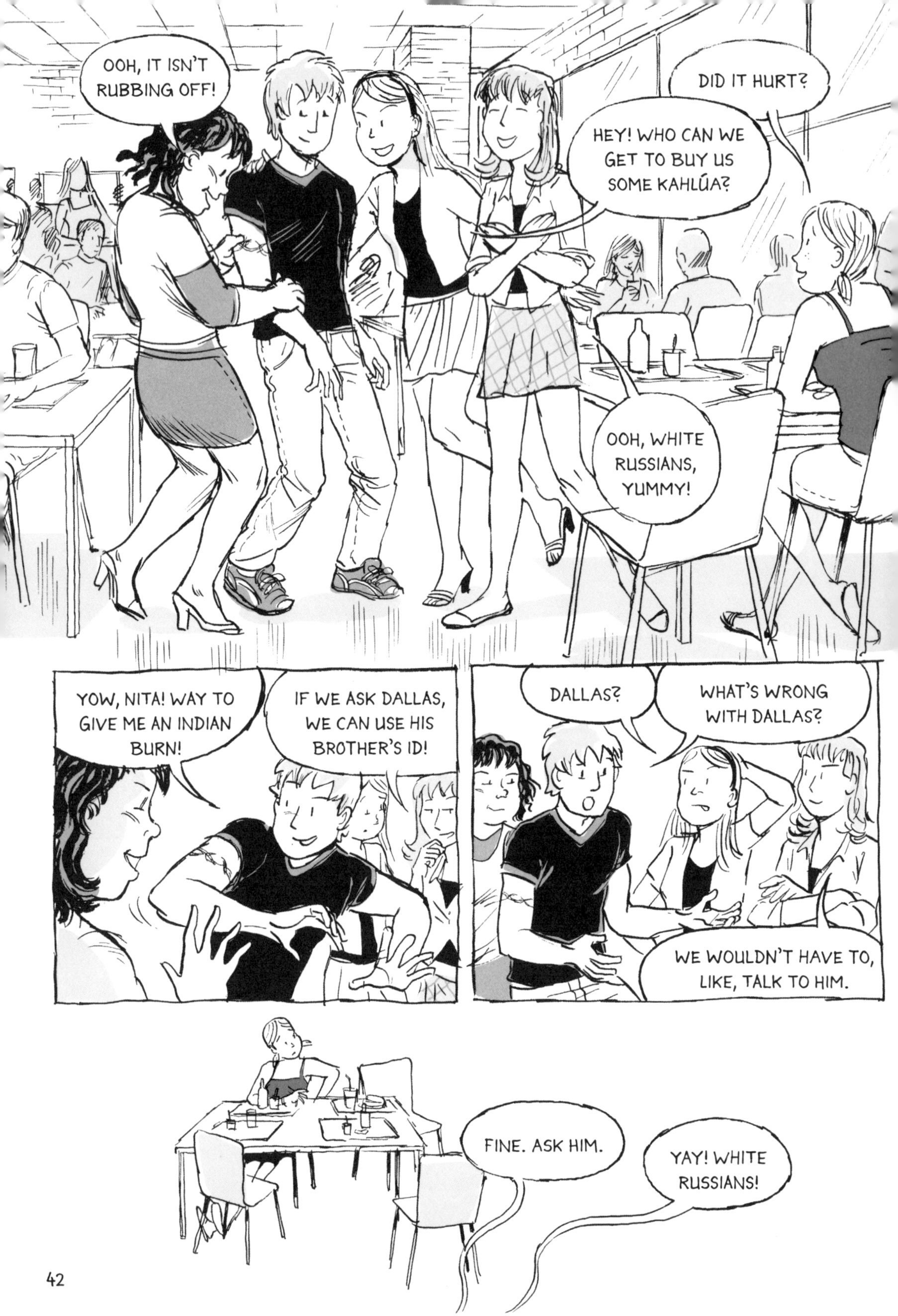
OOH, IT ISN'T RUBBING OFF!
DID IT HURT?
HEY! WHO CAN WE GET TO BUY US SOME KAHLÚA?
OOH, WHITE RUSSIANS, YUMMY!
YOW, NITA! WAY TO GIVE ME AN INDIAN BURN!
IF WE ASK DALLAS, WE CAN USE HIS BROTHER'S ID!
DALLAS?
WHAT'S WRONG WITH DALLAS?
WE WOULDN'T HAVE TO, LIKE, TALK TO HIM.
FINE. ASK HIM.
YAY! WHITE RUSSIANS!

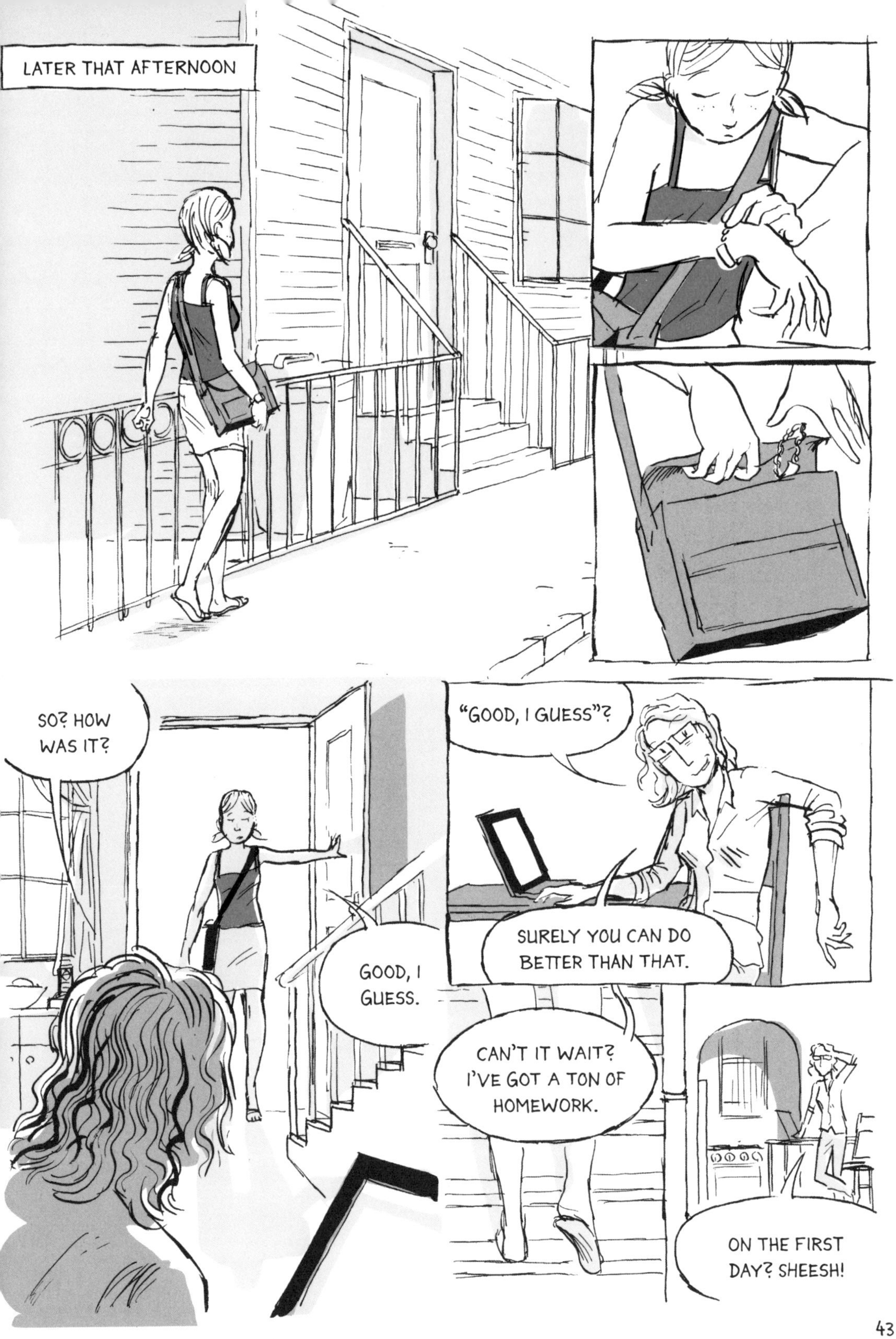
LATER THAT AFTERNOON
SO? HOW WAS IT?
GOOD, I GUESS.
"GOOD, I GUESS"?
SURELY YOU CAN DO BETTER THAN THAT.
CAN'T IT WAIT? I'VE GOT A TON OF HOMEWORK.
ON THE FIRST DAY? SHEESH!

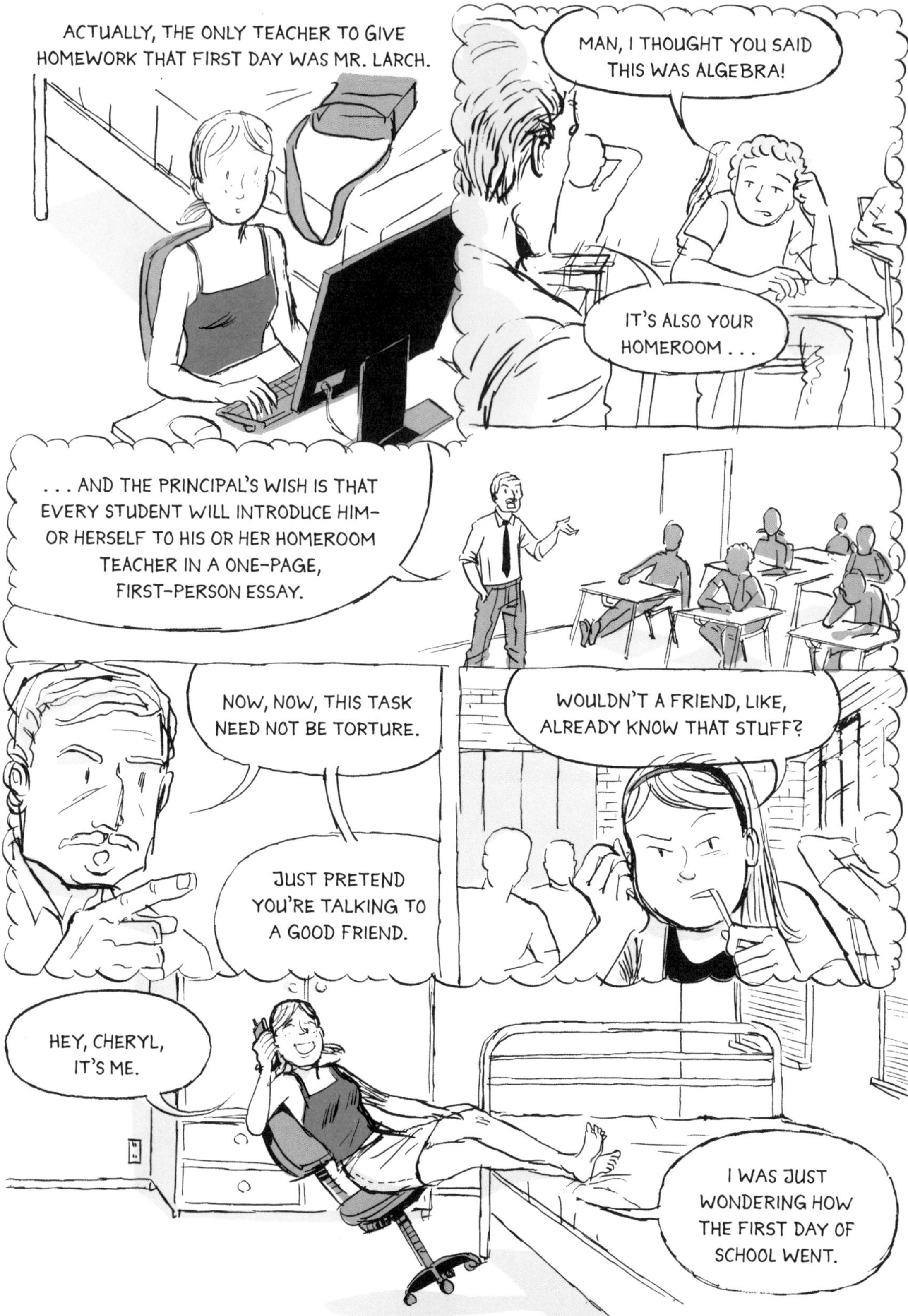
ACTUALLY, THE ONLY TEACHER TO GIVE HOMEWORK THAT FIRST DAY WAS MR. LARCH.
MAN, I THOUGHT YOU SAID THIS WAS ALGEBRA!
IT'S ALSO YOUR HOMEROOM . . .
. . . AND THE PRINCIPAL'S WISH IS THAT EVERY STUDENT WILL INTRODUCE HIM- OR HERSELF TO HIS OR HER HOMEROOM TEACHER IN A ONE-PAGE, FIRST-PERSON ESSAY.
NOW, NOW, THIS TASK NEED NOT BE TORTURE.
JUST PRETEND YOU'RE TALKING TO A GOOD FRIEND.
WOULDN'T A FRIEND, LIKE, ALREADY KNOW THAT STUFF?
HEY, CHERYL, IT'S ME.
I WAS JUST WONDERING HOW THE FIRST DAY OF SCHOOL WENT.

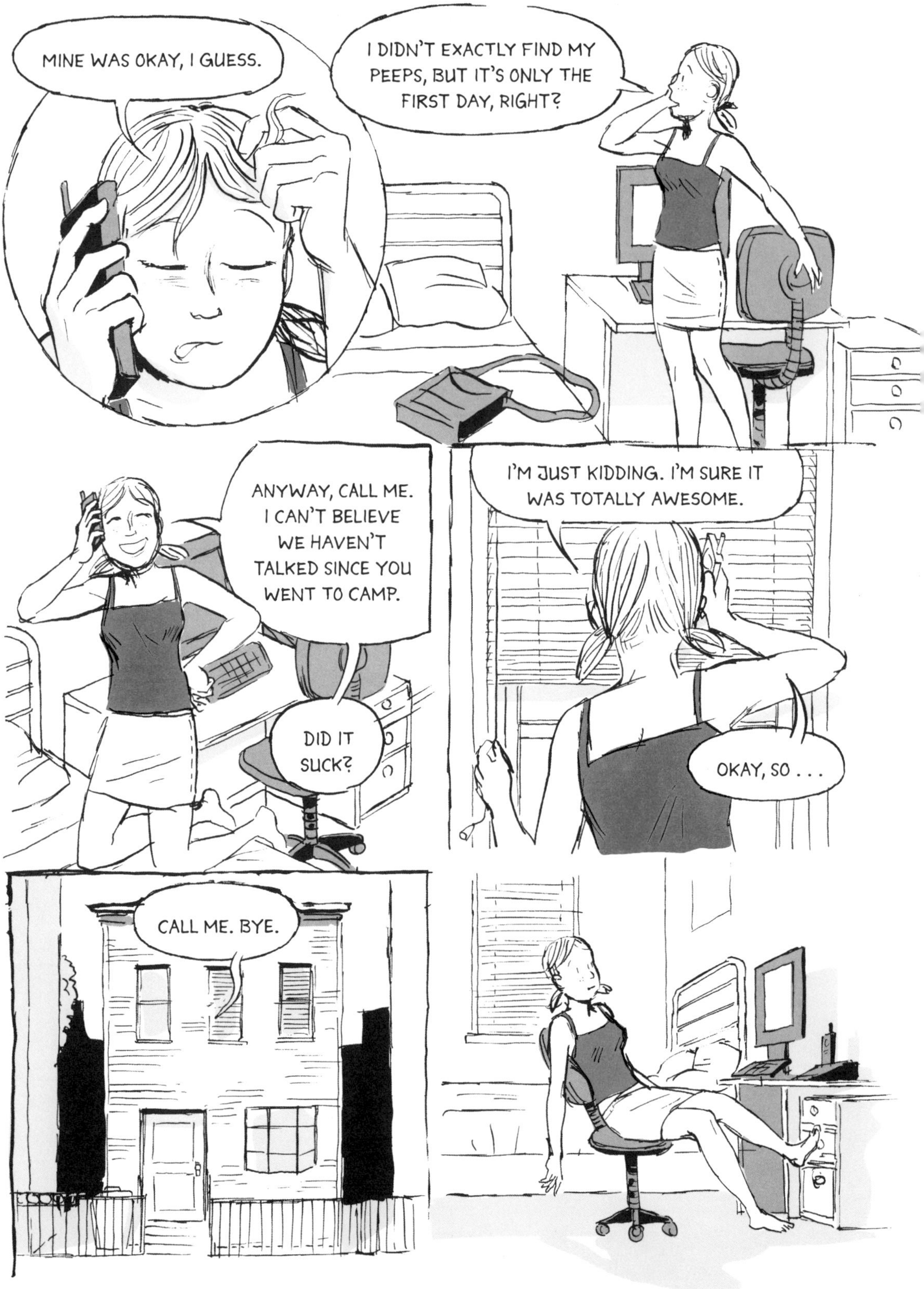
MINE WAS OKAY, I GUESS.
I DIDN'T EXACTLY FIND MY PEEPS, BUT IT'S ONLY THE FIRST DAY, RIGHT?
ANYWAY, CALL ME. I CAN'T BELIEVE WE HAVEN'T TALKED SINCE YOU WENT TO CAMP.
DID IT SUCK?
I'M JUST KIDDING. I'M SURE IT WAS TOTALLY AWESOME.
OKAY, SO . . .
CALL ME. BYE.

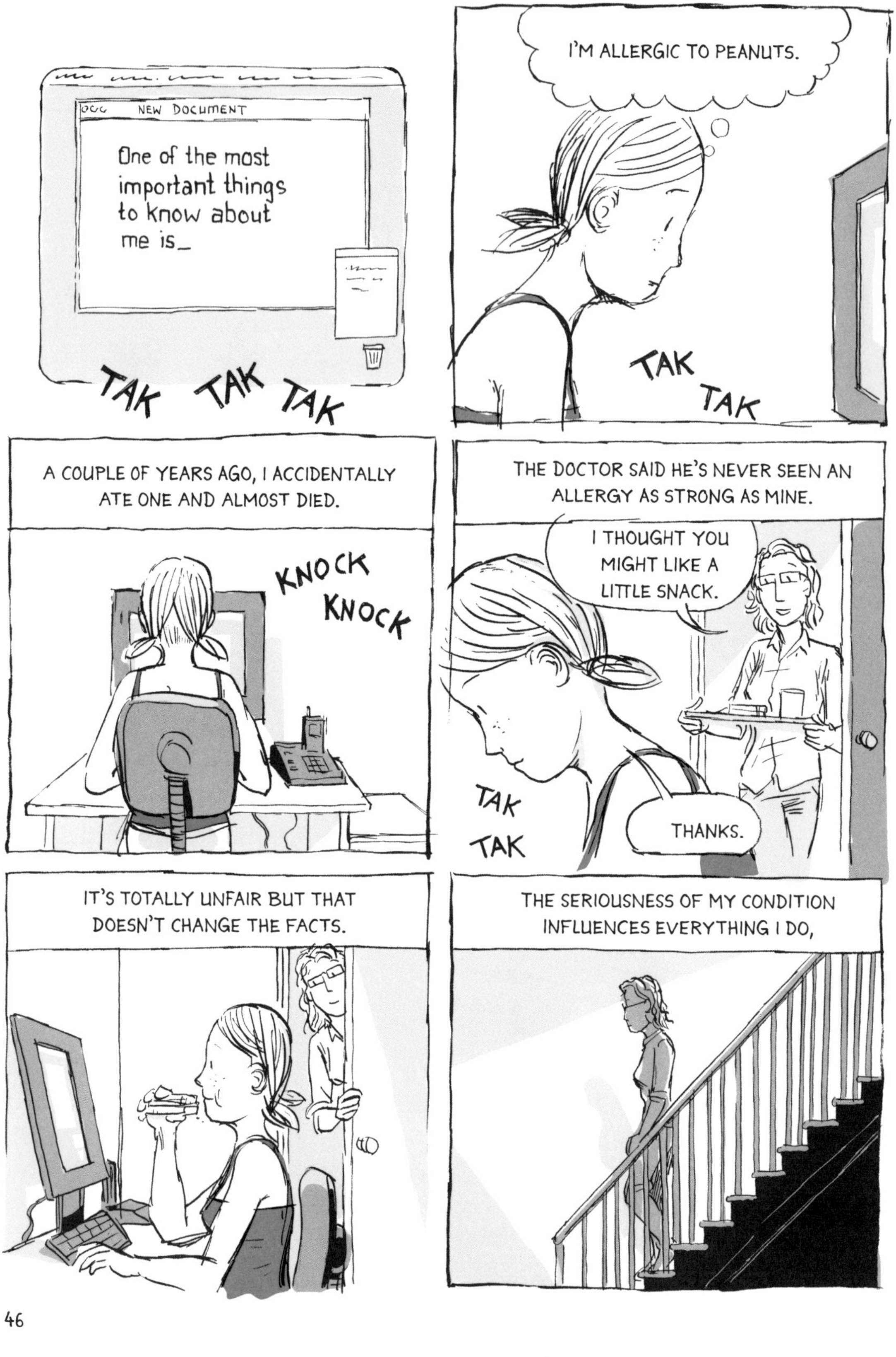
NEW DOCUMENT
One of the most important things to know about me is_
TAK TAK TAK
I'M ALLERGIC TO PEANUTS.
TAK TAK
A COUPLE OF YEARS AGO, I ACCIDENTALLY ATE ONE AND ALMOST DIED.
KNOCK KNOCK
THE DOCTOR SAID HE'S NEVER SEEN AN ALLERGY AS STRONG AS MINE.
I THOUGHT YOU MIGHT LIKE A LITTLE SNACK.
TAK TAK
THANKS.
IT'S TOTALLY UNFAIR BUT THAT DOESN'T CHANGE THE FACTS.
THE SERIOUSNESS OF MY CONDITION INFLUENCES EVERYTHING I DO,

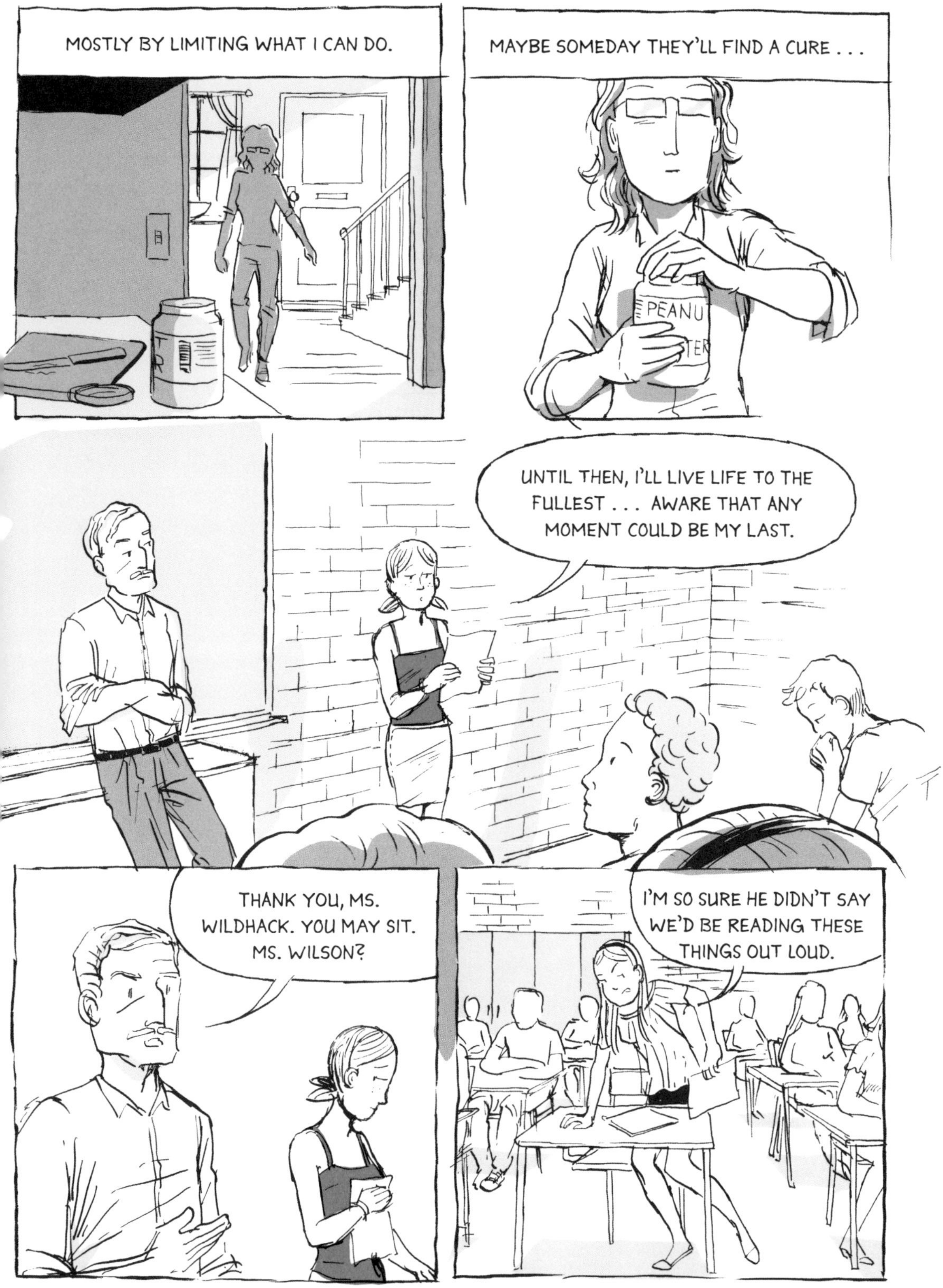
MOSTLY BY LIMITING WHAT I CAN DO.
MAYBE SOMEDAY THEY'LL FIND A CURE . . .
PEANU
TER
UNTIL THEN, I'LL LIVE LIFE TO THE FULLEST . . . AWARE THAT ANY MOMENT COULD BE MY LAST.
THANK YOU, MS. WILDHACK. YOU MAY SIT. MS. WILSON?
I'M SO SURE HE DIDN'T SAY WE'D BE READING THESE THINGS OUT LOUD.

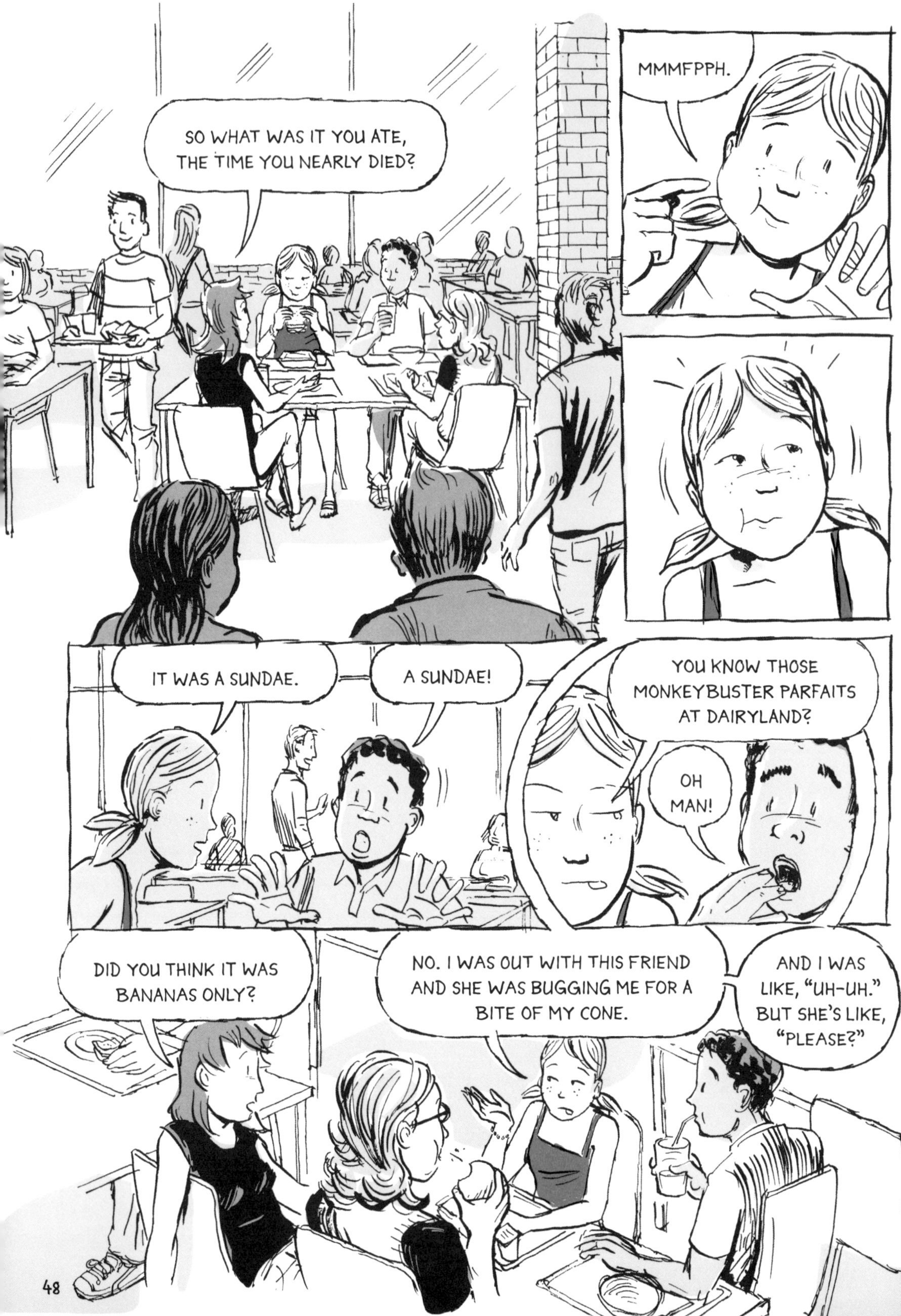
SO WHAT WAS IT YOU ATE, THE TIME YOU NEARLY DIED?
MMMFPPH.
IT WAS A SUNDAE.
A SUNDAE!
YOU KNOW THOSE MONKEYBUSTER PARFAITS AT DAIRYLAND?
OH MAN!
DID YOU THINK IT WAS BANANAS ONLY?
NO. I WAS OUT WITH THIS FRIEND AND SHE WAS BUGGING ME FOR A BITE OF MY CONE.
AND I WAS LIKE, "UH-UH." BUT SHE'S LIKE, "PLEASE?"

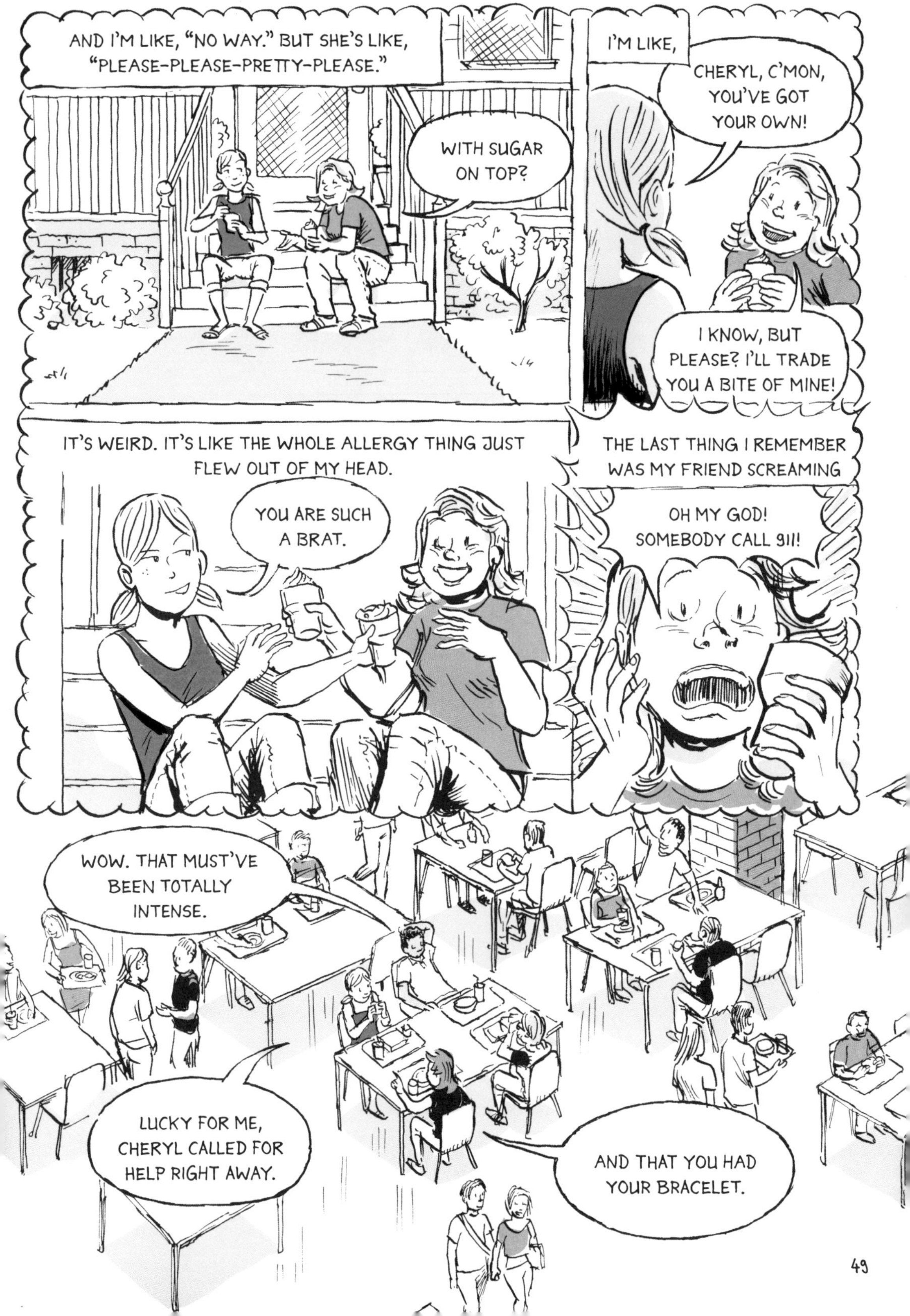
AND I'M LIKE, "NO WAY." BUT SHE'S LIKE, "PLEASE-PLEASE-PRETTY-PLEASE."
WITH SUGAR ON TOP?
I'M LIKE,
CHERYL, C'MON, YOU'VE GOT YOUR OWN!
I KNOW, BUT PLEASE? I'LL TRADE YOU A BITE OF MINE!
IT'S WEIRD. IT'S LIKE THE WHOLE ALLERGY THING JUST FLEW OUT OF MY HEAD.
YOU ARE SUCH A BRAT.
THE LAST THING I REMEMBER WAS MY FRIEND SCREAMING
OH MY GOD! SOMEBODY CALL 911!
WOW. THAT MUST'VE BEEN TOTALLY INTENSE.
LUCKY FOR ME, CHERYL CALLED FOR HELP RIGHT AWAY.
AND THAT YOU HAD YOUR BRACELET.

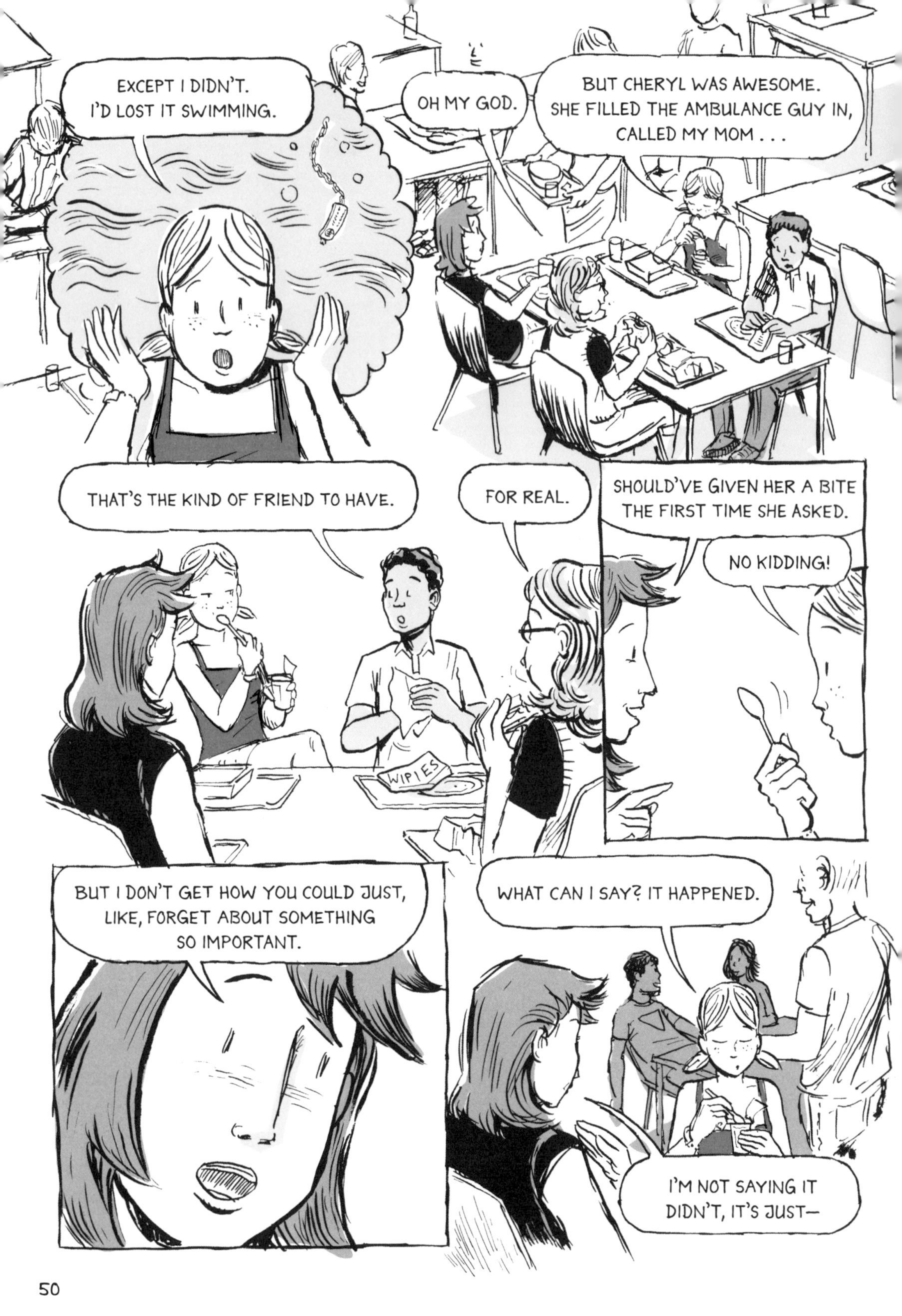
EXCEPT I DIDN'T. I'D LOST IT SWIMMING.
OH MY GOD.
BUT CHERYL WAS AWESOME. SHE FILLED THE AMBULANCE GUY IN, CALLED MY MOM . . .
THAT'S THE KIND OF FRIEND TO HAVE.
WIPIES
FOR REAL.
SHOULD'VE GIVEN HER A BITE THE FIRST TIME SHE ASKED.
NO KIDDING!
BUT I DON'T GET HOW YOU COULD JUST, LIKE, FORGET ABOUT SOMETHING SO IMPORTANT.
WHAT CAN I SAY? IT HAPPENED.
I'M NOT SAYING IT DIDN'T, IT'S JUST—

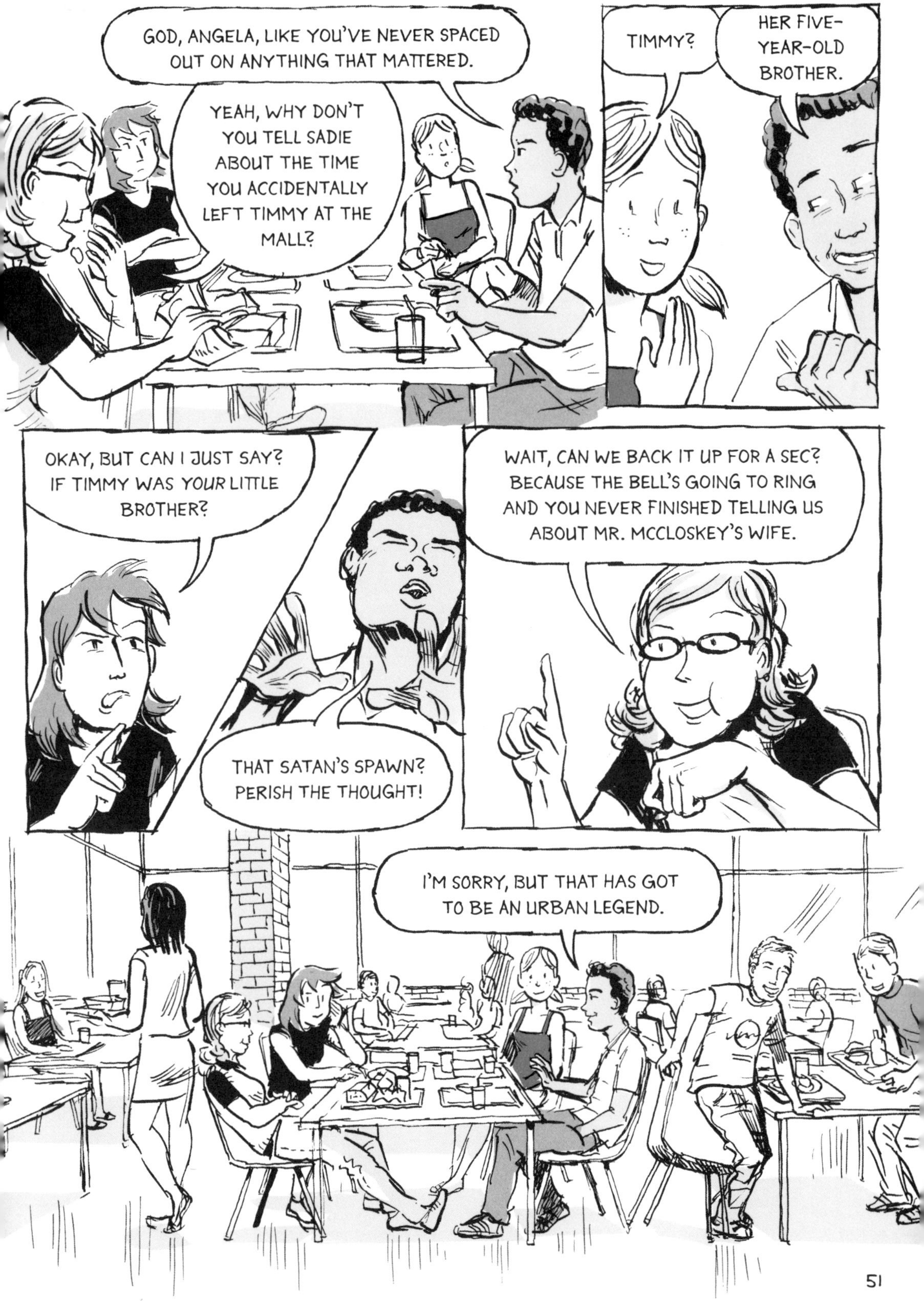
GOD, ANGELA, LIKE YOU'VE NEVER SPACED OUT ON ANYTHING THAT MATTERED.
YEAH, WHY DON'T YOU TELL SADIE ABOUT THE TIME YOU ACCIDENTALLY LEFT TIMMY AT THE MALL?
TIMMY?
HER FIVE-YEAR-OLD BROTHER.
OKAY, BUT CAN I JUST SAY? IF TIMMY WAS *YOUR* LITTLE BROTHER?
THAT SATAN'S SPAWN? PERISH THE THOUGHT!
WAIT, CAN WE BACK IT UP FOR A SEC? BECAUSE THE BELL'S GOING TO RING AND YOU NEVER FINISHED TELLING US ABOUT MR. MCCLOSKEY'S WIFE.
I'M SORRY, BUT THAT HAS GOT TO BE AN URBAN LEGEND.

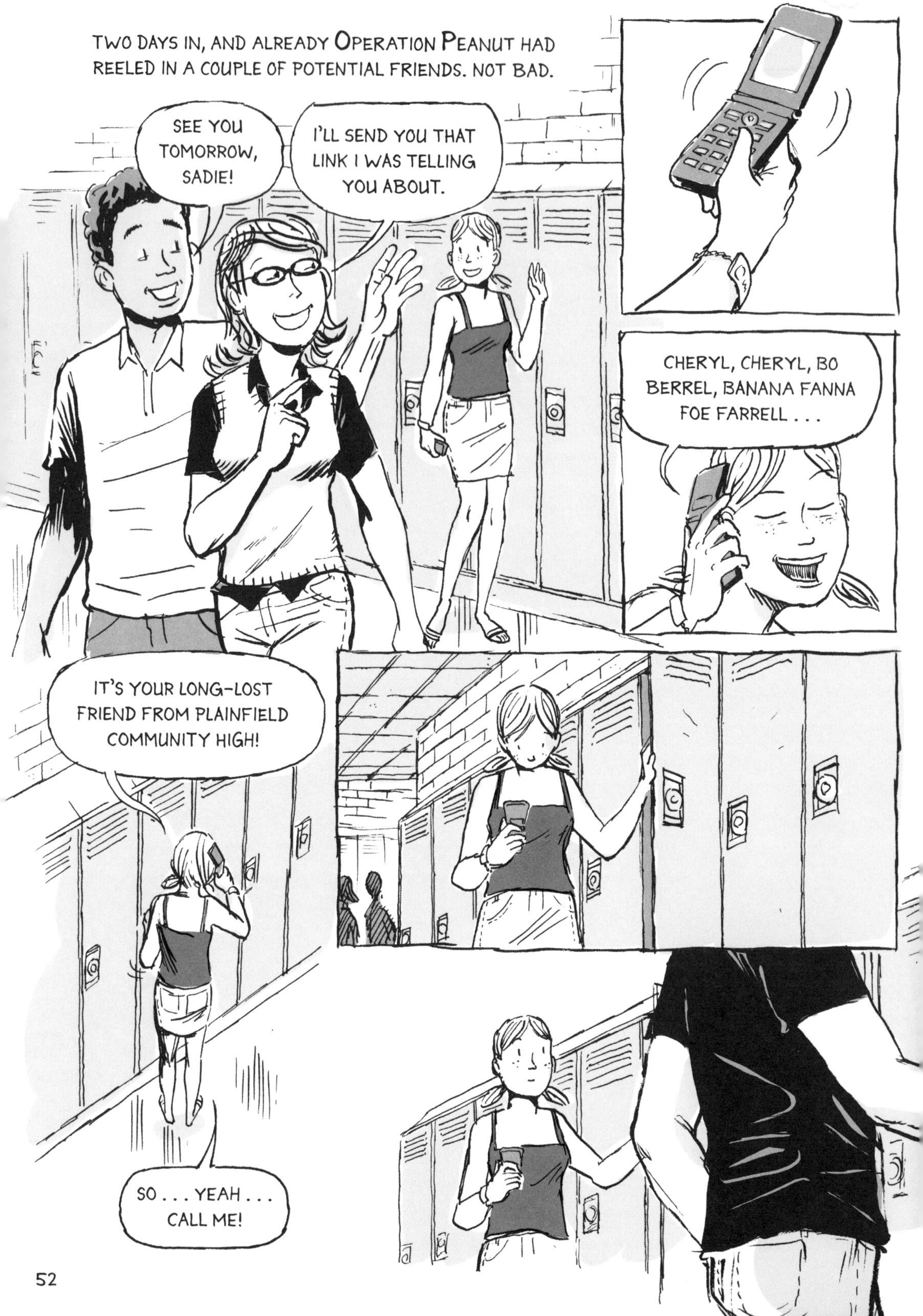

TWO DAYS IN, AND ALREADY OPERATION PEANUT HAD REELED IN A COUPLE OF POTENTIAL FRIENDS. NOT BAD.
SEE YOU TOMORROW, SADIE!
I'LL SEND YOU THAT LINK I WAS TELLING YOU ABOUT.
CHERYL, CHERYL, BO BERREL, BANANA FANNA FOE FARRELL . . .
IT'S YOUR LONG-LOST FRIEND FROM PLAINFIELD COMMUNITY HIGH!
SO . . . YEAH . . . CALL ME!

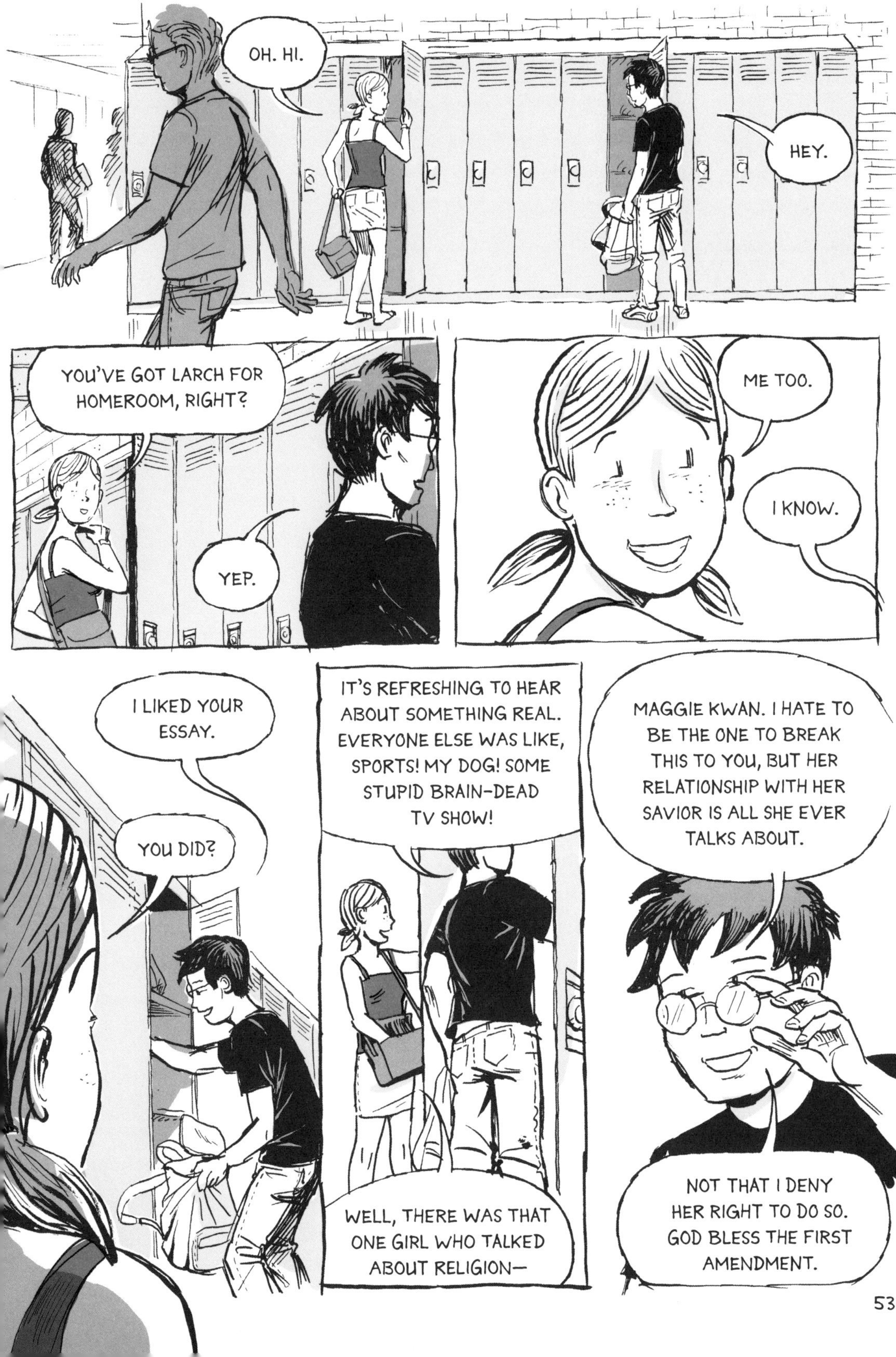
OH. HI.
HEY.
YOU'VE GOT LARCH FOR HOMEROOM, RIGHT?
YEP.
ME TOO.
I KNOW.
I LIKED YOUR ESSAY.
YOU DID?
IT'S REFRESHING TO HEAR ABOUT SOMETHING REAL. EVERYONE ELSE WAS LIKE, SPORTS! MY DOG! SOME STUPID BRAIN-DEAD TV SHOW!
WELL, THERE WAS THAT ONE GIRL WHO TALKED ABOUT RELIGION—
MAGGIE KWAN. I HATE TO BE THE ONE TO BREAK THIS TO YOU, BUT HER RELATIONSHIP WITH HER SAVIOR IS ALL SHE EVER TALKS ABOUT.
NOT THAT I DENY HER RIGHT TO DO SO. GOD BLESS THE FIRST AMENDMENT.

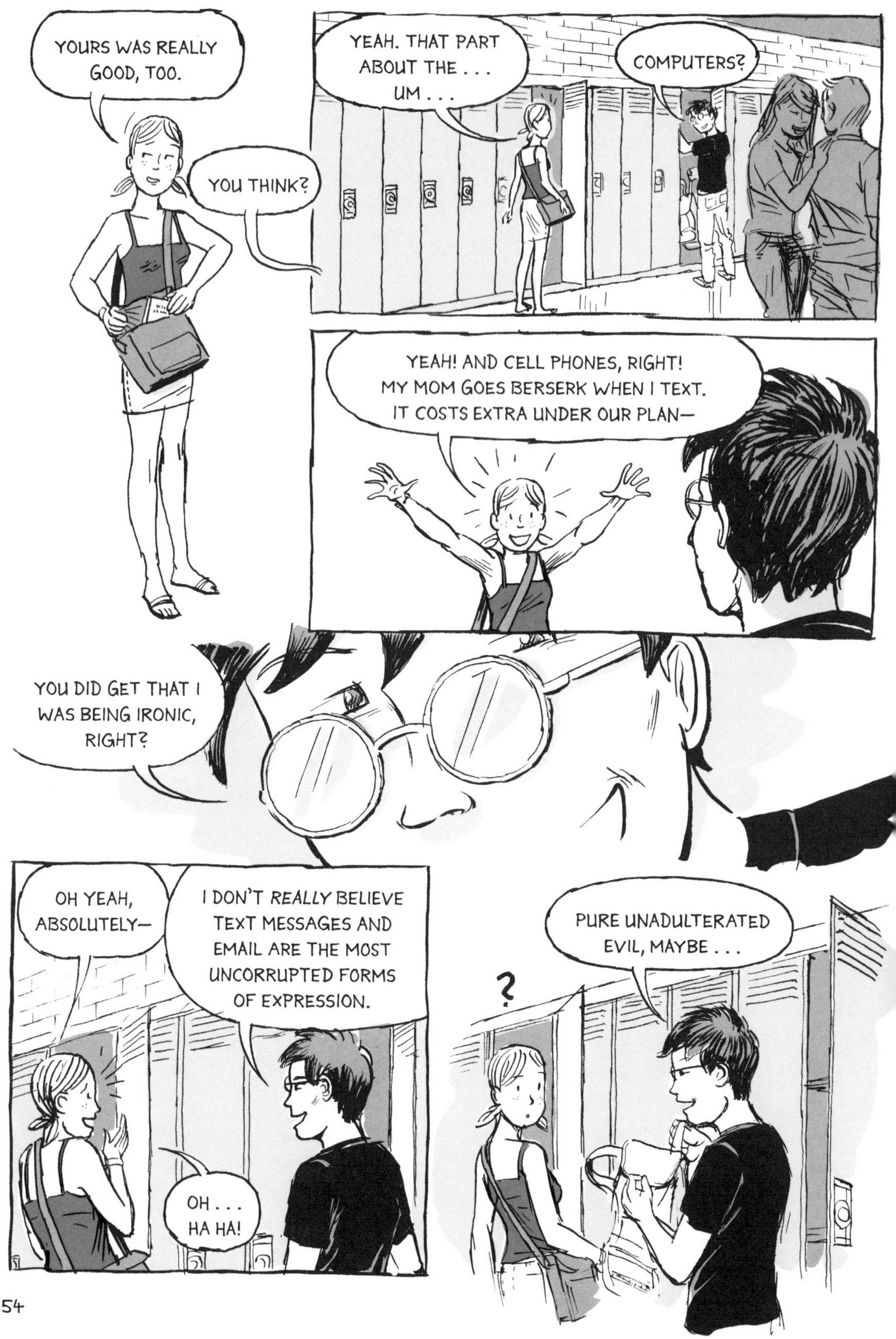
YOURS WAS REALLY GOOD, TOO.
YOU THINK?
YEAH. THAT PART ABOUT THE . . . UM . . .
COMPUTERS?
YEAH! AND CELL PHONES, RIGHT! MY MOM GOES BERSERK WHEN I TEXT. IT COSTS EXTRA UNDER OUR PLAN—
YOU DID GET THAT I WAS BEING IRONIC, RIGHT?
OH YEAH, ABSOLUTELY—
I DON'T *REALLY* BELIEVE TEXT MESSAGES AND EMAIL ARE THE MOST UNCORRUPTED FORMS OF EXPRESSION.
OH . . . HA HA!
?
PURE UNADULTERATED EVIL, MAYBE . . .

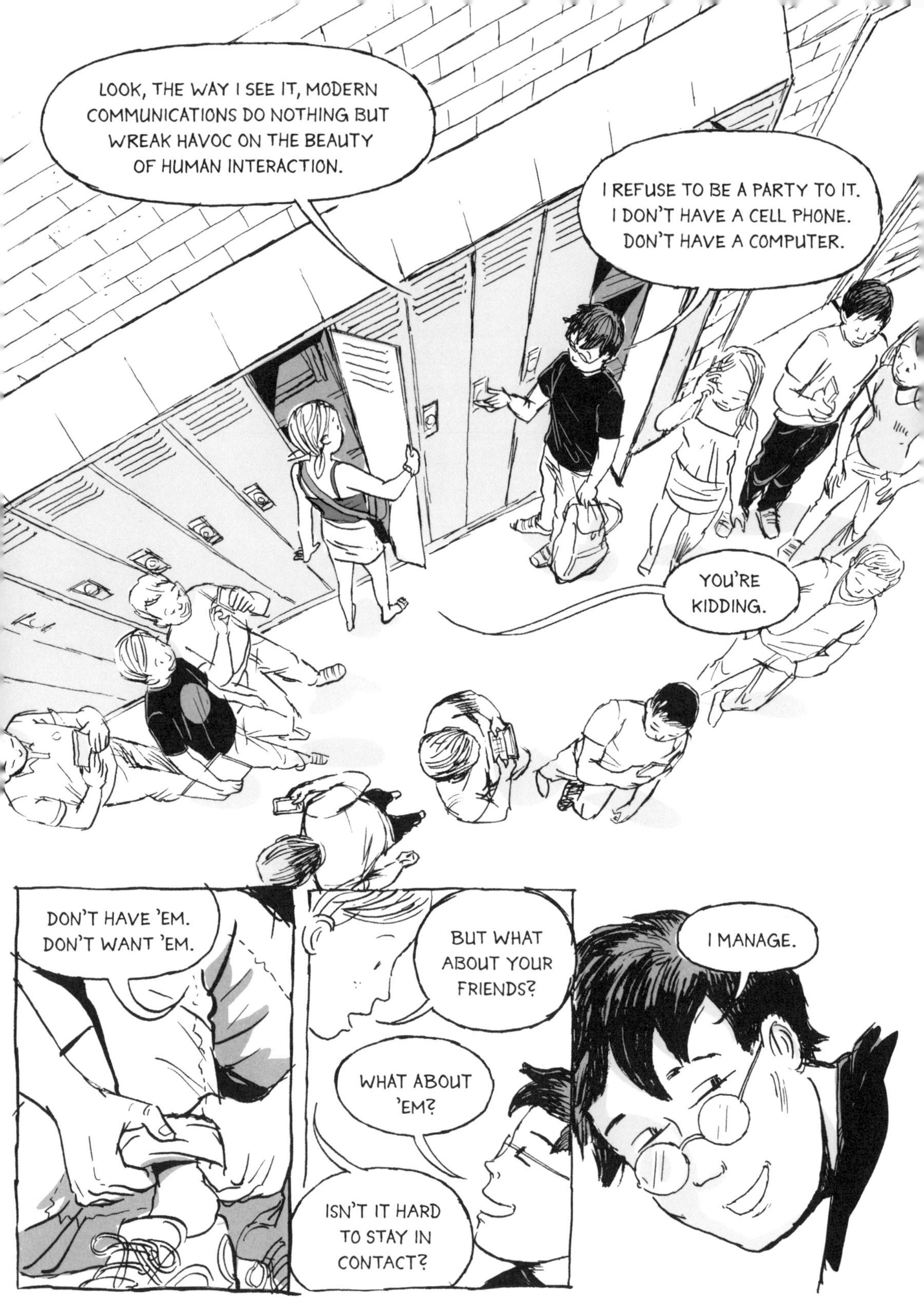
LOOK, THE WAY I SEE IT, MODERN COMMUNICATIONS DO NOTHING BUT WREAK HAVOC ON THE BEAUTY OF HUMAN INTERACTION.
I REFUSE TO BE A PARTY TO IT. I DON'T HAVE A CELL PHONE. DON'T HAVE A COMPUTER.
YOU'RE KIDDING.
DON'T HAVE 'EM. DON'T WANT 'EM.
BUT WHAT ABOUT YOUR FRIENDS?
WHAT ABOUT 'EM?
ISN'T IT HARD TO STAY IN CONTACT?
I MANAGE.

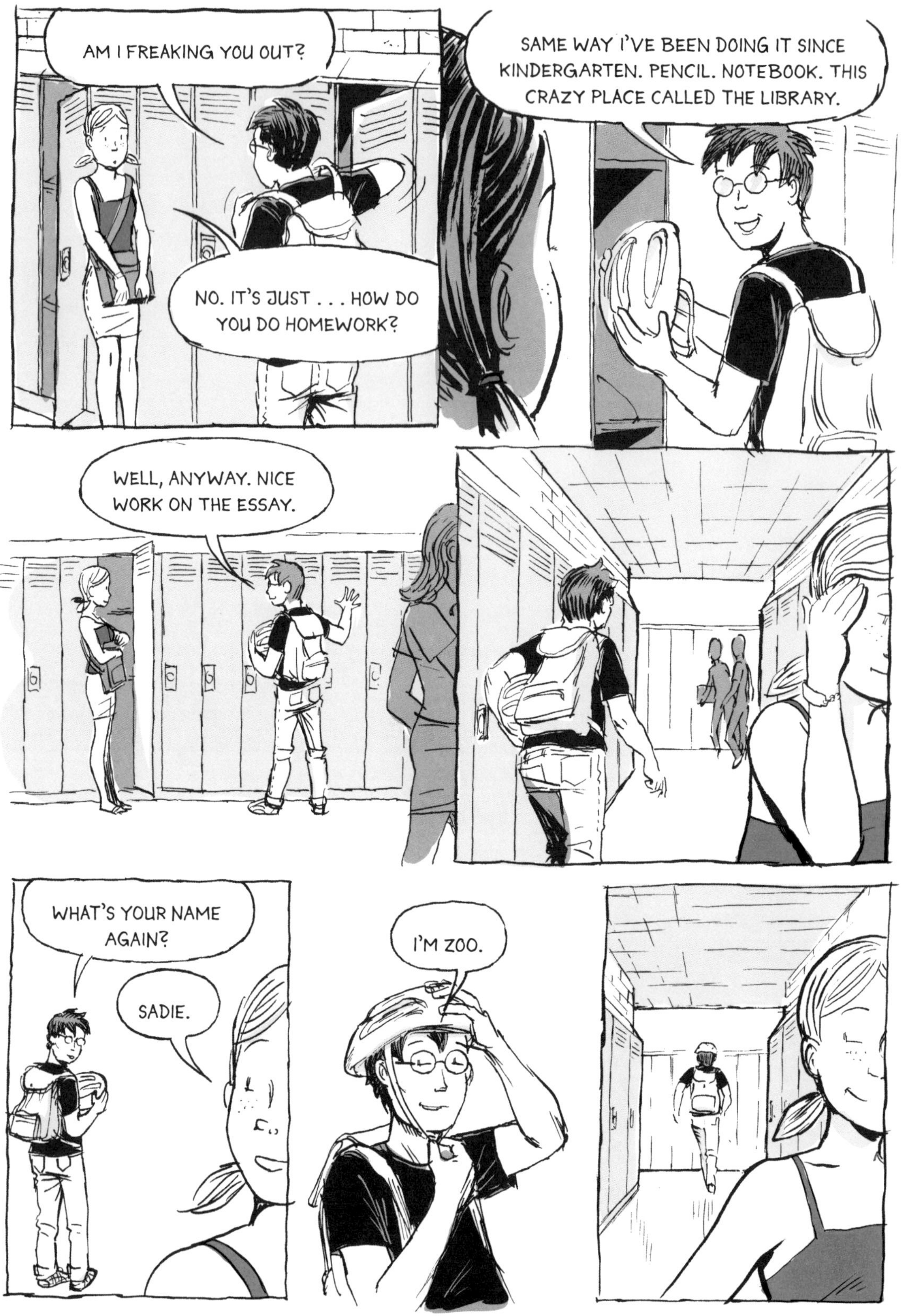
AM I FREAKING YOU OUT?
NO. IT'S JUST . . . HOW DO YOU DO HOMEWORK?
SAME WAY I'VE BEEN DOING IT SINCE KINDERGARTEN. PENCIL. NOTEBOOK. THIS CRAZY PLACE CALLED THE LIBRARY.
WELL, ANYWAY. NICE WORK ON THE ESSAY.
WHAT'S YOUR NAME AGAIN?
SADIE.
I'M ZOO.

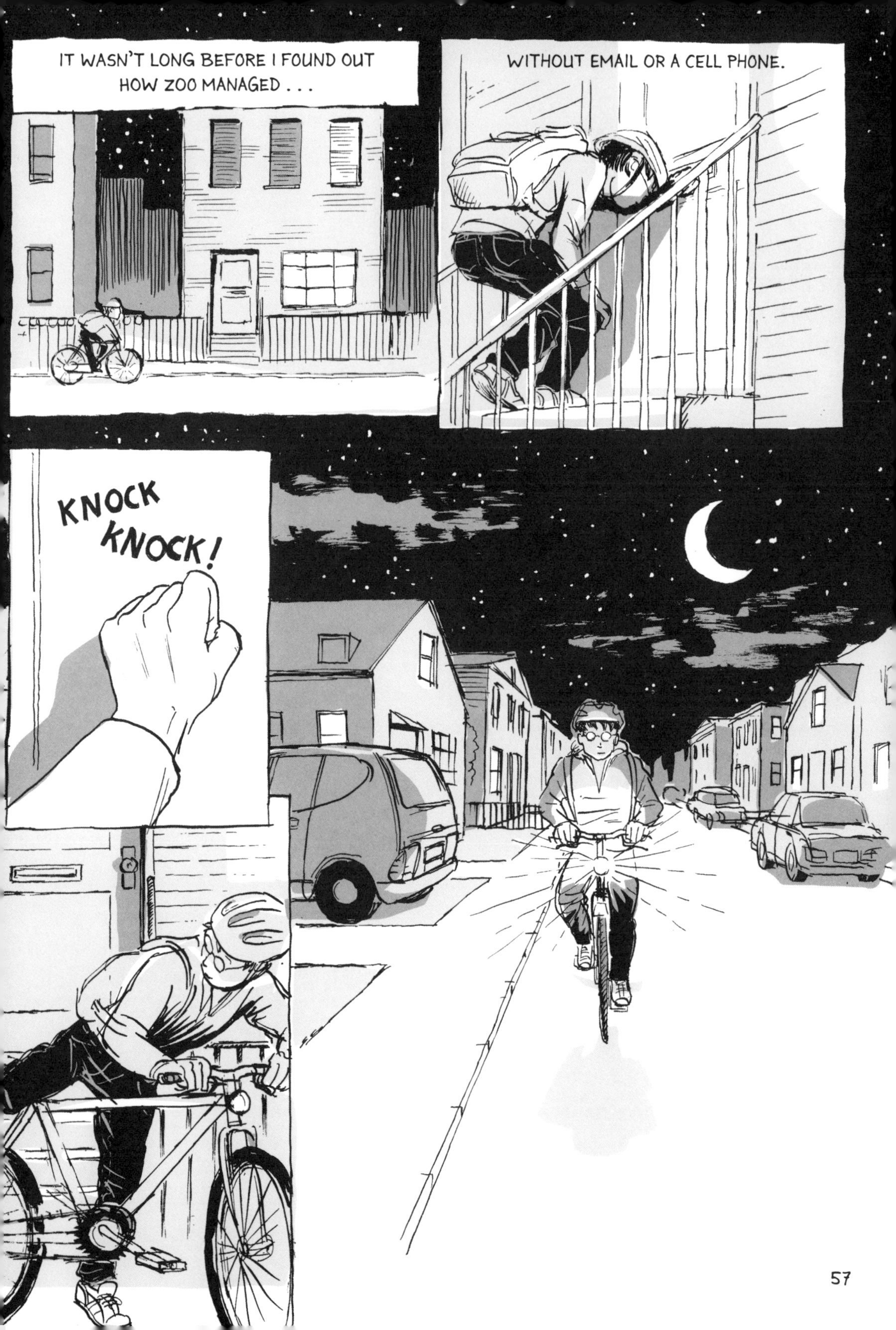
IT WASN'T LONG BEFORE I FOUND OUT HOW ZOO MANAGED . . .
WITHOUT EMAIL OR A CELL PHONE.
KNOCK KNOCK!

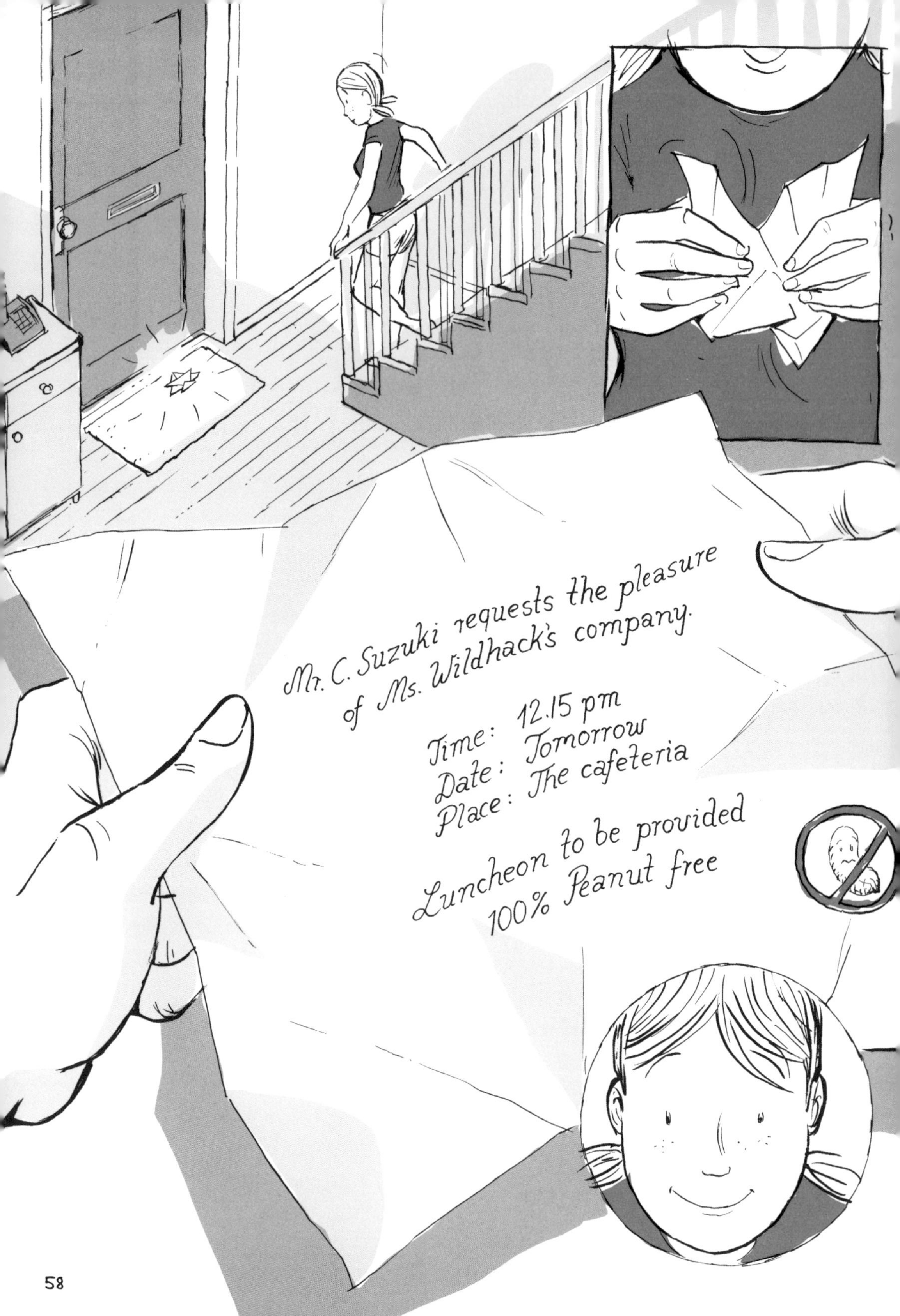
Mr. C. Suzuki requests the pleasure
of Ms. Wildhack's company.
Time: 12.15 pm
Date: Tomorrow
Place: The cafeteria
Luncheon to be provided
100% Peanut free

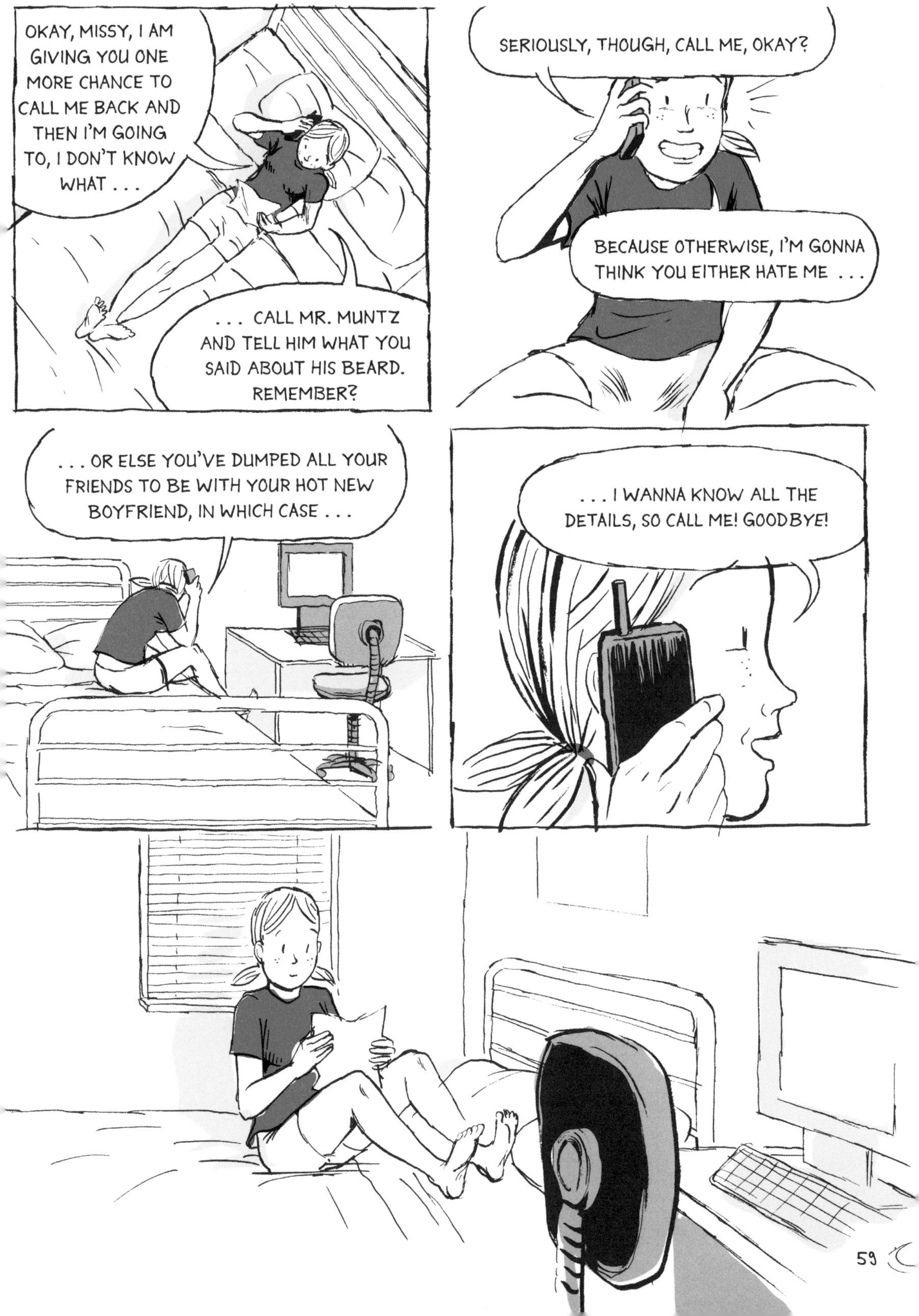
OKAY, MISSY, I AM GIVING YOU ONE MORE CHANCE TO CALL ME BACK AND THEN I'M GOING TO, I DON'T KNOW WHAT . . .
. . . CALL MR. MUNTZ AND TELL HIM WHAT YOU SAID ABOUT HIS BEARD. REMEMBER?
SERIOUSLY, THOUGH, CALL ME, OKAY?
BECAUSE OTHERWISE, I'M GONNA THINK YOU EITHER HATE ME . . .
. . . OR ELSE YOU'VE DUMPED ALL YOUR FRIENDS TO BE WITH YOUR HOT NEW BOYFRIEND, IN WHICH CASE . . .
. . . I WANNA KNOW ALL THE DETAILS, SO CALL ME! GOODBYE!

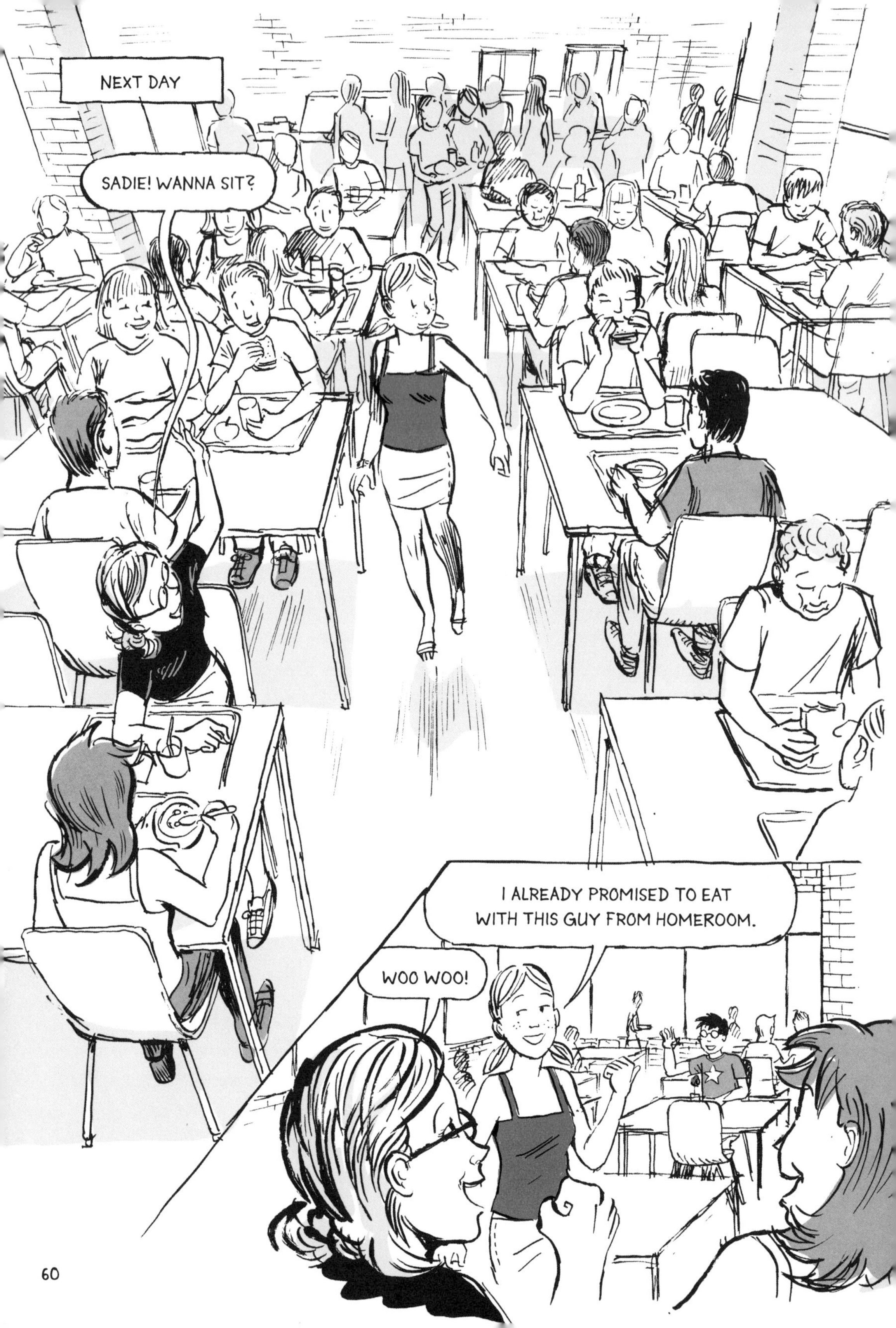
NEXT DAY
SADIE! WANNA SIT?
I ALREADY PROMISED TO EAT WITH THIS GUY FROM HOMEROOM.
WOO WOO!

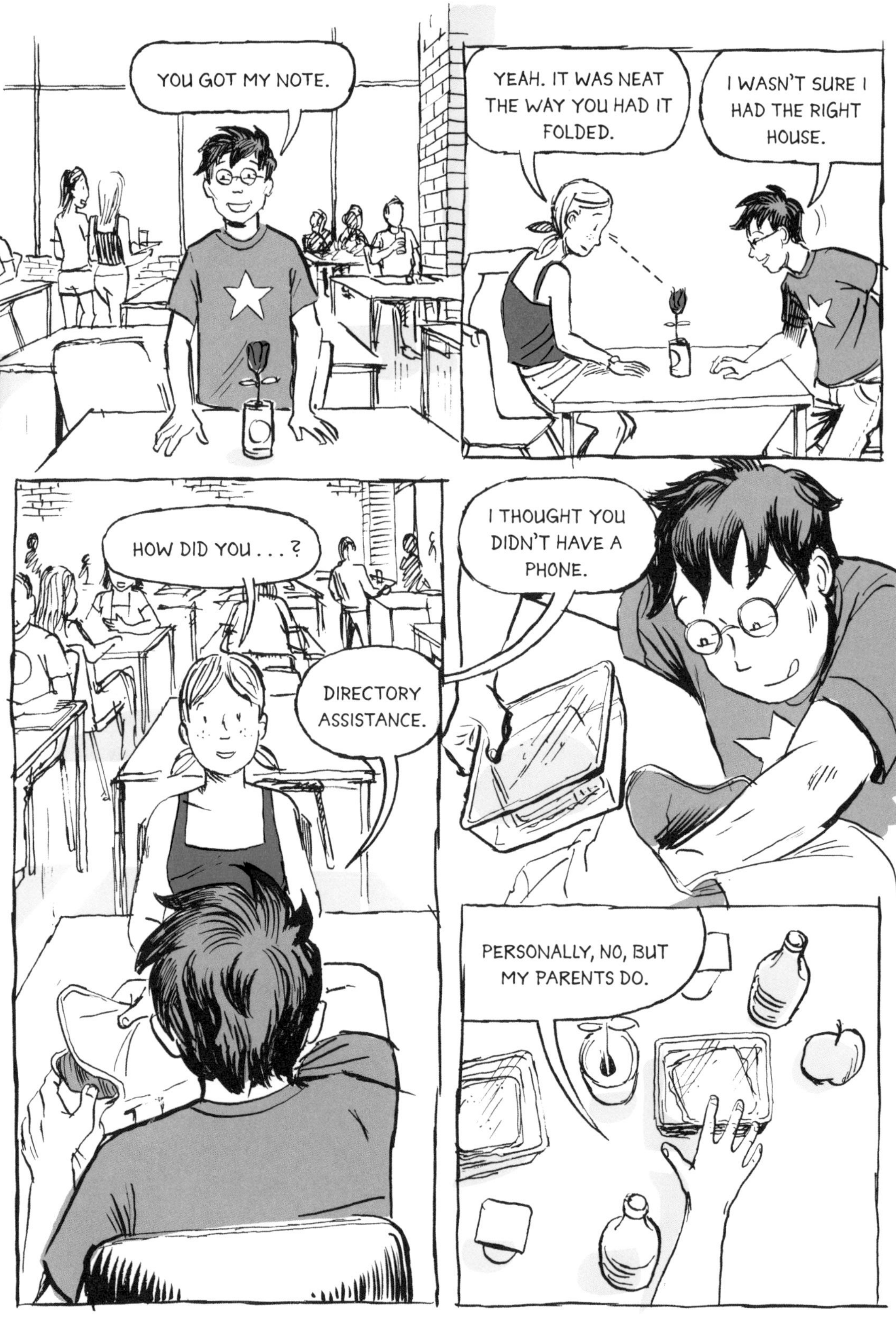
YOU GOT MY NOTE.
YEAH. IT WAS NEAT THE WAY YOU HAD IT FOLDED.
I WASN'T SURE I HAD THE RIGHT HOUSE.
HOW DID YOU . . . ?
DIRECTORY ASSISTANCE.
I THOUGHT YOU DIDN'T HAVE A PHONE.
PERSONALLY, NO, BUT MY PARENTS DO.

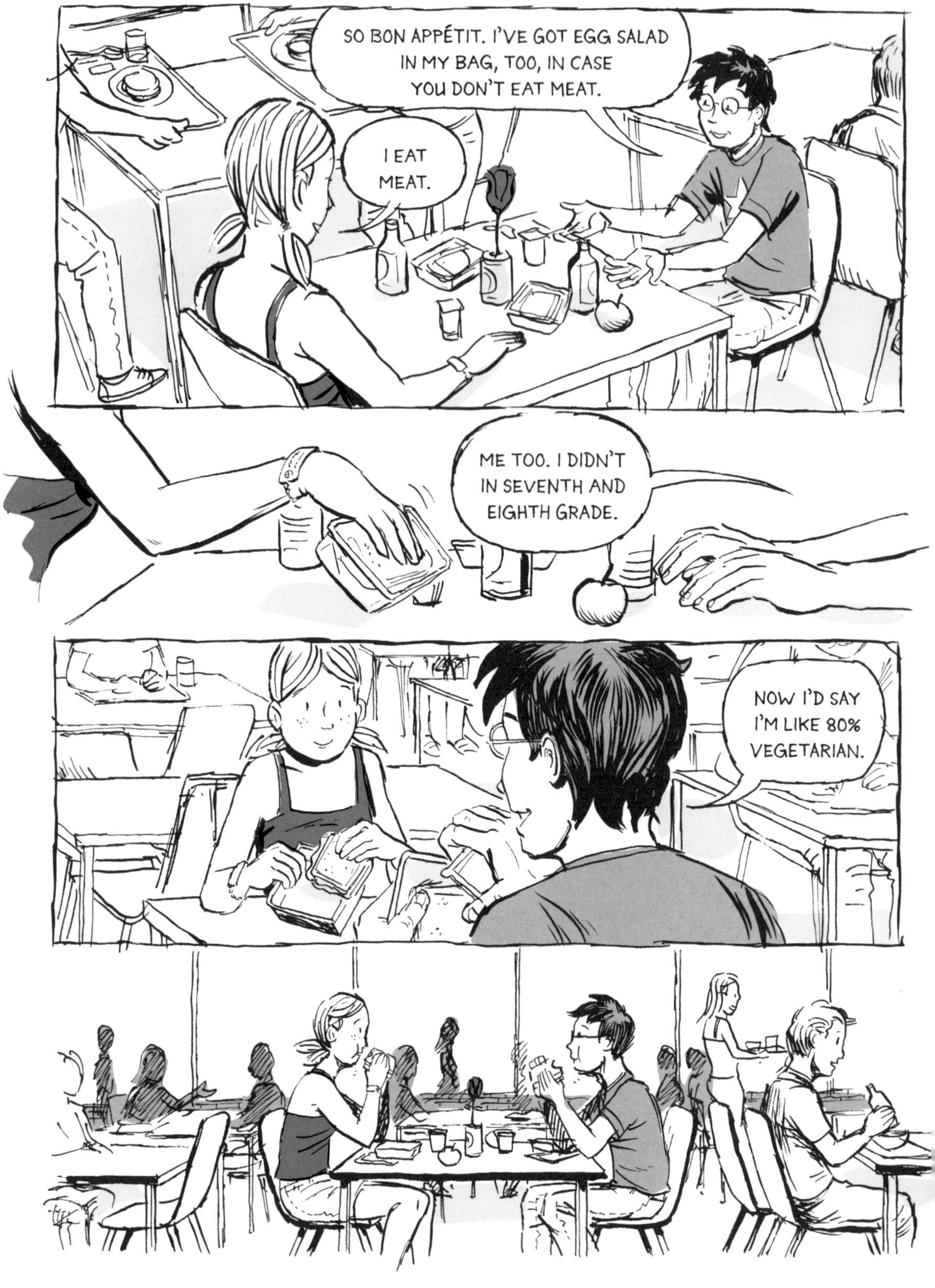

SO BON APPÉTIT. I'VE GOT EGG SALAD IN MY BAG, TOO, IN CASE YOU DON'T EAT MEAT.
I EAT MEAT.
ME TOO. I DIDN'T IN SEVENTH AND EIGHTH GRADE.
NOW I'D SAY I'M LIKE 80% VEGETARIAN.

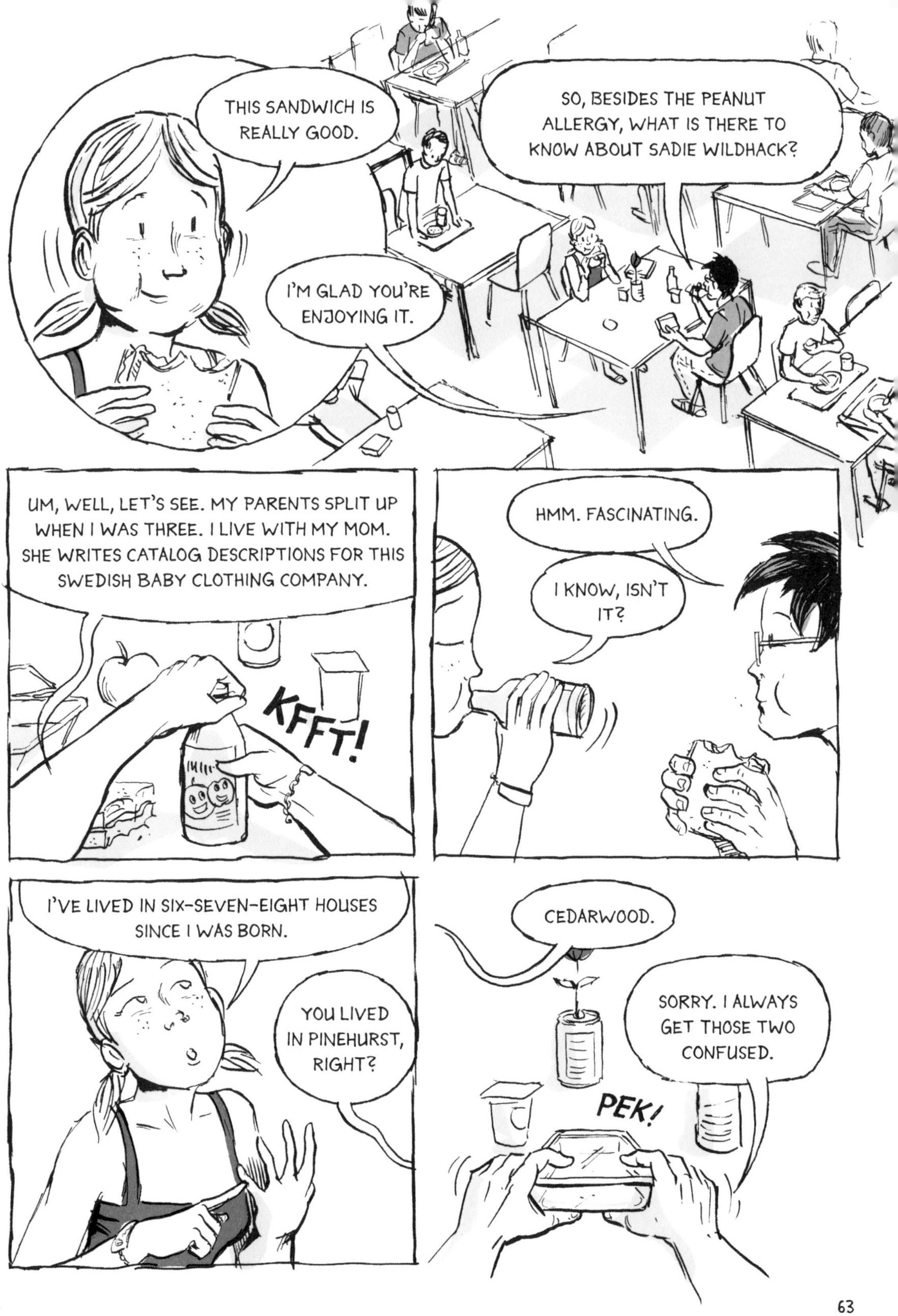
THIS SANDWICH IS REALLY GOOD.
I'M GLAD YOU'RE ENJOYING IT.
SO, BESIDES THE PEANUT ALLERGY, WHAT IS THERE TO KNOW ABOUT SADIE WILDHACK?
UM, WELL, LET'S SEE. MY PARENTS SPLIT UP WHEN I WAS THREE. I LIVE WITH MY MOM. SHE WRITES CATALOG DESCRIPTIONS FOR THIS SWEDISH BABY CLOTHING COMPANY.
KFFT!
HMM. FASCINATING.
I KNOW, ISN'T IT?
I'VE LIVED IN SIX-SEVEN-EIGHT HOUSES SINCE I WAS BORN.
YOU LIVED IN PINEHURST, RIGHT?
CEDARWOOD.
SORRY. I ALWAYS GET THOSE TWO CONFUSED.
PEK!

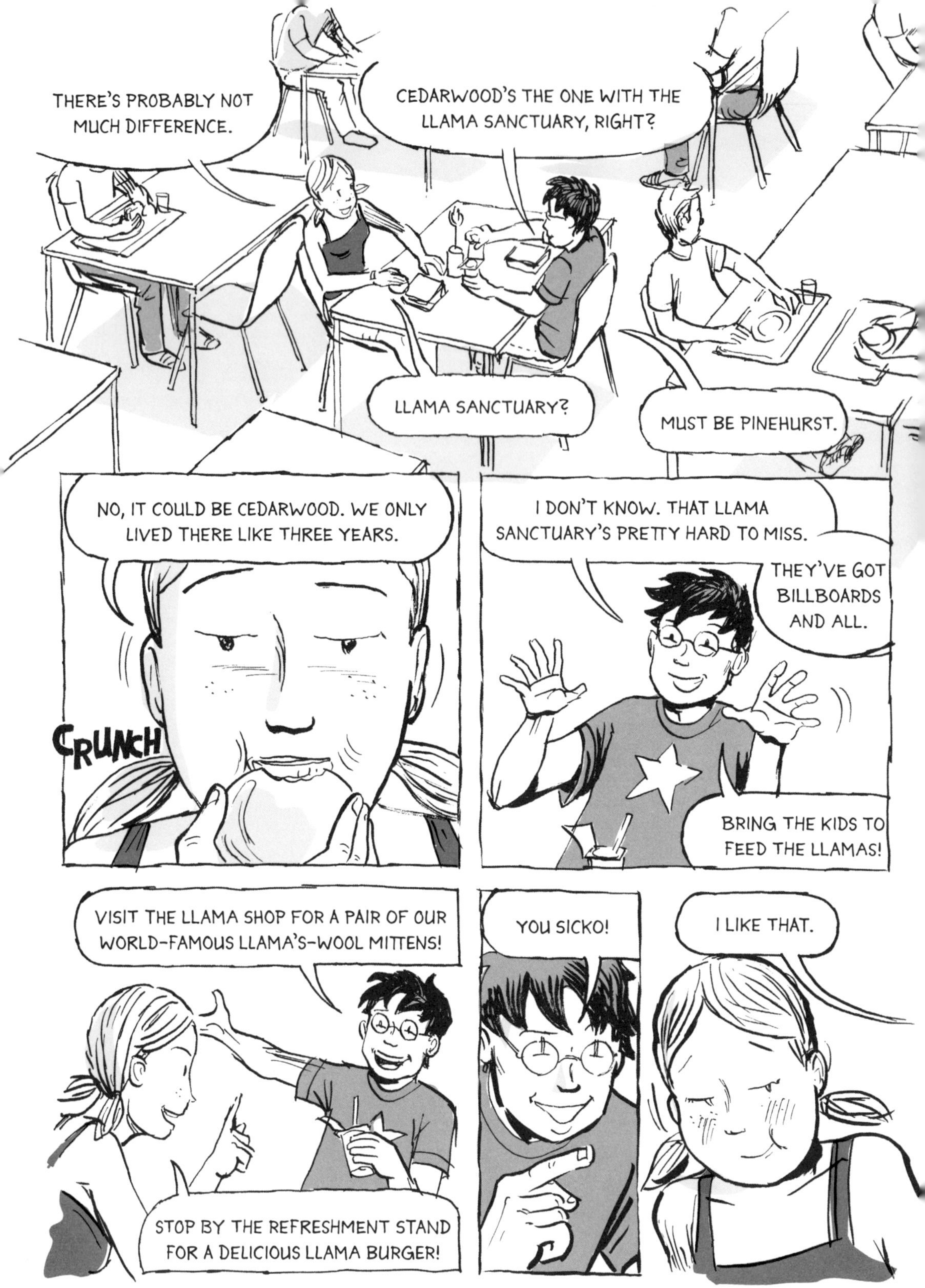
THERE'S PROBABLY NOT MUCH DIFFERENCE.
CEDARWOOD'S THE ONE WITH THE LLAMA SANCTUARY, RIGHT?
LLAMA SANCTUARY?
MUST BE PINEHURST.
NO, IT COULD BE CEDARWOOD. WE ONLY LIVED THERE LIKE THREE YEARS.
CRUNCH
I DON'T KNOW. THAT LLAMA SANCTUARY'S PRETTY HARD TO MISS.
THEY'VE GOT BILLBOARDS AND ALL.
BRING THE KIDS TO FEED THE LLAMAS!
VISIT THE LLAMA SHOP FOR A PAIR OF OUR WORLD-FAMOUS LLAMA'S-WOOL MITTENS!
STOP BY THE REFRESHMENT STAND FOR A DELICIOUS LLAMA BURGER!
YOU SICKO!
I LIKE THAT.

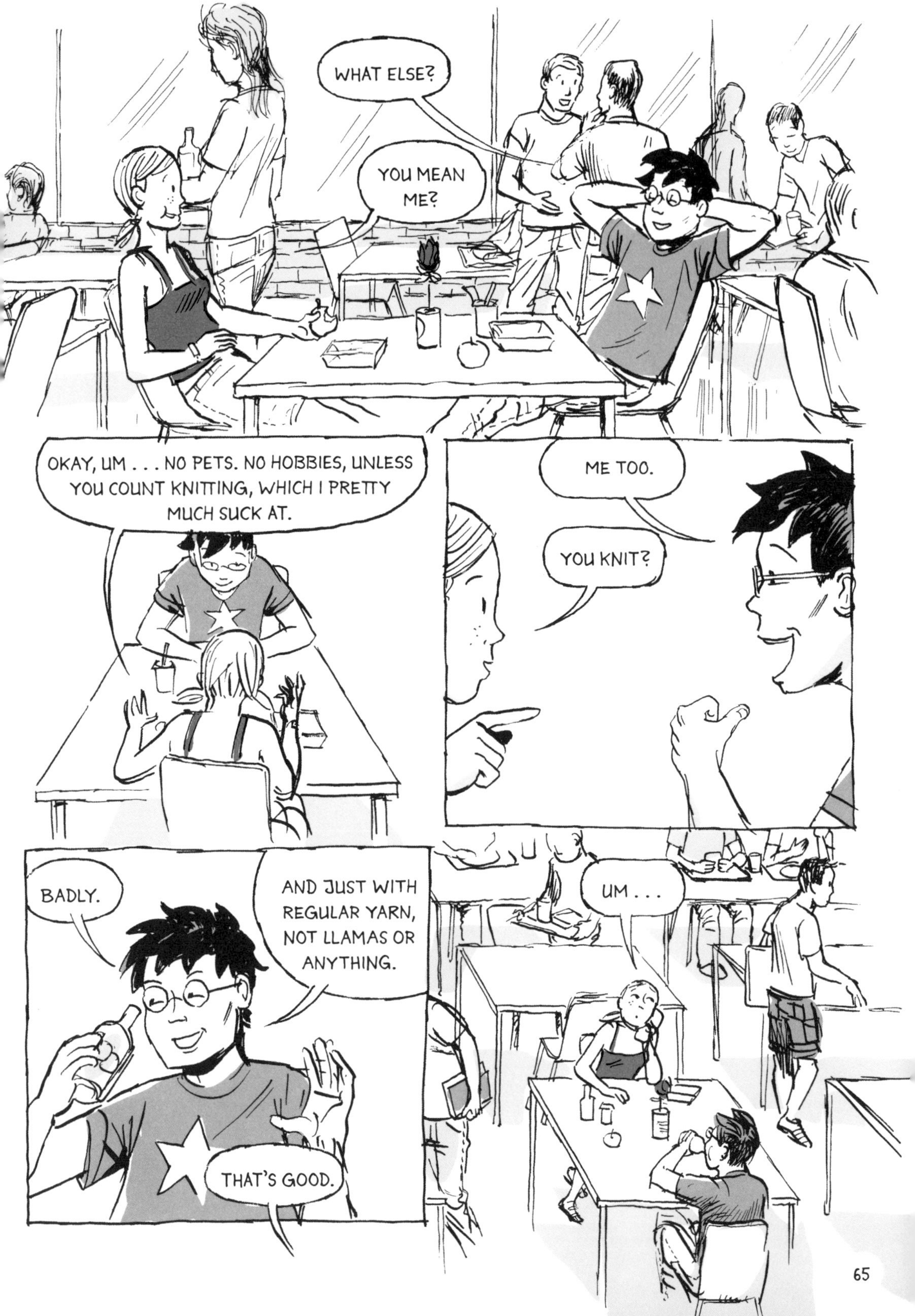
WHAT ELSE?
YOU MEAN ME?
OKAY, UM . . . NO PETS. NO HOBBIES, UNLESS YOU COUNT KNITTING, WHICH I PRETTY MUCH SUCK AT.
ME TOO.
YOU KNIT?
BADLY.
AND JUST WITH REGULAR YARN, NOT LLAMAS OR ANYTHING.
THAT'S GOOD.
UM . . .

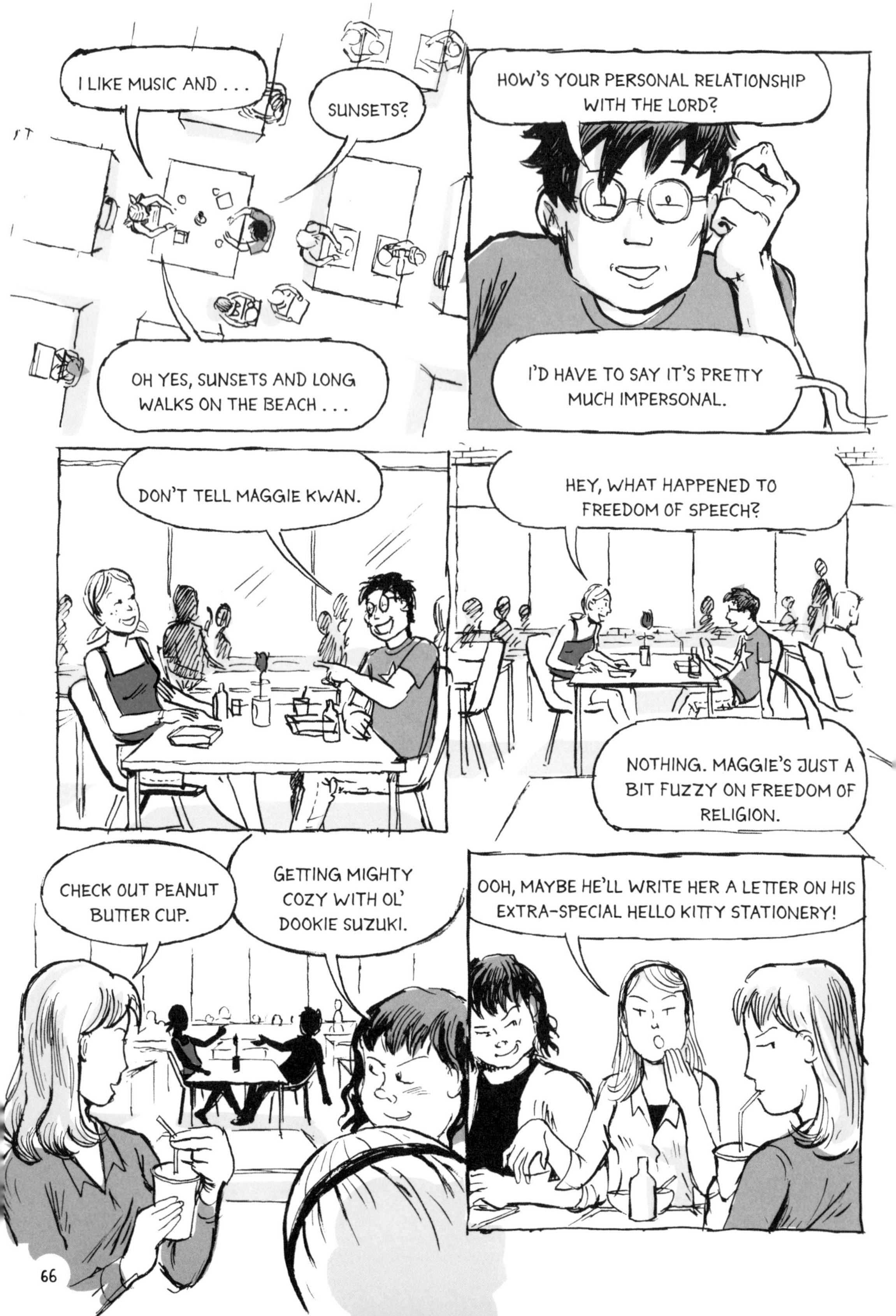
I LIKE MUSIC AND . . .
SUNSETS?
OH YES, SUNSETS AND LONG WALKS ON THE BEACH . . .
HOW'S YOUR PERSONAL RELATIONSHIP WITH THE LORD?
I'D HAVE TO SAY IT'S PRETTY MUCH IMPERSONAL.
DON'T TELL MAGGIE KWAN.
HEY, WHAT HAPPENED TO FREEDOM OF SPEECH?
NOTHING. MAGGIE'S JUST A BIT FUZZY ON FREEDOM OF RELIGION.
CHECK OUT PEANUT BUTTER CUP.
GETTING MIGHTY COZY WITH OL' DOOKIE SUZUKI.
OOH, MAYBE HE'LL WRITE HER A LETTER ON HIS EXTRA-SPECIAL HELLO KITTY STATIONERY!

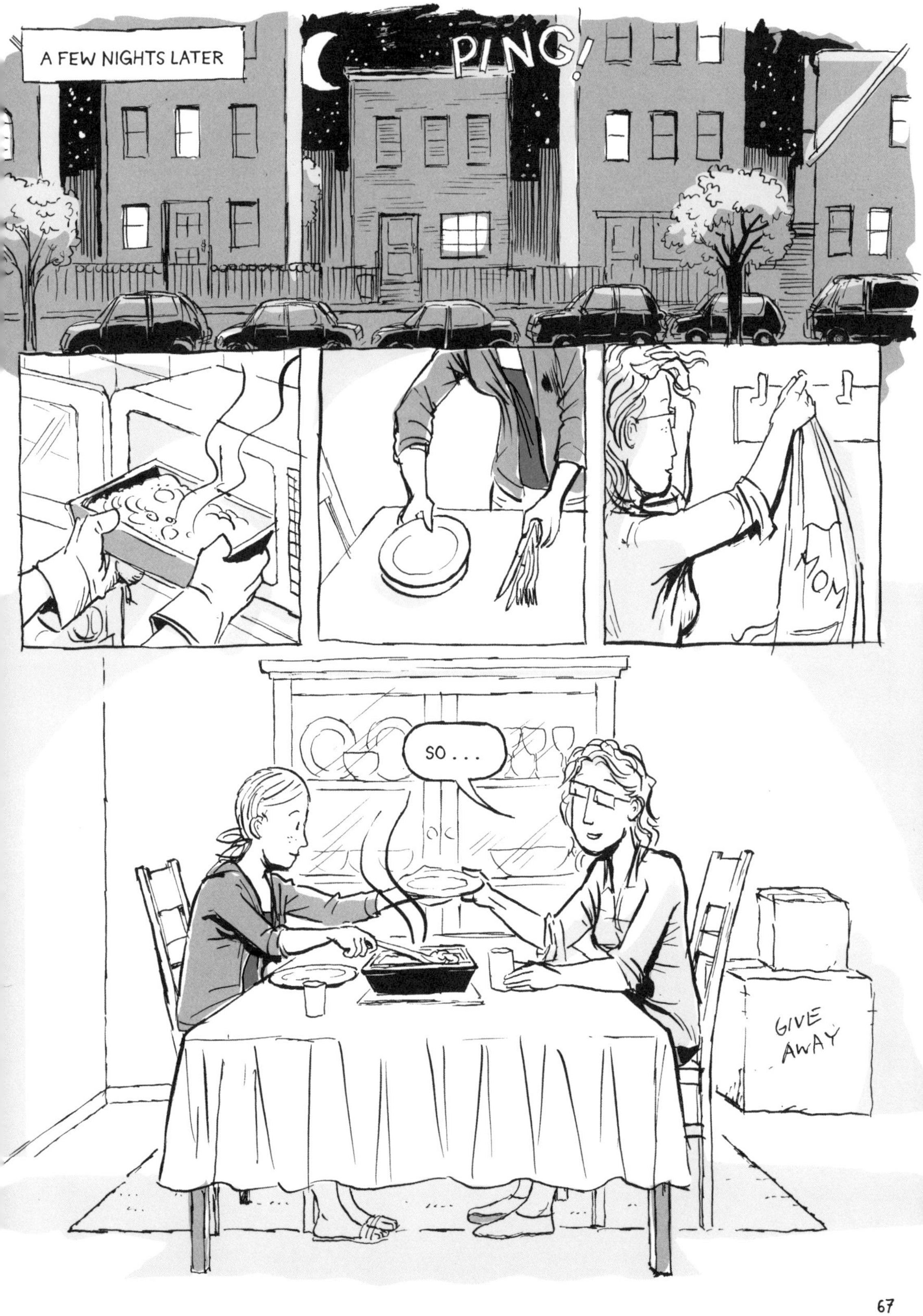
A FEW NIGHTS LATER
PING!
MOM
SO . . .
GIVE AWAY

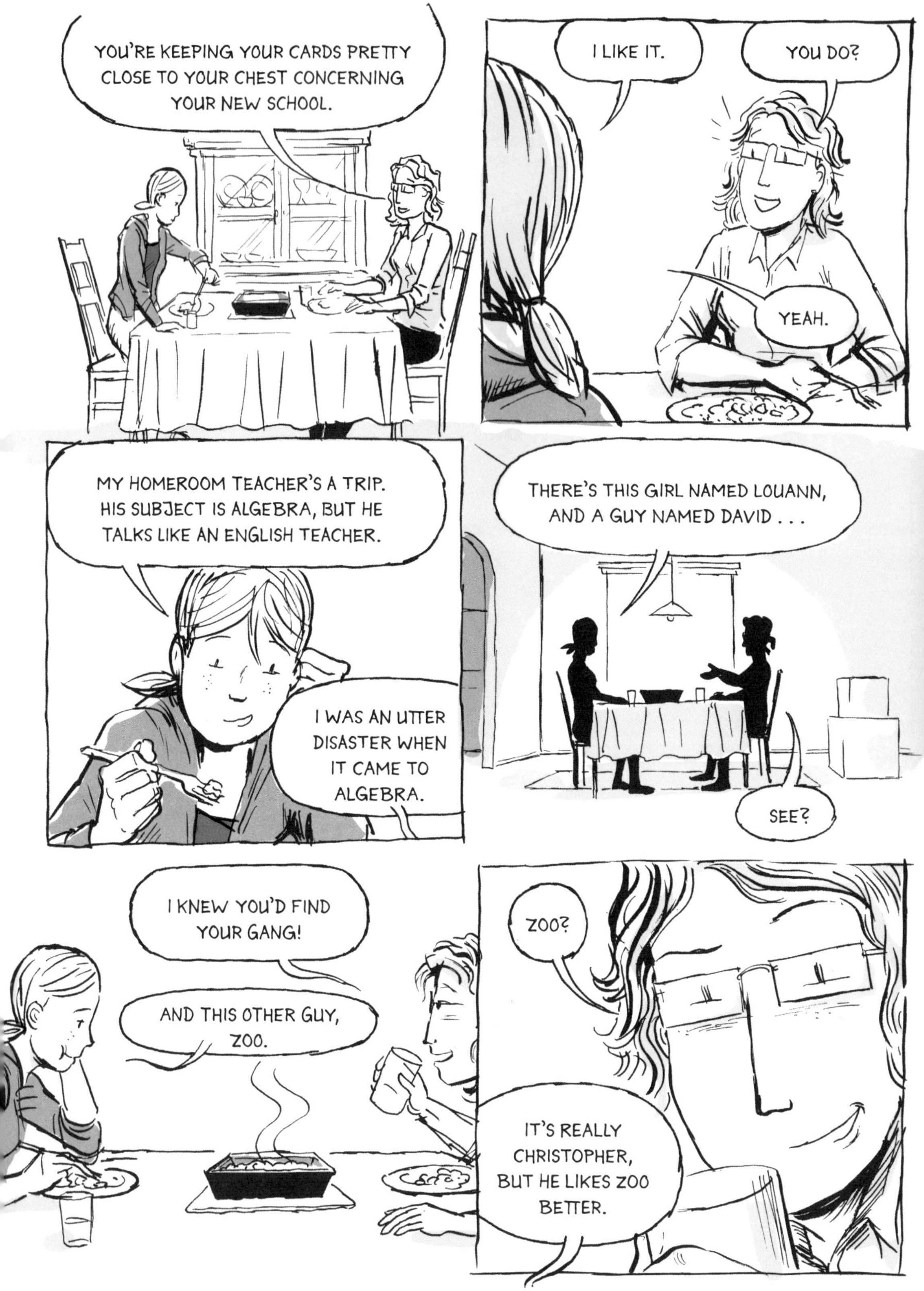
YOU'RE KEEPING YOUR CARDS PRETTY CLOSE TO YOUR CHEST CONCERNING YOUR NEW SCHOOL.
I LIKE IT.
YOU DO?
YEAH.
MY HOMEROOM TEACHER'S A TRIP. HIS SUBJECT IS ALGEBRA, BUT HE TALKS LIKE AN ENGLISH TEACHER.
I WAS AN UTTER DISASTER WHEN IT CAME TO ALGEBRA.
THERE'S THIS GIRL NAMED LOUANN, AND A GUY NAMED DAVID . . .
SEE?
I KNEW YOU'D FIND YOUR GANG!
AND THIS OTHER GUY, ZOO.
ZOO?
IT'S REALLY CHRISTOPHER, BUT HE LIKES ZOO BETTER.

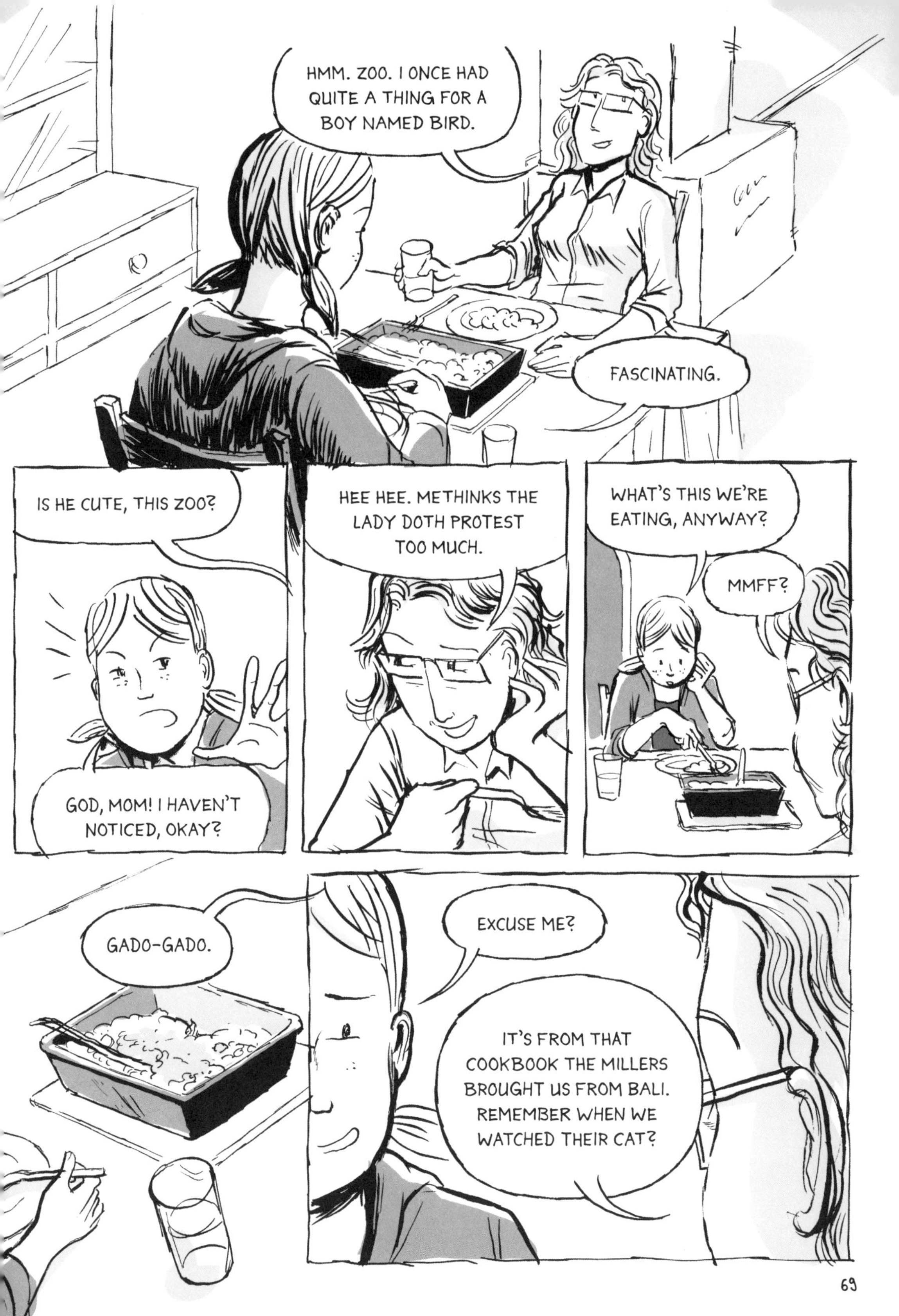
HMM. ZOO. I ONCE HAD QUITE A THING FOR A BOY NAMED BIRD.
FASCINATING.
IS HE CUTE, THIS ZOO?
GOD, MOM! I HAVEN'T NOTICED, OKAY?
HEE HEE. METHINKS THE LADY DOTH PROTEST TOO MUCH.
WHAT'S THIS WE'RE EATING, ANYWAY?
MMFF?
GADO-GADO.
EXCUSE ME?
IT'S FROM THAT COOKBOOK THE MILLERS BROUGHT US FROM BALI. REMEMBER WHEN WE WATCHED THEIR CAT?

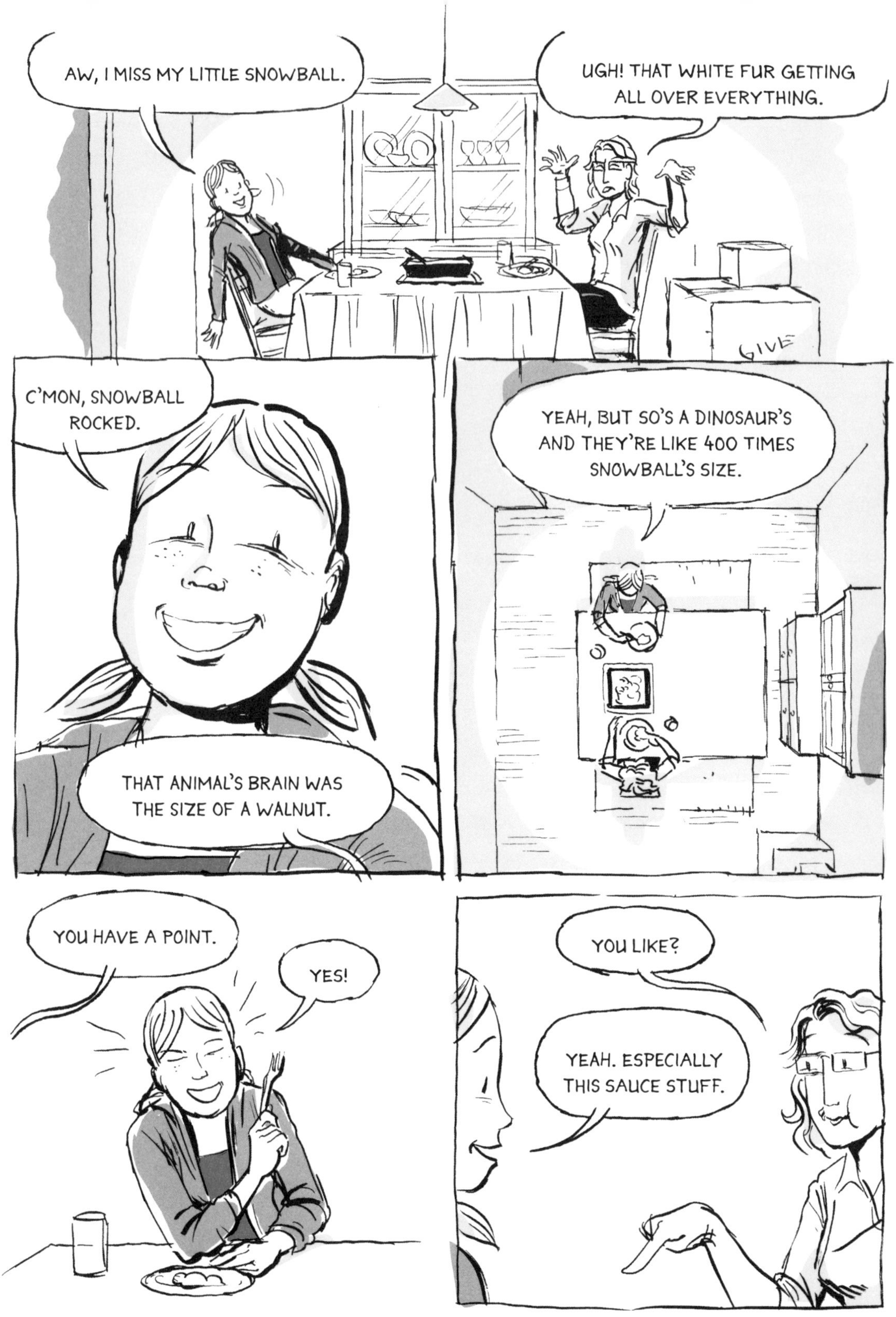
AW, I MISS MY LITTLE SNOWBALL.
UGH! THAT WHITE FUR GETTING ALL OVER EVERYTHING.
GIVE
C'MON, SNOWBALL ROCKED.
THAT ANIMAL'S BRAIN WAS THE SIZE OF A WALNUT.
YEAH, BUT SO'S A DINOSAUR'S AND THEY'RE LIKE 400 TIMES SNOWBALL'S SIZE.
YOU HAVE A POINT.
YES!
YOU LIKE?
YEAH. ESPECIALLY THIS SAUCE STUFF.

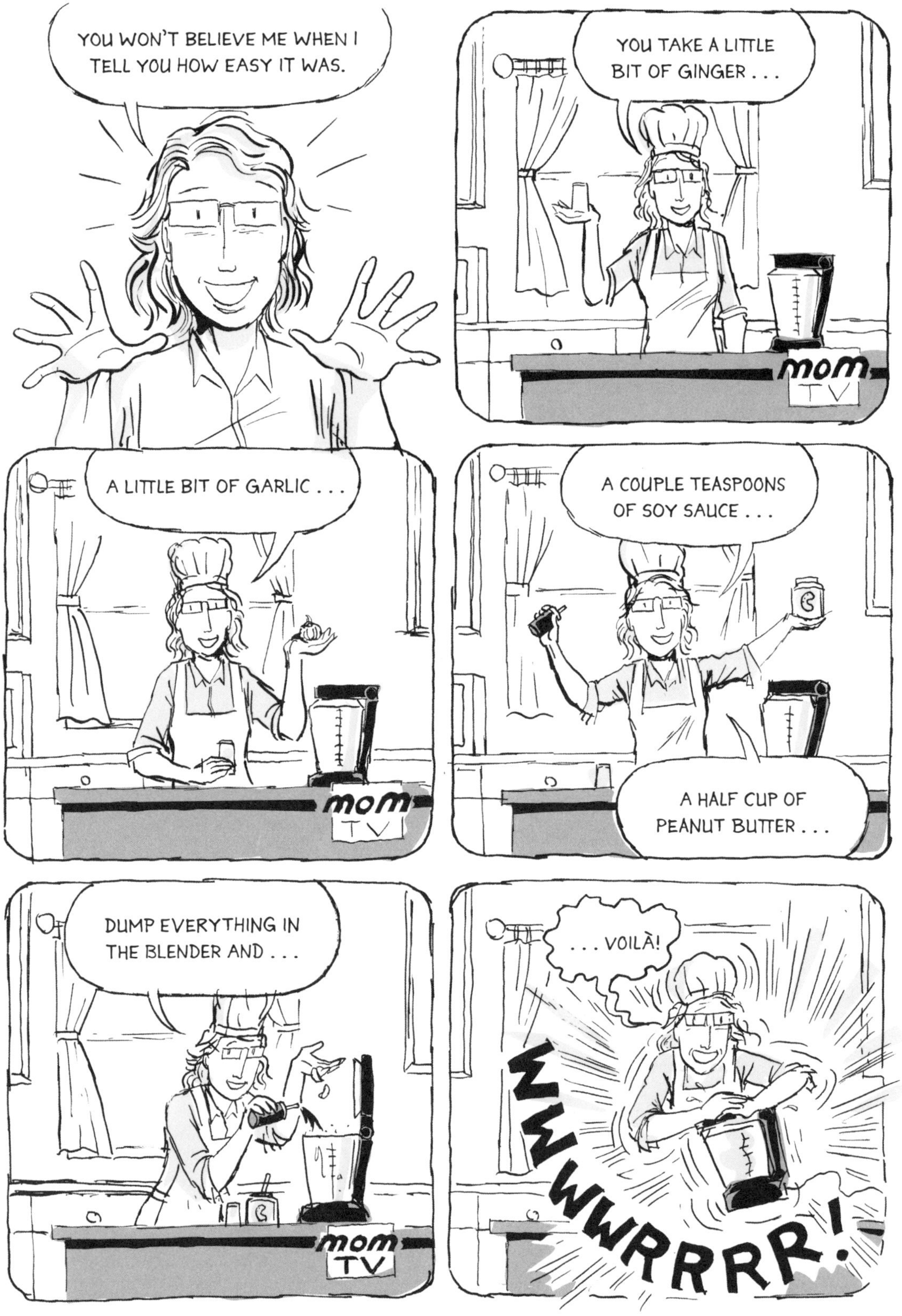
YOU WON'T BELIEVE ME WHEN I TELL YOU HOW EASY IT WAS.
YOU TAKE A LITTLE BIT OF GINGER . . .
mom TV
A LITTLE BIT OF GARLIC . . .
mom TV
A COUPLE TEASPOONS OF SOY SAUCE . . .
A HALF CUP OF PEANUT BUTTER . . .
DUMP EVERYTHING IN THE BLENDER AND . . .
mom TV
. . . VOILÀ!
WWWWRRRRR!

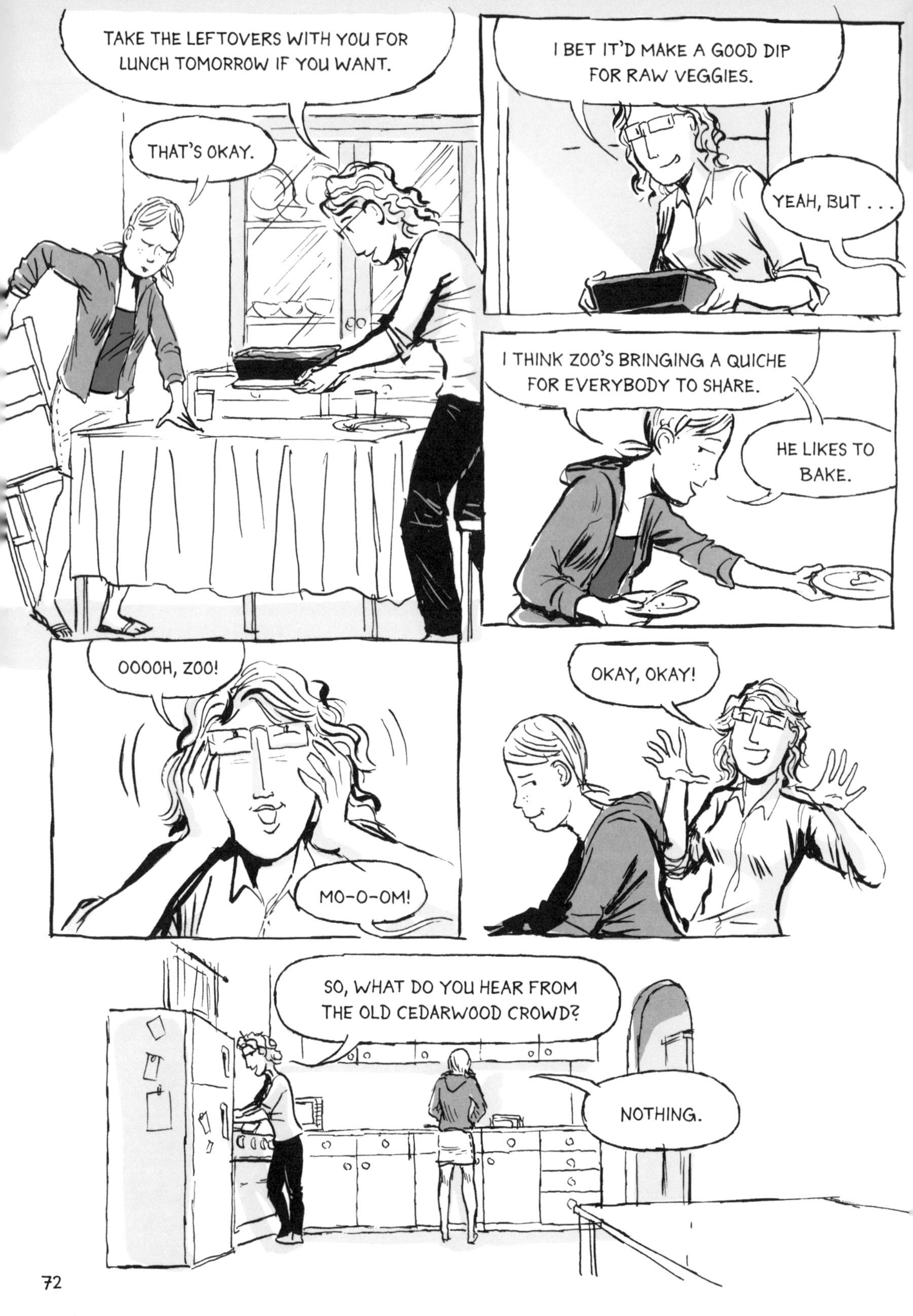
TAKE THE LEFTOVERS WITH YOU FOR LUNCH TOMORROW IF YOU WANT.
THAT'S OKAY.
I BET IT'D MAKE A GOOD DIP FOR RAW VEGGIES.
YEAH, BUT . . .
I THINK ZOO'S BRINGING A QUICHE FOR EVERYBODY TO SHARE.
HE LIKES TO BAKE.
OOOOH, ZOO!
MO-O-OM!
OKAY, OKAY!
SO, WHAT DO YOU HEAR FROM THE OLD CEDARWOOD CROWD?
NOTHING.

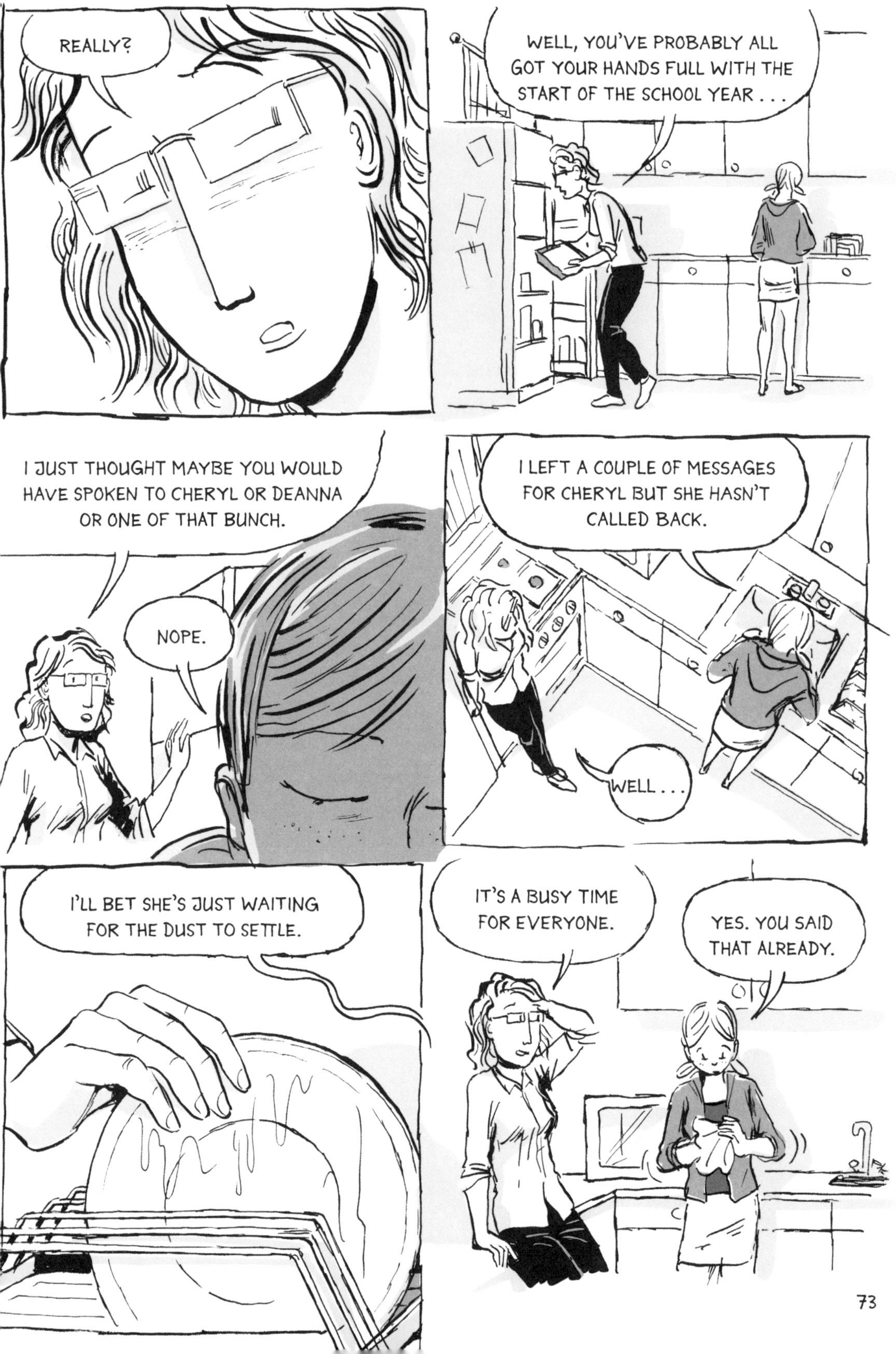
REALLY?
WELL, YOU'VE PROBABLY ALL GOT YOUR HANDS FULL WITH THE START OF THE SCHOOL YEAR . . .
I JUST THOUGHT MAYBE YOU WOULD HAVE SPOKEN TO CHERYL OR DEANNA OR ONE OF THAT BUNCH.
NOPE.
I LEFT A COUPLE OF MESSAGES FOR CHERYL BUT SHE HASN'T CALLED BACK.
WELL . . .
I'LL BET SHE'S JUST WAITING FOR THE DUST TO SETTLE.
IT'S A BUSY TIME FOR EVERYONE.
YES. YOU SAID THAT ALREADY.

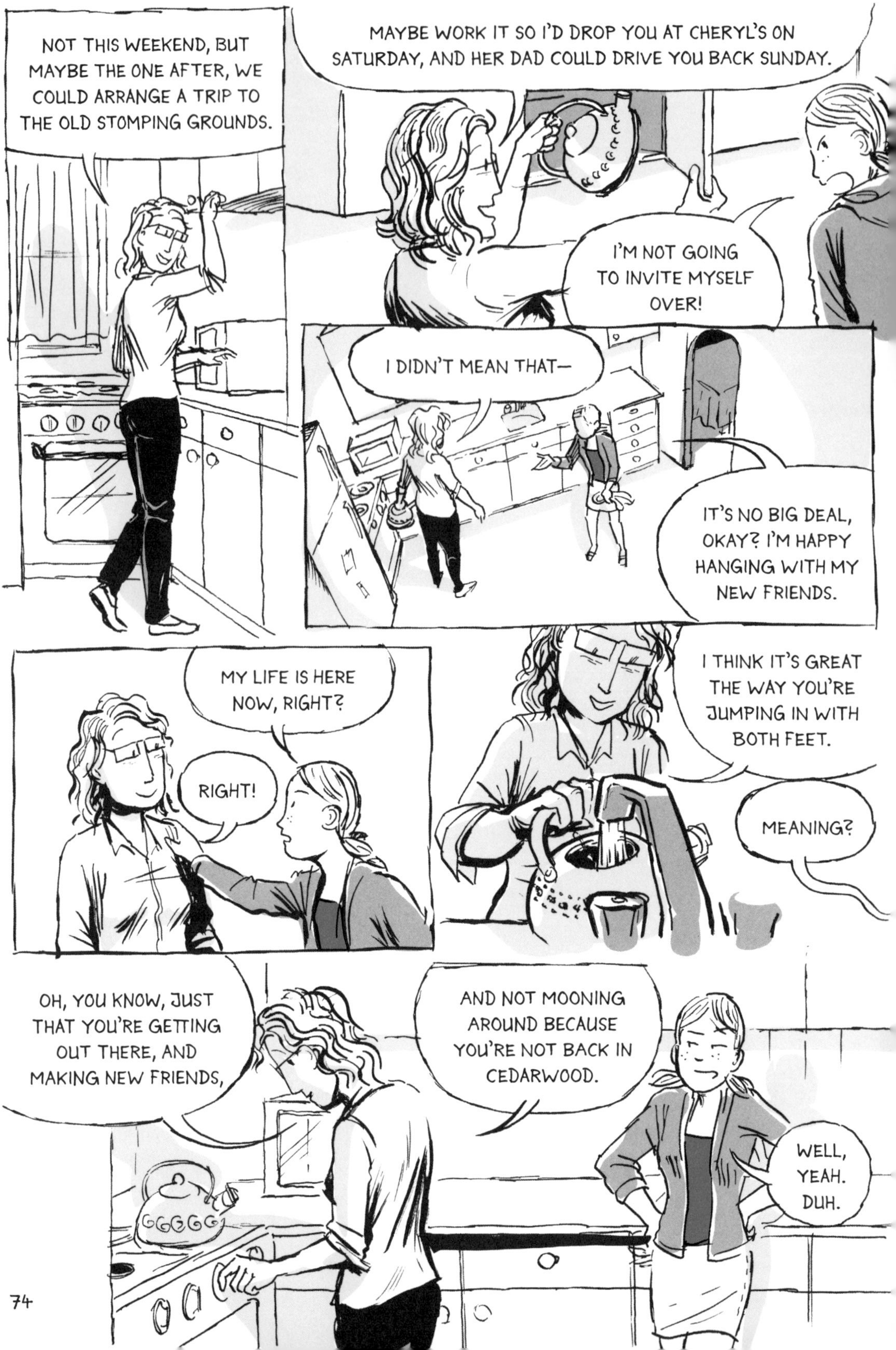
NOT THIS WEEKEND, BUT MAYBE THE ONE AFTER, WE COULD ARRANGE A TRIP TO THE OLD STOMPING GROUNDS.
MAYBE WORK IT SO I'D DROP YOU AT CHERYL'S ON SATURDAY, AND HER DAD COULD DRIVE YOU BACK SUNDAY.
I'M NOT GOING TO INVITE MYSELF OVER!
I DIDN'T MEAN THAT—
IT'S NO BIG DEAL, OKAY? I'M HAPPY HANGING WITH MY NEW FRIENDS.
MY LIFE IS HERE NOW, RIGHT?
RIGHT!
I THINK IT'S GREAT THE WAY YOU'RE JUMPING IN WITH BOTH FEET.
MEANING?
OH, YOU KNOW, JUST THAT YOU'RE GETTING OUT THERE, AND MAKING NEW FRIENDS,
AND NOT MOONING AROUND BECAUSE YOU'RE NOT BACK IN CEDARWOOD.
GGGGG
WELL, YEAH. DUH.

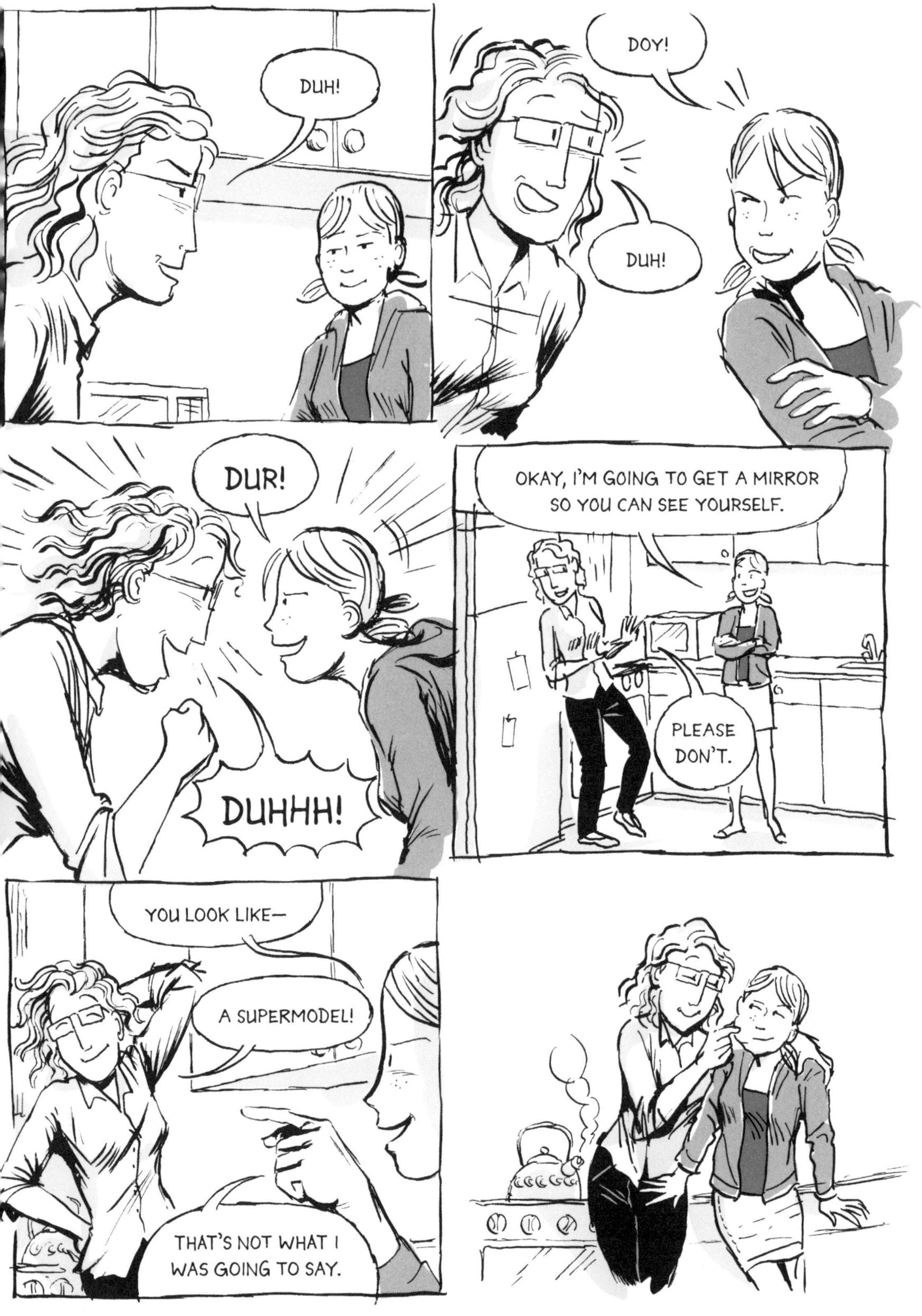
DUH!
DOY!
DUH!
DUR!
DUHHH!
OKAY, I'M GOING TO GET A MIRROR SO YOU CAN SEE YOURSELF.
PLEASE DON'T.
YOU LOOK LIKE—
A SUPERMODEL!
THAT'S NOT WHAT I WAS GOING TO SAY.

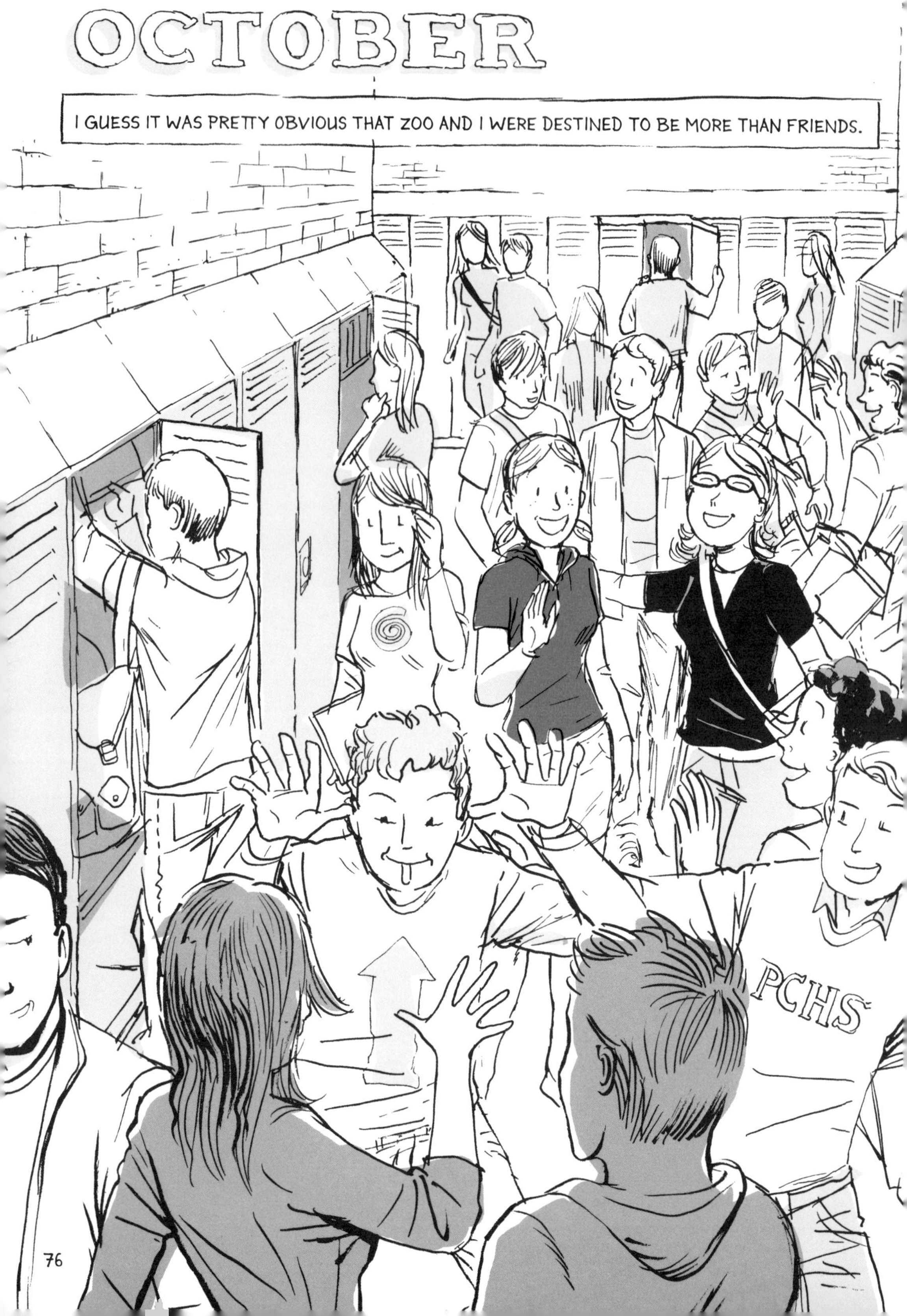
OCTOBER
I GUESS IT WAS PRETTY OBVIOUS THAT ZOO AND I WERE DESTINED TO BE MORE THAN FRIENDS.
PCHS

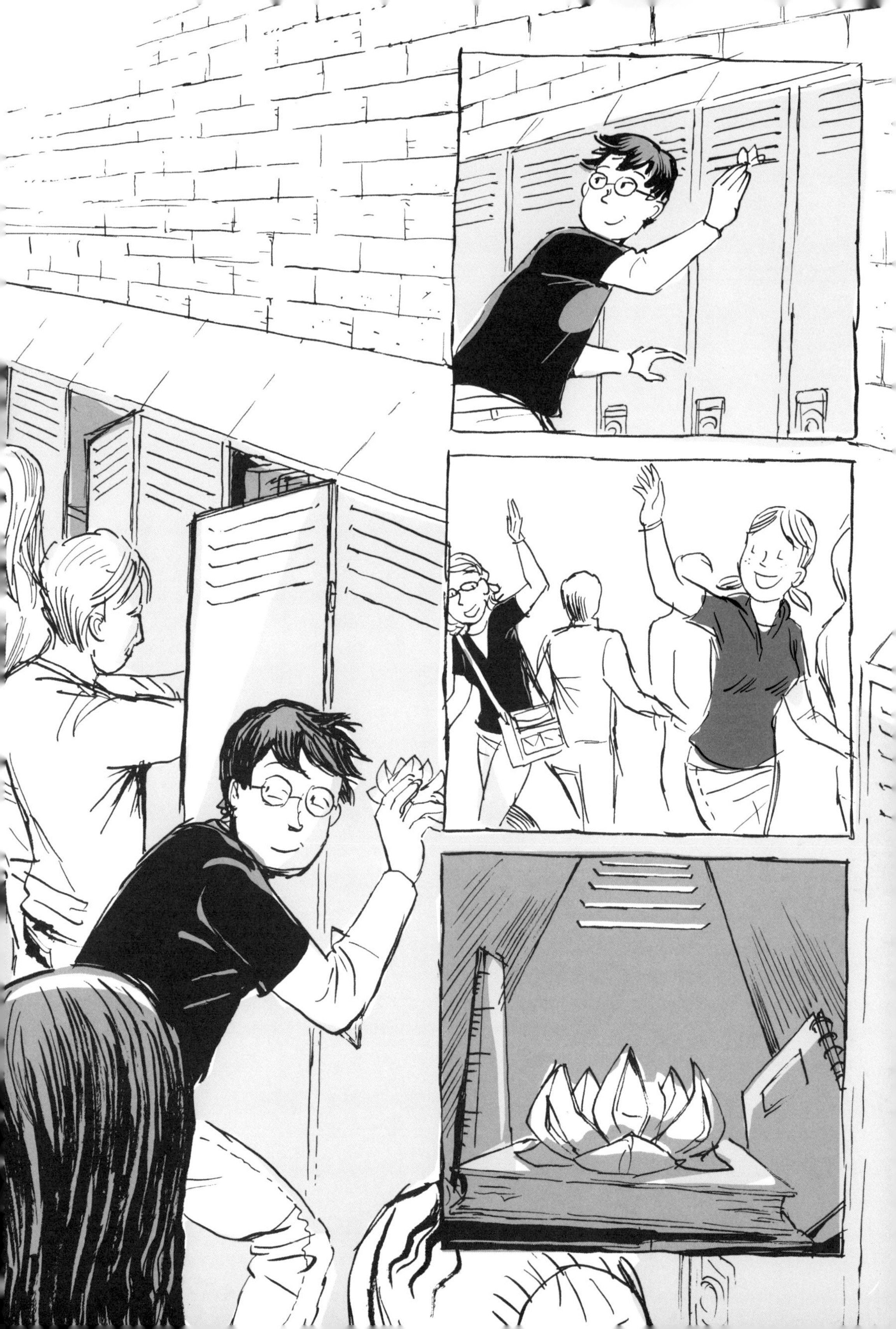

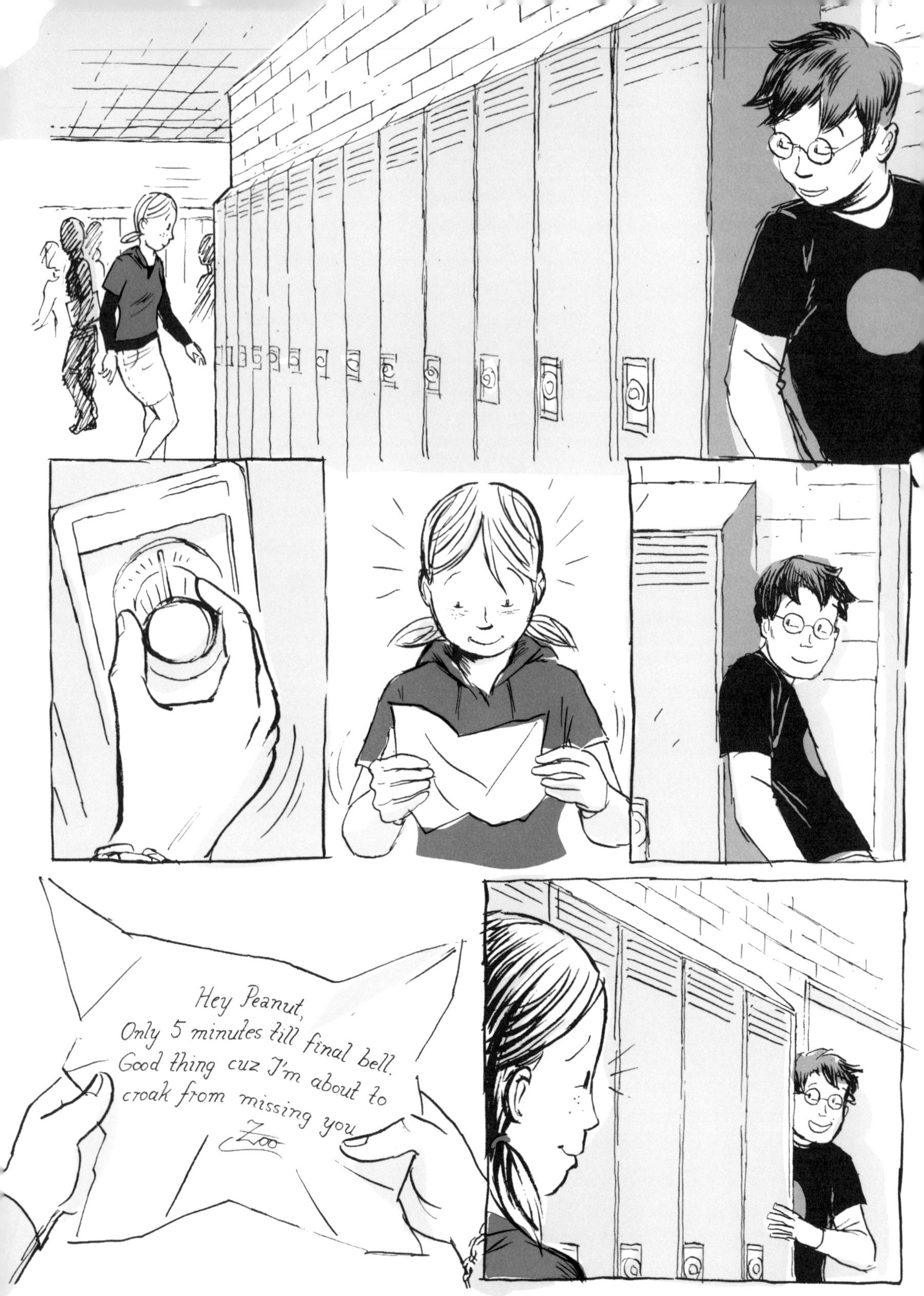
Hey Peanut,
Only 5 minutes till final bell.
Good thing cuz I'm about to
croak from missing you
Zoo

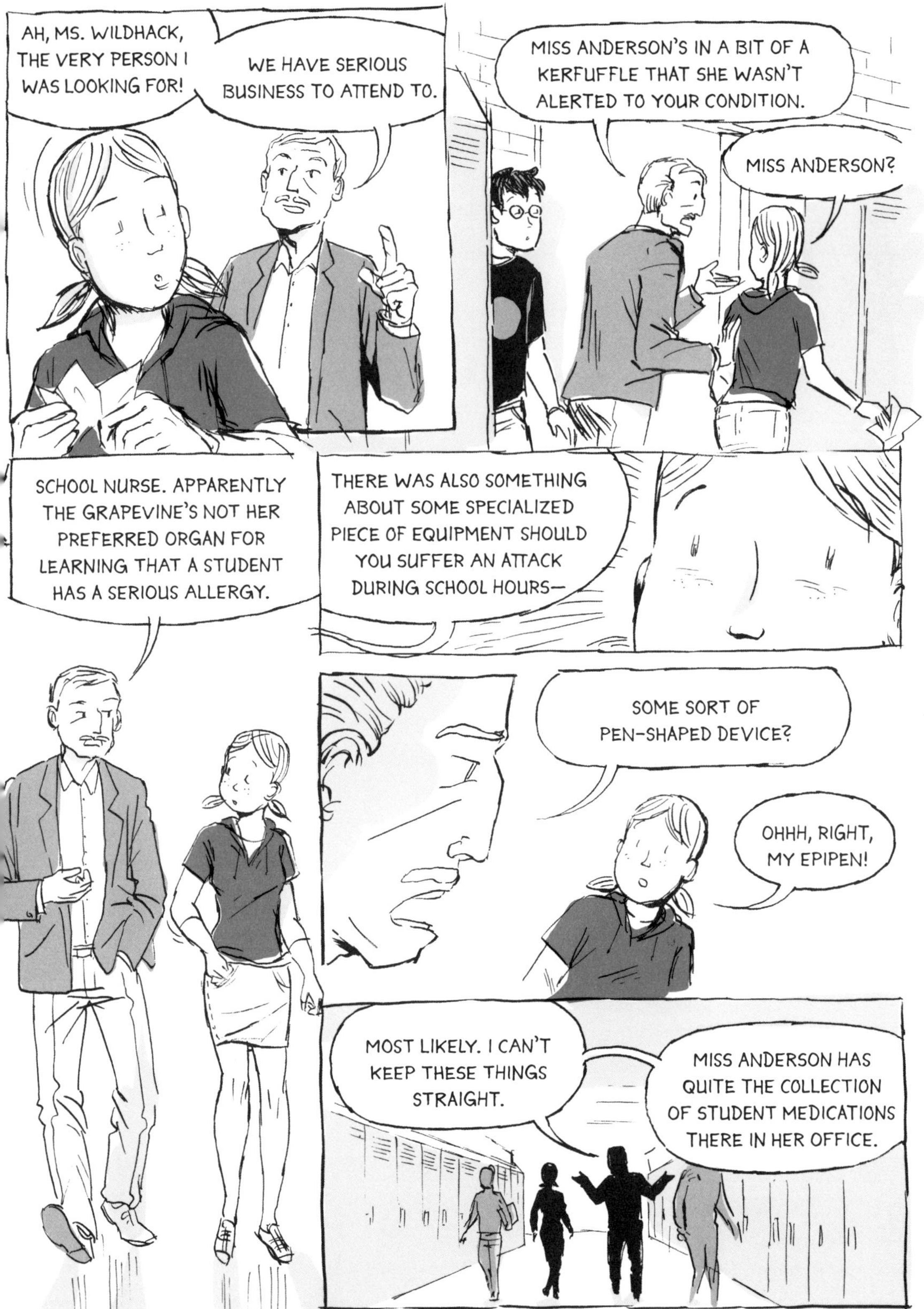
AH, MS. WILDHACK, THE VERY PERSON I WAS LOOKING FOR!
WE HAVE SERIOUS BUSINESS TO ATTEND TO.
MISS ANDERSON'S IN A BIT OF A KERFUFFLE THAT SHE WASN'T ALERTED TO YOUR CONDITION.
MISS ANDERSON?
SCHOOL NURSE. APPARENTLY THE GRAPEVINE'S NOT HER PREFERRED ORGAN FOR LEARNING THAT A STUDENT HAS A SERIOUS ALLERGY.
THERE WAS ALSO SOMETHING ABOUT SOME SPECIALIZED PIECE OF EQUIPMENT SHOULD YOU SUFFER AN ATTACK DURING SCHOOL HOURS—
SOME SORT OF PEN-SHAPED DEVICE?
OHHH, RIGHT, MY EPIPEN!
MOST LIKELY. I CAN'T KEEP THESE THINGS STRAIGHT.
MISS ANDERSON HAS QUITE THE COLLECTION OF STUDENT MEDICATIONS THERE IN HER OFFICE.

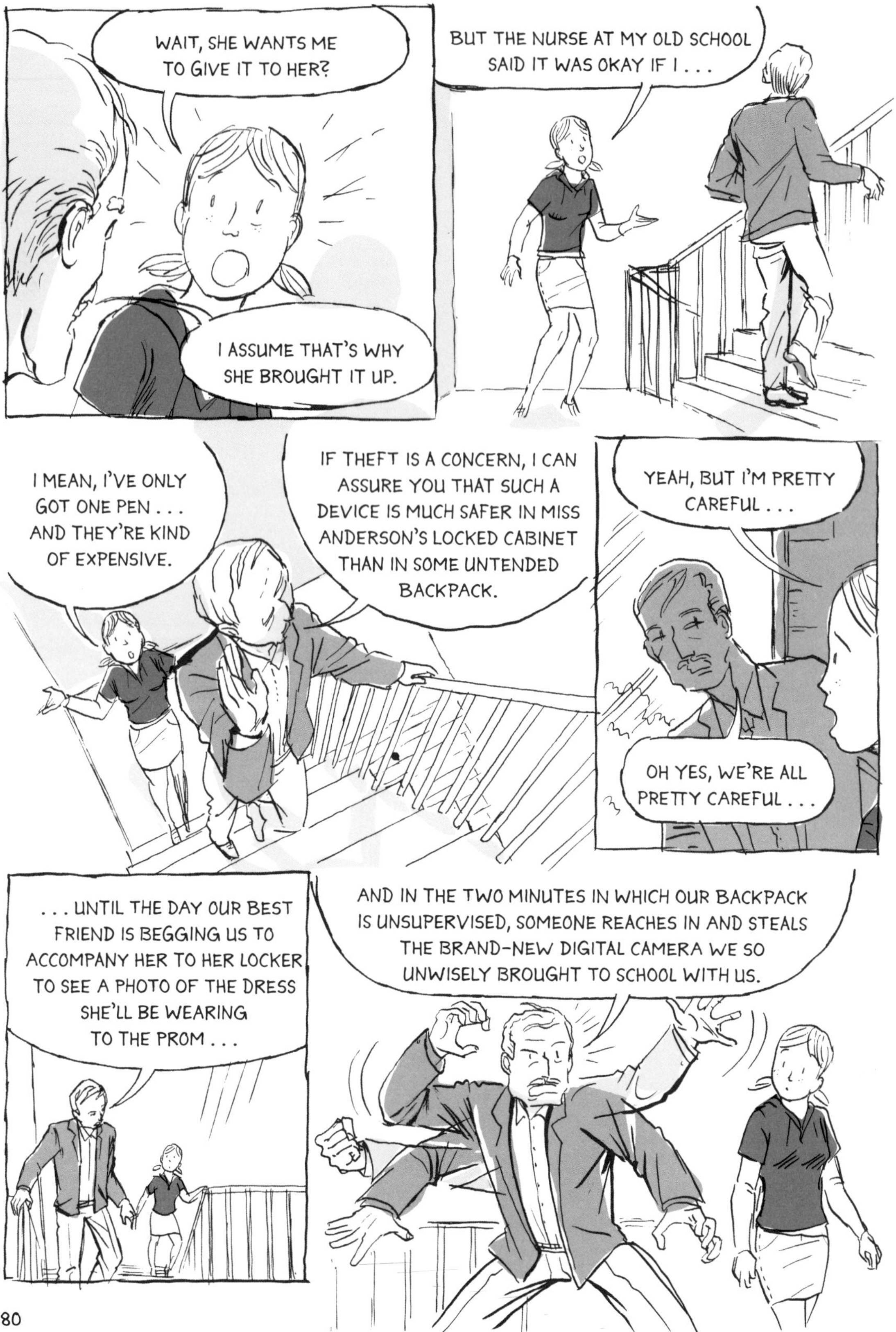
WAIT, SHE WANTS ME TO GIVE IT TO HER?
I ASSUME THAT'S WHY SHE BROUGHT IT UP.
BUT THE NURSE AT MY OLD SCHOOL SAID IT WAS OKAY IF I . . .
I MEAN, I'VE ONLY GOT ONE PEN . . . AND THEY'RE KIND OF EXPENSIVE.
IF THEFT IS A CONCERN, I CAN ASSURE YOU THAT SUCH A DEVICE IS MUCH SAFER IN MISS ANDERSON'S LOCKED CABINET THAN IN SOME UNTENDED BACKPACK.
YEAH, BUT I'M PRETTY CAREFUL . . .
OH YES, WE'RE ALL PRETTY CAREFUL . . .
. . . UNTIL THE DAY OUR BEST FRIEND IS BEGGING US TO ACCOMPANY HER TO HER LOCKER TO SEE A PHOTO OF THE DRESS SHE'LL BE WEARING TO THE PROM . . .
AND IN THE TWO MINUTES IN WHICH OUR BACKPACK IS UNSUPERVISED, SOMEONE REACHES IN AND STEALS THE BRAND-NEW DIGITAL CAMERA WE SO UNWISELY BROUGHT TO SCHOOL WITH US.

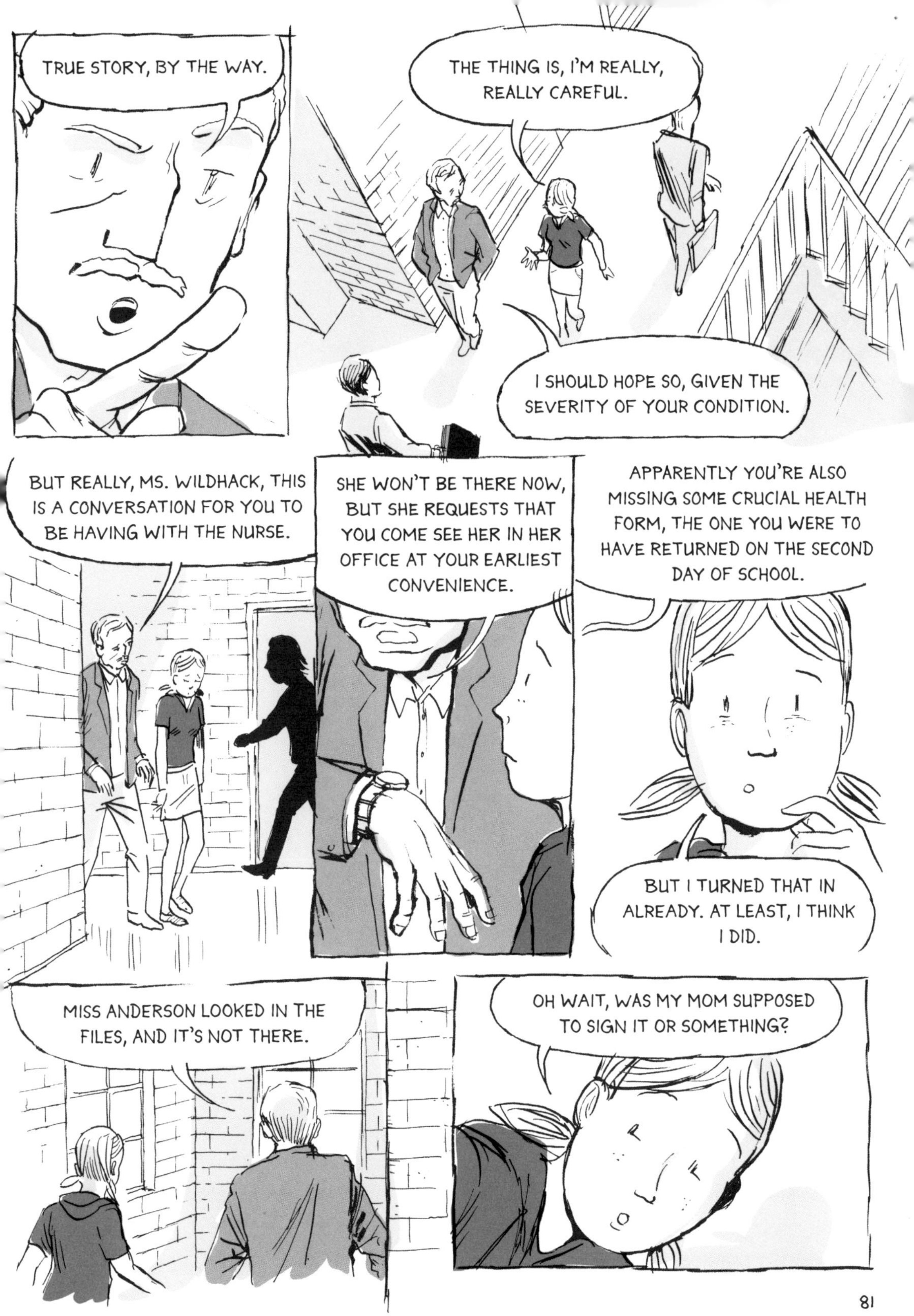
TRUE STORY, BY THE WAY.
THE THING IS, I'M REALLY, REALLY CAREFUL.
I SHOULD HOPE SO, GIVEN THE SEVERITY OF YOUR CONDITION.
BUT REALLY, MS. WILDHACK, THIS IS A CONVERSATION FOR YOU TO BE HAVING WITH THE NURSE.
SHE WON'T BE THERE NOW, BUT SHE REQUESTS THAT YOU COME SEE HER IN HER OFFICE AT YOUR EARLIEST CONVENIENCE.
APPARENTLY YOU'RE ALSO MISSING SOME CRUCIAL HEALTH FORM, THE ONE YOU WERE TO HAVE RETURNED ON THE SECOND DAY OF SCHOOL.
BUT I TURNED THAT IN ALREADY. AT LEAST, I THINK I DID.
MISS ANDERSON LOOKED IN THE FILES, AND IT'S NOT THERE.
OH WAIT, WAS MY MOM SUPPOSED TO SIGN IT OR SOMETHING?

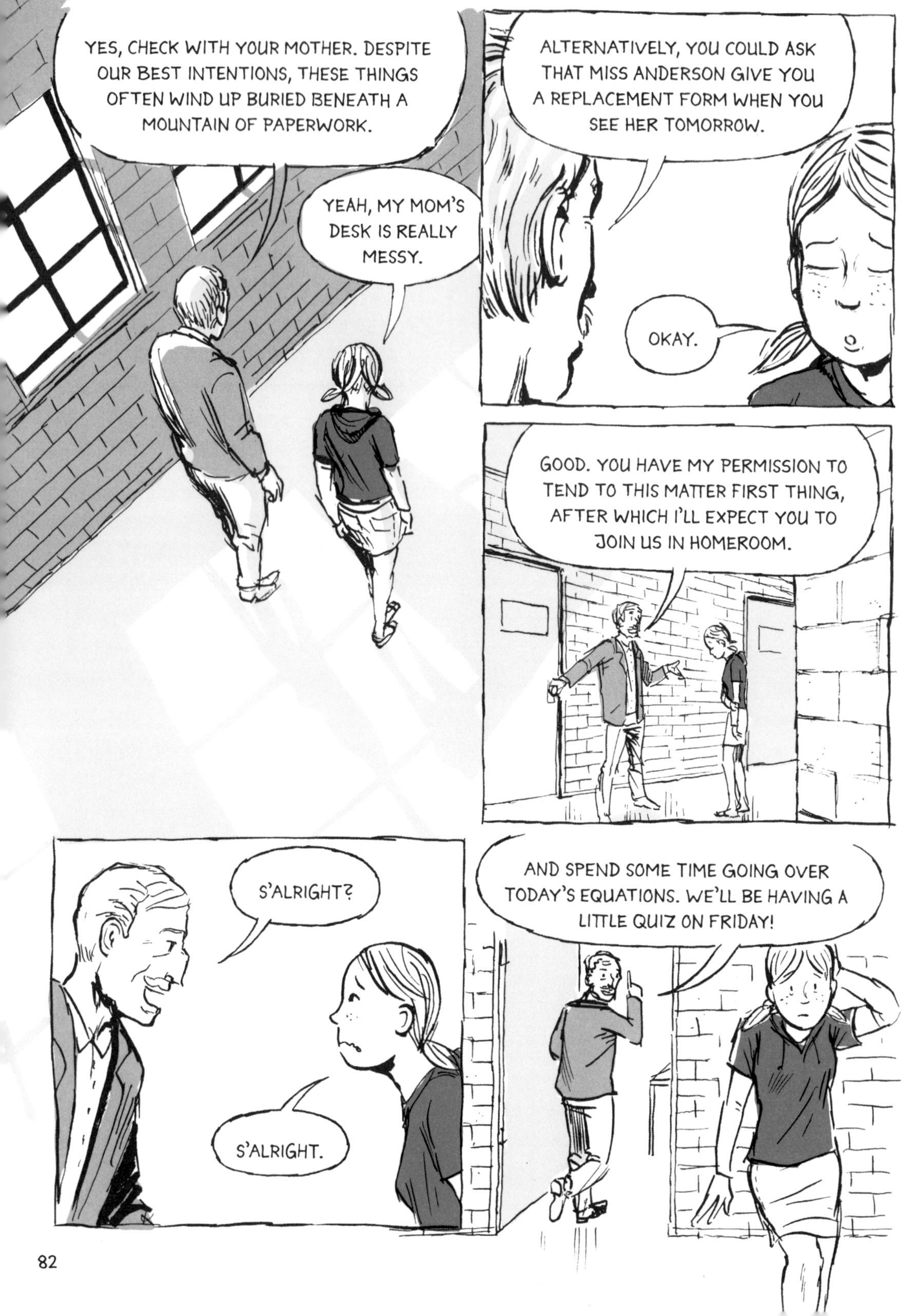
YES, CHECK WITH YOUR MOTHER. DESPITE OUR BEST INTENTIONS, THESE THINGS OFTEN WIND UP BURIED BENEATH A MOUNTAIN OF PAPERWORK.
YEAH, MY MOM'S DESK IS REALLY MESSY.
ALTERNATIVELY, YOU COULD ASK THAT MISS ANDERSON GIVE YOU A REPLACEMENT FORM WHEN YOU SEE HER TOMORROW.
OKAY.
GOOD. YOU HAVE MY PERMISSION TO TEND TO THIS MATTER FIRST THING, AFTER WHICH I'LL EXPECT YOU TO JOIN US IN HOMEROOM.
S'ALRIGHT?
S'ALRIGHT.
AND SPEND SOME TIME GOING OVER TODAY'S EQUATIONS. WE'LL BE HAVING A LITTLE QUIZ ON FRIDAY!

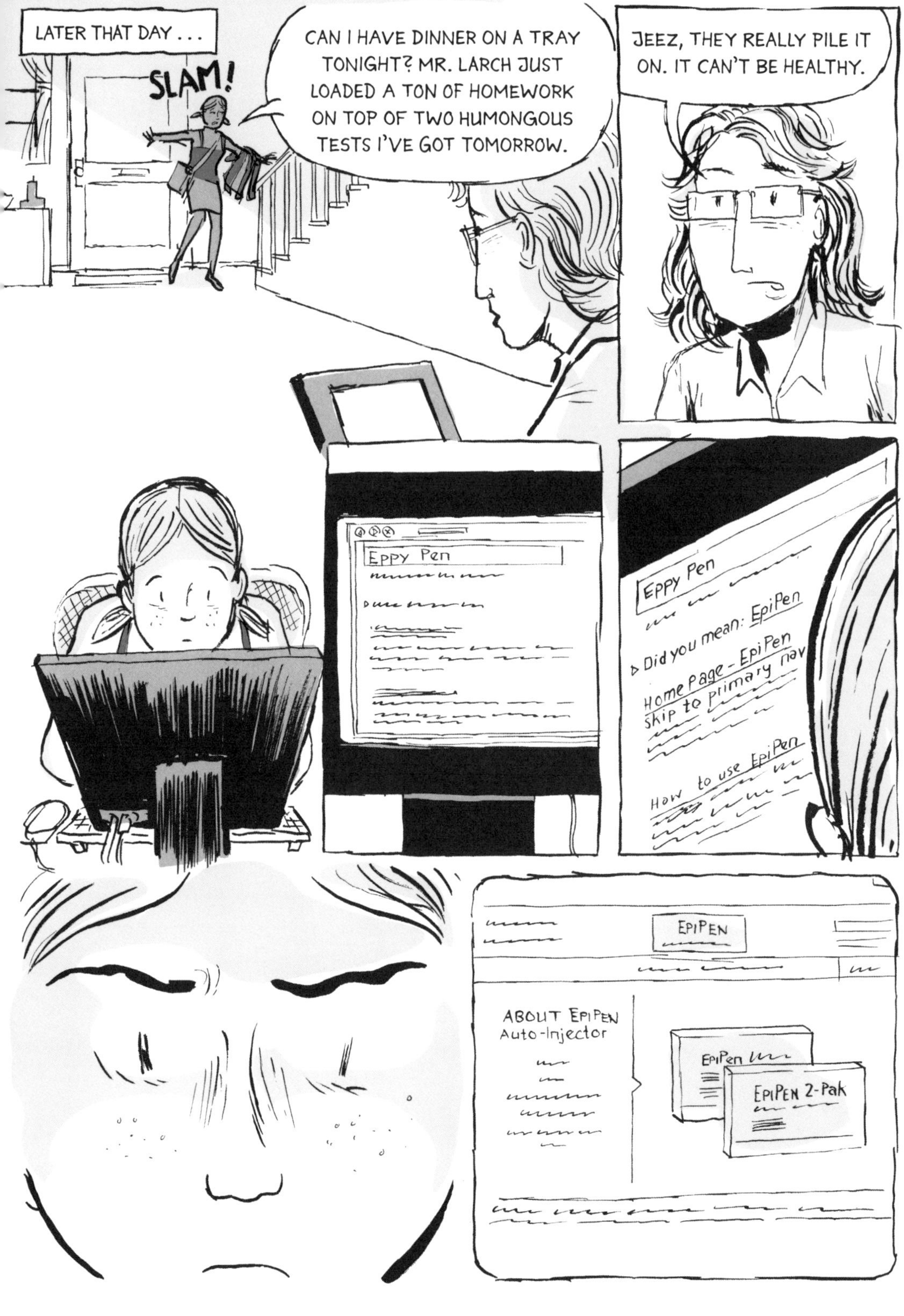

LATER THAT DAY . . .
SLAM!
CAN I HAVE DINNER ON A TRAY TONIGHT? MR. LARCH JUST LOADED A TON OF HOMEWORK ON TOP OF TWO HUMONGOUS TESTS I'VE GOT TOMORROW.
JEEZ, THEY REALLY PILE IT ON. IT CAN'T BE HEALTHY.
Eppy Pen
Eppy Pen
Did you mean: EpiPen
Home Page - EpiPen
Skip to primary nav
How to use EpiPen
EPIPEN
ABOUT EPIPEN
Auto-Injector
EpiPen
EPIPEN 2-Pak

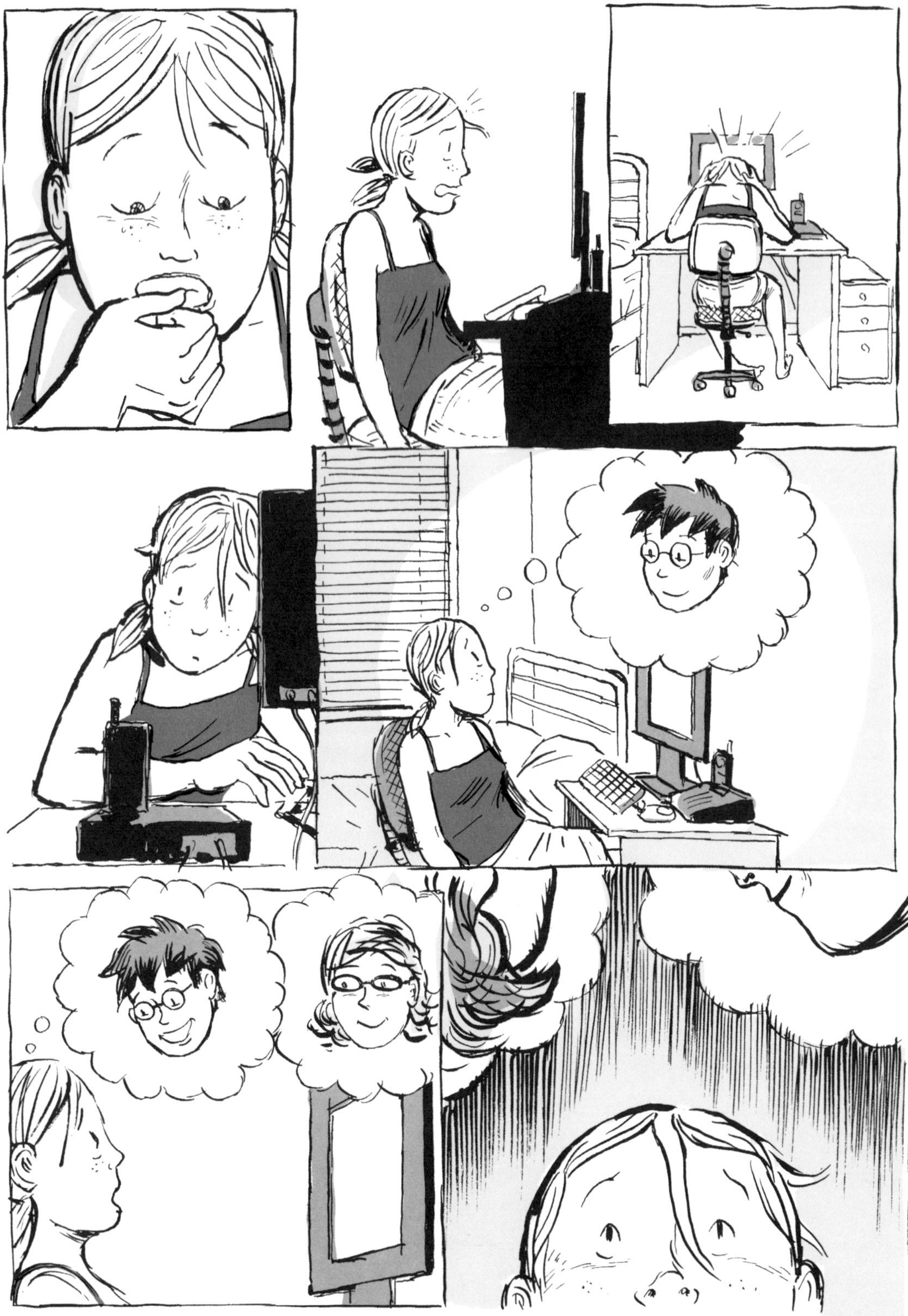

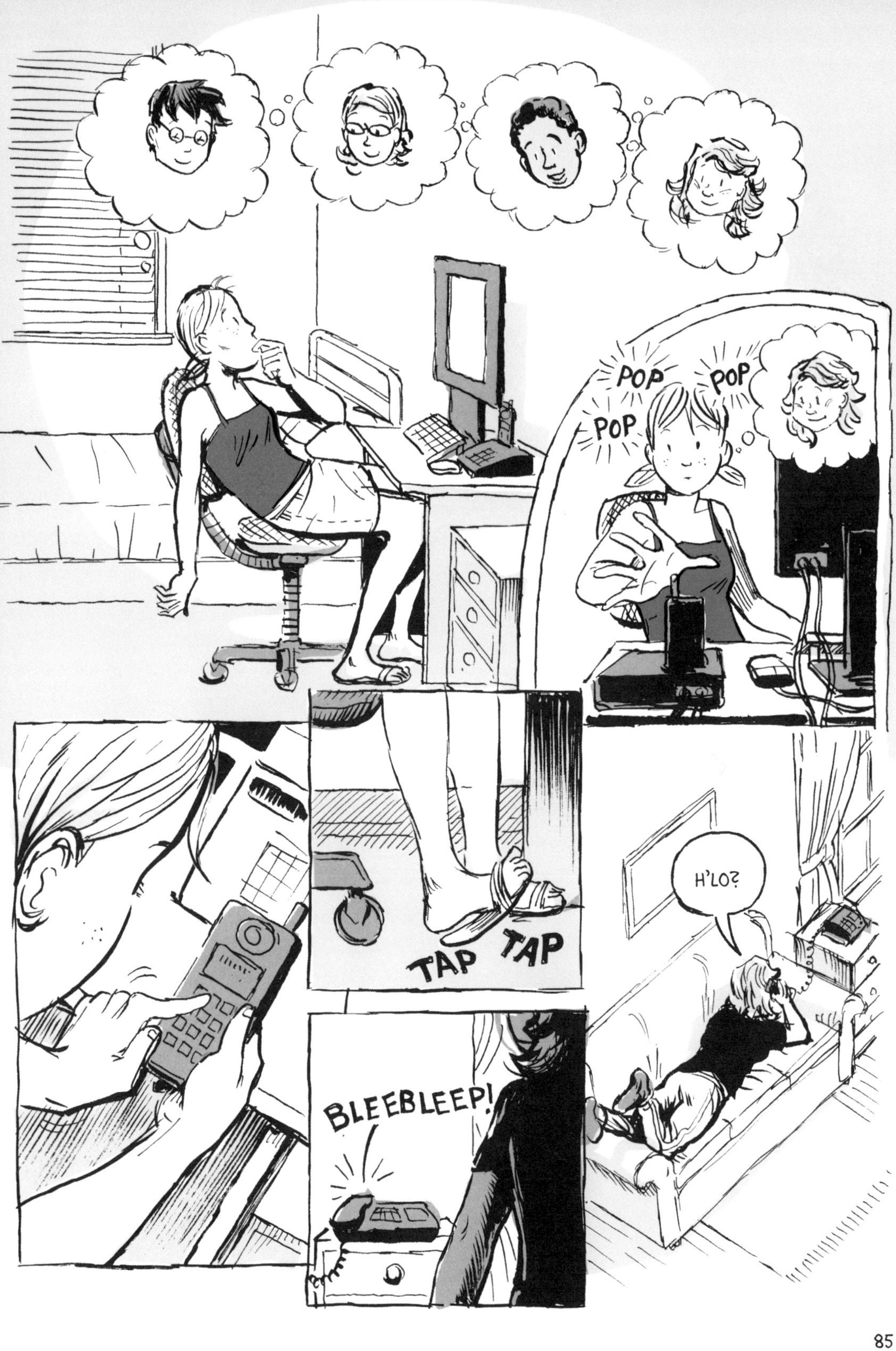
POP
POP
POP
TAP TAP
BLEEBLEEP!
H'LO?

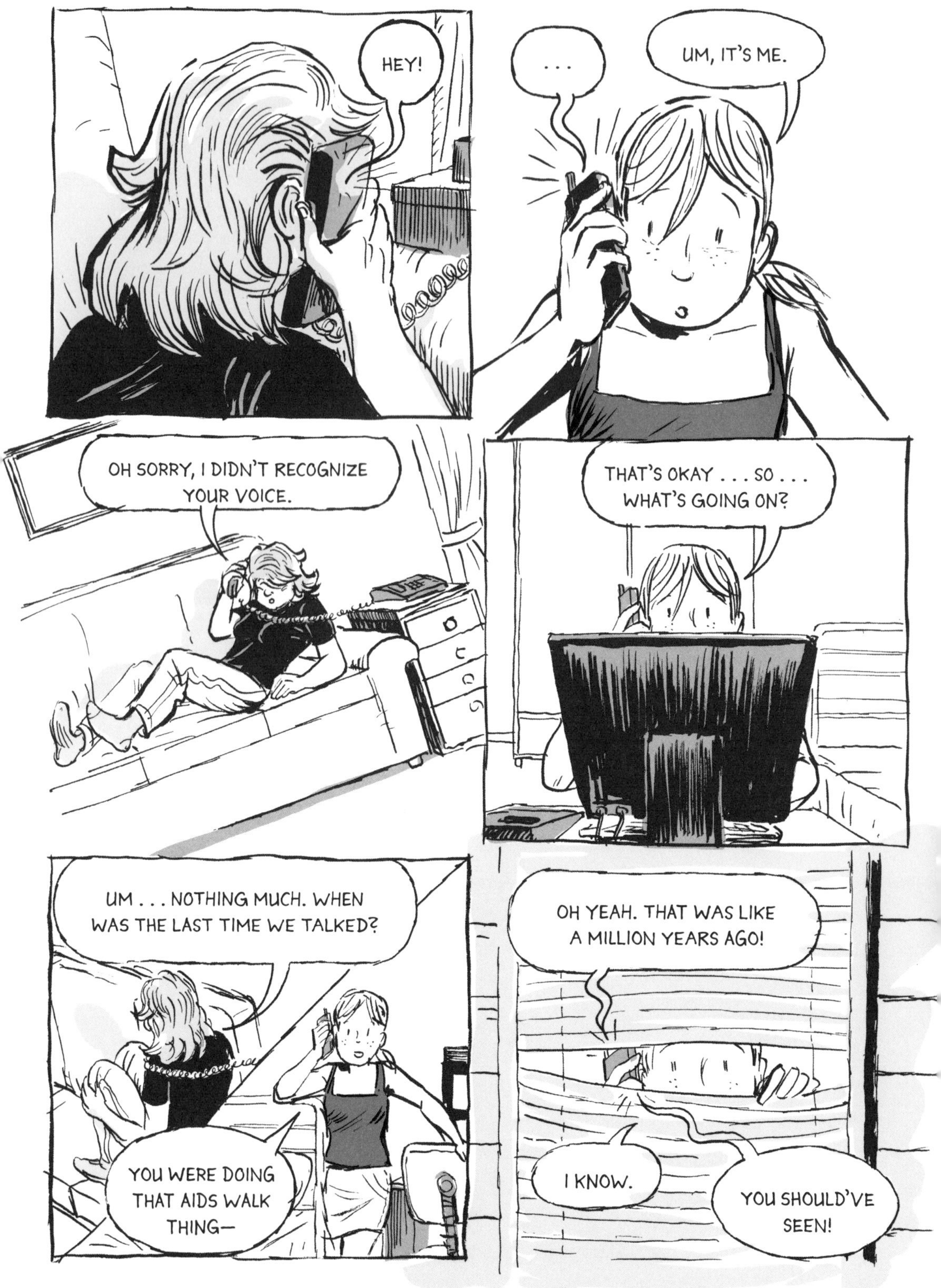
HEY!
. . .
UM, IT'S ME.
OH SORRY, I DIDN'T RECOGNIZE YOUR VOICE.
THAT'S OKAY . . . SO . . . WHAT'S GOING ON?
UM . . . NOTHING MUCH. WHEN WAS THE LAST TIME WE TALKED?
YOU WERE DOING THAT AIDS WALK THING—
OH YEAH. THAT WAS LIKE A MILLION YEARS AGO!
I KNOW.
YOU SHOULD'VE SEEN!

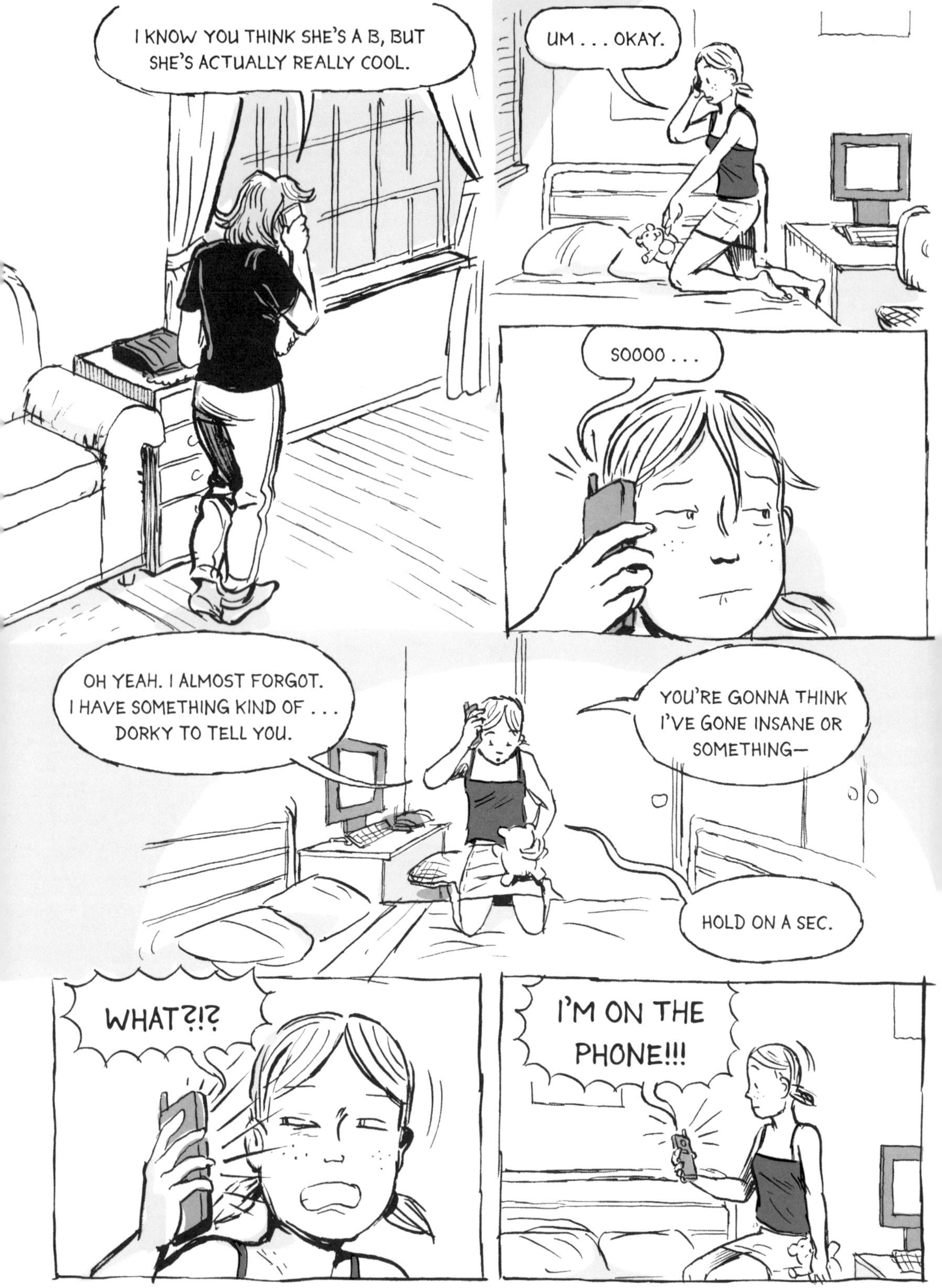
I KNOW YOU THINK SHE'S A B, BUT SHE'S ACTUALLY REALLY COOL.
UM . . . OKAY.
SOOOO . . .
OH YEAH. I ALMOST FORGOT. I HAVE SOMETHING KIND OF . . . DORKY TO TELL YOU.
YOU'RE GONNA THINK I'VE GONE INSANE OR SOMETHING—
HOLD ON A SEC.
WHAT?!?
I'M ON THE PHONE!!!

95

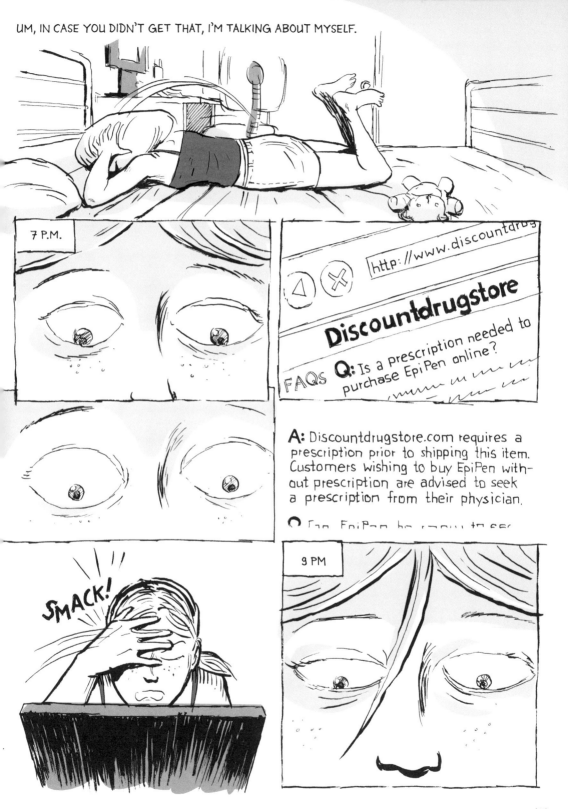

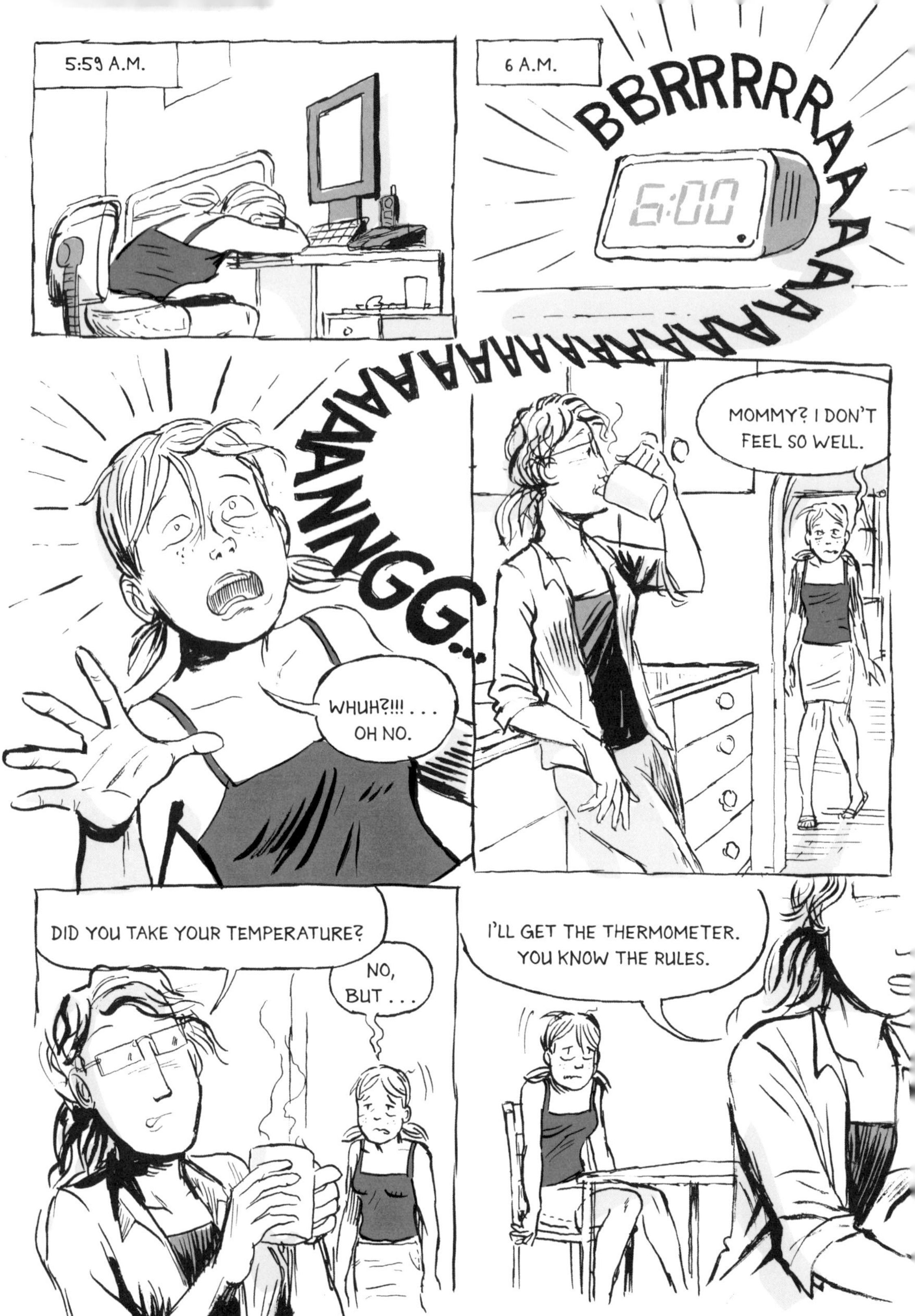
5:59 A.M.
6 A.M.
BBRRRRRAAAAAAAAAAAAAANNGG...
6:00
WHUH?!!! . . . OH NO.
MOMMY? I DON'T FEEL SO WELL.
DID YOU TAKE YOUR TEMPERATURE?
NO, BUT . . .
I'LL GET THE THERMOMETER. YOU KNOW THE RULES.

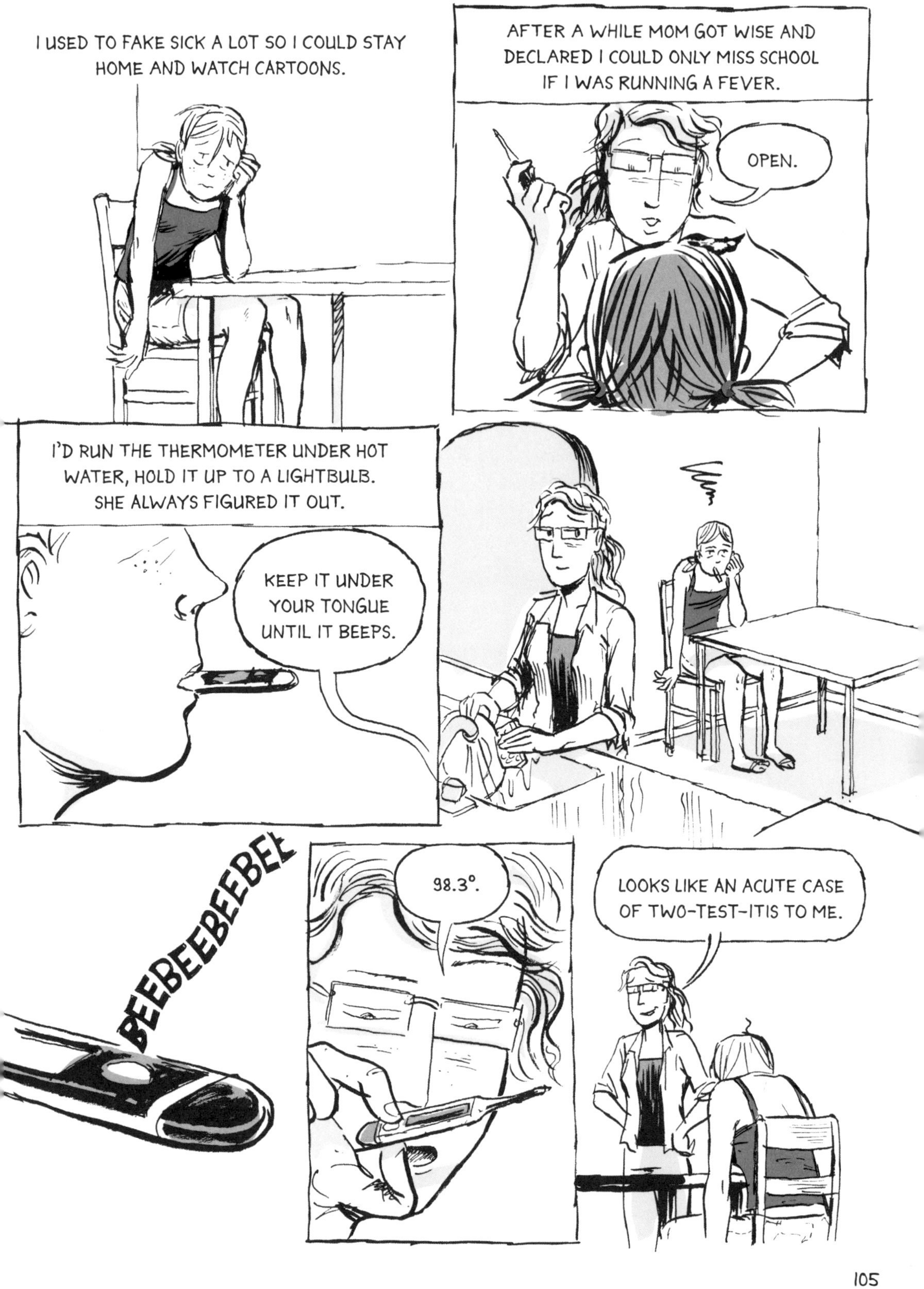
I USED TO FAKE SICK A LOT SO I COULD STAY HOME AND WATCH CARTOONS.
AFTER A WHILE MOM GOT WISE AND DECLARED I COULD ONLY MISS SCHOOL IF I WAS RUNNING A FEVER.
OPEN.
I'D RUN THE THERMOMETER UNDER HOT WATER, HOLD IT UP TO A LIGHTBULB. SHE ALWAYS FIGURED IT OUT.
KEEP IT UNDER YOUR TONGUE UNTIL IT BEEPS.
BEEBEEBEEBEEBEE
98.3°.
LOOKS LIKE AN ACUTE CASE OF TWO-TEST-ITIS TO ME.

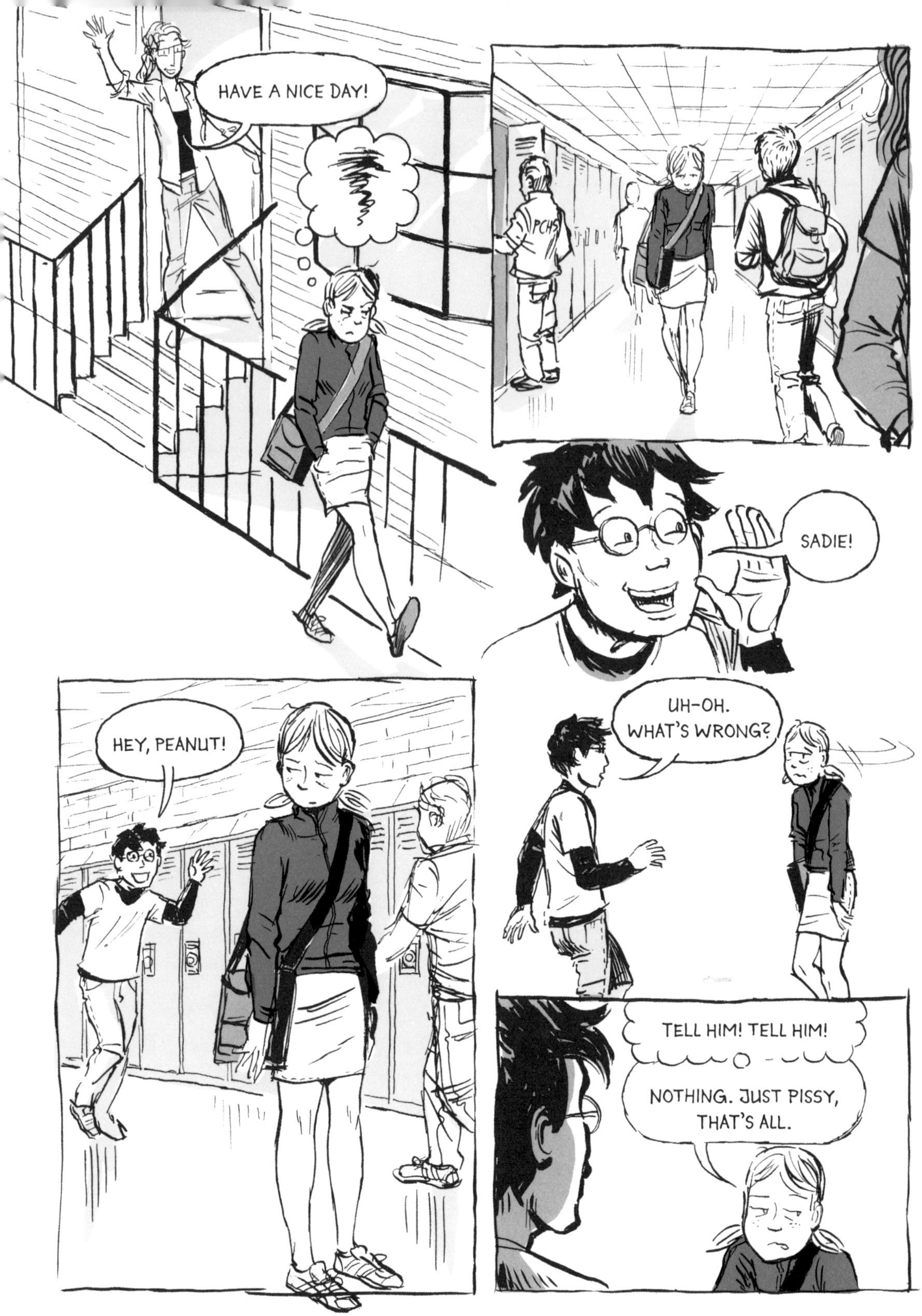
HAVE A NICE DAY!
SADIE!
HEY, PEANUT!
UH-OH. WHAT'S WRONG?
TELL HIM! TELL HIM!
NOTHING. JUST PISSY, THAT'S ALL.

114

115

117

119

125

126

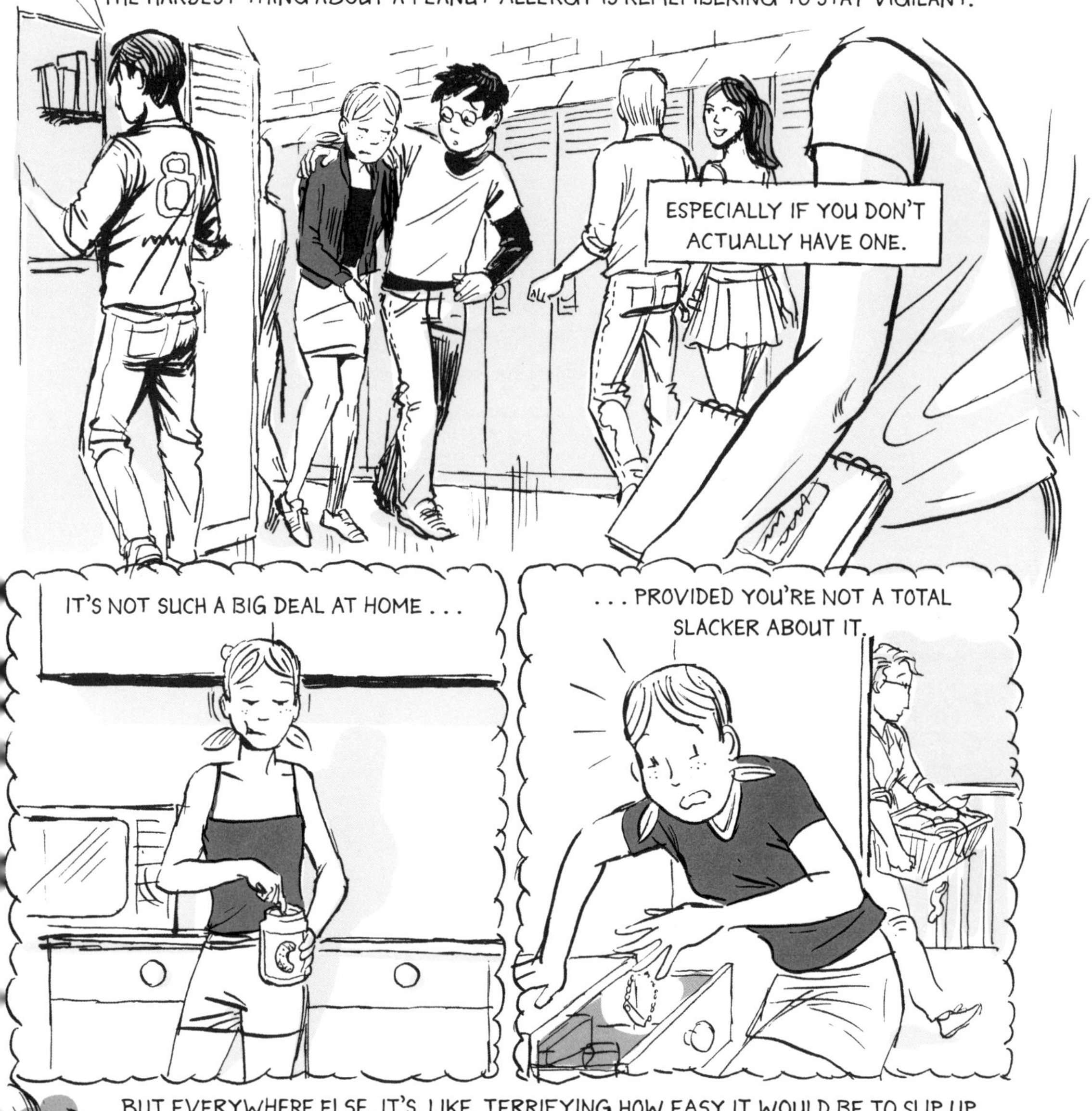
THE HARDEST THING ABOUT A PEANUT ALLERGY IS REMEMBERING TO STAY VIGILANT.
ESPECIALLY IF YOU DON'T ACTUALLY HAVE ONE.
IT'S NOT SUCH A BIG DEAL AT HOME . . .
. . . PROVIDED YOU'RE NOT A TOTAL SLACKER ABOUT IT.
BUT EVERYWHERE ELSE, IT'S, LIKE, TERRIFYING HOW EASY IT WOULD BE TO SLIP UP.

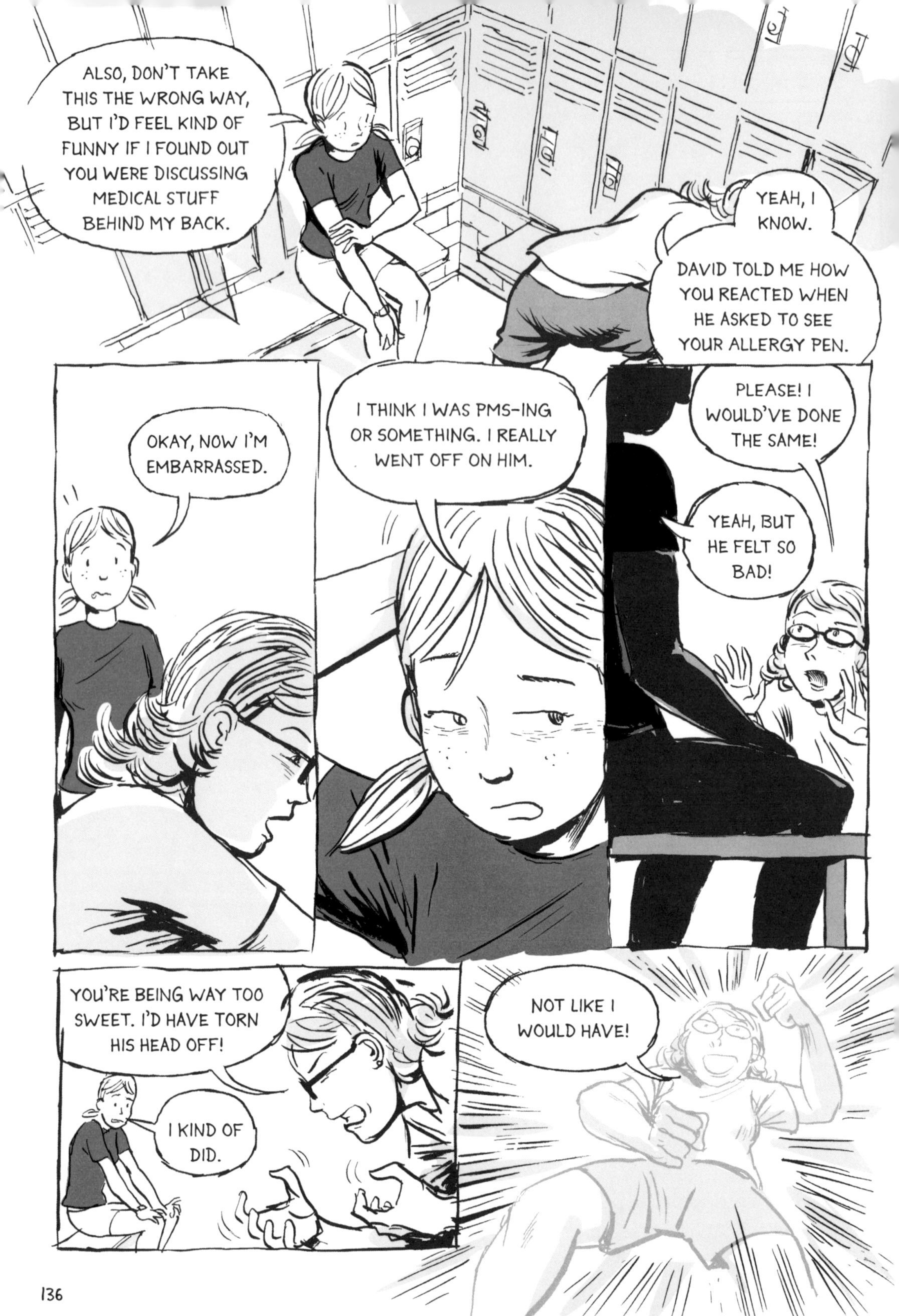
ALSO, DON'T TAKE THIS THE WRONG WAY, BUT I'D FEEL KIND OF FUNNY IF I FOUND OUT YOU WERE DISCUSSING MEDICAL STUFF BEHIND MY BACK.
YEAH, I KNOW.
DAVID TOLD ME HOW YOU REACTED WHEN HE ASKED TO SEE YOUR ALLERGY PEN.
OKAY, NOW I'M EMBARRASSED.
I THINK I WAS PMS-ING OR SOMETHING. I REALLY WENT OFF ON HIM.
PLEASE! I WOULD'VE DONE THE SAME!
YEAH, BUT HE FELT SO BAD!
YOU'RE BEING WAY TOO SWEET. I'D HAVE TORN HIS HEAD OFF!
I KIND OF DID.
NOT LIKE I WOULD HAVE!

144

145

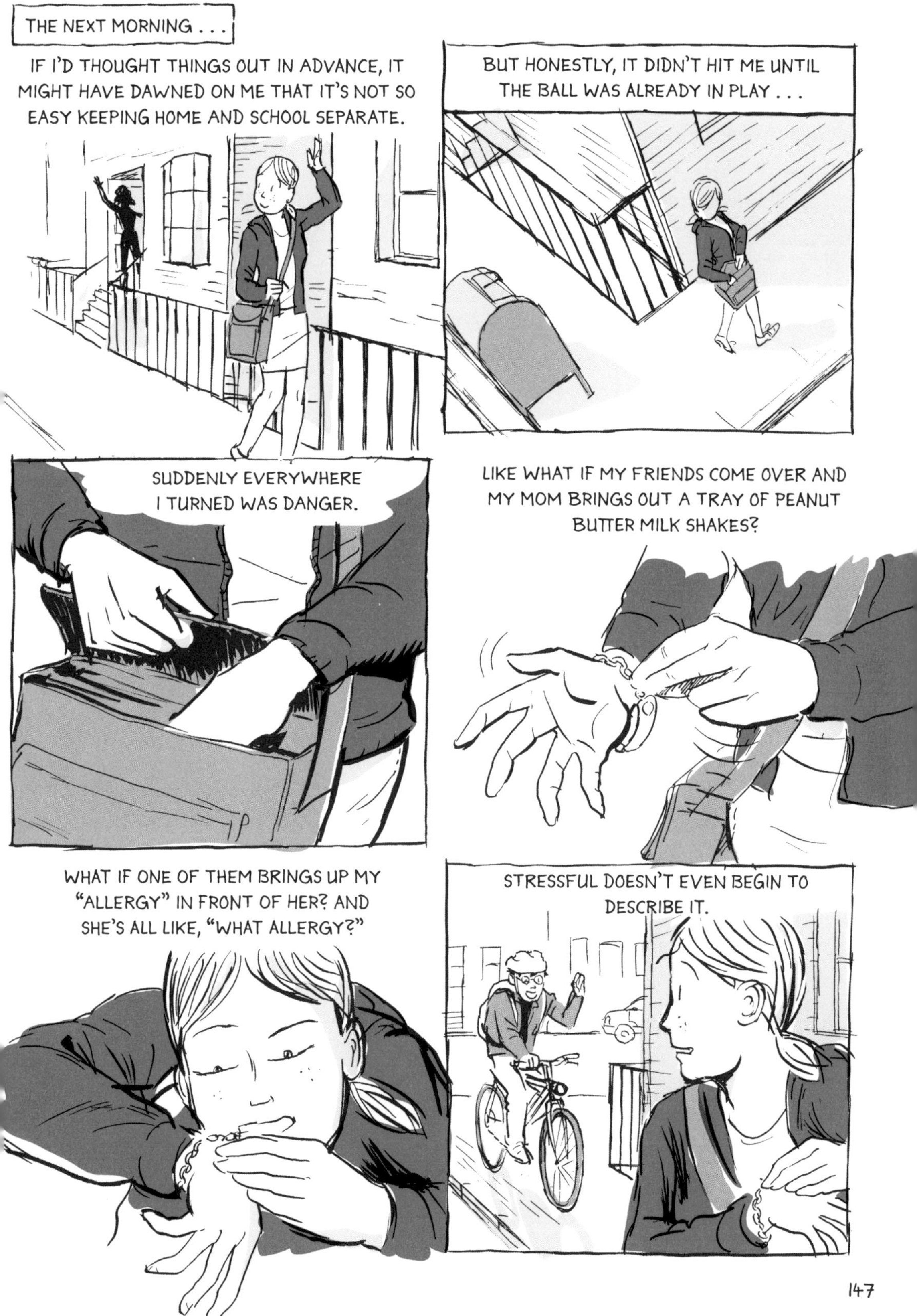
THE NEXT MORNING . . .
IF I'D THOUGHT THINGS OUT IN ADVANCE, IT MIGHT HAVE DAWNED ON ME THAT IT'S NOT SO EASY KEEPING HOME AND SCHOOL SEPARATE.
BUT HONESTLY, IT DIDN'T HIT ME UNTIL THE BALL WAS ALREADY IN PLAY . . .
SUDDENLY EVERYWHERE I TURNED WAS DANGER.
LIKE WHAT IF MY FRIENDS COME OVER AND MY MOM BRINGS OUT A TRAY OF PEANUT BUTTER MILK SHAKES?
WHAT IF ONE OF THEM BRINGS UP MY "ALLERGY" IN FRONT OF HER? AND SHE'S ALL LIKE, "WHAT ALLERGY?"
STRESSFUL DOESN'T EVEN BEGIN TO DESCRIBE IT.

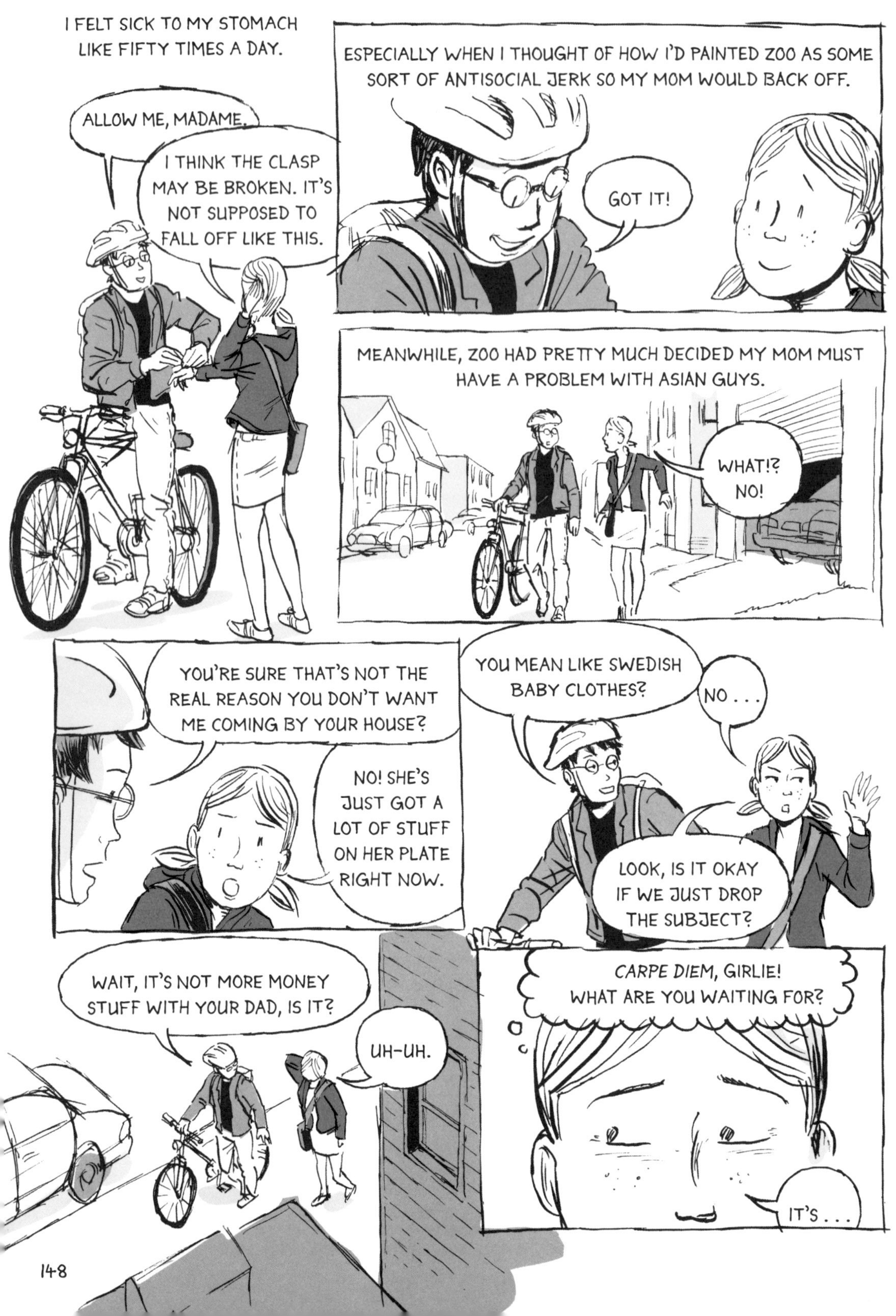
I FELT SICK TO MY STOMACH LIKE FIFTY TIMES A DAY.
ALLOW ME, MADAME.
I THINK THE CLASP MAY BE BROKEN. IT'S NOT SUPPOSED TO FALL OFF LIKE THIS.
ESPECIALLY WHEN I THOUGHT OF HOW I'D PAINTED ZOO AS SOME SORT OF ANTISOCIAL JERK SO MY MOM WOULD BACK OFF.
GOT IT!
MEANWHILE, ZOO HAD PRETTY MUCH DECIDED MY MOM MUST HAVE A PROBLEM WITH ASIAN GUYS.
WHAT!? NO!
YOU'RE SURE THAT'S NOT THE REAL REASON YOU DON'T WANT ME COMING BY YOUR HOUSE?
NO! SHE'S JUST GOT A LOT OF STUFF ON HER PLATE RIGHT NOW.
YOU MEAN LIKE SWEDISH BABY CLOTHES?
NO . . .
LOOK, IS IT OKAY IF WE JUST DROP THE SUBJECT?
WAIT, IT'S NOT MORE MONEY STUFF WITH YOUR DAD, IS IT?
UH-UH.
CARPE DIEM, GIRLIE! WHAT ARE YOU WAITING FOR?
IT'S . . .

NOVEMBER

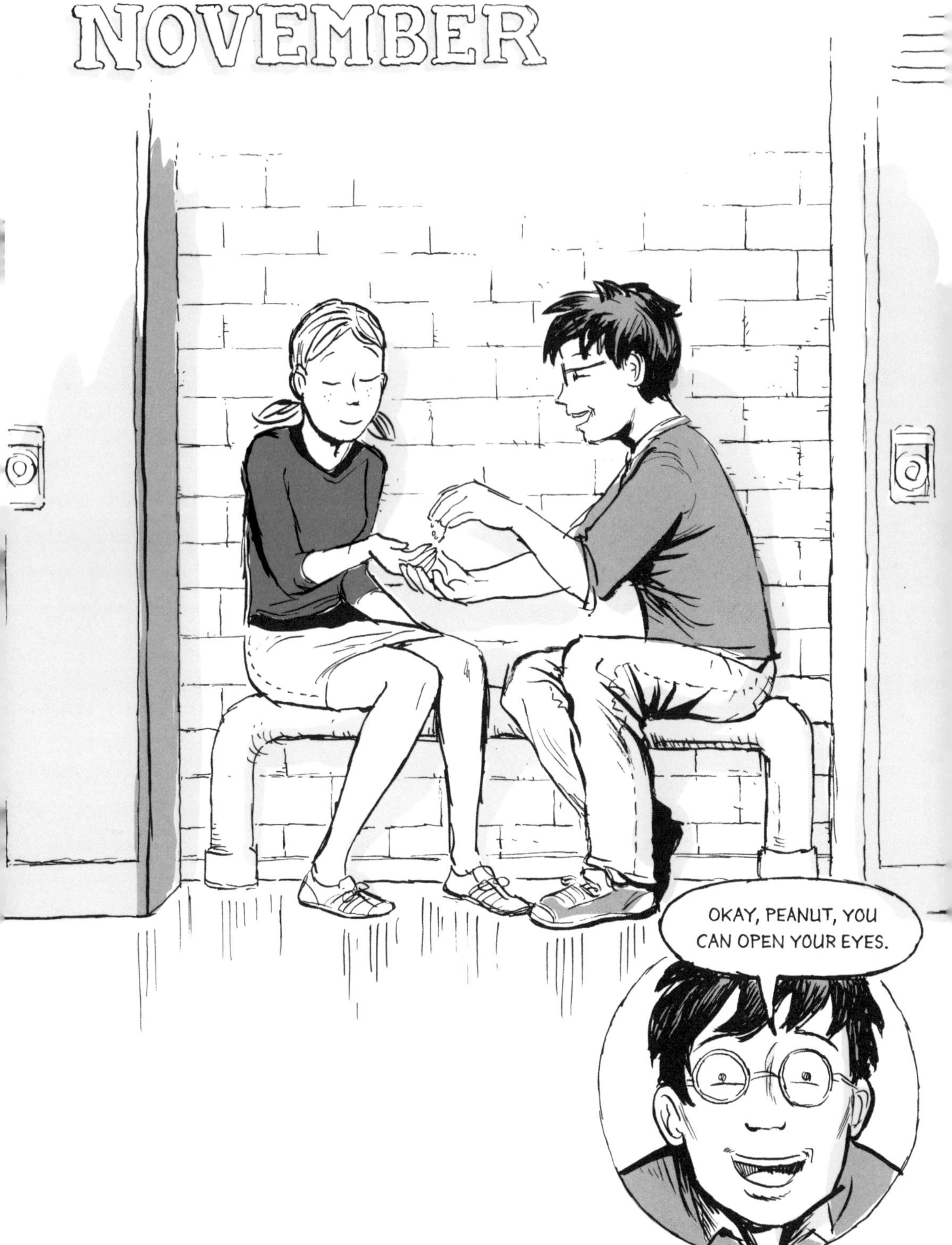
OKAY, PEANUT, YOU
CAN OPEN YOUR EYES.

165

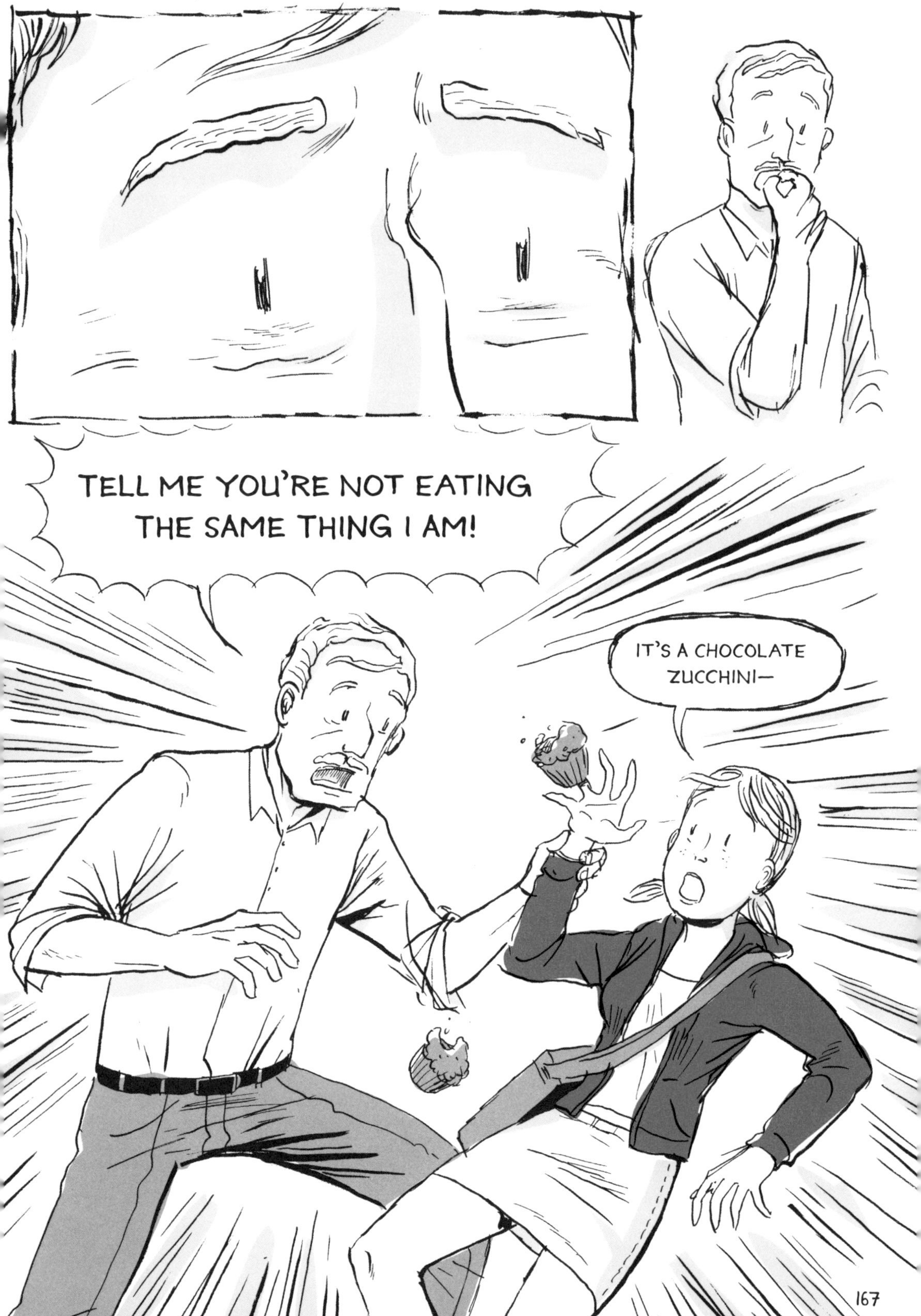
TELL ME YOU'RE NOT EATING THE SAME THING I AM!
IT'S A CHOCOLATE ZUCCHINI—

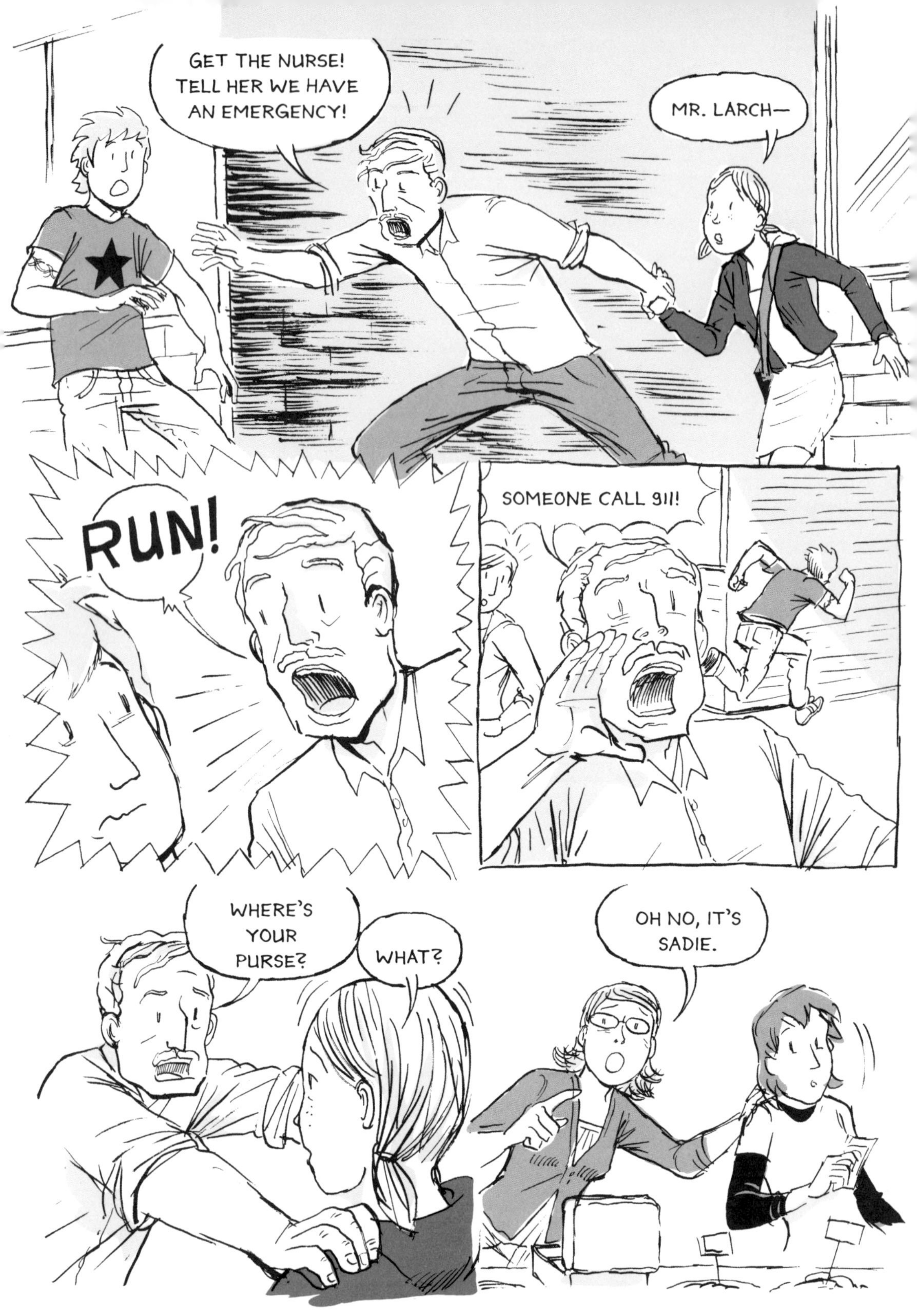
GET THE NURSE! TELL HER WE HAVE AN EMERGENCY!
MR. LARCH—
RUN!
SOMEONE CALL 911!
WHERE'S YOUR PURSE?
WHAT?
OH NO, IT'S SADIE.

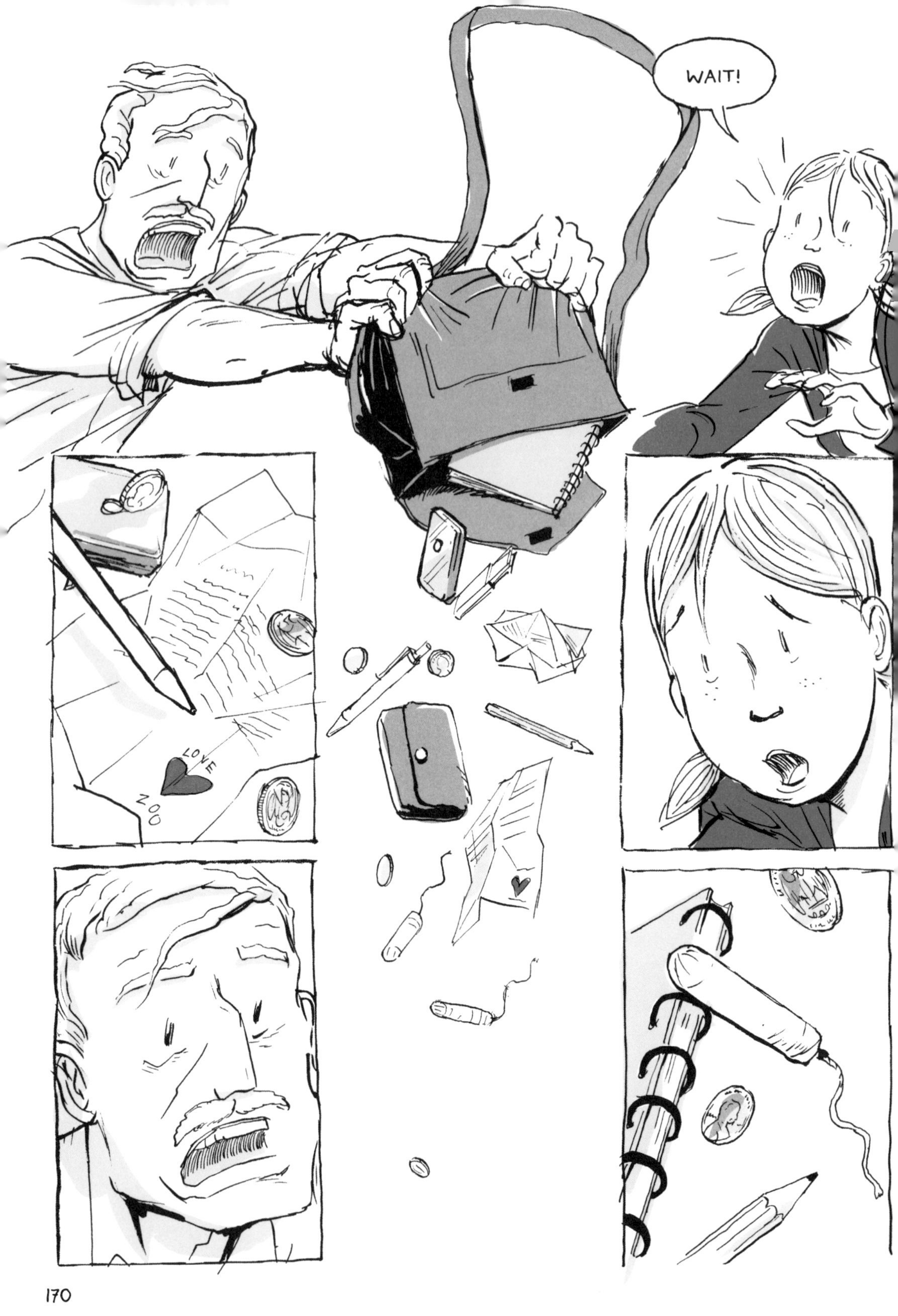
WAIT!
LOVE
ZOO

175

177

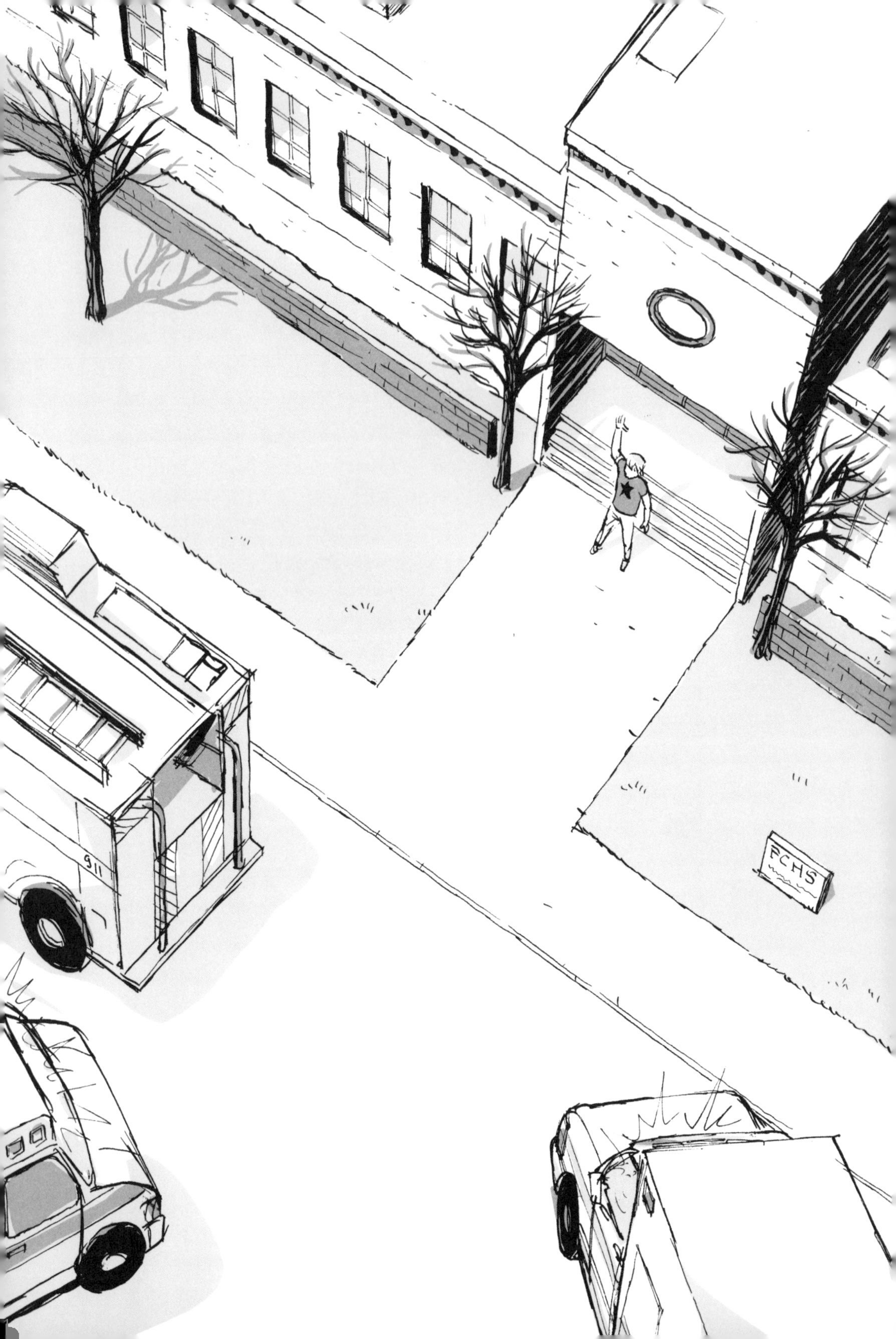
911
FCHS

EPILOGUE

SOMETIMES I WISH I COULD GO BACK TO
MY OLD SCHOOL . . .

. . . THE ONE WHERE NO ONE KNEW
ABOUT MY "PEANUT ALLERGY."

THOUGH, THANKS TO THE MIRACLE OF
MODERN COMMUNICATION . . .

. . . THEY PROBABLY DO NOW.

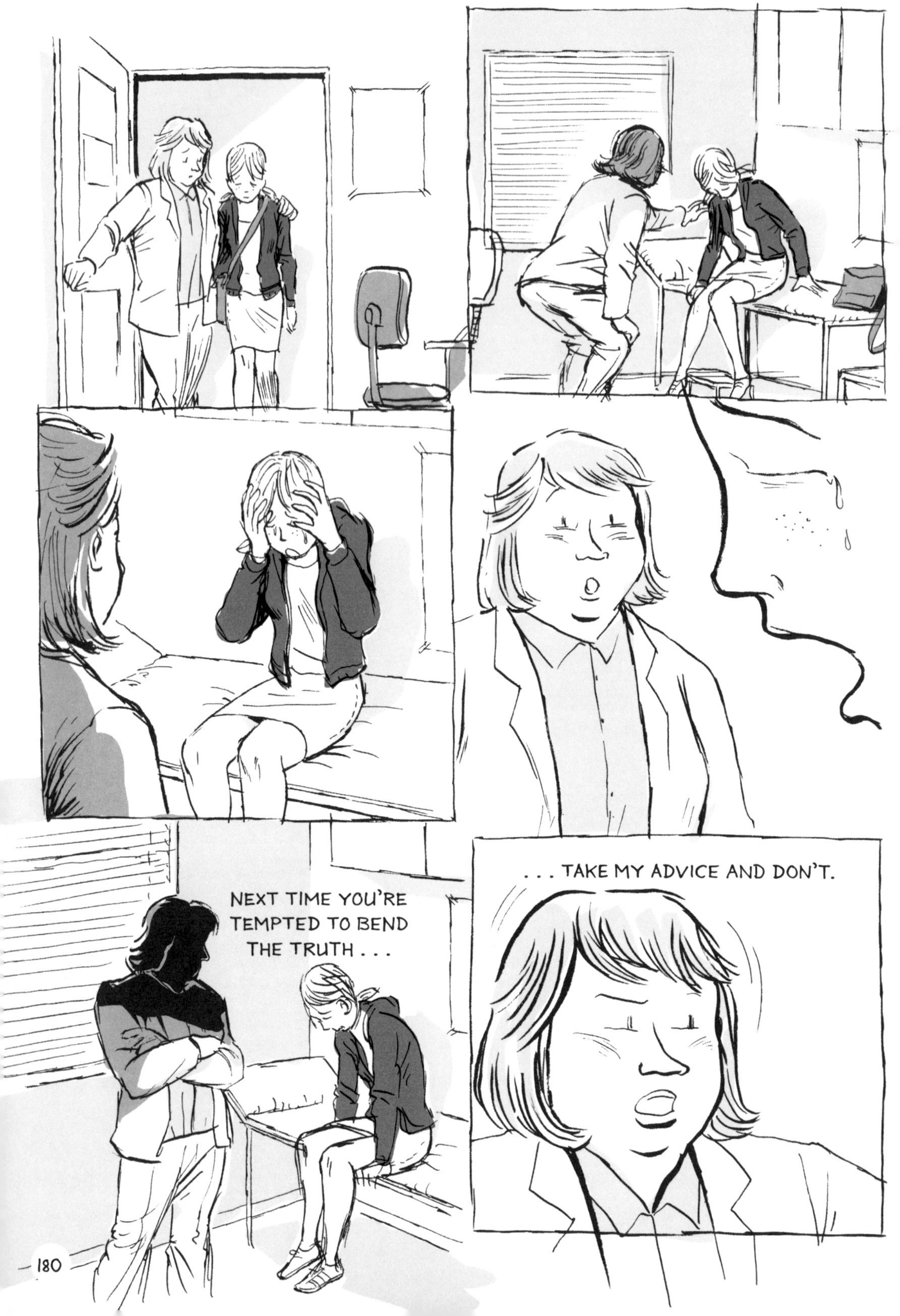
NEXT TIME YOU'RE TEMPTED TO BEND THE TRUTH . . .
. . . TAKE MY ADVICE AND DON'T.

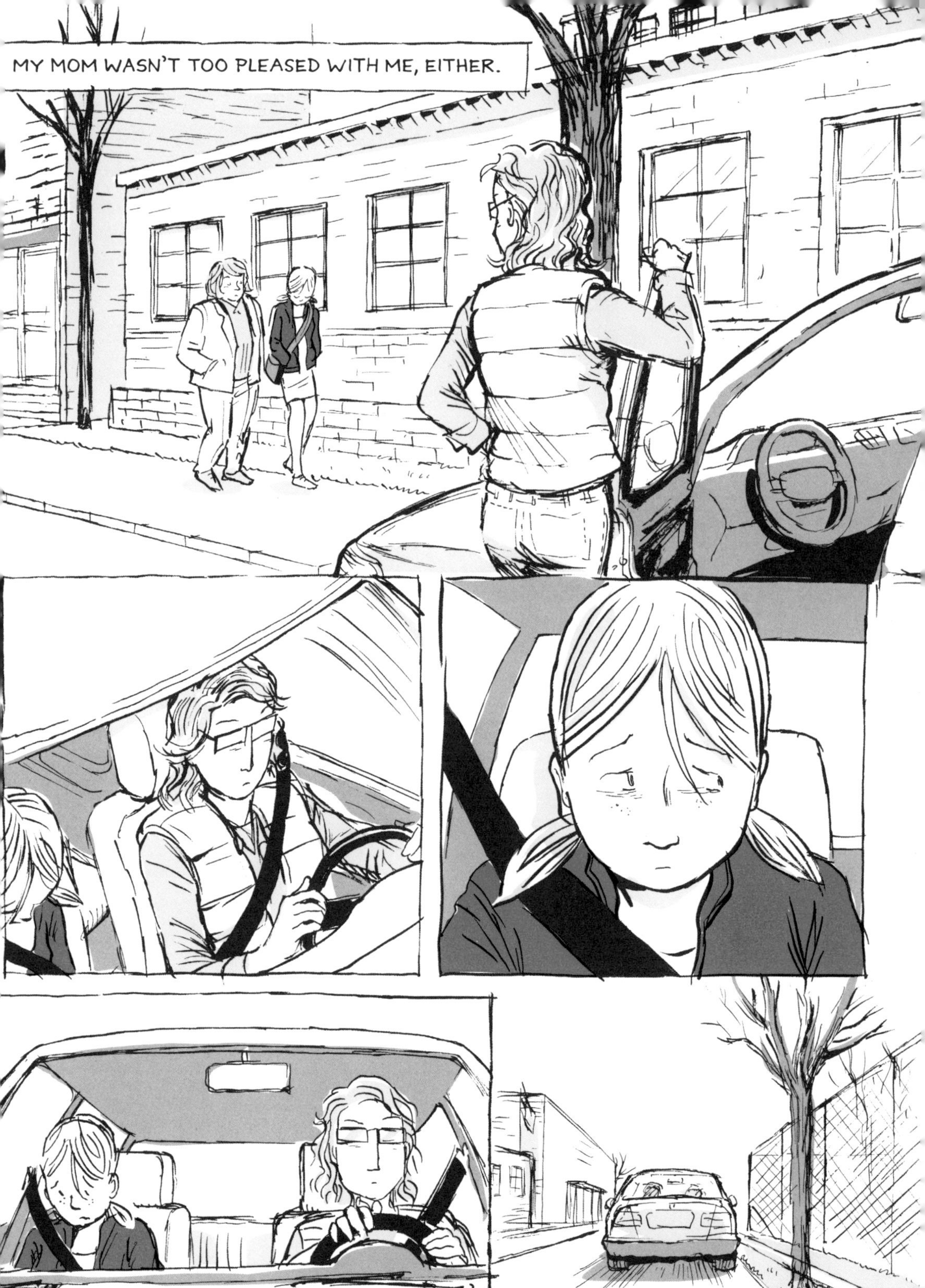
MY MOM WASN'T TOO PLEASED WITH ME, EITHER.

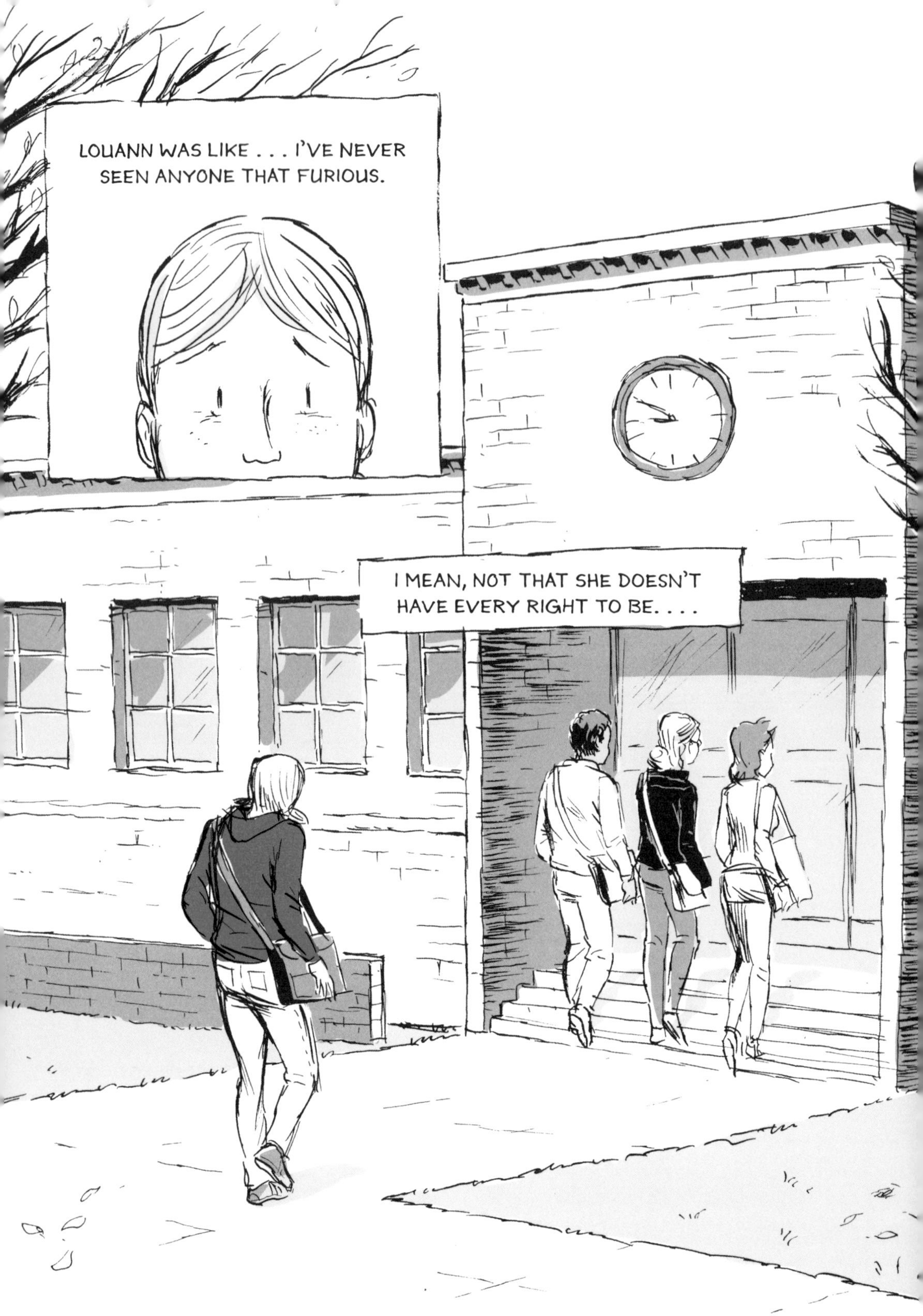
LOUANN WAS LIKE . . . I'VE NEVER SEEN ANYONE THAT FURIOUS.
I MEAN, NOT THAT SHE DOESN'T HAVE EVERY RIGHT TO BE. . . .

WANT TO HEAR SOMETHING FUNNY? THOSE CHOCOLATE ZUCCHINI CAKES? GUESS WHO BROUGHT THEM?

CELIA WILSON

I HEARD HER MOM'S EARTHY-CRUNCHY TO THE NTH POWER. ERGO THE ZUCCHINI.

SURE YOU DON'T WANT TO SPLIT ONE BEFORE YOU TAKE THEM TO THE SALE?

PLEASE! THEY HAVE LIKE 40,000 CALORIES APIECE.

YOU GIRLS WORRY WAY TOO MUCH ABOUT YOUR WEIGHT.

SPARE ME THE SELF-ACCEPTANCE LECTURE, OKAY? JUST BE GLAD I DON'T HAVE AN EATING DISORDER.

WANT TO HEAR SOMETHING ELSE?

SOMEBODY CALL 911!

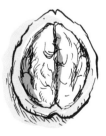
THOSE CAKES DIDN'T *HAVE* PEANUTS.

NOT ONE.

YOU'D THINK SOMEONE AS SMART AS MR. LARCH COULD DISTINGUISH BETWEEN A PEANUT AND A WALNUT. . . .

I GUESS THERE'S A REASON HE DOESN'T TEACH BIOLOGY. . . .

THE MAN'S AS NUTTY AS A FRUITCAKE!

OH MY GAWWD, IT'S THE MISSING HEALTH FORM.

SURE YOU DON'T WANT TO PUT A CHECK NEXT TO SCHIZOPHRENIA?

I'M KIDDING! BUT YOU'VE GOT TO ADMIT THAT I DESERVE A LITTLE FUN . . .

. . . AFTER WHAT YOU PUT ME THROUGH!

191

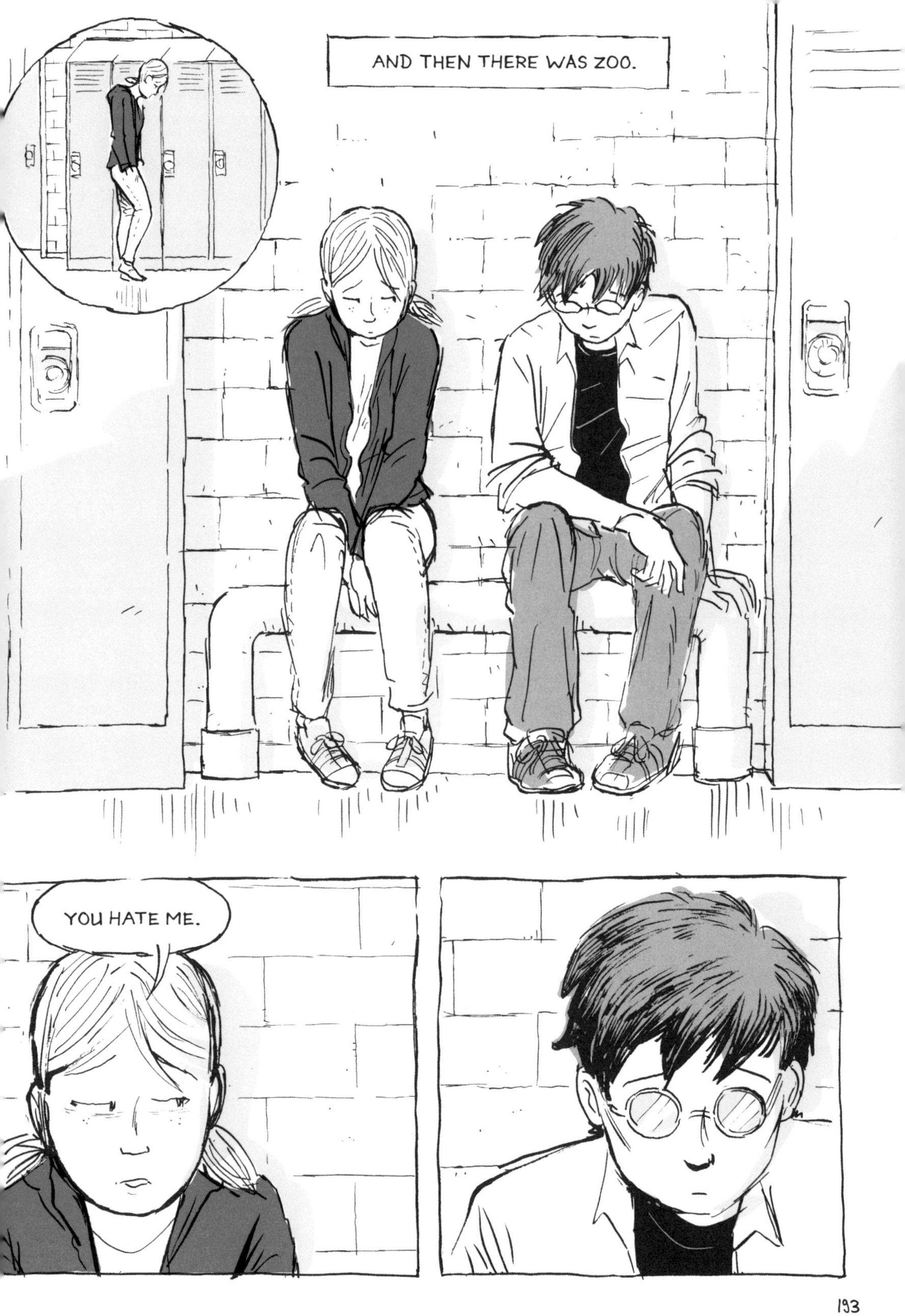
AND THEN THERE WAS ZOO.
YOU HATE ME.

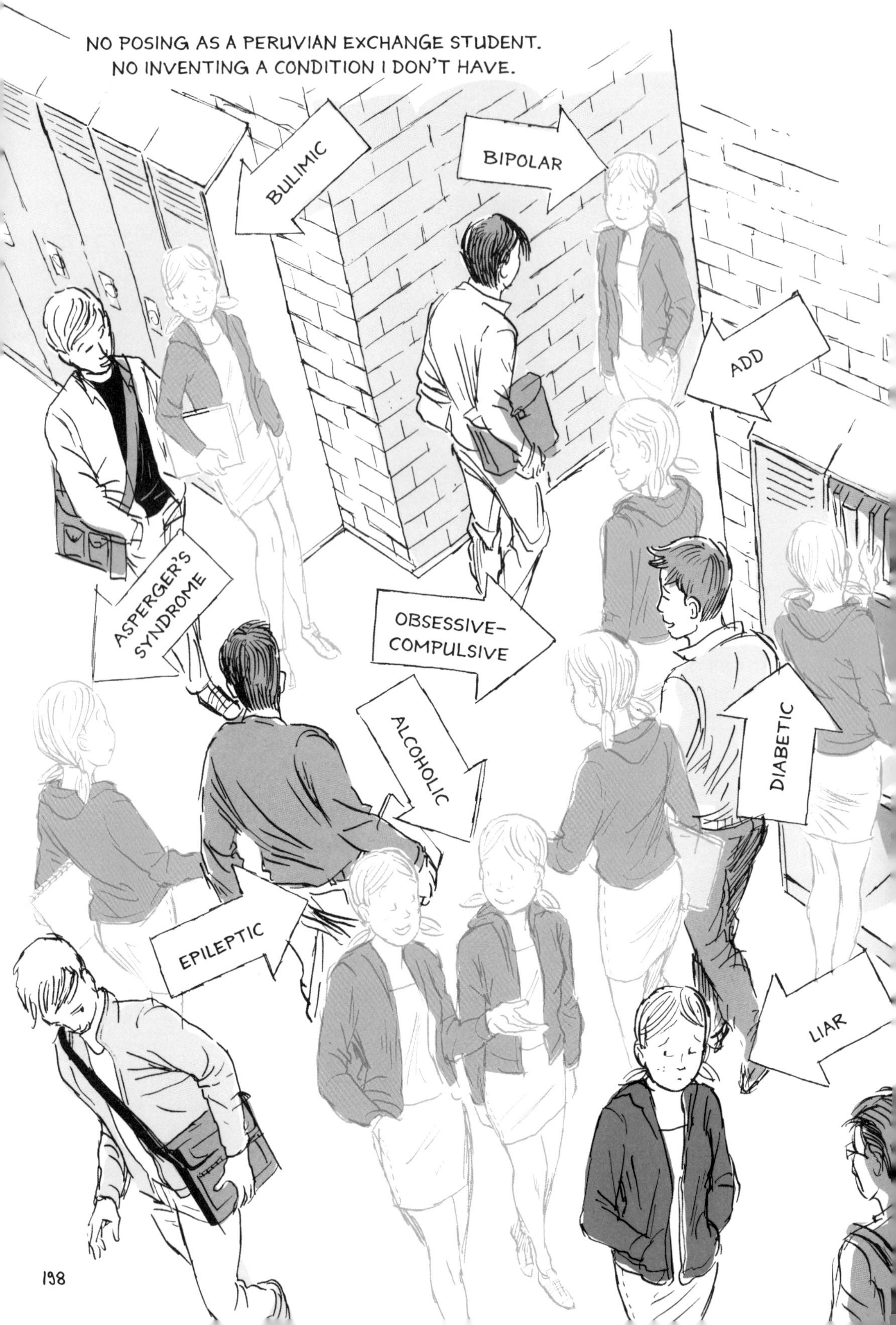
NO POSING AS A PERUVIAN EXCHANGE STUDENT.
NO INVENTING A CONDITION I DON'T HAVE.
BULIMIC
BIPOLAR
ADD
ASPERGER'S SYNDROME
OBSESSIVE-COMPULSIVE
ALCOHOLIC
DIABETIC
EPILEPTIC
LIAR

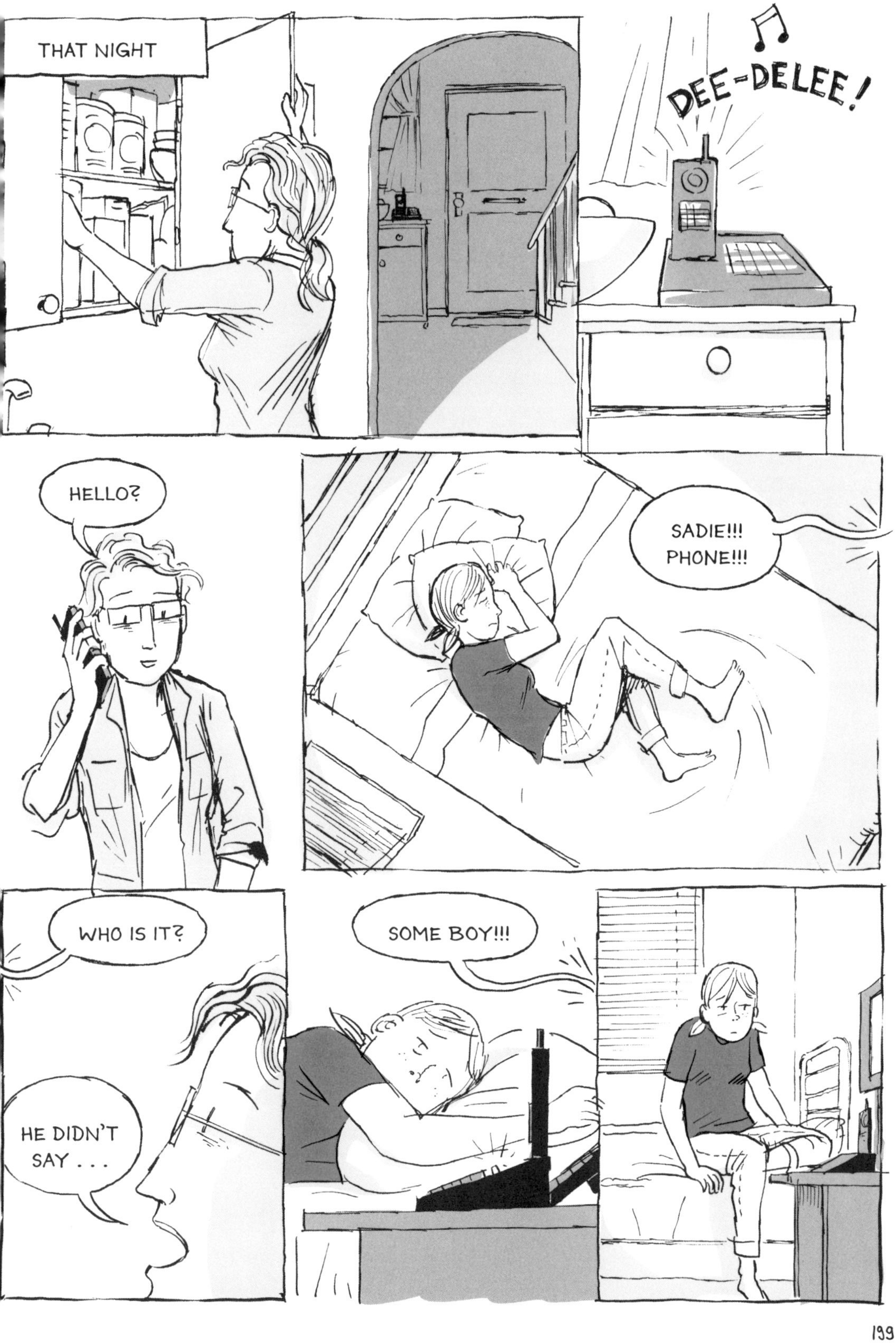
THAT NIGHT
DEE-DELEE!
HELLO?
SADIE!!! PHONE!!!
WHO IS IT?
SOME BOY!!!
HE DIDN'T SAY . . .

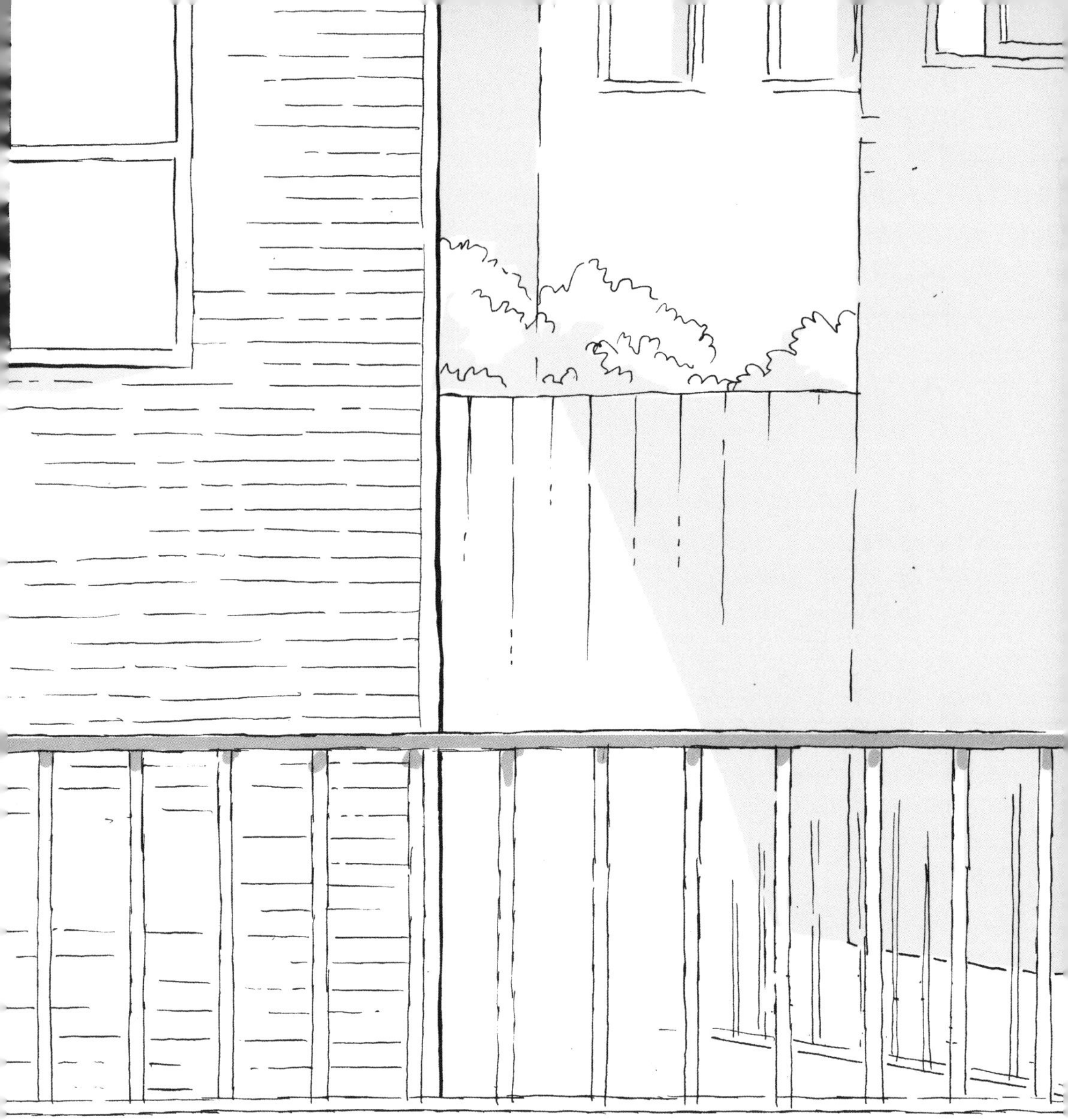

THE END

TEXT COPYRIGHT © 2013 BY AYUN HALLIDAY
COVER PHOTOGRAPH COPYRIGHT © 2013 BY IMAGE SOURCE
COVER AND INTERIOR ILLUSTRATIONS COPYRIGHT © 2013 PAUL HOPPE

PUBLISHED IN THE UNITED STATES BY SCHWARTZ & WADE BOOKS, AN IMPRINT OF RANDOM HOUSE
CHILDREN'S BOOKS, A DIVISION OF RANDOM HOUSE, INC., NEW YORK.

SCHWARTZ & WADE BOOKS AND THE COLOPHON ARE TRADEMARKS OF RANDOM HOUSE, INC.

VISIT US ON THE WEB! RANDOMHOUSE.COM/TEENS

EDUCATORS AND LIBRARIANS, FOR A VARIETY OF TEACHING TOOLS, VISIT US AT
RHTEACHERSLIBRARIANS.COM

LIBRARY OF CONGRESS CATALOGING-IN-PUBLICATION DATA
HALLIDAY, AYUN.
PEANUT / AYUN HALLIDAY ; ILLUSTRATED BY PAUL HOPPE.—IST ED.
P. CM.
SUMMARY: NERVOUS ABOUT STARTING HER SOPHOMORE YEAR AT A NEW HIGH SCHOOL, SADIE DECIDES
TO MAKE HERSELF MORE INTERESTING BY CLAIMING TO BE ALLERGIC TO PEANUTS, BUT HER LIE
QUICKLY SPIRALS OUT OF CONTROL.
ISBN 978-0-375-86590-9 (TRADE) — ISBN 978-0-375-96590-6 (GLB)
978-0-307-97909-4 (EBOOK)
1. GRAPHIC NOVELS. [1. GRAPHIC NOVELS. 2. FOOD ALLERGY—FICTION. 3. POPULARITY—FICTION.
4. HIGH SCHOOLS—FICTION. 5. SCHOOLS—FICTION. 6. MOVING, HOUSEHOLD—FICTION. 7. MOTHERS AND
DAUGHTERS—FICTION.] I. HOPPE, PAUL, ILL. II. TITLE.
PZ7.7.H36PE 2011
[FIC]—DC22
2009047168

THE TEXT OF THIS BOOK IS SET IN HOPPE.
THE ILLUSTRATIONS WERE DRAWN BY HAND USING PEN AND INK AND COLORED DIGITALLY.
BOOK DESIGN BY RACHAEL COLE

MANUFACTURED IN SINGAPORE

10 9 8 7 6 5 4 3 2 1

FIRST EDITION

RANDOM HOUSE CHILDREN'S BOOKS SUPPORTS THE FIRST AMENDMENT
AND CELEBRATES THE RIGHT TO READ.

AYUN HALLIDAY writes and illustrates *The East Village Inky*, a long-running, award-winning autobiographical zine. She is also the author of the picture book *Always Lots of Heinies at the Zoo*, four memoirs, and a guidebook to New York City. Ms. Halliday lives in Brooklyn, New York, with her husband and two children. Visit her at ayunhalliday.com.

PAUL HOPPE's illustrations have appeared in many publications, including the *New York Times*, the *Wall Street Journal*, and the *New Yorker*. He is the cofounder and art director of the comic anthology *Rabid Rabbit*. He has published two graphic novels in Germany and two picture books for children, *Hat* and *The Woods*. Born in Poland and raised in Germany, Mr. Hoppe now lives and works in Brooklyn, New York. Learn more at paulhoppe.com.